About
a
Girl

Lindsey Kelk was a children's book editor and magazine columnist and is now the author of *I Heart New
York*, *I Heart Hollywood*, *I Heart Paris*, *I Heart Vegas*,
I Heart London and *The Single Girl's To-Do List*.
When she isn't writing or watching more TV than
is healthy, Lindsey likes to wear shoes, shop for
shoes and judge the shoes of others. She loves living
in New York but misses Sherbet Fountains, London,
and drinking Gin & Elderflower cocktails with her
friends. Not necessarily in that order.

Praise for Lindsey Kelk

'Outrageous, witty, exciting and romantic, we simply
adored this sparkling read'   *Closer*

'Leaves you feeling all warm and fuzzy inside'
                                              Company

'Kelk has a hilarious turn of phrase and a sparkling
writing style . . . A frothy and fun read'
                                         Daily Express

'Perfect for those wishing to escape from the reality
of cold winter nights. ✱ ✱ ✱ ✱'   *Heat*

Also by Lindsey Kelk

I Heart New York
I Heart Hollywood
I Heart Paris
I Heart Vegas
I Heart London

The Single Girl's To-Do List

Jenny Lopez Has a Bad Week
(e-only novella)

LINDSEY KELK

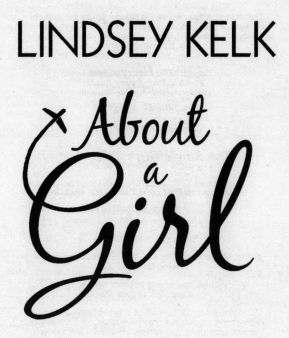

About a Girl

HARPER

Harper
An imprint of HarperCollins*Publishers*
77–85 Fulham Palace Road,
Hammersmith, London W6 8JB

www.harpercollins.co.uk

A Paperback Original 2013

1

Copyright © Lindsey Kelk 2013

Lindsey Kelk asserts the moral right to
be identified as the author of this work

A catalogue record for this book
is available from the British Library

ISBN: 978-0-00-749798-0

Set in Melior by Palimpsest Book Production Limited,
Falkirk, Stirlingshire

Printed and bound in Great Britain by
Clays Ltd, St Ives plc

MIX
Paper from
responsible sources
FSC C007454

About my girls,

Della, Beth, Emma and Terri.

PROLOGUE

I never meant for things to get so out of hand.

I'd lost my job. I'd lost the love of my life. My mum wasn't talking to me. My best friend was epically pissed off. My flatmate probably had a hit out on me by now, and in twenty-four hours I would likely be homeless.

But, you know, swings and roundabouts.

Considering how incredibly cocked up my life was, I felt surprisingly chipper. Happy even. Stretching out as far as I could, I curled the tips of my fingers around the headboard and scrunched my toes up in the crisp white cotton sheets that had found their way to the foot of the bed. Everything was still, everything was calm, and I was smiling. Somewhere across the room, I heard a phone beep. Instead of jumping up to see who needed what and just how quickly I could get it for them, I concentrated on the sound of the shower running in the bathroom and pressed my lips together to refresh the tingling sensation before it faded away. The stubble burn that tickled my cheeks was altogether more stubborn. I was so happy.

1

My best friend had been wrong. Everything was going to be OK. Probably. Not that there hadn't been some sketchy moments over the past week. Not that I hadn't considered having myself committed. More than once. But now it was almost over. I'd survived. This afternoon I would get on a plane back home. I would call everyone who needed calling, and instead of behaving like a jabbering shell of a human, I would be cool, calm and collected and make things right. If I could get through this past week, I could get through anything.

Seven days ago, if anyone had even given me a hint of what was ahead, I would have crawled underneath my desk and refused to come out. But as I had learned from every television show I had ever watched and every book I had thought about reading, you never knew how strong you were until you had to find out. I was definitely stronger than anyone had reckoned. Either that or I was clinically insane. It was a fine line.

The phone beeped again.

It was all going to work out. The photos were taken; the photos were great. Paige was going to be very happy. Mr Bennett was happy. Kekipi didn't seem too bothered either way, but you can't have everything. All I had to do now was spend the rest of the morning lying in this bed reliving all the terrible things I had just done with a terrible man, and by this time tomorrow I'd be practically home.

Rolling onto my stomach, I was very, very glad I couldn't see the state of myself. My too long hair was all tangles, my carefully applied make-up was now carefully applied all over the pillowcases, and, let's face it, post-orgasmic smugness isn't a good look on anyone. If I had seen me right now, I might have wanted to punch me. Not that post-orgasmic anything was a look I was terribly familiar with. Well, the bad hair and terrible make-up, yes, but the smug 'I just got shagged rotten by a very handsome man' part? Not so much. There had to be a way to do post-coital with an air of class, surely. This was something they really did need to start teaching in schools. Maybe at the same time the nurse took the girls away to explain all about the wonderful world of tampons she could give you a rundown on what to pack in the morning-after kit. If there was one thing women needed to know, it was how to get thoroughly seen to without your gentleman friend sandpapering the top three layers of your skin completely off your face in the process.

Three more beeps.

No matter how hard I tried to ignore it, my phone wasn't giving up. With a tiny, sad sniff I realized I was going to have to answer the bloody thing. Only it wasn't on the nightstand where I always left it. Because this wasn't my nightstand. And I had no idea where it was hiding. My beautiful red silk Valentino dress was on one side of the room, my bra on the other. Somewhere in the middle, there was a white shirt and a beach towel. And from deep inside a pile of carelessly discarded man clothes, another iPhone started chiming along in time with mine. It was a veritable chorus of communication. Together, they sounded a bit like a One Direction song. I gave up. Screw you, Vodafone.

'Vanessa?'

I watched the huge bamboo fan on the ceiling spinning round and round and round and tapped out the rhythm of the phones, making no effort to answer either them or the man in the bathroom.

'Vanessa?'

Oh, right. That was me. Sort of.

'Yeah?' I called back, scanning the room for my knickers. The biggest problem with crazy, tear-your-clothes-off sex was that once you'd torn off your clothes and had the crazy sex, the clothes were hard to locate in a dignified fashion. It was impossible not to feel a bit slutty scrabbling around on the floor looking for your pants. It was all well and good if you were one of those girls who slinks around starkers after sexytimes, but I wasn't really a naked person. I was very much an 'always sleep in a nightie in case the house burns down' person. I mean, I still called it 'sexytimes', for God's sake, and as we all know, if you can't say it, you shouldn't be doing it.

'Is that me? Can you answer it?'

'It is. I can.'

And I could, in theory. Although I was very upset at having to get out of bed. Shuffling down the mattress and trying to ignore the streaks of mascara all down the backs of both my hands, I anchored my hair behind my ears and hung over the edge of the bed to comb through the pile of cast-off cotton and silk like a hungry badger. A slutty hungry badger.

The slinky black iPhone was peeking out of my bra, flashing up a private number. I slid off the bed and dived into the middle of the pile of clothes. Classy. 'Nick Miller's phone,' I answered as I clambered back onto the bed. 'Not Nick speaking, obviously.'

'Who is this?'

An unfamiliar and unpleasantly accusatory female voice echoed down the line. Hawaii might be beautiful, but the mobile phone reception was shit.

'This is Tess. I mean Vanessa. Um, yeah, Vanessa.'

Damn it, I couldn't even think straight when I was tired, let alone lie straight.

'I'm trying to reach Nick Miller?'

'This is Nick's phone,' I yawned. 'Can I ask who's calling?'

'Sorry, who am I speaking to? And why do you have Nick's phone?'

'He's in the shower.' I couldn't help feeling that I might be talking myself into a very deep hole. 'I'm Tess. Vanessa! Shit, I'm Vanessa.'

'Put Nick on the phone,' the woman demanded. 'Right now.'

I did not put Nick on the phone. Instead, I did the only thing I could think to do. I pressed the end call button and dropped the very expensive piece of technology into a glass of water at the side of the bed. Because that was bound to help matters. Launching myself off the bed, I scuttled around on the floor searching for my phone. Maybe there was something I could do. Maybe there was still time. Maybe—

'Hey, who was it?'

A very handsome, very naked man appeared in the doorway, rubbing his ash-blond hair with a white towel. I silently begged him to cover up. It was very difficult to concentrate on digging yourself out of the world's biggest metaphorical hole when there was a visible penis in the room.

'No one,' I chirped. 'Wrong number.'

'No one has had a wrong number since 1997.' Nick strode across the room, dropping the towel as he went. I couldn't help but feel this was disrespectful to both the housekeeping staff and the environment. That was a fresh towel. 'Pass me the phone.'

'Um, I dropped it.' I looked up from my slovenly spot on the floor and hoped my naked charms would distract him from the extreme act of iPhone violence I had 'accidentally' committed.

They didn't.

'What the fuck, Vanessa?' He grabbed the glass and choked back a sob, staring at the phone as if it was a tony Damian Hirst exhibit. *iPhone in Water*, a dead cert for the Turner Prize. 'My fucking phone. It's broken. What am I supposed to do without a phone?'

Hot or not, whining was never attractive. After finding them hiding inside one of Nick's shoes, I pulled on my knickers, hoping that the less naked I was, the clearer I'd be able to think.

'It slipped.' I held my hands up in defence, attempting to squish my boobs together at the same time. Misdirection was a magician's best weapon and I was definitely going to need a magic trick to get out of this one. Possibly a miracle. Where was Jesus when you needed him? Or at least Derren Brown. But preferably Jesus. 'I'm sorry.'

Nick carried on pawing his waterlogged lifeline and making heartbroken chuntering noises under his breath, while I continued my search for my ever-beeping, completely annoying phone. I still couldn't believe I'd broken the screen. Maybe it was in my bag? I spotted the slouchy, pretty black silk clutch bag that had come with my dress over by the door where I'd tossed it as soon as we had crashed through it last night. MAC make-up, Chanel perfume, spare batteries and dozens upon dozens of pens spilled out all over the floor. I was a strange creature sometimes. Didn't like to be without a pen.

'Hello?' I answered after finally retrieving it from inside

6

Nick's abandoned boxer shorts. Eww. I fought the urge to hang up and give it a rub down with a wet wipe. This was not the time to relapse into my OCD issues.

'Tess, it's Paige. Where are you? I've called, like, ten times. I've been looking all over for you.'

Brilliant. Paige. Couldn't a girl get five minutes, post-shag peace and quiet?

'I'm in my cottage,' I hedged. 'What's up?'

'No, you aren't. I've just been there.' She paused for a second. 'Are you with Nick?'

'God, yeah, that's what I meant. Nick's cottage,' I looked up at Nick, who seemed to have got over the untimely death of his iPhone thanks to the comforting charms of my tits. 'We were just going over the photos.'

Nick raised an eyebrow and tossed his phone onto the floor. It was amazing how quickly a man could recover from a painful loss if he thought there was even a tiny chance he could put his penis in someone.

'OK, I'm coming over. You need to do something. Stephanie called – she's mega, mega pissed off. I'm going to get fired. What the fuck, Tess – what do we do?'

'OK, don't panic, but don't come here,' I said, trapping the phone between my cheek and my shoulder while slapping Nick's hands away from my newly acquired knickers. 'I've got loads of stuff to show you from yesterday – I left you messages. Seriously, calm down. I'll come to you. Nick's busy, but—'

'Nick is busy,' he said, thumbs hooking around the delicate silk I'd only just managed to get halfway round my arse. 'And so are you.'

He snatched the phone and threw it across the room. I watched it skitter across the shiny wooden floor and vanish underneath the bed, taking Paige's panic attack with it.

'You know, you are an incredibly sexy woman,' he said, running his fingertips up and down my spine and pressing his face against my neck. 'You cannot even begin to know how much I want you right now.'

'I really want to play along with this,' I whispered with my eyes closed and brow furrowed. I wasn't used to being called sexy. Or a woman. Most men didn't actually seem to notice I had a discernible gender at all and so hearing these things from such a ridiculously attractive man was very difficult to resist. 'But this is just about the worst timing ever.'

'Vanessa.' He took my tiny fists and covered them with his huge hands. 'You broke my phone. You owe me. Now shut up and do as you're told.'

Just as it had been since I'd first laid eyes on him, every word out of Nick's mouth went straight to my vagina, but this time I had to resist. I could be strong. As long as I kept my knickers on.

'I'm sorry, but I've really, really got to go,' I insisted, swooping out of his arms and grabbing my bra from the floor in one surprisingly graceful move. 'I'm so sorry.'

'Don't be sorry.' He gave me a dark look and grabbed my wrist. 'Just don't go.'

Before I could come back with an intelligent argument, there was a very loud knock at the door.

'I am sorry and I do have to go.' I shook off his hand and tried to discern what bits, in the tangled pile of material on the floor, had started out last night as my outfit. 'Don't answer it. It's Paige.'

Really, I was impossibly stupid. I had just told Nick Miller not to do something and then expected him not to do it.

'What if it is?' he asked, eyebrows raised. 'We're adults.'

'Oh, don't start!' I had no time for this. He could be such a cock sometimes. Most of the time. In fact, any time when he wasn't actually using his penis, he was behaving like one. 'Just please don't open that door.'

And so, naked as the day he was born, Nick strode over to the door and flung it wide open. A very shocked blonde girl stood on the step and gaped.

'Paige,' Nick nodded. 'Vanessa and I were just going over the plans for tomorrow.'

The tiny blonde girl tried desperately to avert her eyes from Nick in all his naked glory. As it was, the only other thing for her to concentrate on was me in my knickers, and that was doing nothing to improve the situation.

As she recovered herself and put two and two together to make a filthy four, Paige's face fell. I took an ill-advised step forward and got my foot caught in Nick's boxer shorts.

'Paige.' I looked at her.

'Nick?' She looked at him.

Nick just looked very pleased with himself.

'Oh, Tess.' Paige started to laugh and it wasn't very nice. 'Tess, Tess, Tess.'

'Paige, don't,' I begged. I was fully aware that pleading with women didn't usually go very well when they caught you hanging out in your underwear with the man they had designs on. Especially when that man was naked. 'Please.'

'Tess?' Despite how very clever he claimed to be, Nick wasn't always the sharpest knife in the drawer. 'Who's Tess?'

'She is,' Paige said, nodding towards me. 'Aren't you?'

'Vanessa?' Nick placed a hand over his manparts, not

9

looking nearly as smug as he had five minutes ago. If I hadn't been ready for the ground to open up and swallow me whole, it might have been funny. 'What's going on?'

'Nick, I can explain,' I started, entirely unsure how I was going to do that. 'It's a long story. It's a funny story. It's, um, well. I don't know where to start.'

'I do,' Paige chipped in. 'This is Tess. She's an irresponsible, selfish, evil, lying bitchface who's been faking everything to everyone, and I didn't grass her up because I'm an idiot.'

Bit harsh, I thought. A bit harsh, but ultimately accurate. All of a sudden, my knees weren't feeling terribly steady. Nick looked very confused. And also still very naked. Unfortunately, his supreme manliness wasn't enough to slow Paige down now she'd started.

'Long story short, her name isn't Vanessa,' my friend, mentor and confidante stated. She was on a roll. 'Her name is Tess Brookes and she's full of shit.'

Well.

It was a much more concise version of events than I had to offer.

CHAPTER ONE

Two Weeks Earlier

It was more or less a day like any other when it all went wrong.

My alarm went off, I got up, showered in silence and watched fifteen minutes of breakfast news with stuttering subtitles so as not to wake my flatmate. I got dressed, I checked my bag to make sure I had an adequate number of tampons even though my period was a good three weeks away, and after checking I'd turned my hair straighteners off twice, I left for the office. As usual, I was the first in. No one else made it in before ten on Mondays, but I was the kind of irritating person who got a lot more done without the clacking of everyone else's keyboards to distract me. Early mornings and late nights were my friends. And given the frequency with which they occurred, they were pretty much my only friends. But on this particular Monday, I had good reason to be so bright-eyed and bushy-tailed. After seven years' hard slog, I was getting the promotion I'd been dreaming of.

11

I, Tess Brookes, was about to become the youngest creative director in the history of Donovan & Dunning.

Obviously no one was quite as excited about this as me, so it wasn't exactly a shock that I was sitting outside the HR manager's office before she'd even got off the Tube. It was fair to say I was dead giddy.

'Morning, Raquel.' I gave her a cheek-achingly massive smile when she finally appeared at the top of the stairs. It couldn't hurt, I reasoned; after all, today was my day. Some girls had weddings, some had babies, I had my promotion. And that was only sad if you let it be.

'Tess.' Raquel, short, bleach blonde and dead-eyed, motioned for me to follow her into her office. She didn't look surprised to see me. And why would she? We'd been discussing this promotion for the past six months; I figured she'd be glad to see the back of me. All that was left was for me to sign my new contract and then I'd be out of her way. For six months. I was ambitious.

'OK, so let's just get straight to this.' She sat down behind a too big desk and smiled. 'I've got some difficult news.'

'Right.' I sat up straight and put on my 'I'm listening' face. Difficult news? Was she leaving? Maybe she was leaving. I really hoped she was leaving.

'As you know, the company has gone through quite a lot of changes in the past twelve months,' Raquel said, folding her hands in front of her and leaning her head to one side. Such a serious soul was Raquel. Probably because she fired people for a living and everyone hated her. 'And as such, we are having to undertake some necessary measures to ensure a successful restructure.'

'OK,' I nodded. This was a very funny way of giving me a big hug and a key to the executive bathroom. Of course I knew there was a restructure. They were restructuring me into a corner office and a big fat pay rise. Which was much needed to pay for the ridiculously expensive Promotion Shoes that were currently rubbing the fuck out of my feet.

'As you know,' she repeated, 'the original plan for the business was to move you into a creative director role, with the copy and design teams reporting directly to you.'

'The original plan?' I was starting to feel a fraction less giddy.

'The original plan,' she confirmed, never taking her eyes off me.

This didn't sound wonderful. Why wasn't she squealing and giving me a present? And why was she smiling? Raquel never smiled.

'Unfortunately, due to the new restructure, we will not be moving ahead with the original plan. The creative director role you were moving into is no longer part of the planned downsizing of the company.'

Words I officially did not enjoy. Unfortunately. Restructure. Downsizing.

'And as such, your role has been restructured out of the business.'

I was definitely ready for the hug and the present.

'The creative director role –' my voice did not sound nearly as steady as I would like – 'has been restructured out of the business?'

After seven years of overtime, evenings and weekends, I was being stiffed out of my promotion by an HR demon with a gob full of business jargon and clichés.

'Yes.' Raquel gave me the same look you might give a small child who has just successfully worked out that cows go moo.

'So I'm not going to be the new creative director?'

'You are not.'

Poof. There it went. Bye bye, promotion. Hello, God knows how many more years back at my old desk. Hello, shit-ton of overtime I was going to have to do to pay for my new shoes. I stared at an Oxford University mug sitting right on the edge of her desk and fought the urge to move it out of harm's way. Who went to Oxford and then ended up doing HR for an advertising company?

'As you'll see, we've put together a very fair redundancy package,' Raquel continued, switching gears so fast I wasn't sure I'd heard her right. She pushed a stiff cardboard envelope across the desk towards me and tapped it twice. 'Given the circumstances, we understand if you would like to leave immediately. I can forward your personal effects. If you could just leave your phone and security pass with me, I'll take care of all of that.'

I looked down at the envelope and then back up at Satan's minion.

'I'm afraid I'm not following,' I said as politely as possible. 'Redundancy package?'

'The company no longer has a position available for you.' Raquel scratched her nose delicately. I resisted the urge to slap it. Only just. 'At all.'

'So when you say the creative director role has been restructured out of the business . . .' I took a deep breath and tried very hard not to vomit. 'What you are actually saying is that *I* have been restructured out of the business?'

'The creative director role,' she repeated with a nod, 'is no longer viable in the current business plan. You are the creative director.'

'But I haven't even started the job. How can I have

been restructured out of it?' I was aware that my voice was starting to get uncomfortably high. I was even more aware of the fact that I was going to cry. I blinked twice and stared hard at the Oxford mug, trying to regain my composure.

'I understand you are bound to have some questions.' Raquel's shark eyes had already glazed over. 'Perhaps you'd like to schedule some time to go over them on the phone tomorrow.'

'Or perhaps I'd like you to stop being a dick and tell me why I'm being fired?' I shouted.

There was no stopping the tears. Between the blisters on my heels and my blind rage, there was nothing I could do to stem the sobbing. It was neither ladylike nor professional, but apparently I no longer had a profession, so who gave a toss whether or not I was being ladylike?

'Perhaps you could explain to me why I'm being "let go" when you're supposed to be promoting me? Perhaps you could explain to me who exactly is going to lead the creative team? Perhaps you could tell me who is going to win all of your business and lead all of your campaigns and who is going to work on New Year's Eve so you don't lose an account for a toilet cleaner?' I grabbed the cardboard envelope and bashed it against the desk to punctuate my every word before flinging it across the room. '*And* it was crappy toilet cleaner.'

'No one is disputing your commitment to the job,' Raquel said without even flinching. 'And we will be very happy to give you a reference when you find a new situation.'

'A new situation?' There was a chance I was screeching. 'This isn't *Downton* fucking *Abbey*. I'm not a scullery maid. I'm the best creative you have here and you know it. Where's Michael? Where is bloody Michael?'

Michael was my boss. Michael was a cock. When Michael spilled a glass of wine down my top at the Christmas party every year, I laughed it off. When Michael referred to me and my breasts as 'his three favourite employees' in front of a new client last summer, I let it go. When Michael tried to cop a feel under the pretence of performing the Heimlich manoeuvre when I had hiccups *every time I had hiccups for seven years*, I kept my mouth shut. And now where was he?

'Mr Donovan isn't in the office this morning,' Raquel replied, actually sounding bored. 'I do understand you're upset, but really, this isn't a personal issue. It's just a matter of corporate restructuring.'

'Well, I think you need to restructure your face,' I yelled. Not my best comeback ever. 'This is ridiculous. I run that creative team. All of the accounts are working on my ideas. All of them.'

'This conversation really isn't relevant to the decision that has been made.' She stood up and opened her office door. I took this to mean I was supposed to fuck off through it. 'Your role no longer exists within the company. I will forward all your personal belongings and the details of our very generous package to your home address and include my direct line. I'd be very happy to discuss any questions you might have once you've had some time to reflect. We should probably do it over the phone.'

For the want of something else to do, I grabbed the Oxford University mug from her desk and threw it, as hard as I could, onto the floor. It bounced once on the beige carpet and then sat there sadly, a tiny trickle of coffee pooling beside it.

'Feel better for that?' Raquel asked, one eyebrow raised.

'Not really,' I admitted, my chin up high and arm stretched out to knock a stack of files off her desk. Stamping a sore foot, I swiped a Pritt Stick off the shelf and brazenly stuck it in my pocket.

'I'm taking that,' I explained with added petulance. 'You can knock it off my generous package.'

It was strange where your mind went when you were in shock.

Seven years of work and my boss hadn't even had the decency to come in on time to fire me himself. I'd missed weddings and birthdays and dates to meet deadlines, deliver projects, give presentations, and I'd done it all with a smile. While all my friends were out puking in the street and snogging strangers, I'd spent last New Year's Eve sat in the meeting room, throwing a stress ball at a wall for three straight hours while I attempted to come up with an innovative campaign for knock-off Toilet Duck. And I bloody well did it. My flat was full of books I'd bought but never read, DVDs that had gone unwatched and CDs I hadn't got round to listening to. Good God, it had been so long since I'd listened to music, I still had CDs. But it hadn't mattered before. Because this was the plan. No matter how often my two remaining friends had told me to ease up, that work wasn't everything, I hadn't listened. I was happy. I wasn't missing out on my life; my job *was* my life. And now I had neither.

But what really stung, I realized as I rode down to my floor for the last time in the lift that always smelled ever so slightly of cat food, what really stung wasn't the loss of the actual job, it was everything that went with it.

17

Most importantly, it was the dream of moving into my own place and leaving my demonic flatmate behind. Because once I was in my own flat, living would really start. I'd buy fancy dinnerware and nice curtains and learn how to make sushi and buy a cool TV with an amazing audio system. And then I'd invite Charlie round for dinner and we'd end up drinking a little too much and watching a movie which would almost certainly be something starring Emma Stone, and just when she was being her most endearing for the ladies and sexy for the men, I would rest my head on his shoulder and he would realize that I was his Emma Stone and we would kiss and then we would be together for ever. But no. That couldn't happen now. Because I didn't have my job. So there wouldn't be a flat. And there wouldn't be a dinner or an Emma Stone movie night or a kiss or any happiness ever again. Poof, it was all gone.

Having never been fired, let go or otherwise excused before in my life, I wasn't sure what the correct protocol was. For the first time, I was thankful everyone else in the office were such lazy bastards. There was no one to see me snivelling and shoving my belongings into a reusable Tesco shopper, except for a terrified-looking intern and the graphic designer who everyone knew sniffed Bostick in the toilets. The company was going under and I was being let go, but the glue-sniffer kept his job. It was perfect.

I picked up my stapler and stared at it for a moment. I couldn't remember a time when I didn't have a plan. Whether it was setting up the girl's football team in junior school because I had declared the PE teacher sexist, turning a profit on the refreshment stand at the village panto, or making sure I was sitting next to Jason Hutchins on the year ten bus trip to Alton Towers, I always had a plan. And the Cloverhill Panthers had come third from last in our local division, watering down the Ribena at the panto until it was basically pink piss had made exactly four pounds and seventeen pence, and for two precious hours and thirteen minutes, Jason Hutchins had been all mine. I always had a plan and that plan always worked. I dropped the stapler in my bag and walked out the door.

After a ten-minute wander down Theobalds Road, I found myself in Bloomsbury Square, shopping bag in one hand, dignity in the other. Hobbling over to an empty bench, I kicked off my new shoes without worrying what the British summertime mud would do to the gorgeous nude suede and stared vacantly at two dogs running up and down the park. They always looked happy, I thought, as I pulled all the pins out of my elaborate updo one by one. Dogs were always happy. Dogs didn't have a plan. Dogs hadn't been climbing up a career ladder for the last seven years. Dogs hadn't been hopelessly in love with their best friend for the last ten. Well, I couldn't hand on heart say that was definitely true, but it seemed unlikely.

I rifled around in my Tesco bag looking for something to spur on an emotion that wasn't pathetic. All that was in there was my stolen stapler, three framed photos, a brand-new box of Special K cereal bars and about seventeen different pens. (Lots of highlighters. I liked a highlighter.) That was it. Seven years and I'd erased all evidence of my very existence from the office in one half-full environmentally-friendly shopping bag.

I pulled the photos out, one by one, and laid them on my black-clad knee. The first was of me and Amy, little-girl versions of me and my best friend, dressed up as princesses and hugging desperately for the camera. The next one was a more formal shot of me, my sisters, my mum and my grandmother, looking considerably less chipper. We weren't huggers, the Brookeses. Someone basically had to die to convince my mother to go further than a stern pat on the shoulder. When my first granddad had passed away, she had ruffled my hair. It was intense. The third and final photo was of me and Amy again, this time all grown-up and joined by Charlie, my co-worker, best boy friend and the man I had been in love with for the past decade. The three of us were slouched on a sofa in some random Parisian hotel in front of a huge mirror with another one behind us. My face was obscured by the camera that had gone every-where with me that summer, but my denim cut-offs and stripy T-shirt echoed endlessly in the reflections of the two mirrors. Charlie and Amy's reflected faces smiled back at me. Amy was on my left, deep in her *Amélie* phase, black hair cropped close to her head and legs stretched out, draped across me and Charlie. To my right, the love of my life rested his head on my shoulder and held a lit cigarette off to the side, so as not to drop the ash on my bare skin. Even though you couldn't tell by the photo, I remembered I was smiling. We were the three musketeers. Rock, paper, scissors. Amy was the scissors, Charlie was the paper and I was the rock. I was always the rock.

Slowly but surely, I felt my breathing return to normal and the tension in my shoulders ease ever so slightly. Just in time for me to realize someone was sitting beside me on the bench.

'Morning.' An incredibly average-looking man with

a shaved head and a black bomber jacket gave me a sideways nod.

'Morning,' I replied, carefully placing the photographs back in my bag. No reason not to be polite. This was my life now, after all. Just sitting around, talking to the other non-workers-slash-vagrants in London's parks while I lived vicariously through the dog ownership of others. I wondered if the Tesco near Russell Square sold White Lightning. It felt like the day was missing a bottle of White Lightning.

'Don't make a scene,' the man said, moving down the bench towards me and looking straight ahead. 'Give me your wallet and your phone.'

'Sorry?' I wasn't quite sure I'd heard him properly. Was I being mugged? After seven years in London, was I actually being mugged? Not bloody likely.

'Phone and wallet. Now.' He pulled a small Swiss Army knife out of his pocket and gave me as scary a look as he could muster. 'Don't make me make you.'

Still not quite with it, I tilted my head to one side and stared. I couldn't help but think he'd be scarier with hair. He looked like an overgrown baby.

'I haven't got a phone,' I replied. This was actually happening. I was being mugged by a giant baby in a bomber jacket. 'And you can't have my wallet. There's nothing in it anyway and it was a present.'

'Everyone's got a phone.' He sounded a bit taken aback. 'Give it to me now.'

'No, really.' I opened up my handbag and tipped it upside down, emptying the contents out onto the bench between us. Three lipsticks, a powder compact, my keys, more tampons than anyone could ever feasibly need and even more pens clattered against the wooden slats. I

picked up my wallet and stuck it between my knees. I
meant what I said – I'd already told him he couldn't
have that and I wasn't about to go back on my word to
a criminal. 'See? No phone. I just got fired. They took
my phone. Have not got one.'

'You haven't got a phone at all?' The would-be mugger
was visibly shocked. 'That's bollocks, that is.'

'It really, really is,' I agreed.

We sat in silence for a moment.

'Haven't got a job either,' I said as I started scooping
up my belongings and dropping them back in the bag.
It seemed he wasn't nearly as interested in highlighters
as I was. Probably didn't have much call for them in
his game. 'Phone's not such a problem.'

'Me neither,' he replied, grabbing a couple of tampons
and popping them into my handbag for me. 'Had one.
Lost it. Fucking Tories, innit?'

'I suppose the recession has been hard for everyone,'
I sympathized. 'It's a tough time.'

'Do you need to call anyone?' the big baby asked. The
man dug his hand into his non-knifey pocket and
produced a brand-new iPhone. 'You can use my phone
if you want.'

'Actually, that would be amazing,' I said, readily
accepting the handset but ignoring the controversial
cover design. Pretty sure they didn't sell Swastika iPhone
cases in Carphone Warehouse. This was definitely home-
made. 'Thank you.'

'Don't worry, I'll give you a bit of privacy.' He nodded
curtly, stood up and wandered a couple of feet away.
I watched as a worried-looking middle-aged lady in a
waxed jacket and an Alice band took a very sharp and
sudden detour. I looked away as he followed her.

'Hello?'

'Amy.' I would never answer the phone to an unknown number. Amy always would. 'It's me.'

'What phone are you on? What's going on? Did they give you a new phone. Did you get an iPhone? Have you got Siri? Can I ask him a question?'

'It's not my phone.' I cut her off before she could come up with anything filthy to ask the omniscient Siri. 'Are you at work?'

'Yeah.' She didn't sound convinced. 'Until five.'

'Oh. I got the sack and I thought you might want to get very, very drunk.'

'STELLA!' I snapped my head away from the handset as Amy bellowed at her boss without moving the phone away from her mouth. 'I've got a migraine. I'm going home. All right?'

'I don't think you can shout that loudly if you've got a migraine,' I pointed out.

'Be at yours in half an hour,' Amy replied, ignoring me. 'Don't kill yourself before then, OK?'

'OK,' I said. It hadn't actually occurred to me before she brought it up, but the Thames was awfully close by and it would save me from having to sign on. I didn't actually know where the job centre was. Maybe my new friend could tell me. Or maybe I should just kill myself. Amy had hung up before I could ask her opinion and I noticed the phone's owner hovering nearby. I hung up, smiled and held it out to him.

'You know what?' He waved my hand away. 'Have it. I can always get another one.'

'Oh no.' I tried to press it back into his tattooed hand. 'I couldn't possibly. Really, I couldn't.'

'No, take it.' He pressed it back into my hand and

stood up. 'How are you going to get another job without a phone? Just have it.'

'Well, thank you very much.' I gave him my cheeriest smile. 'That's really lovely of you.'

'No worries.' He held up his arm in a salute I vaguely recognized, and not from Brownies. 'And don't worry yourself. Fit bird like you? You'll be fine. Just remember, fuck 'em all.'

'Yeah, fuck 'em all,' I repeated, trying to reconcile the fact that his compliment made me happy with the fact that it came from a man who was clearly some sort of neo-Nazi.

I watched my fairy godmugger wander off across the park, the edges of my stolen, swastika-emblazoned phone cutting into my palm, and just as it started to rain, I started to cry. And I did not know how I was going to stop.

CHAPTER TWO

The girl I met in the mirror at home was not the same girl who had left my flat three hours earlier. Her smart chignon had turned into a tangled mess of sodden curls, and the carefully applied but terribly subtle make-up was all gone, either cried or rained away. The brown eyes that had been so sparkly when they left the house were dull and rimmed with red. My simple black shift dress was wet through, now considerably less office chic – more black-latex-condom-frock with a Pritt Stick still in the pocket. At least now I understood why that little boy had burst into tears when I'd smiled at him outside Superdrug. I was still staring at my reflection, willing what I believed to be three new wrinkles on my forehead to go away, when the front door flew open and a tiny black-haired woman blew inside, hurling herself at me before I could even draw breath.

'Oh my God! What happened? What did you do?' Amy leapt up onto her tiptoes and crushed me in a bear hug. 'Did you punch someone? Did you photocopy your arse? Did you embezzle them for millions?'

25

'Downsizing,' I choked, disengaging my soggy self from her arms. 'There was a "restructure".'

'You know I hate when you use air quotes,' Amy said, slapping my hands down by my side. 'And that's really, really disappointing. You didn't punch anyone? Not even Charlie?'

Amy and I had been best friends since we could speak. Before that, I'm assured that we got on very well. Born six weeks apart, our mums had been besties ever since they'd bonded at an aerobics class in the village hall. We had marked every major milestone together – from first words and first steps right through to most recent snogs and latest hangovers. We were always there for each other in times of need, whether that need was me running out of teabags before there was such a thing as a twenty-four-hour Tesco in East London, or Amy walking out on her fiancé, Dave, three days before her wedding. She never had been good at making a decision and sticking to it. In the past two years she'd had three jobs and four zero percent credit cards, but when it came to me, she was as dependable as Ken Barlow and fiercely loyal. I couldn't fault her.

'I didn't get a chance to punch anyone.' I still couldn't quite believe what had happened. I was redundant. I'd been called a lot of things in my time, but the 'R' word was the worst. 'HR called me in. I thought it was just paperwork stuff for the promotion, and then they told me they were letting me go.'

The words stuck in my throat.

'Nothing dramatic. Nothing exciting. Just restructuring.'

'Are you OK?' She eyed me cautiously, as though I might suddenly lose my tiny mind and bust up the entire apartment. It was fair. If I had been capable of feeling anything at all, there was a chance I might have. 'Your job is, like, your everything.'

Just what I needed to hear.

'I'm not anything,' I said carefully. My mouth felt thick and the words weren't coming out quite right. 'I don't feel anything.'

'Nothing?' Clearly I'd given the wrong answer. 'Not angry or sad or confused or, I don't know, stabby? Sometimes I feel stabby when I get the sack.'

Amy got the sack a lot.

'Nothing,' I repeated. 'Just . . . a bit blank. A bit cold.'

'Emotionally cold?' She was far too eager for my liking. 'Do you feel dead inside?'

'Physically cold.' Maybe calling her had been a bad idea. 'And like I need a wee.'

'Yet more disappointment.' Amy dragged me through the tiny living room and into the kitchen to pop open one of the three bottles of cheap fizzy wine that were clinking together merrily inside a Sainsbury's bag. 'I don't get it. Surely they can't fire you. Everyone knows you're the only one who does anything at that place. Have you gone mad? Did they fire you because you're mad? What did Charlie say?'

'He wasn't in when I left.' I accepted a Snoopy mug full of cava and gulped it down. Cheap fizz burned. Burning was good. 'I don't know if he knows.'

Of course Charlie would know. Everyone would know. Everyone would know that I had been fired. Every. One.

'He hasn't called?' Amy topped me up before helping herself to a packet of Pop Tarts from my flatmate's cupboard and sticking them in the toaster. I didn't have the energy or inclination to stop her.

'HR took my phone,' I said, rummaging around in my handbag for my new-to-me iPhone. 'Happily, I was the victim of a reverse mugging in the park and someone gave me this.'

My tiny bestie snatched the phone out of my hand and examined it carefully without asking me to elaborate. 'Ooh, it's a new one. Good result. Weird case.'

I took it from her, removed the offending cover and handed it back. 'I can't keep it. It's stolen.'

'Swapsies, then? You can have mine.' She pressed several buttons and coughed before speaking. 'Siri, why are Donovan & Dunning a bunch of wankers?'

'I'm sorry, I don't know what you mean by that,' he replied. Very diplomatic for an inanimate object.

I leaned against the kitchen wall, sipping my second, surreptitiously refilled mug of cava and staring out over the East London rooftops. They were exactly how I'd left them this morning. As I concentrated on the unchanging chimney pots, stupid things kept popping into my mind, like what was my mum going to say? What was I supposed to do when my alarm went off tomorrow morning? Would I end up homeless? I didn't know how to go about getting a job. I'd been at Donovan & Dunning since I'd left uni. Before I left uni even – I'd interned there my entire final year. I was going to have to write a CV. Did people still have CVs? Was there something I was supposed to tweet? Maybe there was an unemployment app on my new phone. Most upsettingly, all of the unfinished jobs I'd been doing at work were bothering me. Someone needed to proofread the final air freshener presentation. And who else would take care of the copy for the new baked beans advert? Maybe they'd just lift it from an episode of *Mad Men*, save some time.

For the want of something better to do, I pressed my back against the cold kitchen wall and slid down to the floor. Ahh. That was better. Amy sat on the kitchen top, phone in one hand, Pop Tart in the other, gazing down at me with concern. It didn't feel right. I was supposed to be the one who looked after her.

'Tess,' she said. I peered at her over the edge of my Snoopy mug with wide eyes. 'You're sitting on the kitchen floor in a piss-wet-through dress.'

'I am.' She was not wrong.

'Your head is on the bin. And the bin smells.'

'It is.' Again, stellar observational skills. 'And it does.'

'Do you think you should maybe go and get changed?'

I didn't think I should get changed. I was scared that if I took off my work dress I wouldn't have anything to put on but my pyjamas, and if I put on my pyjamas I might never, ever take them off again. Had Michael remembered about lunch with that awful man from the car company? Eventually, Amy took my silence as a no.

'How about a bath? You must be freezing?'

A bath sounded equally depressing. There was nothing to do in a bath that didn't involve sobbing or razor blades. I wondered if Sandra the designer had remembered to change the colour of the squirrel in that paper towel concept.

'Tess, I'm going to need some verbal feedback from you.' Amy put down her breakfast long enough to snap her fingers in front of me. 'What do you want to do?'

I looked up, pushed my scummy hair out of my face and shook my head.

'I don't know,' I said. 'I honestly don't know. I don't know anything.'

Lindsey Kelk

For the second time that day, I started to cry. My mother would be mortified.

With a sad sigh, Amy hopped down off the worktop and curled up beside me and the bin. 'I know it must feel like shit,' she said, sliding her arm between me and the wall and forcing a hug. 'But you're better than this. You know you're amazing at your job. Whatever reason they have for whatever they've done, it's going to be their loss. That place was killing you. You'll have another job, a better job, at a better agency, this time next Monday. You know I'm right.'

Ignoring the fact that, despite having a first class degree in English and Media Studies, Amy's longest career commitment to date had been as a ticket taker at the local Odeon, I decided to believe her. What choice did I have? I was good at my job. Charlie had once told me I was so good, I couldn't just sell ice to Eskimos, I could convince them that my ice had been hand-carved by pixies and contained the frozen tears of unicorns and that they should thank me for giving them the opportunity to even think about buying it. I just needed a new plan. And some more crappy wine.

'First things first – if you're not going to have a bath, you at least need a shower.' Amy kissed my cheek and jumped up to her feet. 'You're going to catch your death, and, quite honestly, I can't look at your hair like that for one more second. You're pretty rank.'

'OK.' I let her hoist me up to my full five feet and nine inches and wiped my cheeks with the backs of my hands. Sometimes she made me feel like a complete beast, her being all pixie-like and adorable and me being, well, five foot nine. My nan always told me I was statuesque, but really, who wanted to be a statue?

30

'So you get in the shower and I'll go out and get some proper food – you've got nothing in,' Amy said, slapping me on the arse and pointing me towards the shower. 'Hitler's not due back any time soon, is she?'

'Please don't call her Hitler,' I groaned. It was fair to say that Amy and my flatmate did not get along. Luckily, said flatmate was away all week. 'She's not home till the weekend.'

'Thank. Fuck,' Amy declared with exaggerated relief on her face. 'She's the last thing we need.'

'Agreed.' I hated to encourage the two of them when they went at it, but it was true, my flatmate was not the most supportive human in existence. If I could get through this week, get things back on track before she came home, life would be easier.

'Right.' Amy pulled her keys to my flat out of her pocket and used them as a tiny, shiny pointer. 'So, shower and hair wash for you, Sainsbury's and seven chocolate oranges for me, and we'll meet in front of the TV for a *Buffy* marathon in fifteen minutes. And I'm only giving you one day off because tomorrow, every ad agency in the country is going to be fighting over you, and there'll be no time for vampire-slaying then.'

I nodded, hugged her and shut myself in the bathroom, suddenly desperate to strip off my wet outer layer. Flinging the soggy shift against the bathroom tiles, it hit with a satisfying slap and I stepped under the shower with almost a smile. My skin was cold and clammy and the hot water stung in the best way possible. I could feel myself warming up right through to my bones, which at least meant I could still feel something. Seriously, someone needed to let London know that it was summer.

We'd had about three days of legitimate sunshine since May and it was almost July.

'Maybe I'll go travelling,' I told the rubber duck who lived in the corner of the shower. 'Maybe I'll go somewhere warm.'

'With what money?' he asked. That duck was so cynical. 'You haven't got any savings.'

Cynical he might be, but he was also right. Bloody duck. I'd spent the first half of my twenties getting into a really quite impressive amount of debt of both the student loan and credit card variety. Interning and assisting were not well-paid professions, and without the Bank of Mum and Dad to help me through the first few years, I'd had to rely on the kindness of strangers. That is, the graduate loans officer at HSBC. He'd been very ready to help and even more ready to take every penny of interest back. So no, I didn't have any savings, but I didn't really have any debt left either, so that was something. Sort of.

'It'll be fine,' I told the judgemental duck as I lathered up. 'Tomorrow I'll email everyone I know at the other agencies. How many references have I written in the last year?'

The duck didn't answer. He was cynical *and* rude.

'So many. I have written so many. I must have all the emails for the HR people somewhere.'

And I had. Aside from being amazing at my job, I was also one of the longest servers at D&D. They had a pretty high staff turnover, and for reasons I'd never really been able to understand before today, no one liked asking HR for a reference.

'I don't need to panic about this,' I carried on. 'It's a hiccup. I'll be in a new job by Monday. A better job. The best job ever.'

Well, maybe not the best job ever. I was really going to struggle to get the job of Alexander Skarsgård's fang fluffer on the next season of *True Blood*. But still, never say never. I would go and work for a better agency. I would work on bigger accounts. I would manage a team who didn't sniff the permanent markers when I wasn't looking. It was time to dream the big dreams. Maybe I could even leave London. I knew a couple of girls who had got transfers over to New York. Maybe I could go and work in the States for a couple of years, do the whole *Sex and the City* thing. Or maybe even Australia. I'd heard there were a lot of opportunities in Australia. I hoped I'd be able to convince Charlie and Amy to come with me without too much violence.

I stayed in the bathroom, scrubbing away shame and disappointment and the top two layers of my skin until I heard the front door go and the TV come on. Wrapping myself up in the biggest, fluffiest towels I could find, towels that obviously weren't mine, I emerged from the bathroom ready to tell Amy all about my plans. Much to the duck's dismay, I was totally smiling.

For all of three seconds.

'Are those my towels?' My flatmate, Vanessa, stood in the middle of the living room with a very unimpressed look on her face. 'Because if they are, you're going to need to replace them.'

Oh. Fuck.

'Can't I just wash them?' I asked, my fragile positive attitude shattering all around me.

'No. You can't.' She looked so disappointed in me. 'They're towels. You don't share towels. That's disgusting.'

There weren't many people in this world who were genuinely awful. Yes, there were the arseholes like Raquel in HR who got a kick out of making other people's lives difficult, but it wasn't like she went home and kicked puppies for fun. And as I'd learned already that day, even white supremacists could have a heart if you caught them on the right day. But Vanessa Kittler was a genuinely awful human being. I wouldn't have been surprised to find out she had an entire pile of puppies in her room just for kicking around. No one would have been surprised to see her in a Dalmatian fur coat. In fact, if I'd found out she was a member of the BNP, I wouldn't have been shocked. If I'd found out she was the secret underground leader of a fascist group planning the genocide of everyone with an undesirable body mass index or home-dyed hair, I might have raised an eyebrow. Just one, though. She was literally the worst person I'd ever met.

Resplendent in skintight black jeans, an obscenely low-cut white T-shirt and a black leather biker jacket, Vanessa looked me up and down, a small silver suitcase resting by her high-heeled feet.

'Why are you at home using my towels in the middle of the day?' she asked with an expression that suggested she'd just caught me doing lines of coke off the PM while my mum watched. 'Shouldn't you be at work?'

'I thought you were away all week?' I stalled, really wanting not to be standing in the middle of the living room in a towel. In Vanessa's towel. 'Didn't you book a shoot or something?'

'I cancelled,' she replied with a single flip of her shiny blonde hair. 'I got to the airport and they had me booked on easyJet. Fuck that. Why are you in my flat?'

To someone who was so conscientious and sickeningly loyal that they were still fighting the urge to call the office that had just fired her and make sure someone had changed the colour of the squirrel in the paper towel concept, this news caused me near physical pain. Vanessa was a photographer. And by that I mean that once every couple of months one of Vanessa's friends booked her for a job that she occasionally accepted, and she vanished from the flat for a couple of days with the camera I'd had to trade her one month four years ago when I couldn't afford my rent, which she had subsequently refused to sell back to me. I ignored the part where she referred to my home of five years as 'her flat'. I knew for a fact that my rent paid more than two thirds of the actual mortgage, but never having paid a penny herself towards the roof over our heads made absolutely no difference to Vanessa whose house this was. Admittedly, her dad did legally pay the mortgage and had done ever since she had been accepted onto a fine arts programme at Central Saint Martins an undisclosed number of years ago. The deal was that he'd pay until she graduated. She never graduated. He was still paying. As far as Van was concerned, a deal's a deal.

I took a deep breath and started my favourite conversation again. 'I sort of got made redundant this morning.'

'You what?' She blinked and smiled.

'I got made redundant.'

It did not get easier the more often I said it.

'Oh my God.' Vanessa laughed. Actually laughed. 'You lost your job?'

I nodded and rested one wet foot on top of the other, dripping quietly.

'But what are you going to do?' she said as she slowly sat down on the sofa, eyes fixed on me. 'I mean, like, all you do is work.'

'It's OK, it was just restructuring,' I said, reminding

myself as much as telling her. 'I'll be in a new job by next week.'

'Are you high?' she asked. 'Where exactly? If a company that has had you working twelve hours a day for five years doesn't want to keep you around, what makes you think anyone else is going to want to touch you? How are you going to explain getting the sack?'

'I didn't get the sack,' I reiterated, trying not to panic. 'I was made redundant. No one's going to care. I've got loads of experience.'

'Loads of experience in getting fired,' Vanessa replied. 'You know what they say – it's easier to find a job when you're in a job. Who is going to believe you were kicked out for nothing?'

These were not the things I needed to hear.

'If I were interviewing for whatever it is you do, who would I hire? The person who'd applied but still had a job because they were good enough for their company to want to keep them, or the person who'd got the sack for being surplus to requirements?'

Damn her evil logic.

'Honestly, I'm amazed you haven't already killed yourself,' she said, stretching out on the cream settee without taking off her boots. She was truly evil. 'Now you haven't got a job, it must bring all the other tragic parts of your life into focus.'

'All the other tragic parts?'

'No job, no boyfriend, no friends . . .' She ticked off my faults on her fingers. 'That hair.'

I shook the towel turban from my head and grabbed a damp strand. 'What's wrong with my hair?'

'Maybe you could go off on one of those *Eat, Pray, Love* self-exploratory adventures,' she carried on, clearly enjoying herself. 'Although that would actually require some imagination. Can you put the kettle on? I have had the worst morning.'

I pressed my lips together in a grim line. Vanessa had had the worst morning. Of course.

Vanessa and I had come across each other five years ago. I'd been looking for a new flat closer to the office and she was looking for a new flatmate who wouldn't walk out after three months because she was a living nightmare. Of course I didn't know that at the time. We were introduced by a 'mutual friend', aka a friend of Charlie's who was trying to get into Vanessa's knickers, and even though it was hardly love at first sight, her flat was beautiful, right in the middle of Clerkenwell and only a twenty-minute walk from work. She told me she was a photographer, and I'd been a keen amateur photographer until work had completely taken over my life, so I thought that was nice. We made small talk about our mutual love of Bradley Cooper, Kinder eggs and wearing shorts over tights, and within fifteen minutes I'd signed the lease. The day I moved in, Charlie, Amy and I were treated to the sight of Vanessa and Charlie's friend shagging over the back of the settee. I never saw him again. Vanessa I was stuck with.

Within weeks, Vanessa had broken every rule in the flatmate book. She drank my booze, my tea *and* my milk; she never bought toilet paper; she played music so loudly that I had to sleep with earplugs in. Inside a year, she overtook Angelina Jolie on my list of most evil women alive. She fought with my female friends, she slept with my male friends, she took my clothes without asking, and I was fairly certain that on at least one occasion she had stolen money out of my purse. On my twenty-fifth birthday, she performed an impromptu striptease on the bar of the restaurant we were eating at because she was 'considering a career as a burlesque dancer' and called me a boring twat when I asked her to get down. Suffice to say my visiting grandparents were not impressed. The day my second granddad died (not related to the burlesque performance as far as I was aware), she punched me in the arm so hard that I had a bruise for a week and told me to cheer up, it wasn't like I had died. Her favourite term of endearment for Amy was 'Tweedle Twat', and she'd been openly trying to shag Charlie since the day he'd moved my stuff into the flat, despite the fact that she knew how I felt about him. And despite the fact that she was actually being penetrated by one of his best friends the moment they met.

Of course there were reasons why I'd stayed. I hated moving and I hated living with strangers even more. Amy refused to leave her shared house in Shepherd's Bush and I refused to share one bathroom with five nursing students, so that was off the table. And given that Vanessa's dad was paying the mortgage, the rent was so ridiculously cheap that I'd been able to pay off all my student loans without bankrupting myself. And once in a blue moon she would do something human and I'd think she wasn't so bad. We'd spend an evening on the sofa watching bad romcoms and slagging off every man who'd ever walked the earth, or she'd suggest ordering a Chinese takeaway and manage not to insult me more than twice the whole time we ate. And every year, without fail, she bought me a new vibrator for my birthday. Which, for Vanessa, was a Nice Thing To Do. Plus I was very busy and she she was away a lot. Somehow, until now, it had worked.

But when the doorbell went again, I was still standing in the living room wrapped in a towel that was not my own, and I really, really wished I lived in a six-to-a-toilet bedsit in West London.

'Hey, sorry it took so long. I got chatting to this random—'

'Oh, fucking hell, tell me it's not the muffbumper?' Vanessa groaned. 'I can't. I just can't. It's bad enough that you're here without that psycho hanging around.'

'Oh, Jesus Christ, she's home.' Amy froze in the living room doorway, the look on her face switching from impending chocolate binge giddiness to an expression Medusa might find 'a bit cold'.

The second time my best friend and flatmate met, Vanessa had asked Amy if it was hard being a lesbian. As far as we could tell, this question was based exclusively on Amy's choice of shoe and hairstyle. The fact that Vanessa chose to ask the question while Amy was sitting in her fiancé Dave's lap at her own engagement party didn't seem to matter. Ever since, she had filed Amy away in a lovely little box in her brain labelled 'lesbian'. Even though she wasn't even a little bit gay. Did not matter in the slightest.

'Yes, I'm home,' Vanessa replied without taking her eyes off the TV. 'Because I live here. You don't. So you can fuck off.'

'Fairly certain Tess lives here as well, so I'm probably not going to do that.' Amy's voice was laden with faux politeness. 'I thought you were away?'

'Stalking me?' Vanessa asked. 'I've told you before, you're not my type.'

'No, I know. You prefer someone with a cock. Or, you know, anyone with a cock. How is the chlamydia?'

Vanessa sat up sharply. 'Oh my God, you told her?'

Good to know what could get her attention. Obviously I shouldn't have told Amy that my flatmate had caught the clap from, well, we didn't know who exactly, but she had and I had. And in my defence, she didn't need to tell me, but of course she had to. And as the only functioning adult in the flat, I had been charged with reminding her to take her antibiotics every day. It was always nice to be included in things, even your flatmate's venereal diseases.

'It's not Tess's fault you're a dirty skank,' Amy said, dropping the bag full of chocolatey goodness on the side table and rolling up her sleeves. Uh-oh, were we going to have a rumble? Finally? 'Maybe if you kept your mouth and your legs closed for fifteen minutes out of every day, this wouldn't happen.'

Inside the plastic bag, I saw the screen of Amy's mobile flashing. On average she went through one handset every two months – honestly, I'd never known anyone so careless. I wondered how many of her phones my friend from the park had happened upon in the past. But rather than give her a lecture on proper care and management of electronic equipment, I slipped the phone out of the bag and left the two of them at it. They wouldn't notice if I wasn't there; they never did. And I had to answer Amy's phone for her. It was Charlie.

'Amy's phone,' I answered, ever so slightly breathless. Yes, I'd known him for ten years. Yes, I'd worked in the same office as him for the past three. No, it didn't change anything. Worst. Crush. Ever. 'It's Tess.'

'Tess? It's Charlie, are – are you OK?'

Oh, Charlie. So concerned.

'I'm fine,' I lied, closing my bedroom door on the outbreak of World War III in the living room. 'Amy's here.'

'What happened?' He sounded so worried. Bless. 'We just got an email a minute ago saying you're no longer with the company. What is going on? You quit without telling me?'

You had to laugh, didn't you?

'They sent an email saying I'm no longer with the company?' I laid back against my fat marshmallow pillows and closed my eyes. 'That's all it said?'

'Yeah. I emailed you this morning but it kept bouncing back, and then you didn't answer my texts so I phoned HR to see if you'd called in sick. Then they sent this. Tess, what happened?'

'Restructuring?' I suggested. 'Downsizing? Redundancies?'

'Oh. Fuuuuuuck.'

'Yeah.' I felt the first tear in a while trickle down my cheek.

I heard Charlie sighing on the other end of the phone and imagined him sitting at his desk three over and two across from where I used to sit. His hair, almost the exact same shade of dark coppery brown as mine, would be all rumpled as usual. His tie would be loose, as though it were four fifteen on a Friday instead of twelve twenty on a Monday, and he'd be wearing the glasses with clear lenses that he'd bought at Urban Outfitters to try to look a bit cleverer because he had a big client meeting this afternoon.

'Shit, Tess,' he said after the pause. 'I'm sorry. That's bollocks. What a load of wank.'

And that magical way with words was why I was the creative director and he was an account manager. Or at least that's why he was an account manager.

I had been in love with Charlie Wilder for ten long

years but it felt longer. Ever since I'd spotted him sitting outside our halls of residence playing a guitar covered in Smiths stickers, a battered copy of *Catcher in the Rye* by his side, I just knew he was the one. OK, so I hadn't actually read *Catcher in the Rye* and I only knew one or two Smiths songs from films or TV, but regardless, I was smitten. Because these two things meant that Charlie Wilder, unlike every boy I had gone to school with, was Terribly Deep. When you added that observation to the fact that he was six three and therefore taller than me, even in heels, it was hard to fight fate. Unfortunately, it was fair to say that Charlie wasn't hit quite so squarely by Cupid's arrow. It took almost nine months for me to work up the courage (i.e. get drunk enough) to talk to him, and by that time he had a girlfriend. Eventually, after I'd spent two years reading every book I heard him so much as allude to and learning every lyric Morrissey had ever written, we somehow became friends. And once we were friends, I was terrified of scaring Charlie out of my life by confessing my all-encompassing, soul-crushing love for him. As far as I could tell, he wasn't exactly struggling to suppress his feelings for me. There hadn't been so much as a drunken semi-song, and, as Amy routinely liked to tell me, every girl accidentally snogs her boy best friend at some point. Or if you were Vanessa, gave them an STD. Everywhere we went, people assumed we were a couple. When they worked out that we weren't, they wanted to know why not. Charlie always laughed and said I was too good for him. I always laughed and agreed. And then died inside.

But no. So we were the very definition of 'just good friends'. Every Sunday, we went to the pub and ate too many Yorkshire puddings. He killed my spiders; I bought his socks. He was dreadful at remembering to buy socks. But every single time we spoke, whether it was about work, football or the seasonal special at Starbucks, all I wanted was for him to grab hold of me, spin me around and tell me he loved me. It was, admittedly, a little bit sad. As far as I was concerned, there were two kinds of men in the world – Charlie and the Not-Charlies. The Not-Charlies didn't get a look in.

So you can understand why I was a bit slow to process exactly what he'd said.

'Hang on – no one else got laid off? No other redundancies?'

'No. No one. And Michael just announced that we won that air freshener account. Everyone was asking where you were. It's mental. What exactly did he tell you?'

Reluctantly I went over the whole story, my heart sinking through the floor as reality set in. Donovan & Dunning weren't restructuring. The only person being downsized was me, and it was working. I'd never felt smaller in my entire life. I just couldn't understand why. What could I possibly have done wrong?

'I'll try to find out what's going on,' he promised when I'd finished. 'Do you want to come over later? We could get very, very drunk and watch *Top Gun*?'

I did like *Top Gun*.

'And I'll buy all that girl shit you like? You know – wine, those massive cookies, chocolate that isn't a Mars Bar?'

I also liked girl shit.

'Come on, Tess, you'll feel better. You know you want to.'

And I did want to. But the idea of curling up on Charlie's sofa eating chocolates that weren't Mars Bars while he sat there feeling sorry for me was too much to bear. The only thing worse than being in love with someone who didn't love you was being in love with someone who pitied you.

'I think I just want to go to sleep. I'm really tired,' I said, rolling out of my towel and into the nightshirt underneath my pillow. So what if it was only midday. I was unemployed. 'Call you tomorrow?'

'Make sure you do,' he said sternly. 'It'll be all right, you know. Love you.'

'Love you too,' I replied, wincing with every word. Not because he didn't mean it, but because he did. Just not in the same way. 'Oh, and Charlie – I know what you're going to say, but could you make sure Sandra changes the colour on the squirrel?'

'You're hopeless,' he sighed. 'Will do.'

Hanging up, I shuffled my bum up the bed until I could kick my feet under the covers and pulled them up over my head. Vanessa and Amy were still going at it in the living room. I couldn't even make out what they were arguing about at this point – it was just high-pitched squealing. It sounded like dolphins re-enacting *Toy Story 3*. And I hadn't lied – I really was exhausted. Tomorrow I would get up and I would draft my CV. Charlie would have found out exactly what had gone down at work and I'd call all the lovely recruitment agencies and ad agencies and let them know that I was ready for a new challenge. Maybe if I just went to sleep, everything would be better when I woke up. That always seemed to work in the movies, after all.

CHAPTER THREE

In the four days that had passed since I'd been fired I had learned the following lessons. One: what worked in the movies did not work in real life. Two: advertising was the creative industry equivalent of the movie *Mean Girls*. Three: four days wasn't long enough for your hair to start washing itself. Four: if, however, you just didn't get out of bed, you stopped noticing that your hair smelled disgusting after two and a half days, so that didn't really matter.

I had woken up on Tuesday strong, confident and fully committed to writing a new chapter in *The Story of Tess*. Amy called in sick with another migraine and played cheerleader, DJing a motivational mix of music from my largely unplayed music library. By midday, I had an amazing CV, I'd called and left voicemails with every advertising agency in London, and I'd drunk five and a half cups of coffee. Big cups. By four p.m., my CV had gone out to eight recruitment agencies, I'd been to the toilet six times and Charlie had reported back at least a dozen different rumours about my 'no longer being with the company'. The three favourites seemed to be that I had been leaking information to a competitor, that I had blackmailed the company into promoting me, and, my personal favourite, that I'd been sleeping with Michael and that he'd sent me to France to have his baby. Because clearly it was 1852 and that's what we did when we got knocked up by the boss.

At six p.m., after Amy had left for the bar job she occasionally bothered with, after Charlie had emailed me the fifteenth different rumour (that I was completing a sex change and would be coming back in the New Year as Terence), and after I had received the fifth phone call of the day explaining no one was hiring at the moment, that things were really tough right now and asking if I had considered retraining as a teacher, I gave up. As in, I took off my people clothes and put on my most disgusting threadbare flannel pyjamas, ate everything in the fridge and turned off my stolen phone. And when I turned it back on twenty-four hours later, the only people who had tried to contact me were Amy and Charlie. So I turned it back off again. The only bright spot was that when I left my room at *EastEnders* o'clock, Vanessa had mysteriously disappeared and taken her suitcase and toxic personality with her.

For the past seventy-two hours I had only got out of bed to pee, take something out of the fridge or fetch another *Sex and the City* boxset from the living room. No one ever got laid off in *Sex and the City*. And they all got the men they wanted in the end. Even if one of them was Steve. It did not make me feel better. I did not turn it off.

But three days later, the universe and Amy had decided enough was enough.

'Get up, get up, get up!' She started slapping at either side of my head and bouncing up and down on top of my bed. 'It's Saturday. You've got to get up. We're staging an intervention.'

'I don't want to be intervened,' I croaked, pushing Amy away and throwing myself face first into my pile of pillows. 'Leave me alone.'

'No, you're not Anne Frank, you're not hiding from the Nazis. It's time for you to get your arse up and out,' she said, jumping on my back and wrapping her legs around my waist. She was very strong for such a little girl. 'You need to get in the shower. We've got places to go, people to see.'

'Not possible,' I remonstrated, pushing up onto all fours and trying to shake her off, but Amy clung to me as though she was riding a scabby horse. 'Let me go back to sleep.'

'We haven't got time – I'm double-parked. Get dressed, you filthy mare.'

Of course the other person in Amy's intervention was Charlie. I shook Amy loose and tried to push the dead cat on top of my head into something resembling a pony-tail. It wasn't like he hadn't spent more than one night on my bathroom floor holding my hair back while I brought up half of the student union bar, but still, I tried to avoid looking like utter scum in front of him when I could. If I could.

'How are you double-parked? You haven't got a car.' I blinked at the daylight and the very tall, very lovely man silhouetted by my window.

'It's mental, Tess. You just go on the Internet and ask a man if you can borrow one, and then you give him your credit card details and, fuck me, you've got a car,'

47

he replied. Sarcasm was not one of Charlie's strong points. As opposed to his beautiful, floppy hair and wonderful eyes. And his long, long legs. And broad chest. I was going off topic.

'If you hadn't gone the complete Howard Hughes, you'd remember that this afternoon is my niece's christening and we are attending,' Amy said, releasing her kung fu grip and rolling across the bed as she wrinkled her tiny nose. Her black bob was ruffled from over-exertion and her cheeks were flushed. She looked the very picture of health. She looked like my complete opposite. 'So get up and get in the shower because we are on our way up north whether you like it or not.'

Those karma gods were not playing fair.

'Tess! Amy!'

As was tradition, my mum leapt up from the kitchen table as though I was returning from the war and we hadn't called seventeen minutes ago to say we were getting off the M1 and would be there in seventeen minutes. No hugs, though. We didn't hug.

'And Charlie.'

As was tradition, my boy best friend was met with a wildly inappropriate growl of a hello, as he had been ever since the first time I'd brought him home. The only person on earth who loved Charlie more than I did was my mum. I wasn't sure if she wanted him to marry me or marry her. Of course she was already married and my stepdad was possibly the best man on earth, but that didn't stop her from giving him a squeeze that was just half a heart-beat too long. They hugged. They always hugged.

'Nice to see you, Julie,' he squeaked as she copped a sneaky feel. 'You look well.'

'Isn't it a lovely weekend?' Once she had put Charlie down, Mum sat back at the table while Amy helped herself to everything in our fridge. 'It's going to be a lovely christening. Amy, you must be so proud of your sister.'

'Yes, getting accidentally knocked up is quite the achievement these days,' Amy replied, popping the top off a beer. 'And two kids to two different men. She's a living miracle.'

'So proud,' Mum beamed, stone cold smile on her face. 'And what are you doing for work now? Are you still seeing that lovely coloured man?'

I shook my head and planted my face on the cool kitchen table. It smelled of disinfectant wipes and shame.

'No, that was really just a sex thing,' Amy said. She did love going toe to toe with my mum. And the worst part was that she was really only warming up for her own mother. 'But you know what they say – once you go black—'

'I haven't, but that's very interesting.' Mum always got bored before Amy did and so she turned her attention to Charlie. 'And what about you, love? How's work? Tess still acting the slave driver?'

Because the atmosphere wasn't tense enough already.

During the two-hour drive up into the seventh circle of hell, Amy and Charlie had been thoroughly briefed on the situation. They knew that I had not told my mother about my newly unemployed status, and they knew I was not planning to do so. Originally I just hadn't been able to face it. And then I had convinced myself I'd be able to get a new job so quickly that there wasn't any point in telling her. And then I'd spent three days under the duvet eating packet after packet of Hobnobs.

Charlie thought I should tell her. Charlie thought my mum was nicer than Mary Poppins on Xanax. Charlie loved my mum because my mum loved Charlie. Amy did not think I should tell her. Amy thought my mum was a word I'd only ever said out loud twice in my entire life. Amy did not love my mum because my mum did not love Amy. And while no one wants to think badly of their parents, Amy's opinion of my mum was probably closer to the truth than Charlie's. It was comforting to know there was someone out there who knew everything about me and wasn't genetically or legally required to love me but did so anyway. Unfortunately, it also meant that Amy had witnessed all the rows, all the shouting and all the tears, and, as was right and proper for a best friend, she held all the grudges I was biologically denied.

I loved my mum and I knew that she loved me. I also knew that she loved me more when I was doing well. If I got ninety-eight percent in a test, she wanted to know what had happened to the other two percent. If I got a pay rise, she wanted to know why it wasn't a promotion. If I got a promotion, she wanted to see a business card to verify it. She was a pusher. She was a pushy mother. Whenever I got upset about it, I tried to remind myself I should be happy that she focused her efforts on shoving me up the academic and professional ladders, and even happier that reality TV didn't exist when I was a kid. I would almost certainly have ended up on *X Factor*, dancing to Kelis's *Milkshake* in a diamante bra-and-knicker set at the age of six. It wasn't her fault, I reminded myself for the thousandth time that year; she just wanted the best for me. She just wanted me to have the things that she didn't. And she'd watched *Working Girl* too many times in the eighties. It wasn't a coincidence that I was called Tess.

'Oh, you know Tess doesn't work in my team,' Charlie replied with careful diplomacy. 'And thank goodness. She's so good at her job, she'd just show me up.'

He always knew the right thing to say. Mum and I sat across from each other and smiled in tandem. Her hair was shorter than mine and starting to go grey, but we had the same colour eyes and identical gigantic rack. I'd got my Big Bird height, overanalytical mind and physical inability to hold a tune from Dad, but the rest of me was pure Julie.

'So what's the news?' she asked, eventually turning to me. 'How's that fancy office? Have you got your new business cards yet?'

'Not yet,' I said, trying very hard not to tell any lies. 'And really, the creative director job isn't that different from what I was doing before. It's just a different title.'

I actually assumed that was true. Everyone knew you ended up doing the new job for at least a year before you actually got the title.

'Everyone's been very impressed – they can't wait to see you and hear all about it.' Mum wore my achievements like a badge. 'Your sisters will be at the christening.'

Joy.

'Where's Brian?' I asked, looking around the house I grew up in for signs of my stepdad, aka the only sane member of my family. It made perfect sense that he wasn't genetically related to me in anyway. 'Hiding?'

'Hiding,' Mum confirmed. 'He's playing golf. He'll be back by two.'

I nodded and tried not to worry. It seemed like Brian was playing a lot of golf lately.

'Oh, Tess, Amy's mum dropped by earlier and asked if you could take some pictures this afternoon?'

'I would, but I didn't bring my camera,' I said, biting my lip and hoping she wouldn't ask where it was.

It was last summer, when I'd been short on money due to a ridiculous last-minute weekend away with Charlie that I couldn't afford and which had ended in him copping off with a twenty-two-year-old blonde girl while I sat in the B&B sulking, that I'd traded my camera to Vanessa for a month's rent. The camera I'd begged my mother to buy me. The camera I had taken with me everywhere until work had got in the way. The camera that sat on my 'photographer' roommate's desk and never moved.

'She'll just have to manage without, then, won't she,' Mum shrugged. 'I told her it wasn't fair to ask anyway. You've been working all week and then she expects you to take photos of her bloody granddaughter's christening? I mean, you're a bloody director now, for Christ's sake. And it's not like there won't be another one, the way she goes on. No offence, Amy.'

'None taken,' Amy replied. 'My sister is a bigger slag than I am, I know.'

'Hadn't we better go and get changed?' I stood up and grabbed my hastily packed weekend bag, wondering what sartorial treats Amy had shoved in there while I was showering. 'We don't want to be fighting for the bathroom.'

'Fine.' Mum feigned disappointment that we were trying to escape so quickly, but I knew she was relieved. 'Be down here by quarter to three. We'll walk down to the church together.'

I just prayed I wouldn't burn up on entry.

*   *   *

The christening went as well as a small village christening could go. Babies cried, mums cooed and the twenty-something children who had run away at the age of eighteen stood awkwardly at the back fielding questions from their former Brownie leaders about why they weren't married yet.

'We can't get married,' Amy was explaining to our septuagenarian Brown Owl. 'Because we're a triad. Me, Tess and Charlie. Society doesn't understand our love. It's a polyamory thing.'

'Pollyanna-y?' Mrs Rogers looked very confused. 'I don't quite follow, Amy, love.'

'Just what we need,' Charlie whispered in my ear as he fell into the seat next to me. The post-baptismal celebrations were taking place in the pub, 'the true church of the village', as it was written. Almost everyone I'd gone to school with was crammed into the conservatory of The Millhouse, putting back pints and taking pictures of Amy's new niece, Katniss, with their phones and posting them straight to her Facebook page. I had assumed Amy was taking the piss when she'd told me the baby's name, but no. I should have known. Her big sister was called Bella, after all.

'What's that?' I clinked my Diet Coke against his pint of bitter and took a sip. As predicted, Amy had struggled with my wardrobe of sensible work separates, so I was sitting in a Yorkshire pub at my best friend's sister's baby's christening in July wearing black leather knee boots, a gold sequinned miniskirt I'd worn one New Year at uni, and a white cotton shirt that really needed ironing. It was quite the outfit.

'Amy is going round telling everyone that the three of us are a couple,' he said, undoing his already loose tie. 'I think she got bored of people asking about Dave.'

'Amy was bored of people asking about Dave seven seconds after she broke up with him,' I replied, imagining the fun conversation I'd be having with Lorraine from the library and Donna from the post office before the night was out. 'Now she's just bored. Why did she even make us come to this?'

'I'm fairly certain it was to remind you why you left in the first place. Is it working?' Charlie drained his pint and nodded towards my half-empty glass. 'What are you drinking? I'm going to the bar.'

Reaching over, I wiped a frothy moustache from his top lip and smiled. 'Just Diet Coke. I'm not in the mood to drink.'

'God forbid you should make a scene.' He looked over to where Amy was performing a jazz tap routine for the pensioners who lived in the bungalows near her mum.

'I'm not nearly so entertaining,' I replied. 'Thanks for coming with us, anyway. I know it's a ball-ache.'

'Yeah, whatever.' He stood up and stretched. 'Any family is better than no family, remember?'

'And the grass is always greener,' I said. 'Remember?'

Charlie half laughed as he walked away, towering over everyone else in the bar while I watched. It was Christmas in the third year of uni when he first came home with me. His parents were getting divorced, and since I'd been there, done that, I'd told him to come home with me. Never in a million years did I think he'd say yes. Now, eight Noels on, he had a stocking embroidered with his name and a permanent spot at our Christmas dinner table. Just like me, he didn't really see his dad, and his mum had moved to Malta with his stepdad a couple of years ago. Without any grandparents or siblings, as soon as the Boots Christmas catalogue dropped, he was an honorary Brookes.

'Tess! You came! We were worried you might be too busy!'

Only a full-blooded Brookes could be that passive-aggressive. I tore my eyes away from Charlie's arse to the far less pleasant sight of my two younger sisters standing before me, arms full of babies and faces full of judgement.

'Are those new boots?' Melanie asked.

'Your hair is so long,' Liz said.

'And you both look well,' I said, looking down at my niece and nephew and giving them each a curt nod. 'Hello, babies.'

'Here, hold her.' Melanie, twenty-six, married, mother of two, handed me baby Tallulah. 'She doesn't even know who you are. Isn't that funny?'

I bit my lip to avoid pointing out that Tallulah was only nine months old and barely even knew who she was and took the baby with a strained smile.

'Please don't be sick on this shirt,' I whispered to my niece. 'It was a present.'

'Look, you're a natural!' Liz, twenty-two, engaged, mother of one but desperately trying for another by all accounts, thrust out a second baby. 'Take Harry while I get us a drink.'

'I can't hold two babies,' I squealed, taking the even tinier bundle in my other arm and looking around in desperation. 'What if I need a wee?'

'You're not allowed to have a wee,' Mel said, smoothing out her wrinkled-to-buggery dress and sitting down beside me. She picked up a glass of wine that did not belong to her and swigged it back. 'Welcome to my world.'

'I think I read something on the way in about over-population, so I can't stay,' I said. I really wanted to give her one of the babies back, but with my arms full, I had no idea how to offload one. They smelled weird. 'Are they OK? I can't see their faces. How do you do this?'

'Don't overthink it, you'll drop one,' she advised. Her hair, identical to mine, sprang all around her face. While I kept my copper mess carefully tethered in a long pony-tail, Mel had clearly decided to embrace the curls for the christening. It was a controversial gamble that had not paid off. 'Although I realize that telling you not to overthink something is like telling Liz no.'

Mel was the poor put-upon middle sister. While Mum was busy forcing me up an imaginary ladder of success and our stepdad was spoiling little Lizzie with his un-wavering attention, the true child of divorce and official Band-Aid baby Mel sat quietly in the middle of it all, shaking her head and counting down the days until she could get out, get married and fuck up a family all of her own. So far, so good. She had a house, a husband, a Rav 4 and two kids. As far as she was concerned, she was winning. And despite her open disapproval of me, I actually liked Mel. She was funny, dry and desperately honest. We didn't see each other terribly often, mainly because I avoided the village like the plague and she couldn't exactly come gallivanting down to London with two babies under three. It might seem like a strange thing to say about your sister, but if we weren't related, I'd want to be her friend.

'Wiiiiiine.' Liz returned from the bar and handed Mel a glass bucket of suspiciously green-tinged white wine.

'So, Tess, tell me everything. You never update Facebook. Have you got a boyfriend?'

Liz, on the other hand, not so much.

'Me and Jamie are moving at the end of the month, has Mel told you? Right around the corner from her. Isn't it brilliant? All our babies will get to grow up together. Well, all our babies apart from your babies. You really need to get a move on, you know – you're not getting any younger.'

There was nothing like being reminded about your tick-tick-ticking biological clock by your six-years-younger half-sister to put the icing on this shitty cake of a week. And cake should never be shitty.

'Is Charlie going out with anyone?' she asked, tightening her blonde ponytail. Liz was the only one of the three of us who had escaped Mum's dark-hair-big-boob genes. 'He might be up for it now if he's getting desperate. I could talk to him for you?'

'Or I could kill you,' I offered, desperate to offload one of these babies. Preferably whichever one was starting to smell like poop. 'Charlie isn't desperate.'

Liz and Mel shared a not-very-furtive glance.

'And neither am I,' I added.

'You know there's a rumour going round that you and Amy are lezzers.' Liz sipped her wine and narrowed her eyes. 'But I told Karen you weren't. Because you're not. Are you?'

'No, Liz, Amy and I are not lesbians. We're very busy career women who have other things to worry about than babies and boyfriends.' Didn't matter how true that was, it still sounded like an excuse. 'And I think you'll find Amy probably started that rumour to make Karen look stupid.'

'So the new job's going well?' Mel took over the interrogation and one of the babies. Unfortunately, it was not the smelly one. I gave Tallulah the filthiest look I could muster but she just blew a raspberry back at me. No respect, that girl.

'Yes?' I was the worst liar.

'Because I emailed you and it bounced back.'

Bloody email. She couldn't have sent flowers?

'Uh, there was a problem with the server.'

'But not on Charlie's email? Because I emailed Charlie and that was fine.'

So much for her being the nice sister. Along with her hair and boobs, Mel had also inherited our mum's ability to sniff out blood, and once she got a whiff of something not right, she did not let go.

'I didn't want to say anything at the christening' – Amy always told me it was good to start a lie by making yourself look good – 'but I'm not actually working there any more.'

'Then where are you working?' The two of them stared at me as though they already knew the answer but just really, really needed to hear me say it.

'I'm not working anywhere,' I said quietly. 'I got made redundant.'

Mel gasped. Liz reached out and snatched Tallulah from my arms in case unemployment was catching.

'You know that one isn't yours, don't you?' I asked.

'Mum!' Liz grabbed our passing mother's arm, her face completely white. 'Tess lost her job!'

'Oh, for fuck's sake.' I pressed my hand against my forehead and prayed to whoever might be listening to strike me dead on the spot. I could not handle this right now. Silently I cursed Amy for dragging me up here and

wished a plague on Charlie's house for driving the car.
My mother stopped dead in her tracks, her face frozen
in horror, and just in case people hadn't heard Liz, she
dropped a full glass of red wine onto the tiled floor. It
shattered into not really that many pieces (definitely not
crystal) and splattered everyone around us with cheap
red plonk.

'Tess, what is she talking about?' Ignoring the fact that
she'd just ruined about seven people's tights, my mum
looked as though she'd just had a stroke. I really hoped
she hadn't. 'What does she mean you lost your job?'

'I was going to tell you after . . .' I waved my hand
around the very quiet room. 'I got made redundant.'

And with that, the whispering began. Everyone knew
someone who had been made redundant, but Tess
Brookes? Her who had moved away to That London?
With her fancy job? Scandalous.

'But your promotion?' Mum's face was still a very
worrying shade of grey.

'No promotion,' I replied. Thank goodness I hadn't
overreacted. This was exactly as horrible as I had thought
it would be.

'I cannot believe you would embarrass me like this,'
she said through gritted teeth as she looked around at
anyone but me. 'I cannot believe you would come here
and announce that like it's nothing. I cannot believe you
wanted to embarrass me in front of all my friends.'

I dipped my head, pretending my eyes weren't stinging,
and watched the puddle of her spilled wine bleed across
the floor towards a white paper napkin and slowly stain
it a dark ruby red. There were so many things I wanted
to say. I hadn't planned to tell her like this. I hadn't
wanted to embarrass anyone. Liz told her! It was just like

being fifteen again; Liz was such a grass. But just like when I was fifteen, I knew there was no point answering back. She wasn't finished.

'Don't just sit there crying. What did you do?'

Damage done, Liz got up, switched babies with Mel and flounced away, muttering something about needing to change Harry. Mel gave me a quick supportive squeeze on the shoulder and followed. Just like being fifteen. Where was Amy when I needed her?

'I didn't *do* anything – they were just laying people off,' I explained. It didn't help that I didn't actually know what had happened myself. 'I didn't do anything wrong.'

'Well, people don't just lose their jobs for no reason, Tess,' she carried on while a random sixteen-year-old who probably went to my old school started mopping up the mess around us. 'I should have known something was wrong when you came out dressed like that.'

She had a point there. She should have known.

'I can't believe this. After all I've done for you.'

'What? After all you've done what?'

Ahh. There was Amy. And as my best friend stepped up to my mother, the whispering was replaced by a low clinking of glasses, occasionally punctuated by the popping open of packets of McCoy's.

'What exactly have you done?' she asked, forcing her way in between me and my mother, hands on skinny hips, and stamping a very little foot. 'Aside from bully your daughter for the last twenty years?'

Amy and my mum were exactly the same height. For years I'd wondered who would win in a fight, and at last it looked like I might find out.

'I know this is going to be hard for you, Amy, but please don't involve yourself where you're not wanted,' she replied. Ahh, interesting. She was playing the responsible mother card.

'Can we not do this?' I asked as calmly as possible. 'We can talk about this at home. This is . . . Katniss's day?'

Nope, that just did not sound right.

'Oh, we will talk about this at home,' Mum replied, giving Amy the frowning of a lifetime. 'We'll talk about when you decided it was all right to start lying to your mother. And Amy, I think it would be a good idea if you stayed at your house tonight.'

Before Amy could reply, my mum turned on her sensible heel and marched away. As the door to the pub slammed, the silence broke and the party went back to full volume with a new lease of life now they had something scandalous to talk about. Thank goodness me losing my job had served a purpose.

'Sorry.' Amy dropped into my lap and rested her head on my shoulder. Because that would quiet those lesbian rumours. 'I couldn't listen to her going on at you.'

'Oh, I'm sure you only made it marginally worse,' I said, patting her on the head. 'She was going to find out sooner or later.'

'I suppose. Sorry I made you come in the first place, then,' she sniffed. 'I thought coming back and checking out all the losers would remind you how awesome our lives are.'

I looked at her in disbelief. She shrugged. 'How awesome my life is?'

'OK.' I groaned and stood up straight, ignoring the looks and smirks around the room. 'I'm going to go out for a walk. Get some fresh air. Are you all right? I saw you dancing for Mrs Rogers earlier. Nice moves.'

'Can you stop worrying about me for one minute and worry about yourself?' she said, brushing down her inappropriately tiny red dress and straightening out her glossy black bob. 'When am I not fine?'

It was true. She was always fine. So I gave her a smile and, ignoring all my Cloverhill classmates, I pushed my way over to the fire escape and escaped.

CHAPTER FOUR

Behind the Millhouse was the mill pond, a tiny body of water just big enough to have a good side and a bad side. Naturally, the bad side was where all the cool kids hung out and drank cheap, rank booze, while the good side was where the nanas brought their grandchildren to throw bits of old Hovis at the scabby ducks. I had spent so many hours throwing Hovis at those ducks, with and without my nana. After a slow and steady lap of the pond, I found a bench somewhere in between the two poles, my confused ensemble not really fitting in with either crew. The kids had clearly clocked me as too old to hang out with them and too uncool to buy them more bargain vodka, and the grandparents did not want their precious children talking to a lady dressed as a stripper on her way to work in a call centre. I didn't care. I didn't really feel anything. My brain was so full of so much, I couldn't do anything but sit on the bench, try to ignore the splinters in the backs of my thighs and make occasional squeaking noises. I wondered if there was some terrifying astrological event I didn't know about, if all

Capricorns were going through something equally traumatic, but it just wasn't possible. Kate Middleton was a Capricorn – there would have been something on the news if her life was turning as all-encompassingly shitty as mine. There would have been a tweet.

Stretching out my fingers, I stared at the backs of my hands as though I had a laptop in front of me and tried to switch into work mode. I was best in work mode. If I were still an employed, functioning member of society and my shambles of a life was a campaign, how would I pitch it?

The biggest problem was the sheer number of problems. I didn't have a job, I hated my flatmate, my mum hated me, I was in love with my best friend, my best friend was not in love with me, and on top of everything else, even when you peeled away those key issues, I had absolutely no life. Not a single quirky characteristic that could be spun into an adorable side project. As a brand, I was less desirable than Skoda; even I would struggle to spin me. But it wasn't impossible – I needed rebranding. All the successful companies struggled at some point. Even Apple nearly went bankrupt once. And if someone could make Old Spice cool again, I could certainly save myself.

But what was the Tess Brookes brand?

This was why I'd never had an online dating profile – it was too hard to describe yourself. I was loyal, conscientious, creative and logical. I could always see the solution to a problem; I always knew how to make a client happy. Unless the client was me, apparently. Visually, I didn't have a signature look unless you counted bad hair and massive boobs. (Hopefully no one did.) There was no one thing that would make someone sit back and go, 'Oh, that's *so* Tess.' I didn't have a favourite band, a favourite book; I dipped in and out of whatever was on the TV when I turned it on. I could describe every single demographic out there, I could tell you what made someone buy Coke over Pepsi and then switch back again, but I couldn't tell you whether or not I preferred polka dots over stripes. I knew too much about everyone else and nothing at all about myself. How could I convince someone to buy me when there was nothing to buy?

'There you are.'

I looked up to see Charlie striding along the edge of the pond, a frown on his face. His pretty, pretty face.

'I've been looking for you everywhere.'

'To be fair, I didn't get that far.' I glanced around. I wasn't more than five minutes away from the pub. I was sad, but I was also very lazy. 'You missed an awesome scene.'

'I know, I heard. I was in the gents.' He sat down beside me, took off his jumper and draped it round my shoulders. 'But afterwards you missed Amy grabbing hold of the baby and singing "Circle of Life", so I think we're square.'

'Jesus, I've only been out here half an hour,' I laughed, trying not to be upset that I'd missed what sounded like an incredible *Lion King* homage. I did love a Disney movie. There! That was something I knew about myself. I was a twenty-eight-year-old unemployed single woman who loved animated movies made for children. If we were at work, I'd be trying to sell me some cat food and a lovely cardigan about now. Maybe I should just change my name and run away – that would be a pretty decent rebrand.

'Well, I was worried about you,' he said, nudging me with his shoulder. 'Been a shit week, Brookes. How are you still sober?'

'Didn't bring any booze.' I waved my empty hands at him. 'Schoolboy error.'

'Thankfully' – Charlie produced a half-bottle of vodka from behind his back – 'I am not a schoolboy.'

'Oh, you clever man,' I said, gratefully accepting the bottle and taking a deep drink. I had never been a very good drinker. I loved a drink, but drinks did not love me. The two mugs of wine I'd enjoyed on Monday, post-sacking, were the first alcoholic drinks I'd had in a month, but while we were rebranding, I had to consider all my options. Maybe the new Tess would be a drinker. Maybe she'd learn how to make elaborate cocktails and have her friends over for parties. Maybe she'd be a whisky drinker and keep a decanter on her desk like Don Draper. Or maybe she'd do a shot of cheap supermarket vodka by the duck pond and retch in her own mouth.

'Keep it down.' Charlie rubbed my back and took the bottle from me. 'Keep it down.'

'Oh, bugger me, that's disgusting,' I coughed, feeling the burn in the back of my throat. Maybe if I was going to be a drinker, I shouldn't start with four-quid cava and vodka that cost less than a Tube ticket. 'Thank you.'

'You're very welcome.' Charlie took a shot without wincing and passed the bottle back. The sun was already setting across the pond, and the bad side was getting considerably more traffic than the good. 'So, what are we going to do with you?'

'I have no idea,' I replied, turning to give him my best attempt at a smile. 'I was just trying to work that out myself.'

'Well, if you were a client and I was trying to sort you out, I'd start with what you wanted out of your campaign,' he reasoned while I took a second shot. Out of the corner of my eye, I saw him rubbing the centre of his left eyebrow. That meant he was thinking. Rubbing his chin meant he was confused. Nodding and scratching the back of his neck meant he was listening but not really paying attention. There wasn't a thing about this man I didn't know. 'What do you want?'

This was why we were soulmates. He was trying to solve my problems in exactly the same way I was trying to solve my problems.

'My job,' I replied.

'You can't have your job.' He slapped my bare thigh and I had to remember to be offended and not turned on. 'As account manager, it's my role to give you honest feedback and tell you what is and isn't possible. Your old job, off the table. What else do you want?'

'I really do just want my job,' I said, clutching the warm bottle between my knees. 'If I had my job back, I could just put everything back how it was and carry on. That would be perfect.'

'If this week has taught us nothing else, it's that things were not perfect for you,' Charlie said. He turned on the bench until his knee was pressing against mine. 'People lose their jobs every day, Tess. They don't take to their beds for four days and fall apart. They turn to their friends, they go on holiday, they – I don't fucking know – read the great novels or something. Write a great novel. Start a blog. Tell me what makes you happy, aside from work.'

I tried to think about something other than his knee on mine.

'You?' I said as quietly as humanly possible.

'Me?'

'You and Amy?' I wanted to slap myself.

Charlie nodded for a moment and took the bottle back from me without words. The ducks on the pond, full of stale bread, started to make their way over to the rushes looking for their beds.

'I think the problem is, you're so used to being in your head and solving the problem that you don't know how to present it back to the client. That's my job,' Charlie took hold of my hand. His were almost as soft as mine, but so much bigger. I turned, flushed with vodka, proximity and my ridiculous outfit, and looked into his big brown eyes. He was adorable. 'So here's what I see. You are a beautiful, clever, funny woman. You work too hard, you take on too much, and you're far too concerned with other people's expectations. You worry too much about your friends and you live with a mentalist, but aside from that, the basic elements are all there.'

Beautiful. He said I was beautiful.

'Basic elements for what?' I asked.

'A life,' Charlie replied. 'You're amazing, you know?' He knew me well enough to recognize my near-tears whimper and started talking fast. 'You have so much drive and ambition; you're so dedicated to achieving your goals. All you need to do is redirect that energy to a new goal. I'm not saying you shouldn't care about your job – you should. It's just that it can't be the only thing you care about. There can't only be one thing that makes you happy.'

'Are you happy?' I asked him, not letting go of his hand. I was a bit worried I might never let go. 'In general, I mean, are you happy?'

'Yeah,' he nodded slowly. 'I'm happy. I like my job, I've got good mates, I like my flat. There are things I'd change, but overall I'm not complaining. Are you happy?'

'Am I happy?' I repeated. 'I don't think I'm really anything.'

It was hard to say out loud, but as soon as I did, I knew it was true.

'What would you change?' I asked him, waiting to start feeling drunk. I really wanted to be drunk. 'You said there are things you'd change.'

'Oh, obvious stuff.' He squeezed my hand and scuffed the toe of his shoe in the dirt under the bench. 'I'd like my own place. I'd like Arsenal to be doing better in the league. A smoking-hot girlfriend who would do my washing so I didn't keep running out of socks would be nice.'

'I am so sick of buying you more socks. What do you do, eat them?' I asked with the closest thing to a laugh I could muster. Bravely, I rested my head on his shoulder and breathed in. He was wearing the aftershave I'd bought him for Christmas. He smelled cool, spicy and familiar. It made my stomach melt, my fingertips tingle. 'You've got loads going for you. You could get a hot girlfriend if you really wanted one. You've got everything.'

'And so have you.' He dropped his head on top of mine, our coppery curls meshing together, and put his arm around my shoulders. 'You just haven't realized yet.'

'I've got sod all,' I said, trying to pretend that the teenagers weren't totally eyeing up the bottle in my hand. 'As you have quite rightly pointed out.'

'You've got me.' Charlie said. 'And I'm all right.'

'Oh, don't.' I laughed out loud. 'Don't even.'

This wasn't the first time Charlie and I had got drunk

on a bench. This was not the first time one of us had talked the other through a crisis. But it was the first time he'd looked at me with such dark eyes. The first time I'd felt his thumb gently running back and forth over the back of the hand he was holding. And the first time that I had ever felt his heart beating as fast as mine.

'I'm all right, aren't I?' he asked. 'Tess?'

I felt goosebumps on my bare legs and twisted round to get a better look at him. His dark, gingerish five o'clock shadow was starting to come through and his dark, dilated eyes were ever so slightly bloodshot from getting up so early, driving so far and drinking so much. He leaned his forehead against mine and repeated himself in a whisper.

'Tess?'

Words were my thing. Words were my actual job. I used them every day, manipulated them, moulded them, made them dance around in circles, but at that moment there wasn't a word in the world that would help me. And so instead of trying to say something funny or clever, I took a deep breath and kissed him. For a moment, I couldn't tell who was more shocked. Neither of us moved – we just sat there, frozen, Tess pressed against Charlie. My cold, vodka-burned lips against his cold, vodka-burned lips.

And then he kissed me back.

It was slow at first and I wasn't quite sure it was happening but I was too scared to pull away. And then I felt the slightest movement against my face, the tickle of warm breath on my wet lips. For ten years I had wondered what it would feel like to kiss Charlie Wilder on the mouth, and now I knew. It felt spectacular. The arm around my shoulders tightened and his other hand crept up to my face, cradling my cheek in his palm while our lips became better acquainted. I wrapped my arms around his back and ignored the little voice in my head that was shouting, 'And now we'll never, ever let go!' As well as the vodka, I could taste the beer on his breath. I hated beer but I didn't care. I was kissing Charlie Wilder and Charlie Wilder was kissing me.

'Wait.' Unable to stop myself, I pulled away with a pained expression. 'You're not kissing me because I'm sad, are you?'

'I don't think so,' he replied, his voice broken and just short of breath enough to make my heart pound.

'And you're not kissing me because you've been drinking?' I just could not stop myself from asking these ridiculous questions. Who gave a shit if he was kissing me because he'd been drinking? I hated myself so much sometimes.

'Maybe? A little bit,' he admitted, leaning back in for another kiss. 'Can you stop overthinking this now, please?'

'No,' I replied, pressing a smile against his lips. 'Have you met me?'

The teenagers across the way started whooping at us approximately four seconds into the second kiss, and although the sun setting across the mill pond was as close as my village ever came to beautiful and romantic, they were very, very off-putting.

'Back to yours?' Charlie asked. I took a deep breath and held it in for a moment. He wasn't just suggesting we go home, he was suggesting we Go Home Together. 'Tess?'

'Where else are we going to go?' I asked lightly, pretending I wasn't absolutely bricking myself. I hadn't had sex in almost two years, and while we were being entirely honest, it had not been a good experience. This wasn't just a casual shag after a rubbish party to check I still knew how to do it. This was Charlie. I was going to have sex with Charlie.

'There's always the back seat of my car.'

I pulled away to look at him, not sure whether he was joking or not. Nor sure whether I wanted him to be joking or not.

'But while I know that would continue the dodgy teenage theme of the evening, I think I'd rather take you to bed,' he said, his voice was all low and rough. I'd never heard it like that before. 'If it's not too weird?'

It was weird. This whole thing was weird. I was sitting on a bench wearing a gold sequinned miniskirt, kissing a boy I'd been dreaming about kissing ever since the first night I'd lain on my plastic-covered mattress in my hall of residence. I should have said it could wait. I should have said no, we couldn't sneak into my parents' house and have sex on my bottom bunk. But where was the fun in that? Besides, I'd had a third of a half-bottle of own-brand vodka and Charlie Wilder wanted to have sex with me. I was eighteen again. Whatever happened next, I blamed the sequins.

'It's not weird at all,' I said, practically jumping off the bench and dragging him down the street. 'Let's go.'

And just like that, we were together.

CHAPTER FIVE

The next morning, I woke up wrapped in the same pale blue duvet cover I'd left behind when I'd moved to uni and a pair of arms that were brand new. Too scared to move, I tried to keep my breathing slow and even. I was in bed with Charlie. I was in bed with Charlie and neither of us was wearing any clothes. And the reason we weren't wearing any clothes was because for the last twelve hours we had been at it.

I closed my eyes on my childhood room, my exam certificates hanging on the walls, my favourite photos lining the shelves, and tried to commit as much of the night to memory as possible. It was hard to keep the events straight, not because I'd been drunk but because I was suffering from a distinct case of what Amy always referred to as Boink Brain. Nothing fogged up your memory like a good shag. I was completely overloaded with happiness, and, given how long it was since I'd last had sex, every part of me was aching. Happily, like everyone said, it was just like riding a bike. A really, really fun bike. I remembered sneaking into the dark, empty house, checking for my parents and then kissing in the kitchen, fumbling with buttons and zips, taking far too long to get up the stairs, eventually finding my room. It was strange to know someone so well, to know everything about them, and then find yourself in a situation where you knew nothing. I had never seen Charlie naked. I had no idea what to expect in the trouser department. I had no idea how it would be.

More than once, Amy had tried to counsel me out of my Charlie crush by telling me that he was too nice to be any good in bed, that it would be like shagging my brother. As it was, I didn't have a brother, but if that was how incest went down, I could see why it was so popular in the Deep South. Amy had been wrong. The sex was wonderful. Beautiful. It was like film sex, all deep and meaningful and very, very nice. I pressed my hand into Charlie's, smiling lazily as his fingers instinctively curled around mine. Mine. He was mine.

'Hey.'

I felt him rather than heard him, his words tickling my ear.

'So.' He snuggled up closer to me and I silently congratulated myself on having bothered to shave my legs the day before. 'That happened.'

'That did happen,' I replied, too nervous to turn round and face him. Naked in the dark was one thing. Naked the next day with slept-in make-up and morning breath? Quite another. 'Couple of times, actually.'

We lay quietly and I was glad he couldn't see my smile. I looked like the cat that had got all of the canaries and quite possibly a parrot. I'd only been awake for a couple of minutes, but already it was like I'd woken in a whole new world. A new fantastic point of view.

Aladdin and his magic carpet could piss off. I didn't have a job and I lived with a psycho, but it didn't matter. I had Charlie. My best friend, and now my – well, whatever he was, he was the best at something else too.

With a quick kiss to my shoulder, he rolled away, leaving my back cold and bereft. Since he was stuck on the wall side of a single lower bunk bed, there wasn't really anywhere for him to go. Awkward.

'Amy is going to laugh and laugh,' he said after a moment. 'And then laugh.'

I pulled the covers up over my boobs, ran a finger under each eye to minimize any mascara fall-out and rolled over to look at my conquest.

'She is?' I tried to sound as innocent as possible. 'You think?'

'Oh God, yeah.' Charlie did not look changed. There was no beatific glow about his face. He was not gazing at me with a love so powerful it dared not speak its name. He was pretty much just laughing. Ha ha ha. 'We will never hear the end of it. I feel like she's been expecting this for ever.'

'You do? She has?'

In his defence, I had a lot more evidence to draw on than Charlie did. For the past ten years, Amy had watched me pine and swoon and sulk and had routinely slapped me around the back of the head whenever I'd so much as mentioned the elephant in the room that was Me and Charlie. Or 'Chess' as I may or may not have named us. In public, when it was the three of us, it was different. She did make fun of us. She mocked our in-jokes and routinely told us to get a room whenever we indulged in some platonic snuggling. From Charlie's perspective, Amy had been scoffing at this non-relationship for ever.

He had no idea that she was counselling me behind closed doors. He had no idea how I was feeling. Which meant there was a chance he didn't feel the same. Gulp. Puke. Gulp.

Raking a hand through his beautifully fucked-up hair, Charlie shrugged and yawned.

'Maybe we just, you know, don't tell her,' he said, looking so terribly casual as he went about breaking my heart. 'Just until we've worked this all out.'

'Hmm, that's one idea.' I edged ever so slightly away. 'But actually, it would really help if you could clear something up for me. What is "this"?'

There. My life was complete. I had made air quotes in bed with Charlie Wilder. Amy would actually have had a stroke if she could have seen what had just happened.

'I don't know,' he replied, easy as anything.

A very big part of me just wanted to nod, smile and shut up. I had Charlie in my bed. We had spent a good part of the night making love – not shagging but definitely, one hundred percent gazing into each other's eyes, holding hands, Barry White in the background making love, with an emphasis on the 'lurve'. That part of me did not like to make waves and was fairly certain that if I just lay there quietly, he would remember he had a penis, that he had put it in me fairly recently and would possibly put it in me again. Everyone knew that was the path to true love. But there was another very tiny part of me that really didn't like the sound of this 'I don't know' and 'Maybe we shouldn't tell your best friend in the entire world that we boned.'

'You don't know?'

It just came out. Honestly, I had no control over it.

'I'm not trying to be a dickhead, Tess.' Charlie sat up, hit his head on the top bunk and promptly lay back down. 'I'm not pretending it didn't happen, but we need to be realistic about this. We've been mates for years. We can't just shag once and go back to being friends like nothing happened. That'll just get weird.'

'I didn't say I wanted to,' I said, trying to keep my voice down, but since I was me, it was hard. 'I don't want to pretend it never happened.'

'Good. Because it was amazing.' He reached over to stroke my arm and gave me a silly half-smile that I half recognized. 'We just need to work it all out and I'd rather do that without Amy getting involved. She'll be marching us down the aisle and getting ordained online or something.'

Wedding jokes. He was making wedding jokes. How to send a girl from bad pukey sick feeling in her stomach to good pukey sick feeling in her stomach in one easy step. And, little did he know, Amy was already ordained online. Handy.

'Yeah, you're right.' I threw in a light laugh and a toss of the head for good measure, sort of a cross between a total sex goddess and a smallish pony. 'I get it.'

'It's just tricky, the whole friends with benefits thing,' he said with a smile, combing his fingers through my hair. Or at least he tried to comb his fingers through my hair. Long curly hair plus an all-night sex session equals many, many tangles. 'It never seems to work, and you're my best mate. I don't want you to get hurt in this.'

Ohhh.

It was amazing how much damage you could do with so few words. Friends with benefits. Best mate. And

77

thank goodness he didn't want me to get hurt. THANK GOODNESS.

'I think I need a shower,' I said, grabbing a towel off the radiator and holding it against myself as I clambered out of bed. 'Yes, I do.'

'Wait, you're not pissed off, are you?'

I span on my heel and stared down at the man in my bed. Tall, cute and, as it turned out, a bloody good shag. And weirdly, it felt like that was all I knew about him.

'Why did we, you know . . .' I started, not sure where I was going. 'Last night. Why did you have sex with me?'

'Because you kissed me.' Charlie was doing a much better job of keeping his voice down than I was and looked as though he would really like me to try harder.

'And if I hadn't kissed you, we would never have . . .' I just couldn't bring myself to say it again.

'I don't know, because you did.' He was talking to me, but his eyes were definitely scanning the room for his boxers. 'Is this just regular post-sex crazy girl behaviour or what?'

'I wouldn't know.' I snatched up his pants and threw them in his face. M&S cotton boxers, definitely bought by his mother. 'Because I don't have enough casual sex to know whether or not it turns me into a crazy girl.'

'Can you not shout?' he mumbled, pulling the boxers off his face. 'Your mum is going to hear.'

'And we wouldn't want that, would we?' I bellowed. Not shouting, bellowing. 'We wouldn't want anyone to know that I forced myself on you.'

'Bloody hell, can you calm down?' Charlie hissed, shuffling out of the bed and trying to put his giant hands on my shoulders. 'What is wrong with you? All I said was I didn't want to tell Amy that we slept together until we'd had time to work out what was going on. What's not OK about that?'

'Everything,' I replied. I would not cry. I would not cry. I would not cry.

I didn't want a shower any more. I just wanted to leave. Shaking his hands off my shoulders, I pulled on my knickers, my skinny jeans and a baggy black jumper Amy had the foresight to include in my packing. While crying.

'Don't, please.' His voice had changed from confused and angry to confused, angry and a little bit scared. 'Just sit down and talk to me.'

'I don't want to sit down,' I said, my eyes burning bright red. 'I don't want to talk to you. I don't want to work out what's going on. I already know what's going on. You're a wanker.'

'Why am I a wanker?' Charlie asked, incredulous, as I grabbed my handbag and checked for all the essentials. It felt like it would really ruin the moment if I had to manhandle myself into my massive bra, so I picked it up and threw it in my handbag instead. 'What have I done that you didn't want me to do?'

'Nothing,' I said as I curled my hair around itself and fastened it in a topknot. 'I did want to kiss you and I did want to sleep with you but I do not want to be your fuck-buddy, Charlie.'

There wasn't a lot of point pretending I wasn't crying now, and so I turned to face him, tears streaming, nose running, the whole ugly crying extravaganza.

'I have been in love with you for so long, and I had no idea how not to be. I didn't think actually sleeping with you would be the way to sort it out, but apparently it was. So thanks.'

Before I could launch into legitimate sobs, I opened the bedroom door, slammed it shut behind me and ran downstairs. Mum and Brian were drinking Sunday morning coffee in the kitchen in complete silence.

'I think me and you need to have a talk, young lady,' Mum said, cool as a cucumber.

'I do not agree,' I replied, slipping my feet into my Primark ballet pumps. 'Brian, can you please run me to the station?'

'Course I can, love,' he said, coffee on the table, car keys appearing from his jeans pocket. 'Come on.'

'Don't you dare walk out of this house, madam.' Mum sounded shocked. It was fair. It was, after all, the first time in my entire life that I'd answered her back or not done as I was told. Fairly impressive at twenty-eight. 'You sit down at this table and tell me what exactly is going on with you or you don't come back to this house ever again.'

'I'll leave my keys with Brian then,' I shouted as I passed through the front door. Probably a bit rash. I probably wasn't thinking entirely straight. Or walking straight just yet.

'Oh dear God, it's drugs, isn't it? I knew it. All those late nights in the office, never having any money, fired for "no reason". What is it? Heroin? Are you doing the heroin?' She was shouting just loud enough for the neighbours to have that on Facebook in the next ten minutes.

'Yes, Mum,' I replied as calm as you like. 'I'm doing all of the heroin. Track marks up and down my arms, can't get enough of the stuff. It's aces.'

Marching towards the door, all I wanted was to be out of that house.

'Tess Sigourney Brookes, you come back here this instant.' My mum did not sound amused.

I didn't turn round. I didn't reply. I just got in the car.

'Sorry to be a pain in the arse, Brian.' I gave my lovely stepdad an apologetic smile as I buckled my seatbelt. 'Just not having a very good week.'

'Happens to the best of us, love,' he said as he started the engine and backed out of the driveway. 'Happens to the best of us.'

When I finally arrived back home, the flat was gloriously empty. The battery was flat on my phone and I'd left the charger at my mum's, so there was very little to do but have a bath, wash away every trace of Charlie Wilder and collapse on the settee with a big bag of Wotsits. Or four big bags of Wotsits.

A week ago, I'd been prepping for my first day in my big new job. Seven days on, I had no job, I had no prospects, I'd shagged Charlie, I'd fallen out with Charlie, and I was relatively certain my mum had a bit of a bag on with me. I had excelled myself. An entire decade's worth of drama in one week.

'Sometimes things need shaking up,' I'd told the rubber duck in the bath. 'You've got to test the limits sometimes.'

He didn't reply. He was getting a real attitude.

I was deep into my third episode of *Come Dine With Me* when I heard someone hammering on the front door.

'Yay, Vanessa,' I whispered, pulling my stripy blanket up under my chin.

'Tess, are you in there?'

Not Vanessa. Charlie.

It was too late to run into my room and hide under the bed, so I did the next best thing I could think of. Pull the blanket over my head and shout, 'No.'

But when I pulled the blanket down over my eyes, I saw a tall, creased-looking boy in the corner of my living room. All six feet three inches looking sad and stooped. My ovaries wanted to leap out of my body and never let him go.

'Your mum gave me your spare key.' He held it up before tossing it to me. 'I didn't think you'd let me in.'

'I wouldn't have,' I replied, wishing I was wearing anything other than a giant Eeyore sleep shirt and a scrunchie. 'So you can go now.'

'I need to talk to you.' He stepped towards the sofa with caution, staying as far away from me as it was possible to be, and rubbed at his eyebrow as he sat down. I curled up into a not-so-tiny ball and pouted. 'I need to say I'm sorry.'

'Yes, you do,' I acknowledged. 'So say it and then piss off.'

'I'm sorry.'

'And you're still here.'

Charlie took a deep breath in and stared at his feet. I pulled my knees up over my nose and peered at him over my blanket. This was horrible.

'Do you remember the first time you talked to me?' he asked. 'Not in a seminar or anything, but the first time we properly had a conversation?'

'Yes.' Of course I bloody remembered, arsehole.

'It was the Christmas party in the union, and you and Amy were wearing those stupid matching fairy outfits and all of the lads from my floor had a bet on which of them could get off with the two of you first.'

Oh, university. Hallowed halls of learning.

'And then we were at the bar at the same time and you were not sober,' he said with a smile. 'And you asked if I'd done the reading for our media studies class, and I said I never did the reading for the media studies class, and you looked horrified.'

'I was a very straight student,' I muttered.

'And then we were just chatting, and that girl I was seeing came up and kissed me.'

'Sarah Luffman.' Sarah bloody Luffman. I still wouldn't accept her Facebook friend request to this day.

'Sarah, yeah. Of course you remember.' He rested his hands on his knees as though he was bracing himself. 'Anyway, she came up and kissed me and I saw your face fall. You looked, like, properly heartbroken. And I didn't know why, but it made me so sad because all night, all I'd been thinking about was kissing you.'

'Because of the bet?' I asked.

'No,' he shook his head. 'Because I thought you were beautiful.'

Oh.

I wondered if it would be appropriate to ask him to wait while I went and changed. This conversation could not take place while I was wearing something I had bought for a tenner from the Disney store in the January sale.

'But when I looked again, you were gone. And the next time I saw you, my flatmate told me you were going out with that bloke off the PE course. So I didn't make a move. But we had so much in common and we were in all the same classes and, you know, that was that.'

'And you never thought to bother again?' I said, shuffling my feet a little bit closer to him. 'In ten years?'

'I know your mum and dad got divorced, Tess, but if

you'd lived through what I've lived through, you wouldn't be so quick to swap a friend for a shag. By the time we were both single, we were such good friends. We had so much in common – the books and the music and everything – and I didn't want to ruin that. I was twenty. I couldn't even think about anything long-term. But you were long-term to me.'

'You do know the only reason I read all those books and listened to all that music was so that I'd have something to talk to you about in the first place, don't you?' I asked, looking at a knot in the floorboards. 'Because I liked you.'

'Sneaky cow.' He pulled the sleeves of his jumper over his hands and smiled. 'Anyway, I just wanted you to know why I might have freaked out a little bit this morning.'

'I'm not quite sure I do know,' I said, my heart pounding. I really needed to hear him say it. 'You might want to clarify.'

That's when I saw the full trademarked and copyright Charlie Wilder grin break out across his face. 'I freaked out because I didn't know what it was. Or what you wanted it to be. I could never just do the friends with benefits thing with you because you're my Tess. I love you.'

'You love me?'

They were words I'd heard a thousand times before, they were words I'd said a thousand times before, but they'd never, ever mattered until he said them now. It felt like Cupid, the Andrex puppy and a selection of assorted kittens had taken up residence in my stomach. There was far too much fluffy fluttering going on in there for my organs to work properly.

'You love me?' I said it again just to make sure.

'Of course I love you,' he repeated, taking hold of my hand. 'You're my best friend.'

And with that, Cupid, the anonymous Labrador and assorted kittens froze and turned around to look at me very, very slowly.

'I'm your best friend?'

My French teacher had always told me the best way to understand something was to repeat it until you'd really drilled everything into your brain, but I was just not getting this.

'My best, best friend.' Charlie squeezed my fingers so tightly I thought they might snap, and I inched back ever so slightly on the sofa. 'And we both know how important that is.'

'We do?'

'How many times have you seen me ruin a relationship?' He let go of my hand and threw his arms up in the air. The arms that had been around me all night long. 'I'm the worst! I can't keep it together with a girl, you know that.'

I did know that. Charlie had a different girlfriend approximately once every five months. And once every five months I absolutely did not spend (on average) two hours online stalking the shit out of her and praying to a god I didn't believe in that she would just go away without me having to resort to violence. So far, those prayers had been answered. I probably owed every major religion at least a fiver: the girlfriends never lasted more than a couple of months. One did almost six, but Charlie was travelling around Australia for three of them and I knew for a fact that he'd cheated. Not that he was a cheater. Most of the time.

'There's a reason we've never got together.' Charlie seemed to be choosing his words very carefully. I hoped they were the right ones. 'What if it doesn't work out and we end up hating each other? I'll let you down, Tess, I will. I don't want you to hate me; I want you to be checking the football scores for me in the old people's home when I'm too old and blind to read the screen. I want you to be in my life for ever.'

One by one, Cupid, the puppy and the kittens limped away, whispering awkwardly between themselves. I assumed they were uncomfortable with tears because dear God was I about to bring out some pretty impressive crying. The tears I'd busted out that morning were nothing compared with the biblical flood that was about to drown everyone in the room.

'Ah, fucking hell – this is what I'm talking about. We're not even going out and I've made you cry.' Charlie dived across the sofa and pulled me into a hug, trying to stem the sobs. 'See? It would never work.'

'But . . . but we did it?' As the words came out of my mouth, I wondered if I'd actually gone mad and we had, in fact, not 'done it' at all.

'I know.'

'After ten years? After never doing it at all?'

'I know.'

To his credit, he looked terribly guilty. Not that it mattered in the slightest. My heart hurt. My everything hurt.

'Why?'

'I honestly don't know,' he replied.

We sat locked in silence on the sofa, half disengaged from the least sexy embrace in the history of embraces. I was staring at Charlie's messy hair, his pale face, his sad eyes. He was staring at my Eeyore nightie. All I wanted to do was hug him again and tell him it was all going to be all right, that it didn't matter and that we could just pretend it had never happened. We would just go back to being best friends and I'd go back to waiting for him to work out that I was the one. Even though I could still feel the red-hot tears spilling over my cheeks, every single part of me just wanted to make him feel better. Somewhere in the corner of the room, my self-respect shook her head in disgust. He didn't say anything else. I couldn't say anything else. Luckily, someone else didn't have quite the same struggle.

'Oh Jesus Christ, what's going on now?'

In the midst of all our emo-drama, I hadn't heard the front door open. And I hadn't seen Vanessa loitering in the hallway. But I heard her.

'Don't tell me you two are shagging?' She hung her keys on my hook next to the door and inspected her nails. 'Don't bother, Tess, he's shit in bed.'

'What did you just say?' I couldn't possibly have heard her right.

'I said don't bother, he's shit in bed,' Vanessa repeated slowly, disappearing into her bedroom. 'And between me, you and Mr Wilder, he's not exactly packing down their either. Not. Worth. The. effort.'

I let go of Charlie at exactly the same time he let go of me, and slid off the sofa into a graceless pile of too long limbs and donkey T-shirt at his feet.

'You?' I pointed at him. 'And her?' I pointed to Vanessa.

'OK, don't go mental, but—'

'Oh my God, you and her.'

It was too late; I was freaking out. The Andrex puppy

had morphed into a Rottweiler and Cupid had traded his bow and arrow for an AK-47.

'It was nothing,' he said insistently, grabbing hold of my wrists a fraction too tightly. 'It was just one of those things. I don't even know. It was nothing.'

'It was several times,' Vanessa called from behind her closed bedroom door. 'Your place, this place, that hotel for the weekend in Wales.'

'You went to Wales?' I breathed. 'You went on a mini-break?'

Truly this was the last straw. Everyone knew that a mini-break was the universally accepted sign of true love. Bridget Jones said so.

'Remember you asked me not to tell Tess until you "knew what we were"?' she called. Exactly what he had said to me that morning. 'And because she'd probably have a nervous breakdown.'

'I didn't say that.' Charlie squeezed my wrists until they hurt. 'I didn't. Tess, it wasn't anything. It wasn't worth upsetting you.'

'I didn't say anything because, really, it wasn't worth upsetting you,' she agreed from her bedroom. 'It wasn't worth upsetting my yeast infection either.'

'Oh, fucking hell,' I whispered to Eeyore. From the look on his face, he really got it.

'And after all the effort he put into getting into my knickers, I never even came. I've had more fun with an electric toothbrush,' Vanessa said as she reemerged, holding her passport aloft. 'And he was such a whiner afterwards. I'd let you listen to the messages, but I deleted them after that time I played them at the comedy phone messages open mike night. Anyway, Tess, are you even listening? I'm going to be away for at least a week, longer if I can help it. Honestly, I know you don't care, but I have had such a stressful few days. Council tax is due next week – pay it, yeah?'

Of course she didn't bother to lock the door behind her, which made it all the easier to grab hold of Charlie and bundle him out of it. By his face.

'*Get out*,' I shouted, grabbing hold of a handful of hair and physically pushing him away from me. I couldn't get rid of him fast enough. My skin was crawling at the thought of Charlie and Vanessa. Him kissing her. Her touching him. 'Get out of my flat.'

'Tess, I love you,' he said, desperately clinging to the door frame.

'Please fuck off!' I slammed the door, really not giving two shits whether his fingers were still inside or not. I sort of hoped that they were. Eeyore approved. 'Go away, Charlie. Don't come back.'

I counted to ten, panting hard and waiting for the pleading to stop and the crying to start. Eventually, all that was left was silence. He was gone. Charlie had said he loved me. Charlie had had an affair with Vanessa. The council tax was due. So this was what heartbreak felt like? Bollocks to that. Having never actually been in love with any of my boyfriends before, I'd never actually had my heart broken before. I waited to feel the urge to consume large quantities of ice cream and cry. But I didn't want to cry, and I certainly didn't want dairy products. I felt sick. I felt angry. I wanted to break something. I couldn't break Vanessa, but I could break some of her things.

With my hands curled into tight little fists, I kicked Vanessa's door open (entirely unnecessary but it felt right) and looked for something to destroy. Her room was, as usual, a complete shithole. My room was generally a bit of a mess, but it was a clean, white-walled, cream-carpeted, orderly mess. A teetering stack of unread magazines here, a collection of credit card statements there. Vanessa's room was disgusting. My room was more of a disappointment. In all the years I'd been here, I hadn't got as far as putting up a single picture or photo on the wall – they all lived on my desk at work, my first home. There was a framed print of a Warhol I'd seen at the Tate Modern with Charlie sitting on the floor by my chest of drawers. He'd been coming over to hang it every Sunday for the last six months, but he'd never quite made it. And so on the floor it had stayed. My room looked like a corporate crash pad rather than somewhere a real person lived. It was where I crawled under the covers at midnight on a Wednesday after a client dinner and where I hung all of my smart separates, still in their bags from the dry-cleaner's.

Staring at Vanessa's overflowing wardrobe, I suddenly hated all of my clothes. It felt like everything I owned was black, blue or white, unless Amy had picked it, and then it was sequinned, short and generally unwearable. Even my jeans were 'casual Friday' appropriate. The toes on my Converse were bright white. My heels, aside from my Promotion Shoes, were all sensible. I hated everything. I hated myself.

Vanessa's wardrobe was a tumble of colour and texture. I barely touched the door and the entire contents burst on to the floor, making a desperate bid for freedom. Red strapless dresses, printed palazzo pants, skintight liquid leggings, silk and satin and velvet and leather, all pooling around my feet and begging to be rescued. I stomped on a particularly ridiculous pair of leather hot pants I remembered seeing her swan around in and sulked. Her room was just so her. Two of her walls were painted deep red and the other two hot pink. It shouldn't have worked, but it did. It clashed, it was too bright, too bold and a little bit gross, but it looked amazing. Just like Vanessa. If Vanessa's room was her, was my room me? Was my sad little white-walled, devoid-of-personality shell of a bedroom really me?

There was no discernible carpet under my feet, just a collage of dirty clothes, open mail and magazines. Dirty mug upon dirty mug upon dirty mug sat everywhere you looked, and half-empty takeaway boxes, plates and forks were balanced precariously on every available surface. No knives, though. Vanessa never used a knife and I found it infuriating. Even more infuriating was the lack of things available to break. The dirty pots looked like they were about to get up and crawl to the kitchen themselves so I wasn't touching them, and I wasn't rock and roll enough to put the telly through the window. The only other things I could see that were legitimately worth money and fuck-up-able were her dead 'work' BlackBerry and my old camera. I couldn't bear to do it. I let out a little frustrated scream through my gritted teeth and punched a pillow, shaking from head to toe.

I was a rubbish woman scorned. Hell totally hath seen fury like me. I'd seen waitresses in Pizza Hut with more fury. I was a complete failure. Back in the living room, I heard the landline ring. There wasn't a single person on earth I wanted to talk to. But of course I answered it anyway.

'Hello?' I steeled myself for the worst. Charlie. Vanessa. My mother.

'Ohmygodareyouokay?' garbled Amy.

'What?'

'Are. You. OK?' she repeated. 'I've been going mental up here. Why isn't your phone on?'

'I left my charger at my mum's,' I answered. 'Amy, did you know that Charlie has been sleeping with Vanessa?'

'Um, no?'

'AMY.'

'He's such a cockwomble!' she shouted down the line. 'Don't be angry. I only know because he said something about being in Wales and she said something about being in Wales and I asked him about being in Wales and he admitted it, but I didn't tell you because he said it wasn't really a thing and I didn't want to upset you and—'

'No, no, no!' I banged the receiver against my forehead, trying to bash the reality of this into my brain. 'You knew? And you didn't say anything?'

'Look at it from my point of view,' Amy replied with a whine. 'You were working, like, a billion hours a day on that pitch for those rank organic lollipops you made me eat loads of.'

I mentally pegged this as six months ago. Those lollipops were rank.

'Plus you were sort of showing an interest in that bloke you met at Floridita and I didn't want to distract you, and then by the time I'd got Charlie's balls in a Vulcan death grip, he swore it was over, that it was only one time and that it was done but he didn't want to upset you, and—'

'Only one time?' I interrupted.

'Yes.'

'Even though you knew they'd both been in Wales together. Having sex.'

What was that taste in my mouth? Oh yes, bile. That was bile.

'Oh. Yeah. Well, I didn't find out about that until ages after.'

'Amy. I can't believe it.'

'I just couldn't bear to tell you,' she said softly. 'He said it wasn't anything. I knew it would break your heart, and I thought you were going to move out soon, and . . . Oh fuck. I fucked up. Fuck fuck fuck.'

It was confusing. I was mad at Amy. She knew about this and she hadn't told me, but I was so mad at Vanessa and even more so at Charlie that all my reserves of rage were accounted for. After a few beats of silence I found my voice.

'I slept with him.'

'*You did?*'

I had no idea precisely where in the country Amy was, but I was fairly certain there were now some deaf Highland cattle up in Scotland. She could be awfully loud when she wanted to be.

'Is that why you left? Are you in Gretna Green? Are you married already? Was it amazing? Tell me everything. I always knew this would happen if the two of you got together . . .' She was on a roll – there was no way I'd be able to interrupt her successfully a third time. 'I'll just cease to exist. It'll just be like, oh, ha ha ha, let's have some wine and a dinner party, and, ooh, do you remember that funny little dark-haired girl who used to hang around? I wonder where she is now? Except you won't even wonder because I'll be dead and you won't care.'

'Are you done?' I asked.

'Are you married?' She countered.

'No.' I replied.

'Then, yes. Hang on, did you sleep with him before or after you found out about Vanessa?'

'Before.'

'Ohhh. Shit.'

'Yeah.'

I held the phone to my ear and we shared a comfortable silence. There really wasn't anything else to say.

'Are you OK?' Amy broke first. As always.

'Not really.' I wasn't any more. I was too tired.

'Are you mad?' she asked.

'I am mad,' I confirmed.

'With me?'

'With everyone alive,' I said. 'Except maybe Ryan Gosling.' Who could be mad at Ryan Gosling?

'Shall I come over when my train gets in?' she asked. 'We can burn pictures of the two of them? Or we could just break loads of her stuff?'

That best friend of mine, what a mind reader. We'd done a lot of picture burning when Amy had ended her engagement. Even though she had been the one to break it off, she was not one to leave that relationship without some righteous anger. It had been a fun time for everyone who wasn't her ex-fiancé. I imagined he missed his twenty-year-old comic collection almost as much as he missed Amy. Possibly more so.

'Yeah, I might be asleep, so let yourself in,' I said. The exhaustion was overwhelming. My limbs felt so heavy I didn't even know how I was holding up the phone. 'See you in a bit.'

'OK. I love you,' she said, making kissing noises down the phone. 'Don't do anything stupid.'

'I've never done anything stupid in my life,' I replied. 'I wouldn't know where to start.'

Collapsing on the closest soft surface, Vanessa's bed, I exhaled loudly and tried to have a Feeling, the phone still in my hand. But there was nothing there. My brain felt like a clown car, crammed full to overflowing with rainbow wigs, red noses and tutu-wearing bears. I should get out of Vanessa's room. I should get dressed. I should call my mum and apologize for my behaviour. But I didn't actually want to. At some point, I was going to have to speak to Charlie. And, must not forget, the council tax needed playing. Priorities, Tess.

Before I could decide which item on my did-not-want-to-do list was up first, the phone rang again. Once again, just in case it was about the council tax, I answered it.

'Hello?' I answered, so, so tired.

'Kittler,' a woman snapped down the line. 'Don't say a single fucking word. I am fucking furious with you.'

Oh no. There was no way I was taking an earbashing on Vanessa's behalf. Not today.

'I'm not—' I started.

'I said not a fucking word,' the woman continued. 'Do you know how hard it is for me to get you jobs? Do you?'

'No?' I answered. Because I didn't.

'No, of course you don't, you selfish bastard. It's really fucking hard. And after last week's fucking no-show . . . I should fire you. I should refuse to even put you up for jobs. And now your fucking BlackBerry is out of service? What the fuck is wrong with you?'

I had, by this time, worked out that I was speaking with Vanessa's agent, Veronica. She had a certain way with words that gave her away. That way was commonly known as 'swearing'.

Vanessa's career as a photographer was, at best, patchy. I'd only ever seen maybe ten photos she'd taken. For the most part, she seemed to take a lot of portraits of her friends, who used them for vanity projects and then randomly got her hired for fashion jobs or indie magazine shoots that never seemed to pan out. My shutterbug sensibilities were offended. The pictures that I had seen were flat, oversaturated and, quite often, completely out of focus. I'd seen better shots on Instagram and I hated Instagram. But no one cared what I thought. They cared that she was stupid hot, knew all the right people, and did I mention she was stupid hot?

Before I had a chance to explain to Agent Veronica that (a) I was not Vanessa and (b) just exactly what was wrong with my flatmate, namely that she was a see-you-next-Tuesday (incidentally one of Agent Veronica's favourite terms of endearment), she had already started shouting at me again.

'Luckily for you, someone is desperate. This new magazine has landed a last-minute interview with Bertie Bennett and they need a photographer.'

'Bertie Bennett?' I didn't know who Bertie Bennett was.

'Don't fuck around with me today, fuckface. Bertie. Fucking. Bennett.' Agent Veronica snapped. Agent Veronica liked swearing a lot. 'It's a piece of piss. Couple of portraits of Bertie, couple of shots of some of his favourite archive pieces, his favourite up-and-coming pieces. Nothing even slightly resembling hard work. It's a better job than you deserve, and if I wasn't shit out of luck with the first three people I'd called, you wouldn't even be hearing my dulcet fucking tones right now.'

She did have a lovely voice.

'You're on a plane to Hawaii tonight. You'll be back by Friday.'

'Hawaii?'

'What the fuck is up with you this afternoon?' she asked. 'You sound like you're stoned. Are you on a juice detox or something? You haven't been fucking born again, have you? I can't be dealing with God botherers.'

'Sorry, I'm not—' My mouth was open and words had started to come out of it. All I needed to do was finish the sentence. All I needed to say was 'I'm not Vanessa' and then I could go back to watching shit telly in my shit Eeyore T-shirt on my shit settee, hating my own guts until Amy came over and agreed with me about how shit everything was.

Or I could go to Hawaii.

'Kittler, you've got exactly ten seconds to say yes or I'm never putting your tiny fucking arse up for a job ever the fuck again. So say yes.'

Ten seconds.

Hawaii.

Piece of piss.

I looked up at the mirror above Vanessa's bed (no, really) and took a moment. Ratty hair. Sad donkey T-shirt. No job. No boyfriend. No friends. Shit family. Council tax due. Turning opinion round on Tess Brookes was going to be hard bloody work. But what if I just wasn't Tess Brookes any more? What if I was Vanessa Kittler? Just slightly less slutty and with a faint Yorkshire lilt?

'Three. Two.'

'I'll do it,' I told my reflection and Veronica in my best Lahndahn drawl. 'I'll go.'

'Too fucking right you will,' Agent Veronica replied. 'I need to email you the brief. I know you're a twat about flights, so book the ticket yourself and claim it back and don't give me any shit about how expensive it's going to be. I'm sure there's room on Daddy's credit card.'

'No, that's fine.' My pulse was starting to race again. For different reasons this time. 'Uh, my BlackBerry is, um, fahcked. Can you send it to my flatmate's address? It's Tess S Brookes at googlemail. And, uh, I'll give you another number. Don't call the BlackBerry.'

Hawaii.

'Whatever. Just get your shit together, Kittler.' Agent Veronica sounded very unhappy with Vanessa. Agent Veronica needed to get in line. 'I won't have you fucking up on me again. This is it. Your last fucking chance. These photos need to be as good as the photos that got me to sign your pathetic arse in the first place and not as wank as the ones you sent in last month. We did discuss the fact that they were indeed wank, did we not?'

'Yes?' I really wished I could see those photos. Presumably she'd been drunk when she took them. Or possibly she'd been too busy shagging Charlie to concentrate. Who knew? There was a world of possibilities.

'Too fucking right, yes,' she snapped. 'This is your last fucking chance. Do not let me down.'

Last chance. Fresh start. It was all the same, really.

CHAPTER SIX

It was only when I arrived at Honolulu international airport and saw a driver waiting in arrivals with a big sign saying 'Vanessa Kittler' that it occurred to me exactly what I'd done.

I didn't know why I'd told Agent Veronica that I would go to a place I'd never visited and take pictures of someone I'd never heard of for a magazine I'd never read. I didn't know why I had picked up my old camera, grabbed Vanessa's kit bag and started packing. I couldn't explain why I wrote a note for Amy that just said, 'Gone to Hawaii. Call you when I get there. So sorry. xxx' and stuck it on the front door. I had a sneaking suspicion it had something to do with the fact that my life had become an unspeakable disaster and I didn't really fancy living it any more. And it wasn't as though the real Vanessa was doing such a spectacular job of her existence, wherever she was. It all seemed to make sense at the time. Same way as two plus two equals three and one. It wasn't wrong; it just wasn't quite right.

Clutching the sweaty plastic handle of my badly

packed suitcase, I tripped over my own feet on the way over to the driver and nodded with as much authority as I could muster when he waved his sign in my direction. It wasn't a lot of authority. Nonetheless, he nodded back, opened the back door and took my suitcase. Success. I had officially fooled one person. By not speaking and almost falling over.

Packing for my spur-of-the-moment career change had been trying. What did photographers wear? My wardrobe was mostly made up of relatively sensible office separates. There was a lot of black, a lot of blue, and a lot of Dorothy Perkins. Vanessa swanned around in swanky designer stuff she snagged from her friends and bought with Daddy's money. Happily, it transpired that the only thing she and I had in common, aside from Charlie Wilder's penis, was our inside leg measurement. Given that I was already borrowing her job, her name and her camera, I didn't think she'd mind if I nicked a couple of pairs of skinny jeans, an entire drawerful of T-shirts and the odd frock. And two pairs of very expensive-looking shoes, just in case. And a nice jumper for the plane. Vanessa and I both had curves, the difference being that hers were in all the right places whereas mine were everywhere. Sitting on my arse in an office for the last seven years had done nothing to help me out. Luckily, I discovered that with the help of some very restrictive underwear and a lot of breathing in, I could fit into most of her things. Which made me much happier than it should. I did pack my own pants, flip-flops and bikini. My poor, ancient bikini. I couldn't exactly remember when I'd bought it, but I was certain it was old enough to be sitting its GCSEs.

It had been a drizzly, grey afternoon in London when

I'd boarded my flight at Heathrow, but when the plane touched down at LAX eleven hours later, it was bright and beautiful. And I was tipsy enough to believe this was a sign from the gods that I had made the right choice – I was being rewarded for my bravery with sunshine and teeny tiny bottles of booze. But now it wasn't a grey Sunday afternoon at Heathrow or a sunny Sunday evening in LA; it was a blazing Monday morning in Hawaii and the reality of what I'd done was starting to sink in. Not that reality was really a concept I was ready to get to grips with just yet. Instead of riding on a bus through the winding streets of London, I was sequestered away in a chauffeur-driven car, rolling along the highway. Instead of staring at bus stops and analysing their ad campaigns, I was blinking vacantly at bright blue skies and palm trees. Without a second thought, I'd traded the Thames for the Pacific Ocean. It was all too much.

Before I could beg the driver to turn round and take me back to the airport, my car pulled up in front of a house that looked exactly like the *Blue Peter* model of Tracy Island that I had not made as a kid. The three-storey palace was built into the side of a hill, all floor-to-ceiling windows and soft, curving angles crowned by a giant round balcony on the very top. It was very sixties futuristic, but at the same time looked like it had been there for ever, like the house had grown out of the hill. Bertie Bennett had to be richer than Jesus. Or J.K. Rowling. It hadn't occurred to me how incredibly rich this man would be. He was clearly not a man who usually had his photo taken by a girl whose most recent photography experiment ran to Facebooking her dinner every night for a week and downloading apps that showed you what you'd look like if you were morbidly obese. My eyes stayed fixed on the architectural wonder as the driver waved a key card at an invisible sensor and sailed through a pair of giant iron gates, leaving the mansion behind us as we swept behind the house down a driveway that led through lush green grounds with what looked like a mountain on one side and a completely deserted beach on the other. Before I had a chance to shut my goldfish gape of a mouth, we pulled up and the engine cut out.

'Miss Kittler? *Aloha, e komo mai.* Welcome to Oahu.'

The door to the car opened and a short, stocky man in a plain black uniform held out his hand. I sat there staring at him. Didn't people speak English in Hawaii? Had I overlooked something else epically important? His broad smile slipped into a squint when I didn't make a move, but all I could do was stare at him. His big brown eyes were far too pretty to belong to a man. He had eyelashes that would make Bambi blush.

'Miss Kittler?'

'Hi, yes,' I croaked, my first words since immigration, and eventually reached out to take his hand. I was an idiot. 'I'm here for the photo thing? For *Gloss*?'

I was also at my most eloquent when straight off a plane. Eloquent and stinky.

'Yes, of course,' my host replied, very politely and in perfect English, leaning in to place a lei around my neck without so much as wrinkling his nose, even though I knew for a fact I was rank rotten. Long-haul flights were the worst. Was this Bertie Bennett? I was so confused. 'I'm Kekipi. You must be very tired from your trip. Let me show you to your cottage.'

To my mind, a cottage was something small and thatched with roses round the door and either a talking hedgehog wearing an apron or a witch inside. The house I was taken to was not a cottage. It was beautiful, with sparkling white-washed walls and a sloping slate roof – an immaculately decorated piece of heaven. And from where I was standing, I could see another four of them dotted along the beach, each one a perfect miniature of the main house complete with tiny veranda, huge windows and matching white wooden lawn furniture. Child Tess had watched too much *Wish You Were Here . . .?* and adult Tess enjoyed an awful lot of *Location, Location, Location*. If Kirstie and Phil could see this, they would die. Everything was so beautiful, I could hardly bear it. It looked as though someone had turned up the contrast on the TV. The blue sky was more vivid than I'd ever seen it and dotted with cotton-wool clouds that flew fast overhead, even though the breeze by the shore was perfect and light. The sea was clear, the sand was white, the trees were a bright, lush green and punctuated with pretty hot-pink and purple flowers. If ever there was an argument for intelligent design, this was it. It was paintbox perfect, every colour bright and bold but beautifully balancing out the next. All I wanted to do was pull out my camera and capture every single sight right away. Surely that had to be a good sign?

'I manage the estate for Mr Bennett,' said the man in black, interrupting my house porn moment and carefully resting a hand on my shoulder as he gently sheepdogged me through the front door of my new home. 'The cottage is fully stocked for you, but please call me if there is anything at all you should need. Just press 1 on any of the phones and someone will come down right away. Mr Bennett would like to invite you up to the house for dinner this evening – he usually dines at eight. Until

then, please do make use of all our facilities. I'm happy
to give you a tour if you're not too tired?'

There were facilities? If I were to take Kekipi to my
house, my tour would take in the extra-fast kettle that
boiled in under a minute, the coffee stain on the living-
room carpet that I could not for the life of me get out,
and the magical airing cupboard that, despite its name,
always smelled damp.

'I am a bit tired, to be honest.' I gave him a very
grateful smile and tried not to be too aware of the fact
that even in my Converse I towered over the man. I was
an ashen-faced, tongue-tied, stinky giant. 'But I'd love
to get the tour later? The place is beautiful.'

I waved my arms around like an over-impressed Big
Bird, eyes wild and red. The real Vanessa would have
been mortified by my public display of enthusiasm.

'Of course, Ms Kittler,' Kekipi nodded. 'Just press 1
on your phone whenever you like.'

'Oh, call me Tess,' I said automatically and felt my
eyes widen like saucers. 'Ness! I mean Ness. Or Vanessa.
Because that is my name.'

'Of course, Vanessa.' Kekipi didn't even blink. What
a total pro. '*Mahalo*.'

'Um, *mahalo*?' I repeated with a very stunted bow, not
entirely sure what I should be doing.

'It means "thank you",' Kekipi said with a small wink
that I might have imagined. 'In case you were worried
that I was swearing at you in a foreign language.'

After he had rolled my suitcase into the cottage, Kekipi
aloha'd me again and then left me alone to relax. I stared
out of the window in disbelief. How could I possibly be
here? And what was I supposed to do now? Chuck on
my swimsuit and head out to the beach? Dig out my

shorts and hike up that beautiful mountain we'd passed on the way in? Bash my head against the closest brick wall until I knocked some sense into it? These were all good options. However, another option was to storm the kitchen, root through each and every cupboard, then rifle through the fridge until I found a box of chocolate-covered macadamia nuts and a huge bag of Cheetos. And so, right there in the kitchen, in the middle of paradise, I stood in all my post-flight skanky glory and troughed every last nut and every last Cheeto. Because what else was a girl supposed to do?

'Tess, thank God.' Amy answered her phone on the first ring. When I'd turned mine on, it had been full of panicked messages from my best friend demanding that I call her immediately and asking which mental institution I was in. 'Where are you? What are you doing? Why has your phone been off for an entire day? Where are you?'

'Oh, Amy.' I leaned against the kitchen counter, wiping Cheeto dust off my fingers onto my jeans, and stared out of the huge French doors that opened onto my own little patio just steps from the beach. 'Remember when we were little and I didn't want to go on Brownie camp so I ran away?'

'Are you under the tree at the bottom of my garden again?' she asked. 'Because you only lasted two hours before you had to come in for a wee last time and you've already been out all night long. Tell me you haven't wet yourself.'

'I haven't wet myself,' I replied hesitantly, mentally checking that that was in fact true. 'I left you a note. Didn't you see the note? I'm in Hawaii.'

What if Amy hadn't seen the note? What if burglars had seen the note? What if they'd broken into the flat and stolen my precious . . . oh. Never mind.

'That's the most ridiculous thing you've ever said,' she said after a moment's consideration. 'And bear in mind I was there that time you announced to the entire pub that you were going to win the *X Factor*.'

'I still think that if I had entered the year the singing binman won—'

'*Off topic, Tess*,' Amy shouted down the line. 'Tell me you are not in Hawaii.'

'I am, though.' I wasn't sure if I was trying to convince her or myself. A quick peep out of the window confirmed I was not in Clerkenwell. 'Dead sure about it. I can see the sea and everything. Deffos in Hawaii.'

'You aren't, though.'

'I am, though.'

'You can't be.'

'I know. But I am.'

'But you're not.'

'Amy.'

'*Tess.*'

Somewhere halfway around the world, my best friend made a clucking noise in a West London flatshare that echoed down a long-distance phone line all the way to the middle of the Pacific Ocean. Sighing in agreement, I pulled off my socks, shimmied out of my jeans and tiptoed across the floor to the patio. The AC kept the tiles cool and I left little half-footprints as I went, footprints that dissipated into thin air almost as soon as I left them behind.

Bertie Bennett's bay curved around his property gracefully, the pretty, clear water lapping against the white sand, the white sand giving way to green grass and the green grass hugging the little cottages at the bottom of the hill, each one surrounded by huge, swaying palm trees. It looked like the kind of place Vanessa would hang out. She was last-minute getaway in Hawaii; I was a wet weekend in Brid.

'So you're actually in Hawaii?' Amy asked. 'Why? How? Have you been watching too many romcoms? Because people don't actually get up and leave the country at the drop of a hat unless they're Julia Roberts or very stupid.'

I stepped off the deck and felt the fresh grass against my toes. It was just a hop, skip and a jump to the beach, but I only had a hop and a skip in me. After that, it was a bit of a slog.

'Then by that definition, I might be very stupid.'

It took a surprisingly short time for me to catch Amy up on my first-ever documented case of spontaneity and/ or a psychotic episode. Understandably she didn't say very much while I was talking, but when she did, it was with great reverence.

'This,' Amy exhaled loudly, 'is amazing.'

Not what I was expecting her to say.

'You don't think I've gone mad?' I bit my thumbnail gently and made my way towards the sea. It was cool and delicious against my hot sweaty feet.

'Oh, I absolutely think you've gone mad,' Amy confirmed quickly. 'But it's about time you went mad. This is brilliant.'

'I'm standing on a beach in my pants pretending to be someone I'm not because I lost my job and, apparently, my mind, and that's a good thing?'

'Yes!' she gushed. 'Like I said, it's brilliant. Can you

see a hula girl? Are there coconuts everywhere? Is there an erupting volcano?'

As stupid as I knew all that sounded, Amy still appeared to know an awful lot more about my destination than I did.

'Coconuts maybe. There are a lot of palm trees,' I confirmed, looking past my immediate surroundings for the first time. Oh, what a shock – everywhere was painfully beautiful. 'Zero hula girls, but there's a great big fucking mountain behind me. I don't know if it's a volcano or not. I hope not because if it is and it erupts, I'm definitely going to die.'

'Where are you exactly? I want to Google it,' she said, still sounding far more excited than I did. It was oddly reassuring, like maybe I wasn't completely insane after all. 'You really have gone completely insane,' she added. So much for the feeling of reassurance.

I held my hand over my eyes to get a better look at a small black rock that popped up out of the ocean like a sombrero and vaguely wondered whether or not I could swim it. I couldn't.

'Is it bad that I don't actually know?' I said, closing my eyes. I needed a break from all the ridiculous natural beauty that was burning my retinas because – oh, bugger me – as soon as I opened them, there was some more. Every time I turned around, I got another eyeful of gorgeousness. Hawaii did not have a bad angle. Hawaii was the Ryan Gosling of destinations. 'I flew into Honolulu, and we didn't drive that far. Somewhere near there, I suppose?'

'Find out – I want to know everything. Text me every second. Or email me. Or Facebook me. Or all of those things. In fact, get on Twitter. TWEET.'

'I thought I might have a shower before I work out what the actual fuck I'm doing first,' I said, squinting at the sunshine. 'I'm knackered and I smell. Oh!'

As I turned back to the cottage, a sweaty shirtless man appeared from nowhere and almost knocked me to the ground.

'I don't know about knackered, but you could smell sweeter,' he grunted, half out of breath. He grabbed my shoulders and stood me up straight. 'Nice knickers.'

Without another word, the topless man spun me round so that I was facing the ocean again and sprinted off.

'What was that? Was that a man?' Amy screeched down the phone. 'You're on a freebie trip to Hawaii, sticking it to Vanessa, and there are men there? I'm getting on the next plane.'

'Unlike me, you've got work,' I reminded her as I watched the man's back, and backside, run away from me. My forearm shone with a slight sheen of his sweat, left behind after our brief collision. Gross. 'Actually, I've got to work too. For a job I don't know how to do. I should go.'

'Extreme Makeover: Life Edition,' she sighed. 'But, um, actually . . . about the me having a job thing. I might have got fired again. So I could totally come.'

'Oh, Aims,' I said with as as much sympathy as I could muster for her third job of the year. 'One quarter life crisis at a time?'

'Whatever. I hated that job anyway.' She gave me a verbal shrug down the phone, her voice painfully care-free. 'By the time you get back, I'll be all sensible and employed again. Or I'll have fucked off to Cuba masquer-ading as a spy.'

'And I'll probably be in handcuffs,' I muttered. The

man had completely vanished from sight. 'Are you all right? Do you need anything?'

'A drink and a ticket to Hawaii?' she asked hopefully.

'I was thinking help with your rent?' I felt horrible for being so far away. Amy needed me. 'You're sure you're OK?'

'I'm sure I am,' Amy shushed me and clapped down the line. 'You're doing your bit right now. Go and roll around in the waves for me. I'll talk to you later on.'

'You bloody well will,' I agreed. 'Daily sanity checks needed. For both of us.'

Hanging up, I looked out at the stupidly beautiful ocean one more time.

'Oh, just shut up, Hawaii,' I muttered at no one in particular.

Maybe hourly sanity checks.

Back inside the cottage, I plugged in my phone with the lead I had bought at the airport and placed it carefully on the bedside table, the same spot where it lived at home. It felt good to do something normal. Looking around the bedroom, I shook my head and felt my heavy curls flap around the back of my head in a limp ponytail. If this was the guest cottage, I was almost too scared to see the main house. It was all so perfect. I'd been impressed by the living room and kitchen – they were so shiny and neat – but they weren't even the half of it. A small hallway led through to an open, airy bedroom filled by a huge bed made up with the softest white linens I'd ever had the privilege of rubbing my face against and giggling into. Off to one side was a small, dark-wood dressing table, a matching desk with accompanying squishy white leather office chair, a huge

MacBook Pro and a very swanky-looking printer. Oh yeah, I was here to work. On the other side of the bed was a wall of fitted wardrobes, all white wood, no sticky fingerprints or evidence of a late-night Dairy Milk binge to be seen. Resting on a white floating shelf was a bright pink ukulele. I fought every urge in my body to pick it up and start playing it badly. That time would come.

Peering out of the bedroom window, I saw a narrow path that wound its way through the gardens and up to a huge, tented terrace and the back of the main house. Aka Bertie Bennett's palace. The only people who could legit live in a house like that were Bond villains, the final six in *America's Next Top Model* or P. Diddy. If I got up there for dinner and Beyoncé was a house guest, I was going to lose my shit.

After tearing myself away from the view, I tore myself away from the rest of my clothes and locked my skanky self in the bathroom. Thanks to Boots at Heathrow I had some bare essentials in my suitcase, but there was no need to bust out the miniature Pantene. Mr Bennett had supplied everything a lady could ever need – Molton Brown toiletries, Diptyque candles and even a proper girl's razor, not the individually wrapped things you get in hotels that slice your legs to ribbons. A proper lady's razor. He had to be gay.

After the world's longest and most delicious shower, I settled down in the leather chair with my laptop on my knee. Having been trapped on a Wi-Fi-less plane for the best part of twenty-four hours, I hadn't been able to do nearly as much research into Mr Bennett as I'd have liked. I'd bought every fashion magazine and photography journal on the stands at the airport, read every single one cover to cover, and by now I knew that my battered H&M denim jacket should be a luxe leather bomber, my loose linen trousers should be cropped cotton, and everything else I owned should be neon. Most of the items I'd plundered from Vanessa's wardrobe were as far away from my conservative clothing collection as I could stomach, not that there weren't an awful lot of monochrome options, but I'd been brave and pilfered all of one bright yellow dress as well. Glancing over at the case full of stripey T-shirts and skinny jeans, I sighed loudly. I'd been pitching for a continental chic sort of look, left-bank sophistication and all that jazz. According to *Marie Claire*, *Elle*, *Vogue*, *InStyle*, *Gloss*, *Belle*, *Grazia* and even *GQ*, which I'd picked up by accident, I'd dropped a major bollock. Shocker.

Once I was connected to Bennett's Wi-Fi network, I clicked through my emails as quickly as possible. I ignored the four Lolcats from Amy, pretended I didn't care that there was nothing from Charlie, and opened the brief that Agent Veronica had sent over. It was nearly ten pages long. Suddenly I got the impression that I wasn't the only one who didn't consider Vanessa to be the sharpest knife in the drawer. Not that I was complaining. In this instance I needed all the help I could get, and she really did make the job sound relatively simple. Cue sense of epic relief. Scanning the info from the magazine, I saw that the art director from *Gloss* was going to be here to direct the actual shoot. I was literally in charge of pointing the camera at the right spot, pressing a button. The only thing that made me sweat was the portrait of Bertie Bennett. What if he was a complete bastard? Not that I hadn't managed more than a few of them in my time. And given that my only other option was to fess up, go home and face Charlie,

King of the Bastards, I figured I'd stay here and take my chances. After all, it was only taking a few pictures. How hard could it be?

With a new sense of confidence, I stretched out on the bed and looked at the itinerary, biro between my teeth. So, Monday. According to the official document from *Gloss*, I was to arrive in Honolulu, get to the Bennett compound and meet Bertie. According to Agent Veronica's notes, added in a bright red font, I was to get to Honolulu, get to the house, 'keep my fucking mouth shut and my fucking knickers on'. Neither of those had ever really been a problem for me. Tuesday morning I was to meet with Paige, the art director, to discuss the shoot, and then Bertie, Paige and I were supposed to go over the clothes he wanted to shoot for the main spread. Again, Veronica had added her own note that advised, 'Do not piss him off.' Harsh but fair. On Wednesday, I'd be shooting the fashion spreads, locations TBC. Thursday was set aside for the portrait of Bertie, and then we had Friday open 'just in case' before we all flew home on Saturday night. Agent Vanessa had added a couple of other general asides in what had to be at least a 32-point font – mostly motivational statements like 'Fuck this up and I'll destroy you' and 'Even a chimp with a camera phone could do this.' Perhaps a chimp with a camera phone could do this, I thought, but chimps had also been sent into space and could count cards if they put their minds to it. I couldn't do either of those things. Fuck fuck fuckity fuck.

After printing out the itinerary and sticking it to the mirror above the desk with a tiny roll of invisible tape I found in the drawer (swoon, stationery), I gave my host a quick Google. In just two minutes and three clicks,

I had discovered that Bertie Bennett was (a) a mental and (b) the owner of a super-cool department store in New York called Bennett's. Fact (b) was easy to find out. Bennett's had a huge web presence and pretty much every fashion site referenced it. I imagined that if I'd ever been to New York instead of just watching a lot of *Friends* and all of *Sex and the City*, that would be something I might know. Fact (a) was easy to ascertain due to the photos I'd found of Bertie dressed in ridiculous costumes and doing ridiculous things. There were far fewer pictures than I'd anticipated, but the ones I found were corkers. The three years he'd spent dressed as a ringmaster every time he left the house in the late seventies was quite well documented. I hoped he was still wearing the top hat – he looked very dapper. The five-month stint he'd spent masquerading as an astronaut in the sixties was barely documented at all, which seemed a shame. For such a major figure in the world of fashion, Bertie really had managed to keep a low profile: there was basically nothing on him at all after the mid-seventies. Times really had changed. If he'd been starting out now, he'd have had a reality show and a 'Designers at Debenhams' deal by now. All of the shots I did find showed a young, vibrant man with a penchant for a bit of fancy dress and a Barbra Streisand show. Incredibly well turned out and definitely what my mum would call a 'dandy'. Possibly what my nan would call a 'confirmed bachelor'. Why northern women over fifty-five couldn't just say 'gay' was beyond me. But there was nothing after he started to turn a wee bit grey. I did find his name in a few society features, mostly schmoozing at Fashion Week events all over the world, but that didn't surprise me – fashionistas flocked together, didn't they? That's why I didn't know any. Gnawing on the barrel of my pen, I wondered what had changed his mind about sitting for a photographer again. Maybe he'd been on the Just For Men and wanted to show off. And I was the lucky snapper. Eeep.

After re-reading the brief another seven times, I opened up Facebook, clicked on Charlie's page and felt my newly acquired balls slip away completely. He hadn't posted anything for days – he rarely did – and so the screen was mostly filled with pictures uploaded by his friends. I clicked the 'pictures of you and Charlie' button and choked up faster than you could say 'emotional cutter'. It was like I was seeing every single one of the photographs with fresh eyes, and not a single one made me feel better. In almost every picture, I was leaning into him or staring up at his face with big shining eyes. In almost every picture, he was looking at someone else or staring at the camera with happy, beery ambivalence.

I remembered every last moment of every last minute we had ever spent together. I remembered going to the cinema to see one of the Bourne movies and barely being able to breathe for nearly two hours because it was so warm out that we were both wearing shorts, and every so often our legs would touch and the skin-on-skin contact took my breath away. I remembered all the times he would walk by my desk and throw a packet of Skittles at my face without speaking because he knew they were my favourite. I remembered going over to see him when his granddad had died, him opening the door with red-rimmed eyes and spluttering sobs. We didn't even say anything, just sat on the sofa watching episode of *Top Gear* after episode of *Top Gear* until we both fell asleep. I woke up in his bed in the middle of the night and

115

found him passed out on the sofa surrounded by photos of his family. He never really talked about them and it broke my heart to see him in so much pain, but I just covered him with a blanket and went back to bed. When I got up the next morning, he was business as usual. The photos were gone and his sore eyes put down to a bad case of hay fever.

It was still incredibly early, barely ten in the morning, but my jet-lagged brain could not process any of what was happening. I slapped my laptop shut and rolled under a soft white blanket, pulling it up to my chin. Either I had never been this tired in my entire life or this bed was made out of clouds. Before I could even turn over and check my phone, I was fast asleep.

CHAPTER SEVEN

It is a little-known fact, but when you combine jetlag and stomach-churning terror, it's quite possible to sleep through an entire day. When I eventually woke up, the sun was already starting to dip below the horizon. The sky was a soft pale blue painted with broad strokes of gauzy pink and orange, a world away from the cloudy grey sunset I'd watched over the village duck pond just two days before.

It was already almost seven, which gave me just under an hour to get myself together for dinner with Mr Bennett. My first real test. Every time I closed my eyes and every time I opened them, this seemed less and less plausible. The craziest thing I'd ever done was call in sick in 2004 because Amy had tickets to see Justin Timberlake and I was scared that if I didn't go with her, she would end up in prison or at the very least with a restraining order. Plus it was Justin.

'All I need to remember is that my name is Vanessa,' I told the slightly concerned face I saw reflected in the dressing-table mirror. 'That's the only thing I need to remember. The rest of it will be easy.'

Ha. Easy.

At five minutes to eight exactly, I picked my way up the torch-lit path to the main house and headed towards the veranda, practising some very steady breathing and rehearsing my key notes in my head. This was just a pitch like any other – I was selling a campaign like I did every day. Except today I was the campaign and Bennett was the client. How hard could it be? I'd pulled my hair back into a tight fishtail braid as I hadn't had enough time to dry it properly, and there was a very real danger of it turning into an unwelcome afro as soon as I stepped outside, and I'd chosen a simple yellow shift dress, one of only two colourful items of clothing I'd packed, paired with leather flip-flops from my brand-new borrowed wardrobe. I had no idea how fancy dinner would be, but I had a feeling turning up in jeans wouldn't really be ideal and I was aiming to invite as few questions as possible. Simple outfit, simple hair, as elegant and classy as possible when you were a cack-handed mare with a make-up brush. All I was going to do was show up, eat my dinner, be polite and ask lots of questions without drawing any attention to myself. One of the things I'd learned from working in advertising all these years was that people liked talking about themselves. As long as you made the right noises and kept the conversation going, no one noticed that you weren't actually saying anything. Between the million questions I had prepared and the fact that I intended to eat until I burst and, most importantly, avoid all alcohol, I didn't anticipate any major problems at dinner.

Which was, of course, my first mistake.

Kekipi and his great big doe eyes were waiting for me with a glass of champagne at the top of the staircase that led onto the veranda.

'Miss Kittler.' He handed me the glass. I took it. I hated to be rude. 'You look delightful.'

'Vanessa,' I corrected him, quietly proud of myself for remembering my new name. 'Please, just Vanessa.'

Behind my host I saw a table set for someone dressed way more fancy than me, but I refused to be defeated. I knew which fork was which. Most of the time.

'Mr Bennett wishes me to pass on his apologies. He won't be able to make dinner this evening, but he has asked that you please stay and eat. The first course will be out shortly.'

Necking the champagne, I nodded and followed him to the table, equal parts relieved and annoyed. It felt the same as prepping for a big meeting and then having your boss call in sick – you didn't really want to have to go through with it, but you were so psyched up you couldn't help but be a little bit disappointed. But it was hard to be too upset with a glass of champagne in my hand and a soft Hawaiian breeze blowing around my bare legs. Even a best-case-scenario Monday back in England would be two-for-one at Wagamama's with Amy. Charlie always had football practice on Mondays. Not that I was thinking about Charlie. At all.

'Mr Miller is just inside,' Kekipi said, refilling my champagne. I did not neck this one. 'Dinner will be served in a few moments.'

'Mr Miller?'

'The gentleman who is conducting the interview with Mr Bennett,' he offered with a smile. 'He'll be out in a moment.'

It hadn't occurred to me that the actual interview would be happening at the same time as the shoot. This was all I needed. Some irritating fashion journo bitching and whining and judging ensembles that weren't even my ensembles.

I took my seat at the table and waited patiently. Never something I'd been good at. While the painful seconds ticked by, I took a chance to check out Bertie Bennett's palace. The veranda where dinner was to be served was part of a bigger deck that wrapped all the way round the house. To the left, up a couple more stone staircases, was a huge infinity pool with neighbouring hot tub that looked out over the private bay. My muscles ached and I was dying to sink into the warm water, even if it did seem a bit rude given that the ocean was right there in front of us. To the right was another deck, dotted with squishy armchairs, sunloungers and parasols. I ran my hand down the smooth wood of the straight-backed dining chair and tried not to think about how wonderful it would be to lie back on one of those chairs with a very large cocktail and maybe a little shoulder massage. Poor me – here I was sitting at this beautiful table with a glass of champagne waiting for someone to bring me my dinner when I could be in a hot tub. Life was hard here, but I was pretty sure I could get used to the difficult decisions.

Despite my best efforts to avoid it, I caught my reflection in the huge window behind the table. Hair looked OK, dress was a little bit bright, but the lights were dim and the sun had almost set. Everyone looked better at sunset. See how much I knew about lighting? I was definitely a natural photographer. Just then the window slid open and a man stepped out.

'Vanessa Kittler.'

Oh. Of course.

It was the man from the beach.

He walked round the table with an easy grace, dressed in perfectly fitted jeans, bare feet and a white shirt that set off a disgustingly good tan. He had an English accent with a transatlantic lilt, but he obviously hadn't spent a lot of time in the UK over the past few months, unless that golden glow was a sunbed tan. And I really hoped it was, because that would make him a complete dickhead and that would distract me from how very handsome he was.

'Hello.' I cleared my throat, stood up, held out my hand and made a concerted effort not to knock anything over. 'Nice to meet you.'

'Oh, we've met, on the beach this morning? You don't remember?' He sat down in the seat opposite me, ignoring my outstretched hand. Hmm, rude. I wished I had a presentation to give. I was definitely a PowerPoint person. Without it, I only had my mouth to rely on, and my mouth was stupid. 'You dressed for dinner. How thoughtful.'

'I didn't know how formal it would be.' There was a slight stammer in my voice and I felt every inch of my skin burning. I wanted to slap myself. And then him. And then myself again. 'T-shirt and knickers seemed a bit casual.'

'Gutted.' He reached over the table and pulled a sweaty bottle of white out of a silver wine bucket and poured himself a glass. Didn't even offer to pour me one. 'I'm Nick.'

'Nice to meet you.' I couldn't stop staring. My blood was up and I wasn't sure whether I wanted to slap him or shag him. It was not my natural state. I was very confused. 'Again.'

He inclined his head very slightly. 'So. Vanessa.'

'Yes?' I waited for his follow-up but nothing came.

After almost a minute of silence, I realized Nick wasn't asking me a question. He was just fucking with me. Instead of filling the air with polite and meaningless small talk like normal people, he just sat there holding his wine glass close to his lips, a small smile threatening to make an appearance on his face. I pushed my champagne glass as far away from me as possible to avoid chugging the whole thing just for something to do. Silence made me nervous. Attractive men made me nervous. Unanticipated situations made me nervous. I was fucked.

'So how long have you been out here?' I asked, looking past my dinner companion and into the house. It was a ghost town. A cool glow lit up one of the windows on the top floor for just a moment, but it flickered out almost as soon as I noticed it. 'Did you get in today?'

Nick didn't answer me. Instead his smile broadened and he sipped his wine. My breaking the silence meant he had won – it was written all over his face. I pressed my lips together in a tight line and forbade myself from speaking again. I would not say another word. I would just sit here and look at his self-satisfied grin. And his crinkly light blue almost grey eyes. And the perfectly toned forearms that were peeking out of his rolled-up shirt sleeves. I was a mug for forearms and crinkly eyes. It all came off a bit Daniel Craig as James Bond, but with fewer physical beatings and marginally better hair. There was no point pretending otherwise – he was hot. But not my type. My type was, after all, pretty specific.

'So you're staying in one of the cottages too?'

The words were out before I realized it. My mouth was such a traitor.

'I can't believe we haven't met before.' He spoke with a slow, steady voice and I knew right away why he was such a good journalist. Between the baby blues and the slightly gravelly but desperately sure-of-itself voice, I couldn't imagine anyone holding out on him in any way, shape or form. 'I know you by, well, reputation.'

'As a photographer?' I asked.

'Sure,' he replied, unable to keep from laughing. 'I know your reputation as a photographer.'

Brilliant. I'd escaped my shitty situation in London and stranded myself in a tropical paradise with a hot, rude man who thought I was a slag. And as much as I considered myself a feminist, I couldn't really blame him. Vanessa was, to be fair, a bit of a slag. Silence seemed like my best defence, so I reached over to my champagne, tried to sip slowly, and prayed for dinner to come out quickly. I was starving.

'You think you're up to this job?' Nick leaned back in his chair and folded his arms. 'Seriously?'

'Do you think *you're* up to this job?' I bounced the question back, classic holding technique. 'Seriously?'

'Yes,' he replied without missing a beat. 'I'm the best at what I do. That's why I'm here. Are you?'

'If I wasn't, I wouldn't be here,' I said as confidently as I could. 'Would I?'

'You're here because Dan Fraser, Oliver Voss, Erica Ishugruo and at least five other photographers, as far as I'm aware, were already booked and this was the only week in the next six months Bennett would give us.' Nick didn't flinch, didn't pause, didn't look away. 'You're here because your agent has the editor of *Gloss* in her pocket. You're here because no one else could be.'

'Right. Brilliant.'

That was me told.

'And just repeating my questions back to me won't work,' he said, rolling up his shirt sleeves a tiny bit further. 'I'm a journalist. I ask questions professionally.'

'Right. Brilliant.'

I pressed my lips together, making my mouth into a terribly attractive tight little line, and stared back at the man across the table. He was really, really starting to piss me off.

'It would have been easier if I had taken the photos myself.' Nick's voice was low enough that I couldn't quite tell if I was supposed to be able to hear him or not.

'You're a photographer as well as a writer?' I asked with forced brightness.

He raised an eyebrow and stared me down.

'No.'

Breathing out forcefully, I rubbed my thumb along my fingernail, feeling the ragged edges where I had bitten it on the plane. Didn't help. I prayed for Kekipi to bring out some food for me to shove in my face before I put my fist in Nick's. His gaze was unwavering and I was completely unsettled. Mostly because he looked like he was really enjoying himself. The more awkward he could make things for me, the happier he became. I grabbed a bread roll from the basket in front of me and tore off a chunk, turning towards the horizon and ignoring the fact that I couldn't seem to sit still while I was looking at him. Stupid vagina – it wasn't the boss of me.

'Tell me about yourself, Vanessa.'

Of course he waited until I'd stuffed a fistful of bread into my gob before asking me the world's most annoying question. I chewed, coughed, swallowed and held a hand in front of my face.

'Not much to tell,' I replied. It wasn't a lie, per se. Compared with the people he must have interviewed, I had to imagine that even a newly minted compulsive liar such as myself wouldn't be terribly interesting.

'Favourite book?'

'Um. I don't know.'

'Favourite record?'

'I like all sorts.'

'Favourite piece of art?'

'Do most people have a favourite piece of art?'

'Favourite film?'

'*Top Gun*,' I answered in an instant.

'That's your boyfriend's favourite film,' he replied just as fast. 'What's your favourite film?'

I replied with a stony stare. My turn not to play fair.

'Oh.' He sipped at his wine again. 'Recent break-up, is it?'

With absolutely no idea how to respond, I shoved another pawful of bread into my mouth and chewed slowly. My forced silence didn't seem to have the same impact on Nick as his had on me. In fact, it appeared to have completely the opposite effect. He was grinning right at me.

'Dinner is served.' Kekipi strode out of the main house followed by a small army of waiters, each one laden with a platter of joy. I let the sight and smell of the food distract me from Nick's ridiculous questioning and tried to decide what I would eat first while wondering whether Bertie Bennett always had a small army of waiters at his beck and call. I assumed he did. 'Can I get you anything else?'

'We're fine, thanks, Kekipi,' Nick answered for both of us before I had a chance. Another thing to go on the

List of Reasons to Punch Him in the Face. 'This looks spectacular.'

'*Mahalo*, Mr Miller,' Kekipi replied with his professional smile. 'We'll just be inside. Please ring the bell if you need anything at all.'

Nick did not tell Kekipi to call him Nick. Dickhead.

'Wait, there's a bell?' I couldn't quite believe it when Nick held up a small golden hand bell.

'Fuck me,' I breathed.

'Maybe after dinner,' he replied, carefully placing the bell back on the table far out of my reach while I choked on absolutely nothing. I blushed and quietly pinched myself under the table to check this was actually happening. What an absolute dickhead.

For as long as I could possibly manage, we ate in silence. I piled mounds of pork, chicken and fish onto my plate and attempted to balance it out with a respectable amount of salad for appearances. I was never going to eat that salad. After my second helping of kalua pig, I caved.

'Have you met Mr Bennett before?' I tried to keep my voice light and casual and not give away the fact that I'd spent almost as much time trying to work out what was a safe question to ask as I had trying not to spill a load of pig down my dress. I hoped I'd done a better job of the question than I had of getting food safely into my mouth.

'No.' Thankfully, Nick decided to play nice and just answer. 'He doesn't give interviews. This is kind of a big deal.'

'Have you interviewed lots of fashion people?' I pushed on while I was on a roll. And eating a roll.

'Not many.' He shook his head, looking as though he'd

eaten something unpleasant, which I knew for a fact he hadn't. 'I talk to people with actual stories. There are very few fashion people with real stories.'

'Surely everyone has a story?' I asked. 'Like how they say everyone has a book in them?'

He shook his head and pinched the bridge of his nose before replying.

'Not everyone does have a book in them. Some people don't even have a Post-it note.'

'It's just something people say,' I sniffed, wiping greasy fingers on my heavy napkin and feeling guilty about the greasy finger marks. 'You really don't think it's true?'

'You do?' Nick asked. 'Take you, for example. According to you, you don't have a favourite book, a favourite band, a favourite movie. What story would you write?'

'For all you know, I am a fantastic writer,' I said, starting to get a bit angry again. Fuelled by the over-confidence of far too much food, I slapped the table. It hurt. 'How do you know I'm not writing an amazing novel about a dystopian society where a reanimated Henry VIII falls in love with a squirrel?'

'Well, look at you and your completely insane imagination.' He laughed a little and for the first time it didn't sound patronizing, even if his words were. 'I should get your back up more often if you're going to come out with gems like that. And you should write that book. I'd read it.'

'Whatever.' I was annoyed. He was a game player and I hated playing games. That was one of the many wonderful things about Charlie. He was easily as hand-some as this douche nozzle, if not more handsome, but he didn't mess people around. He never fell for girl tricks and he never said anything just to provoke a reaction. Not that I was thinking about Charlie.

'You're really not going to tell me about the break-up?' Nick asked, pushing a bowl of vegetables at me. 'It was that bad? You should try those, they're good.'

'I don't want to talk about it,' I replied, heaping some carrots on my plate and pretending they were still healthy even if they were dripping with butter. 'There's nothing to talk about.'

'So there was a break-up.' He flashed his eyebrows up and down and I stared at my plate. Tricksy bastard. 'How about a deal. I'll ask you a question and then you can ask me a question. Sound fair?'

'Not really. You're a professional question asker,' I replied tartly, 'and I'm a photographer.'

'Well, I can tell you're not a wordsmith, anyway,' he rallied. 'Professional question asker?'

The wordsmith in me winced. One week out of my job and I'd already lost my grasp on the English language.

'Question: where do you live?' I asked before I lost my temper.

'I have a flat in London and an apartment in New York, but I wouldn't say I live anywhere,' Nick replied. 'I do like a girl with an appetite. Nice. My question: what do you value most above anything else?'

'Oh, I, um . . .' I was stumped. And still trying to work out if he'd just called me fat.

'You don't get to think, you just have to answer,' he said, clicking his fingers over and over and over. 'Come on, Vanessa.'

'My friends.' I shook my head. 'My best friends. Best friend. Amy. My turn: how old are you?'

'Thirty-six,' he said. 'I know, I look great. Question two: what's your proudest achievement?'

'I . . .'

'No hesitation.'

'Getting my first job before I graduated.' I waved my hands in the air, trying to slow myself down. 'Before I was a photographer. Full-time photographer. Me again: do you have a girlfriend?'

'No.'

'Why not?'

'Because I don't,' Nick replied. 'And that's two questions for me.'

I wasn't nearly as good at this game as he was. Over the next ten minutes, I answered every one of his abstract, nonsensical questions. I told him what colour I felt like, I told him I would never move back to where I grew up, I told him I preferred birthdays to Christmas and preferred the city to the country, the country to the beach and that I had never, ever cheated on anyone. All I managed to learn about Nick was that he was born in London, he had lived in New York, Paris and Argentina, that he didn't have a driving licence, was a night owl rather than an early bird, and his favourite colour was blue. He was right – I was not a professional question asker.

'Is this what you do in difficult interviews?' I asked, all out of questions. I sat back in my chair and mournfully nursed my food baby as Kekipi and the gang came to clear the table. There was still so much left, it was beyond wasteful. I wanted to parcel it all up and send it back to poor, jobless Amy. She would have decimated the leftovers in seconds. 'I ask you, you ask me?'

'This is what I do whenever I have to interview children,' Nick replied. 'Difficult children.'

'Right,' I nodded. Just when I'd been starting to warm to him. 'Do a lot of that, do you?'

'Nope.'

'No.' I shook my head. 'Well, I don't see what you managed to glean that would be interesting to anyone else by asking me if I consider myself to be a loyal person. Who would say no to that?'

'This is the thing.' Nick leaned back in his chair, his features almost vanishing into a silhouette as he pulled away from the candle. 'I learned a lot more about you from your questions than you learned about me from my answers.'

'Is that right?'

'OK, here's what I know.' He took a deep drink of wine and then cleared his throat. 'You grew up in a small village but you were desperate to get out. I know you aren't close to your family because you value your friends much more highly than your relatives. You are single, which I would know even if you hadn't mentioned the break-up earlier because you were so quick to tell me how proud you are of your professional achievements. If you were hopelessly in love, that would have come out in your answers, whether you wanted it to or not. Also, the only friend that you mentioned was Amy, which is very *Sex and the City* of you but it also tells me that you aren't in love with anyone. Or at least you're determined not to be. I've got to assume you're unhappily single because so many of your questions to me were about my love life, and since you asked so many questions about my job and where I'd travelled to, I've got to assume that even though you use your job as your main source of validation, you haven't travelled very much even though you'd like to. Which is weird for a photographer.'

Disconcerting was not the word.

'Is that all you've got?' I needed more wine and I needed it immediately.

'Probably go out on a limb and say you're worrying about your age since you asked me mine,' he shrugged. 'And your questions were a bit banal and depressingly literal but somewhat creatively grounded, what with the favourite colour and everything, so I'd say you're someone who likes to solve problems but in a creative way. That makes more sense for a photographer, I suppose.'

Or for a creative director in an advertising firm, I thought to myself. He was quite possibly the best professional question asker I'd ever come across.

'You've gone a bit quiet,' Nick noted as Kekipi reappeared with half of his gang and several platters of dessert. Thank God this dress had plenty of eating room. I was going to go back to England the size of a cow. Two cows, at this rate. 'I'm right?'

'About some of it,' I admitted. 'But it's not like I didn't learn anything about you.'

'Go on then,' he said as one of the waiters poured out two coffees. I hoped they were decaf. 'Stun me with your insight.'

'I suppose what I noticed most was that you were just really vague.' I added cream to my coffee and tried not to look at Nick while I was talking to him. Too distracting. 'Favourite colour, driving licence, yes and no questions, all really easy, but the rest of it . . . I don't think you like people knowing too much about you.'

'Interesting theory,' he commented. 'Go on.'

And so I did. 'I don't know. I mean, I'm not the journalist, obviously, but just all of it – the quick comebacks, the bare feet, the black coffee. Single at thirty-six, can't commit to a city, nowhere you call home. Maybe you can't commit to anything?'

'I don't think you're breaking any new ground

suggesting a single man in his thirties might have commitment issues,' Nick said with forced boredom. I glanced up from my coffee cup. He might have sounded bored, but he looked really annoyed. Amazing. 'Although you realize commitment issues were invented by women? No man has commitment issues. When a woman says that, what they really mean is, "He doesn't want to commit to me," It's a little bit sad.'

'Wow,' I replied, leaning towards the candles to get a better look at him. 'Are you angry at all women, or is there just one who really pissed you off?'

'Oh, that would be original, wouldn't it?' He moved back out of the light and I couldn't quite see his face. 'Wounded, damaged and heartbroken, I spend my days writing the stories of others so I never have to think about my own. Constantly trying to outrun my feelings until one day I meet the woman who changes everything?'

'I never said heartbroken,' I said quietly.

'Well.' Nick tapped his fingers on the table and smiled down at the tablecloth. 'Well, no, I suppose you didn't.'

The pretty evening breeze rustled the palm trees overhead and I busied myself by concentrating on the lights inside the main house and pushed a stray wisp of hair out of my eyes. I wondered how many people lived in there. It couldn't possibly just be Bertie Bennett – it was far too big.

'So tell me more about Vanessa Kittler, photographer extraordinaire.' Nick broke the silence first. Even though I'd been at a complete loss for something to say, I chalked it up as a win. 'I still want to hear your story.'

'Nope.' I picked up a piece of pineapple from the platter in front of me and used it as a delicious fruity pointer. 'I'm not the storyteller, you are. Maybe you should be a writer.'

'Hilarious,' he replied flatly. Somewhere in the past five minutes, something had knocked the comedy right out of him. Instead of looking bemused by the whole situation, he just looked pissed off. I was ever so slightly pleased with myself. 'Must have been a terrible break-up,' I said, eyes wide with feigned innocence. 'You poor, broken man, you.'

'Yeah, I think you've seen too many films.' Nick chugged the remains of his coffee and snatched the piece of pineapple out of my hand. 'And you clearly haven't read too many books.'

'I read,' I snapped back. He stole my fruit! And, yes, there was an entire plate of pineapple, but that wasn't the point. 'I read all the time.'

'The *Fifty Shades* books don't count.' Nick pushed his chair back.

'I didn't read them, actually,' I announced with triumph. He didn't need to know I hadn't had the time and had read the Wikipedia synopses and then down-loaded the dirty bits instead.

'Like I said, not a reader.'

With just as much grace but significantly more purpose than when he had sat down, Nick stood up, walked round the table and placed his hands on the armrests either side of me, leaning in close. I jerked backwards, eyes locked on his. They were such a strange colour. He bent down until his lips were right beside my ear, and I breathed in suddenly, his fresh, soapy shower gel and shampoo just barely covering the traces of a darker, warmer scent that made my stomach flip.

'Goodnight, Vanessa,' he whispered before pushing

away from my chair and jogging off down the steps and back towards the beach.

'Well.' A little stunned and incredibly flustered, I grabbed another bit of pineapple and took a big bite, waiting for my heartbeat to resume normal service. 'That was just rude.'

'It was a little,' a voice said in the semi-darkness. It was Kekipi. 'I think you touched a nerve.'

I laughed self-consciously, happy to have an ally and only slightly embarrassed at being caught talking to myself.

'How is the pineapple?' he asked, filling up my coffee and pouring himself a cup before sitting down in Nick's empty seat and throwing his bare feet up onto the table. I wondered if he was like this with all of Mr Bennett's guests. I wondered if Mr Bennett had many guests.

'Bloody delicious,' I replied, my mouth completely full. With Kekipi as my witness, it was the best bloody pineapple I had ever eaten. The little plastic pots from M&S would never, ever do the job again. 'Perfection, actually.'

'Good to hear.' Kekipi sipped his coffee and sighed. He looked so contented and comfortable, the opposite of my earlier dinner date. 'They do say you've never eaten pineapple until you've eaten it in Hawaii.'

'I'll have to make sure I eat lots while I'm here then,' I said.

'We can ensure that your cottage is well stocked.' Kekipi gave me a wink and nodded down the hill, where a light flickered on in the cottage next door to mine. Nick was home. 'Mr Miller was an interesting dinner companion?'

'I just hope I haven't bitten off more than I can chew,'

I said, tugging at the end of my plait. 'I've got a funny feeling I'm going to have trouble with that one.'

'I've got a funny feeling I'd like to have trouble with that one,' he replied. 'And that funny feeling is right in the middle of my trousers. He would be just my type.'

'Not mine.' My eyes were still fixed on the glowing window. He was probably taking his shirt off. Right. That. Second. 'Never been a blond fan.'

'I'm sure you could make an exception if you put your mind to it.' Kekipi heaped a giant spoonful of sugar into his cup and stirred. 'He is one of those men everyone wants. He's like pizza and George Clooney. Everyone wants a slice. He'd charm your mother and flirt with your grand-mother while impressing your father with his in-depth knowledge of knot-tying and single malt whiskies.'

'He knows about knot-tying?' I looked back at Kekipi.

'Probably.' He shrugged. 'I think he might be the least gay man I've ever met. I'm trying very hard not to fall in love with him. Can I suggest you do the same?'

'I promise I will not fall in love with him,' I said, laughing alone until my chuckles tailed off into awkward silence. Kekipi stared at me with a less-than-convinced expression.

'I won't,' I said, unnecessarily defensive. 'Seriously. I am not going to fall in love with him.'

'I'll remind you of that at the wedding,' he said.

'You can be head bridesmaid,' I muttered, turning my gaze back towards the cottages and watching the little light in Nick's window flicker and blink before the bay was bathed in darkness.

CHAPTER EIGHT

Tuesday morning was almost as confusing to my poor little brain as Monday evening had been. I woke up with the remains of jetlag fug clouding my mind as I tried to recount the events of the past twenty-four hours. Hawaii, Amy, sleep, dinner, Nick-baiting and then two hours on the veranda with Kekipi. According to my new best friend, it had been years since the estate had seen any real guests and he was ecstatic to have a captive audience, even if only for a week. In exchange for my rapt but sleepy attention, he told me endless amazing stories about his adventures as the only gay in the Hawaiian village and during all the years he'd worked for Bertie Bennett. His tales of wild parties at the Bennett mansion reminded me of *The Great Gatsby*. Which reminded me I should finish reading *The Great Gatsby*.

But that was last night and this was this morning. Today was the first real day of my new double life, my first full working day as Vanessa Kittler. I'd decided, somewhere between two and three a.m. – when all best decisions are made – that if I was going to be Vanessa for a week, I was going to *be* Vanessa for a week. As much as I hated to admit it, all that verbal sparring with Nick had been fun, and while picking a fight didn't feel like a very Tess thing to do, it did feel like a very Vanessa thing to do. And why shouldn't I indulge in flirty banter with the handsome man? I was a free agent. And, as far as that handsome man was concerned, possibly a bit of a slag, according to my reputation. Stretching my arms above my head until I heard something crack, I tried to make myself get up. I only had this life on loan for a week – I really should try to make the most of it. Instead, I rolled over and curled my arms around my pillow, smiling at what I saw. My camera, safely tucked in beside me, resting half under the covers and half on a pillow. Apparently I'd felt like a one-night stand with my Canon when I got home. Nothing like slutting it up with electronic equipment to start a week away. I reached out and stroked it gently, careful not to press any buttons and wake it from its slumber. We had a hard day ahead of us.

Leaving my lover in bed, I slunk into the kitchen in my T-shirt-come-nightie and noticed two things that hadn't been there when I'd finally rolled myself into bed. A plate full of yet more delicious-looking fresh fruit and a thick white envelope resting beside it, addressed to Vanessa. Inside was a stiff white note card with a gold crest and a couple of lines of perfect handwriting.

Dear Ms Kittler,
Unfortunately I will not be available for our appointment today. Please accept my sincerest apologies. Kekipi is at your disposal.
Yours,
B. Bennett.

Hmm. He had cancelled again. I wondered why he'd blown us out this time. That mill trouble Kekipi had been talking about? Stuck at an orgy with Jack Nicholson, Mick Jagger and half the Playboy mansion? More likely he just couldn't make his mind up between the hot tub and the sunloungers on his terrace. I understood his pain – it was almost exactly the same predicament as in *Sophie's Choice*.

'It's fine,' I announced to the empty kitchen, placing the card back on the worktop and twisting my hair into a dodgy topknot. 'Gives me another day to get to grips with the camera.'

And if the worst came to the worst, I still had a spare day at the end of the week to play around with. *Gloss* was a proper magazine with proper contingency plans made by proper planning-type people. They just didn't have a proper photographer. But they didn't know that. Regardless, what this really meant was that I had a completely free day in Hawaii . . .

The beach was deserted and utterly silent when I ventured outside. Instead of a starchy white shirt and badly fitting black trousers, I was wearing one of my super-soft T-shirts and a pair of denim cutoffs that had previously lived life as my 'painting jeans'. It felt good to be out of uniform. The breeze from the day before had vanished and the sun warmed my bare skin through in a heartbeat. It wasn't too hot, it wasn't too humid – it was just right. Goldilocks weather.

'Must remember you're here for a reason,' I reminded myself, sliding the wide, webbed camera strap over my head. 'Must take pictures. Pictures must be good. Or at least good enough for a professional to Photoshop.'

There was no one anywhere to be seen on the beach or up by the house and so I began to wander. Everything looked so calm, so peaceful. Either the entire island was medicated or Kekipi had slipped some Xanax into my coffee the night before. Tiny red-crested birds fluttered around me as I walked along the beach, the floury sand sticking to my feet like little white socks, and I took deep, full-to-the-bottom-of-my-lungs breaths of fresh, flowery air to wash away the grey smog of home.

'Hi.' I nodded politely at a little white bird who was jogging along the edge of the beach, his little head bobbing back and forth. He paused for a moment, looked at me with his head on one side, and then went about his business. I was officially a million miles away from London's scabby one-footed pigeons.

After not really very long at all, the backs of my calves began to burn from walking in the sand. It was time to sit down. Somewhere between the cottages, the ocean and the middle of nowhere, I found a comfortable spot, checked for random men running down the shoreline, and once I was certain I was alone, I turned on by beloved camera. She clicked, whirred and flashed into life, blinking at me as I found my grip.

Trading my camera to Vanessa in lieu of rent had broken my heart, but at the time I hadn't had any choice. And as my mum liked to tell me all the time, what was the point in wasting my time taking pictures when I should be worrying about my work? But now, with my camera back in my hands, the strap rubbing against the back of my neck, it didn't feel like it was going to be a waste of time. And it wasn't just because I was sitting on a beach in Hawaii and didn't have a job to worry about anymore – it just felt really, really good. I fiddled with the settings for a moment, changed the lens, tinkered with the exposure and the shutter speed and then held the viewfinder up to my right eye. The camera had a digital screen on the back, but I still loved to line everything up myself.

'Let's do this,' I mumbled, focusing the camera on a small sailing boat out in the bay and pressing the shutter button. There. I had taken my first photo. It was blurry, overexposed and basically terrible, but still, it was a photograph taken in Hawaii. Baby steps.

For the next couple of hours, I wandered up and down the beach taking photos of everything I came across. Happily, Hawaii was a very giving subject. Everywhere I looked, there was something else that was ridiculously beautiful. Before I knew it, I'd filled an entire memory card with warm-up shots.

'Having fun?'

And before I knew it, I'd tripped over a man sitting in the middle of the beach. I hit the deck hard, managing to hold my camera aloft but dropping to my knees with a force that would definitely leave a bruise. The camera strap jarred on my neck, and, completely incapable of controlling myself, I started to cry.

'Oh dear, oh. Oh don't, please.' The man jumped to his knees, sprightly for an old fella, and placed an awkward hand on my shoulder. 'There, don't cry. Really, I can't bear to see a woman cry. I'm very sorry. Are you all right?'

'Yes.' I gasped for air. I felt like a five-year-old who had skinned her knees. 'It, doesn't, really, hurt.' I choked. 'I just, can't, stop, crying.'

My human tripwire gave me another pat on the shoulder and waited for me to stop making a complete show of myself before speaking again. Once I had wiped away the last tear and was able to press my hand over my raw kneecap without weeping, I gave him a smile and he sighed with relief.

'I'm sorry, I didn't see you.' I held out my non-bloody hand and he shook it heartily. 'I didn't kick you or anything, did I?'

'No, no,' he replied, still shaking my hand. 'I'm the villain of the piece. I saw you coming along but you seemed so engrossed in your pictures, I didn't want to interrupt. I just assumed you wouldn't actually walk into an old man.'

'Never assume,' I said with a mock serious expression. 'I am quite stupid.'

Taking a better look at my beach buddy, I realized he wasn't joking. He was an old man. Dressed in a washed-out blue Nike T-shirt that had probably seen the tumble dryer a thousand times since 1989 and a pair of granddad-appropriate shorts, he looked like Father Christmas on a senior's beach getaway. A big and impressively full white beard obscured a lot of his face, but what I could see of it was pleasantly wrinkly and he had white panda eyes from wearing sunglasses in the sun. He had to be in his seventies, but if it weren't for his white hair and wrinkles, you would never know.

'Oh, I don't believe that for a second,' he said, finally letting go of my hand and gesturing for me to give him the camera. Reluctant but too polite to resist, I handed it over. 'I'm Al – pleased to meet you. You're on holiday?'

'Working, actually.' I watched him flick through my morning's snapshots quickly. 'I'm Vanessa.'

I tried not to be a little bit sick in my mouth as I said it.

'And what are you working on in Hawaii, Vanessa?' he asked with a mixed-up traveller's accent, handing back my camera. 'They're very good, by the way, your pictures.'

'Thank you,' I said, turning my baby off to save the battery life. It hadn't been great five years ago; it wasn't going to be any better now. 'I think it's probably hard to take a bad picture out here, though, isn't it?'

'I don't know.' Al squinted into the sunshine. 'Even the most beautiful woman can look ugly if you've got the wrong man behind the camera.' He waved a regal hand towards me. 'Or woman, of course.'

'Well, I hope you're right,' I replied, nursing the camera in my lap as the throbbing in my knee died down. 'I'm here taking photographs for a magazine.'

'A shutterbug, are you?' He combed his fingers through his magnificent beard as he stared out at the ocean and I fought the urge to reach out and give it a tug. He made the Santa in Selfridges look like an amateur. And I would know because Amy made me go and sit on his knee every bloody year. 'Wasn't sure if you were just at this for fun. And what are you taking pictures of?'

'I'm doing something for this fashion magazine called *Gloss*? I'm taking pictures of Bertie Bennett?' Now I was going up at the end of my sentences, just like nobhead Nick. 'He owns this beach, actually. Do you know him?'

'Know of him,' Al said. 'He's a character.'

'He's a character that's cancelled on me twice since I've got here. Fingers crossed he's not avoiding me.'

'Maybe he doesn't know what a pretty young thing you are,' he said, giving me a twinkly grandpa grin. 'I'm sure he'd be happy to sit for a snap or two if he did.'

I wasn't sure if it was the sea air or the fact that I'd

clearly gone completely insane, but I looked away and giggled. Somewhere in the back of my mind, London Tess gave me a disgusted look. But I liked Al. He reminded me of my granddad. He reminded me of everyone's granddad. And he just seemed so nice.

'Do you live nearby?' I asked, slipping my feet out of my leather flip-flops and wiggling my toes until they had disappeared into the sand. 'It's so gorgeous here.'

'I do,' he said, pointing over at a little cabin a way down the beach. 'That's me. Just in the summer, though. The wife never likes to be away from the city in the winter.'

The cabin looked too tiny for anyone to live in it, let alone two people. 'You're married?'

'Was,' he clarified. 'I lost Jane two years ago. Still not very good at remembering she's not here any more.'

'I'm so sorry.' I winced. Hurrah! Another awkward conversation! 'Were you married for a long time?'

'Thank you. We were married fifty years,' Al replied, clearly used to fielding condolences. 'I do miss the old girl, but she's in a better place now. No one wants to drag these things out, do they?'

'They don't,' I agreed readily. Amy and I had a reciprocal pull-the-plug-pact that I secretly worried I would never be able to see through. I was not concerned about her ability to make the same tough decision. 'So you're retired now?'

'Semi.' He shook the misty look out of his eyes and wiggled his bare toes at the sea. 'I was doing something I loved and then I was asked to stop doing it. Now I'm not sure what to do with myself.'

'I understand completely,' I nodded, not wanting to ask unwelcome questions and make him feel awkward.

'So is there a Mr Vanessa?' Al asked in classic elderly-relative style. 'A paramour back at home?'

'It's a bit of a long story.' I heard my voice break ever so slightly and pressed my fingernails into my palm to distract myself. 'But to make a long story short, no, there is not.'

Al nodded gravely, his baseball cap bobbing up and down. 'Ahh, to suffer the slings and arrows of young love again.'

My spluttering laugh squeezed out a lone tear that I wiped away quickly before Al could see. 'Quite.'

'These things all work themselves out when you're young,' he said, smiling gently. 'Tell me more about these photos of yours. Have you been doing it long? Must be a bit of a big shot if you're taking pictures for this fashion magazine.'

'That's actually an even longer story than the boy nonsense,' I said, slipping the camera strap back around my neck and hoping that the longer I wore it, the more I would feel like a real photographer. 'I used to do quite a bit of photography stuff, then I did something else for a while, but I lost my job so now I'm back into it.'

'I'm glad you found your way back,' he said. 'You looked so happy when you were taking those pictures, like you were in another place.'

'Just concentrating,' I laughed, oddly unable to accept the compliment. Usually I rolled around in professional praise like a pig in shit. 'Just trying to get it right.'

'Trust me –' Al tapped me on my uninjured knee – 'when you get to my age, you can tell these things. I know when someone's got a passion for something. You were a million miles away.'

'I suppose I was,' I said, looking down at the camera.

She gazed back up at me with love. Maybe this was meant to be. Or maybe Al was a crazy old beach bum who didn't have a blind clue what he was talking about.

'Don't waste time worrying about the things you don't have,' he went on, imparting his pensioner wisdom. 'This is what you should be doing.'

'I hope you're right.' I unconsciously stroked the camera case and looked at Al. He was nodding sagely.

'I always am,' he said, hopping to his feet far faster and with more grace than I ever could and holding out his hand again. 'Well, I have places to be, things to do. What a pleasure it was to meet you, Vanessa.'

'And you, Al,' I said, sad to see him go. 'Thank you for being so kind about my pictures.'

'Just honest,' he corrected me as he took off in a jog. An actual jog. 'Hope to see you again.'

'Maybe I'll jog back to the cottage,' I murmured, turning to look at the mile or so I'd wandered in the past couple of hours. Hmm. Maybe I'd just have a lovely walk.

CHAPTER NINE

The walk back to the cottage might not have helped me look any better in my bikini, but it did give me time to think and develop a little bit more confidence in my photos. So far I hadn't quite managed to cock up entirely, but I wasn't doing terribly well with my double identity. I was still very much Tess, and, as I'd established, Tess was not working for me. I needed to work on Brand Vanessa. Obviously my Vanessa wasn't going to be quite the same as the original, but there was definitely some room for improvement on my previous personality. Settling down at the desk, I pulled a pad of thick white paper and a couple of coloured markers out of the drawer. Coloured markers made everything better. I drew a thick black line down the middle of the page, and on one side, at the top, I wrote 'TESS', and on the other 'VANESSA'.

'Right – work mode,' I whispered, shifting around to edge the last remaining grains of sand out of my bikini bottoms. 'What is Brand Tess?'

Taking the cap off my green pen, I started with words I was sure of. Loyal, honest, dedicated, hardworking, a good friend, quite funny, relatively clever. Genuine. I stopped. I had run out of steam worryingly quickly. Looking at the list over and over, I began to wonder, was I a good friend? Amy and I had been besties since before we were born, and, yes, I had plenty of work buddies, but how many other genuine friends did I have other than shithead Charlie? Who was I forgetting? My sisters were hardly beating the door down to hang out with me. With gritted teeth I added some more words to the list that I didn't like nearly as much. Shy. Walkover. Lazy. Boring.

I sort of knew I was boring. Amy might not have had a steady job in ten years, but she was always trying something new or going off on an adventure. Before this, the furthest my passport had taken me in the past two years was on a work trip to Brussels, and I'd spent most of the time throwing up after some dodgy *moules frites*. And I'd only had the *moules frites* because someone had made me. That was the old Tess Brookes, someone who thought eating shellfish and chips was a wild night out. The girl who had been waiting for her best friend to fall in love with her and kick-start her life. But my life didn't need kick-starting; it needed a crash cart and a shot of adrenaline straight to the heart à la Mia Wallace. By coming to Hawaii and pretending to be Vanessa, I'd effectively *Pulp Fiction*-ed my own existence. But what now?

I had to change. I couldn't sit through another meal blushing at Nick Miller and start sobbing on the beach every time a complete stranger even hinted towards a romantic interest back at home. If Tess was boring and lazy and cowardly, what was Vanessa? I took the lid off the red pen.

Bitch. Slut. Selfish. Mean. Gorgeous. Lazy.

Well, what do you know – we had something in common: we were both lazy mares.

'Not that I would mind adding slut to my column as well,' I told the empty room. The empty room was sympathetic.

Not only had sleeping with Charlie been the worst idea since Amy had tried to make toast at university by ironing a loaf of Kingsmill, but it had also reminded me that my ladyparts didn't exist exclusively to cause me agony once a month and keep hot-water bottle companies in business. I had the raging horn and there was nothing I could do about it. Well, there was quite literally one thing I could do – Nick Miller. But I was almost certain that would be the second worst idea since Amy's amateur Heston Blumenthal moment. However, that was exactly what Vanessa would have done, I thought to myself – she would have shagged him then and there last night. Over the table. Probably with Kekipi filming the whole thing. I might hate her, but when she wanted something, she took it. I'd spent ten years waiting for Charlie to get drunk and bored enough to put it in me. Presumably Vanessa had put less than ten minutes' work into getting him to shag her with such enthusiasm – and then he'd taken her on a mini-break to Wales within a week. Granted, I had very little interest in going on a mini-break to Wales, but I was sure there was a lesson to be learnt some-where in there.

Putting pen to paper, I scribbled down some more words. Assertive. Bold. Fickle. Sexy. Carefree. Un-self-conscious. Proud. Adventurous. Exciting. Confident. Basically, Vanessa was all the things I wasn't. I noticed the Vanessa column was a lot longer than the Tess column. And a lot more interesting.

With all my keywords written down, I moved on to the next part of my rebrand. My visual message. After several deep breaths, I locked myself in the bathroom and stripped off. OK. It wasn't so bad. I'd definitely seen worse on *Embarrassing Bodies*. Clearly I'd spent considerably more hours sitting on my arse than hammering the treadmill, but I was only twenty-eight, I'd mostly stayed off the pies, and gravity hadn't been too cruel a mistress. My ridiculous boobs balanced out my slightly too big arse, and my middle wasn't squishy to the point of offence. I could wear a bikini and get away with it if I tried not to slouch and breathed in. All the time. And no one really had arms like Jennifer Aniston, did they? Like most things in life, it was all about finding the right angle.

I untangled my plait and fingered my hair into loose, frizzy waves. With the right amount of Frizz Ease, this could be managed. Or maybe I could cut it all off and dye it blonde. Or shave my head. It had worked for Miley Cyrus. Not so much Britney. Maybe just a trim. But something was still missing? Vanessa still had something I didn't, aside from a gap between her thighs. I was missing an attitude, confidence. Vanessa just didn't give a shit.

Grabbing either side of the sink, I leaned in towards the mirror and stared myself in the big, brown, bloodshot eye.

'You don't give a shit,' I told myself. I didn't look convinced. I mostly looked a bit cold. The AC was on very, very high. 'You are brave and bold and you get what you want out of life.'

I'd always been very, very good at selling my campaigns to clients, even when I thought they were ludicrous. The trick was to find a way to believe it, to find the truth in what you were saying and selling. But where was my truth? Retying my bikini, I dashed back out into the kitchen to look for my phone. I needed to call Amy. Amy would know how to make this make sense. The front door was still wide open and the warm breeze was so much more tempting than the frigid air-con that I padded outside while pulling up her number.

'Working hard?'

Across the way, Nick was sitting outside his cottage, laptop set up under a huge white cotton parasol on a white wooden table. The upkeep on all this white paint must be insane. I made a mental note to ask Kekipi about it. And then immediately erased that note. That was a Tess note. I was not Tess. I was Vanessa.

'And what would Vanessa do?' I whispered under my breath.

Phone in hand, number undialled, I marched over to Nick, barefoot and wearing nothing but my striped bikini. I could not think about what I was about to do or it would never happen. Nick rose as I approached, looking as annoyingly bemused and irritatingly handsome as he had at dinner. Pushing my hair back from my forehead, I stopped dead, right in front of him. At five nine in bare feet, I was almost eye to eye with him. I figured he couldn't be more than five eleven, maybe even five ten if he wasn't wearing shoes. But this was not the time to take in his choice of footwear. This was the time to take in his golden skin, his ashy-blond hair and his grey-blue eyes.

'Can I help you?' he asked.

Without saying anything, I grabbed him by the collar of his pale blue shirt and pulled his face down to meet mine. The kiss was an explosion. As soon as I felt his scratchy stubble against my tender, sunburned skin and his full, firm lips pressing against mine, I was lost. I pulled him closer, kissed him harder until I forgot to breathe. Nick recovered from his surprise like a pro, and before I'd even closed my eyes, his hands were sliding around my back, down my spine. His skin was hot on my air-con-cool body and while my bikini might have afforded me ample support in the boob department, according to the warm hands currently cupping my backside, the bottoms were much skimpier than I remembered. Suddenly, the shock of physical contact was too much. Just as Nick's hands began to move up and around my body, I pushed him away, pressing the back of my hand against my bruised lips.

Nick stared at me like I'd slapped him round the face. I stared back as though I might.

'So I can help you?' he asked with a wounded, dark tone.

'No.' I shook my head and tried to pull my bikini bottoms out of their semi-wedgie as subtly as possible.

'Vanessa.' Nick coughed and laughed all at once, one hand held out to me, the other rearranging his linen shorts. I tried very hard not to look, but obviously I did. And woah. 'Come here.'

'I'll see you later,' I said, backing away before turning towards my own cottage and sprinting inside. As soon as I stepped through the door, I slammed it shut, my hand still pressed against my lips. So that's how it felt to be Vanessa. And it was not awful.

I set my phone carefully down on the worktop and

pretended I wasn't shaking from head to toe. Someone was hammering on the front door, but rather than answer it, I made the perfectly rational decision to run into the bathroom, lock the door and start running a shower to drown out the knocking. It had to be Nick, and if I opened it up, I had no idea what would happen. Either I'd have to shag him on the kitchen counter or he'd slap me round the chops. Neither solution would be productive, even if one would be considerably more fun than the other. Why hadn't I just called Amy? What on earth had possessed me to do something I had never, ever done in twenty-eight years? I blamed the sun. And sand. It was Hawaii's fault. It was Vanessa's fault. Tess didn't walk up to a man she barely knew and definitely disliked and kiss him as if the world was about to end. Tess sat in her seat and watched her best friend kiss said man and then judged her quietly from behind a bottle of Pinot Noir. I needed to get out of my bikini and into some more sensible clothes. I ripped it off. Who could make good decisions while they were prancing around in tiny triangles of fabric?

'I need to relax,' I told myself. 'And I need a drink.'

I cautiously opened the door and sprinted to the kitchen. Glasses seemed surplus to requirements and so, classy gal that I was, I opted to swig straight out of the bottle and ran back to the bathroom with it. I was really just saving Kekipi a job. I was really just very thoughtful.

'Hello?'

Why hadn't I locked the front door?

'Just a minute,' I yelled, clanking the wine bottle far too loudly against the marble sink and grabbing a towel to cover myself.

'Vanessa?' The voice came closer and closer. 'It's Paige, from *Gloss*?'

'Hi.' I flung the bathroom door open, towel tucked around my boobs, steam billowing out behind me. 'Hello.'

'Christ, it's like a Bananarama video.' The blonde girl in front of me stared back with wide eyes. 'Nice hair.'

'Thank you?'

'Sorry, didn't mean to drag you out of the shower.' She could not stop staring at me. I subtly glanced down to make sure my boobs hadn't escaped from my towel. 'I was looking for Vanessa?'

'Oh, of course, that's me.' I casually stretched my leg out backwards and kicked the bathroom door shut, hoping she couldn't see the open wine bottle. My work brain had helpfully clocked on to remind me that Paige Sullivan was the art director from *Gloss* magazine and would be arriving on Tuesday. Today was Tuesday and, bugger me backwards, here she was.

'Vanessa Kittler?' Paige stretched out a confused hand.

'Yes?' I took it reluctantly but shook it with as much enthusiasm as I could muster. There were only two absolutes in this world – nobody put Baby in a corner, and nobody liked a dead-fish handshake. 'Vanessa Kittler, photographer extraordinaire.'

There was nothing like trying a little bit too hard sometimes.

'Oh, OK, sorry, not quite with it from the flight,' Paige said, smiling back at me with a bright, lipstick-commercial confidence that didn't quite make her eyes. 'Just literally got in. Delayed for bloody ever. Literally just landed. Just now. I know, I feel like shit. I look like shit.'

She did not look like shit. Her blonde hair fell around her shoulders in perfectly manageable loose curls, her eye make-up smouldered and her lips were painted a perfect Old Hollywood red. She was so pretty, she looked as if she should be famous.

'And I suppose I'm a bit distracted because I can sort of see your vagina.' She pointed to the hem of my towel but kept her eyes up.

'Oh, shitting hell,' I muttered, crouching down and looking for a new, longer cover-up. 'Sorry. I was just having a shower.'

'And a drink?' She craned her neck, looking over my shoulder to where the bathroom door had mutinously swung open.

'Little one,' I said, pinching my thumb and forefinger together. 'The tiniest one it's possible to have, really.'

'Sounds bloody good to me,' Paige said, slipping out of a quilted bomber jacket to reveal perfectly toned arms in a white cotton vest, complete with peekaboo neon-pink bra straps. Brilliant. 'Maybe we are going to get along. Tell you what, why don't I go and unpack, and then we'll meet back here for a beverage. We need to talk about this shoot, yeah?'

It irked me ever so slightly that she pronounced the end of the word 'beverage' the same way you would pronounced 'barrage', but aside from that, I couldn't see a problem with her plan. It was better than anything I had lined up, after all, and what harm could it do me to have the art director of the magazine on my side?

'Yeah, sure,' I agreed, still stooping. I bet she had a genuine diamond vajazzle under her spray-on jeans. 'I'll even put some clothes on.'

'Oh, you and your scandalous ideas.' She gave me a quick blast of a dirty laugh that made me like her even more. 'Not too many, eh? Might be the odd eligible bachelor out here. Speaking of, don't suppose you've run into our journo boy yet, have you?'

Run into, eaten dinner with, snogged the face off.

'Nick? I have had the pleasure,' I replied, considering how best to explain to this complete stranger who was sort of my boss that I had sexually assaulted our journo boy about thirty minutes earlier. 'He's in the cottage next door.'

'Oh, good – I should, you know, check in,' she said, immediately preening and peering out of the window. 'Do you know if he's there now? Do I look OK?'

Oh. Shit. She liked him.

I nodded and kept schtum, hoping Nick would do the same. Now I really was starting to feel like Vanessa. Forty-eight hours into the job and I'd already snogged my boss's boyfriend.

'So, back here in, like, two hours?' Paige grabbed a huge square bag decorated with interlocked Cs from the worktop and waved her sparkly watch at me. 'Cocktails and catch-ups?'

'Cocktails and catch-ups,' I confirmed, a little bit excited to have a potential new girlfriend. 'Two hours.'

As long as it wasn't cock-ups and catch tails, this could be a grand old time.

Almost three hours later, I was perched on the arm of the overstuffed sofa in my living room, watching the ceiling fan spin round and round and wondering whether or not red wine on an empty stomach had been a good idea. I'd spent almost forty-five minutes out of the previous hour blow-drying and straightening my hair while swearing at the humidity, begging it to play nicely and not embarrass itself next to Paige's perfectly coiffed

155

locks. It had half listened and, as such, I had only had to half pin it up.

Eventually, Paige knocked once on the door and let herself in, just like before.

'We're twins,' she exclaimed, holding up her arms in delight.

We were not twins. We looked like a before and after. Paige had painted a pair of dark blue denim jeans onto her pin-thin legs and wrapped black masking tape all around her torso until it resembled a racer-back vest. I had squeezed myself into a slightly too small pair of Vanessa's stolen jeans and disguised the resulting muffin top with a slightly too big black T-shirt. That said, we did appear to be wearing the same shoes.

'Don't you just love Tribs?' she asked, pointing a foot at me. 'I know YSL shoes are stupidly expensive, but they're so bloody comfy. As soon as I got my first pair, I was like, fuck, no more Choos or Looboos for me. Tribs all the way.'

'All the way,' I agreed. I had certainly not had enough wine. I didn't even know I was wearing YSL shoes.

'So, this guy who works here, Zippy or something?' Paige opened up a much smaller version of the same Chanel bag she'd brought in earlier and produced a little black bullet of lipstick. 'He came over earlier and said there was this little luau thing on the beach a bit further up. It's not an official work thing, but he said it would be fun. There will be drinks and there will be boys.'

I assumed that by Zippy she meant Kekipi, but I let it go.

'I like drinks and boys,' I said, watching her reapply perfect red lipstick straight from the tube without a mirror. 'Should we maybe not wear massive high heels on sand, though?'

'Good point.' She smacked her lips together and dropped the lipstick back into her bag. 'But I can't wear jeans without heels – my legs look like tree trunks.'

'I can't imagine for a second that they do.' I refused to play the 'I'm so fat, you're so fat' game with a creature this well put together. It was insulting to both of us. 'It'll be fine.'

'No, I'll have to go and get changed,' she said, shaking her head resolutely. 'If I wear trousers without heels, I basically look like that little guy from *Game of Thrones*, and he's the only one who's getting away with being four feet tall and hot. He's hot, yeah?'

'He seems very nice?' I hoisted myself to my feet and waited the obligatory three seconds until I felt comfy in my heels. 'Do you want to go and change, then?'

'No need.' Paige clapped and looked at me like she'd just solved world poverty. 'I'll borrow something from you. I'm sure we're about the same size.'

We weren't, but I was so flattered-slash-worried she'd suffered a serious head trauma, I let her push me out of the way and disappear into my room.

'Oh, Vanessa.' She stood in front of my wardrobe looking at all my rejected outfits for the evening with her hands over her mouth. And by all, I meant three. Because I only had three other outfits. The yellow dress I'd worn for dinner the night before, a black silky number and my newly cut-off denim cut-offs. 'Is this all you have?'

'I didn't think there was going to be a lot of call for black tie,' I said, standing shame-faced in the doorway. 'And I came in a hurry.'

Paige turned her back on my dressing room in disgust and fixed me with a very odd look. 'Back to mine, then.'

It shouldn't have been a shock that Paige's wardrobe was bursting to the seams, but I was still a little astounded that her plane had been able to take off with all the shit that was spilling out of her bedroom. I was sitting on her bed waiting for her to show me outfit number three, and so far I'd counted seven bikinis, two swimming costumes, ten pairs of shoes and three striped American Apparel T-shirts that were *exactly the same*. And that was just what was on the floor. Inside the wardrobe, all manner of silk and satin concoctions threatened to leap out and make their bid for freedom.

'What about this?'

She stepped out of the bathroom in what looked like an oversized white shirt with pleats on the front and no collar, and even though I'd already shown her mine earlier in the day, I was a bit worried that at any second she was about to show me her lady garden. At least when I'd done it, it was by accident.

'It's Derek Lam.' She threw her arms out as though that should mean something to me. 'It's last season, though. Is it horribly obvious that it's last season?'

'Paige,' I said as calmly as possible. 'We're going to a Hawaiian luau. In Hawaii. I don't think it's going to matter if it's last season or if it pre-dates the Koran. I just don't think white silk is a good idea when there's going to be rum punch.'

'Good point,' she said, whipping the dress over her head to show me her nude bra and knickers before grabbing a multicoloured shift dress with a neon-pink bib in the front. It looked like a high-fashion Care Bear costume. 'Thakoon?'

'Bless you?' I shrugged.

With a second disturbed look, Paige pulled the dress on, grabbed a pair of nude strappy sandals and shook her curls out in the mirror. 'Fine.' She pulled a grumpy face and then wiped off her red lippy with a tissue. 'It needs a nude lip.'

I collapsed back on the bed. I had a feeling I was going to be there for a while.

CHAPTER TEN

It took another forty-five minutes of primping before Paige could be persuaded to leave for the luau. I had traded my heels for my brown leather flip-flops but kept my jeans and T-shirt. The night air had cooled slightly, but I was still really too warm. I was also incredibly conscious of the swathes of black eyeliner Paige had insisted I wear. To be fair to her, she didn't do a horrible job, but it was just too hot for so much make-up and I wasn't used to looking like a sexy panda. If there was such a thing. There was a reason pandas didn't do it all that often, and I strongly suspected it had something to do with their amateur smokey-eye look in the Chinese humidity. Eventually, with Paige in her expensive toddleresque ensemble and me in my stolen clothes and borrowed make-up, we found Kekipi's luau. And it was full of gays.

'You came!' Kekipi dashed up to me with a coconut that was not full of coconut water and gave me a huge hug. 'I told missy to bring you. It's not a real luau, just a bit of a boys' get-together, but we do have tiki torches, dancing and a disgusting amount of pig.'

'You had me at pig,' I promised.

Kekipi laughed and clapped. He was my favourite. 'Since Mr Bennett stopped giving his parties, we've made it a tradition to invite fabulous women to our own whenever there are fabulous women to invite.'

'I believe Paige definitely falls into the fabulous category,' I said, accepting a coconut cocktail of my own as well as a hot-pink lei made of delicious-smelling flowers. Across the way, Paige was trying to negotiate with a half-naked man for a baby-blue garland as the pink was 'too matchy matchy' for her outfit. 'I think I'm just filler.'

'Fabulous filler.' Kekipi slipped his arm through mine and walked me over to an empty table. 'So I have to ask you, have you seen Mr Twenty Questions today?'

'I have,' I confirmed and swiftly changed the subject. 'But I have to ask you, what's going on with Bertie Bennett? How come he keeps cancelling things?'

'Oh, don't,' Kekipi said, waving his hand in my face. 'I haven't seen him in days. I don't know where he's hiding. I just find notes dotted around the house. It's family business issues – don't concern yourself with it.'

'Not the best time to invite journalists over, then.' I found the straw in my cocktail and took a sip. It was so wonderful, I feared I might never drink any other type of drink as long as I lived. 'Interesting.'

'Hmm.' Kekipi clearly didn't want to talk about it. 'But it does seem a little silly to invite a group of people over to interview you and take pictures then decide that's the week you want to do a Dietrich.'

'It does a bit,' I agreed, finding the bottom of my drink far too quickly. Maybe it had only been half full. Maybe I was a complete lush. 'These are really good.'

'They are almost as delicious as Mr Miller.' He took

my empty coconut from me and set it on a table. 'I'm not refilling until you tell me what he said to you today. Was it saucers of milk at table two? Did you scratch each other's eyes out?'

'Not exactly.' I really wanted that coconut back. 'Not yet, anyway.'

'Oh, amazing.' Kekipi clapped and an obscenely fit young man with long black curtains of hair parted in the centre appeared with two more drinks. I imagined that being in charge of hiring and firing had its perks when you were Bertie Bennett's estate manager. 'Did you hate-fuck him? You hate-fucked him, didn't you?'

'No!' I tried to look scandalized. I had awkward issues with people using the eff-word to mean, well, effing. I failed. 'I absolutely didn't.'

'But you wanted to.' He pushed my new drink across the table towards me. 'Don't worry, I get it. He's hot, he's an asshole, you're in Hawaii. It happens.'

I forced a stray strand of hair back into the kirby grips at the back of my head and gave one firm, decisive nod. 'Maybe so, but it's not going to happen to me.'

'I guess we'll find out about that later, won't we?' Kekipi stood up and backed away, wiggling his eyebrows at me.

I sat alone at my table, happily watching Paige and what I assumed to be the rest of Bennett's staff dancing to the sounds of someone's iPod under several strings of perfectly hung fairy lights. Tiki torches marked out the dance floor and someone had wrapped spare leis around the palm trees. It looked like we were in an all-gay, Hawaii-based remake of *Dirty Dancing*. If I tuned out the music, which was always difficult when someone was playing Beyoncé at full blast, I could hear the sea lapping against the shore and everything smelled sweet. Not least my delicious cocktail. I closed my eyes and breathed in deeply. I should have started making stupid decisions years ago. I really wished Amy was here. Not Charlie, though. Because I wasn't thinking about Charlie.

I continued to not think about Charlie for two more drinks and almost an hour of the Beyoncé, Rihanna and Robyn megamix. I'd almost got to my feet for that 'Call Me Maybe' song, but Kekipi dashed over to stop me, declaring the song 'so last year', apologizing for its inclusion and refreshing my drink. I knew putting away so many cocktails on a school night was a bad idea, but since all my bad ideas had been going so well, I figured I might as well keep up the good work. Plus it made the music so much more bearable. After a rousing group rendition of 'Single Ladies', Paige wandered over, zigzagging across the sand, and sat down in the chair beside me with a sloppy smile.

'I think I'm jet-lagged,' she sighed, head tilted up towards the stars. 'I feel a bit weird.'

'Do you want to go back?' I asked, not really wanting to head home, but Tess the Martyr was always lurking in the subconscious background. 'We can go back.'

'No, no, I'm fine.' She patted my hand and leaned over to my straw to take a sip of my drink. 'That helps.'

'I don't think it does,' I said, passing her a skewer of barbecued chicken and a can of Diet Coke.

She held up her hand and made a pukey face which I took to mean she didn't want them. Just as well, because I really did.

'Shouldn't we talk about the photo shoot?' I asked, watching her mouth the words to whatever Lady Gaga song was playing with a glazed expression. 'Like, what you want me to actually do.'

'I have it all planned.' Paige closed her eyes and piled her hair up on top of her head and then let it fall down her back. 'It's just an amazing concept. The portrait we're going to do at the house, and then, for the fashion shoot, we're going to Iolani Palace. It's this amazing old palace where the kings of Hawaii used to live, so we're going to shoot the dresses there with Bennett on a throne, like the king of fashion. It's going to be major.'

Major? It was going to be major? I nibbled on a chicken skewer and nodded as confidently as I could.

'I have one question for you, though.' Paige opened her eyes and turned to face me fully, pushing her hair behind her ears. 'Why are you pretending to be Vanessa Kittler?'

I dropped my chicken onto the sand.

'Why am I what now?' I hoped she was drunk enough that a grammatically awkward question might flummox her.

'Why are you pretending to be Vanessa Kittler?' she repeated with careful and precise enunciation. 'Because you're not her.'

'I am,' I replied, forcing a laugh. 'Of course I am. Who else would I be?'

'Fucked if I know.' Paige shrugged and leaned forward, arms across the table. 'But you're not that bitch Kittler. So I'll ask you again and hopefully you'll have an answer that won't involve the police or the need for me to call them. Why are you pretending that you are?'

Shit. Shit shit shit.

'Oh God, I should have known this wouldn't work,' I said, giving up on trying to think of a good excuse and hoping she was feeling charitable. 'But the quick version is, Vanessa is my flatmate, she was out of town, I'd had the worst week on record, then I took the call from her agent about the job and this all seemed like a good idea at the time.'

'What, flying to Hawaii, lying to a bunch of people and pretending to be Vanessa?' Paige asked. 'Not to mention an evil, slaggy bitch no one in the industry can stand?'

'Yes?'

She waved at Kekipi's drink-delivery buddy and waited for him to bring over a fresh coconut before she said anything else.

'Vanessa Kittler shagged my ex-fiancé about two years ago.' She started slowly and I could tell she was trying very hard to remain calm. 'He wasn't my ex at the time. He was my fiancé.'

'Sounds about right.' I didn't want to say too much. There was still too much opportunity for this to go horribly wrong. 'Sorry.'

'When the picture desk told me they'd got her for this job, I went mental. I'm sure they'd tell you that would be putting it politely. But it was all so last-minute. I was away last week and no one else was free. Allegedly.'

She stopped to neck almost half her drink in a oner.

'Obviously I tried to get her taken off the job. Because, you know, it's not just that I hate her, she's a shit photographer. Yeah, OK, she took, like, four really good photos once upon a time, but that's it. People only book her now because they want to shag her. It's pathetic.'

'Again, all sounds about right,' I replied. 'Apart from the four good photos bit.'

'Years ago.' Paige flapped her hands around. 'They're,

like, legendary. In that they're absolutely beautiful and everything else she's ever done has been shite. Not that I've actually seen them because I won't work with her. Which is handy, given that you're not her.'

'So what now?' I stared through the wooden slats of the table at my toes, a crushing feeling weighing heavy in my stomach. 'Are you sending me home?'

'How can I?' she asked. 'I don't have another photographer. I can't take the pictures. Unless one of these beautiful, beautiful men happen to be a proficient photographer, I would be even more fucked than I am now, wouldn't I? Do you have any idea how hard it was to get this interview organized?'

'No, I don't,' I admitted. 'I know this is insane. Or at least I am.'

Paige rubbed invisible worry lines away from her forehead and stared at me.

'I didn't say anything earlier because I was trying to work out what was going on. I thought maybe there were two Vanessa Kittlers, or that maybe you'd just dyed your hair and, I don't know, had a complete personality makeover. Like, maybe you'd had a stroke or something. I tried to find her on Facebook, but of course she's not on Facebook because she's too fucking cool. But wow, this is actually happening. You are not Vanessa Kittler. But you are pretending to be Vanessa Kittler. In Hawaii, on a photo shoot, even though you're not actually a photographer.'

'That would be it in a nutshell, yeah.' It was hard to have such a serious conversation with One Direction as a backing track, but somehow we managed.

'Are you at least a good photographer?' she asked. 'Jesus, you are actually a photographer, aren't you?'

'Let's just go with yes.' I winced at Paige's hopeful expression. 'I'm sorry, I don't really know what else to say.'

'Say that that you're going to take some fucking brilliant pictures of Bertie Bennett, that I'm not going to get fired, and that come Monday, when we land in London, this is all going to seem like it was a very strange dream.' She looked as serious as it was possible to look for someone who had been drinking bootleg Malibu out of hollowed-out coconuts for two hours.

'I'm going to take some fucking amazing pictures of Bertie Bennett, you're not going to get fired, and come Monday, I really hope we find out this has been a dream, otherwise I've got a really difficult week coming up,' I replied. 'And if it helps, Vanessa isn't not on Facebook because she's too cool; she deleted her profile because people kept leaving really, really horrible comments on her wall and she hated having to untag unflattering pictures.'

'How do you live with her?' Paige asked. '*Why* do you live with her? Aside from this psychotic episode, you seem like a relatively normal, nice person. Do you hate yourself or something?'

'Or something,' I confirmed. 'Definitely or something. And maybe I'm not that keen on myself.'

'Right then – glad we've got that out of the way, *Vanessa*.' She raised her drink in the air. 'Can you please just tell me what your actual name is? Even if it's probably best if we don't tell anyone else about this.'

'It's Tess.' I clunked my coconut against hers, so relieved to have told someone, anyone, the truth. 'Tess Brookes.'

'Cheers, Tess,' Paige toasted. 'God, it's going to grate me calling you Vanessa in front of the others.'

'Just call me bitch,' I suggested. 'We'll pretend we're in *RuPaul's Drag Race.*'

'I like your thinking,' she said, straw wedged in her mouth. 'Let's just hope I like your photos too. Thank God I'm an amazing art director.'

'Thank God,' I agreed.

'Oh, you have to dance with me! I love this one.' Paige pushed her chair away from the table too quickly and it tipped backwards into the sand. 'If another one of those blokes grinds on me again, I'm going to trip and fall on his penis.'

'I'm fairly certain they're all gay.' I let her lead me onto the smoothed-out sand of the dance floor while Maroon 5 blasted me from all angles. 'All of them.'

'I don't care,' Paige shouted back. 'Gay men love me.'

It was good to know where she drew the line.

They say time flies when you're having fun, but when you're having fun drinking and dancing with Hawaii's most fabulous, it vanishes into a black hole and comes out again shaking maracas and dancing a cha-cha. It was almost one when I looked at my watch and refused my first drink of the night. Paige had long since decided it was time to take a nap face down on one of the tables. I'd tried to take her to bed, Kekipi had tried to take her to bed, assorted half-naked men had tried to take her to bed. She had declined any and all invitations, claiming each and every time that she was 'waiting'. We just didn't know for what.

I was deep in a vintage Madonna groove when I noticed we had a gatecrasher. Nick was standing at the edge of the party, half hidden by a palm tree, wearing his standard self-satisfied expression. The first thing I remembered was how annoyed I had been with him the night before. The second thing I remembered was kissing him outside his cottage that afternoon. He cocked his head back, gesturing for me to come over. Silently I declined by turning my back to him and trying to commit to the song. Yes, Madonna, life *is* a mystery, everyone *must* stand alone. But Nick did not call my name, he just stood there looking smug, so I continued to dance my arse off.

'Nick!'

By the sounds of it, someone else at the party was not nearly as committed to playing hard to get as I was. After being completely catatonic for nigh on an hour, Paige sprang to life and sprinted across the sand, throwing herself into Nick's unwelcoming arms. I couldn't quite hear her over the music, but I did manage to dance around Kekipi and my other new GBFs, Makani and Aikane, to get myself within hearing distance. Paige had her arms slung round Nick's neck and seemed to be trying to lure him onto the dance floor with some very dodgy moves. It was painful to watch. Thankfully, even full of cocktails and surrounded by hot twinks, Kekipi never forgot his job.

'Ms Sullivan. Paige, darling.' He cut in on the world's most awkward dance party and scooped Paige up in his arms. Although he didn't look big enough to manhandle a grown woman, this was clearly not his first time. 'You're Cinderella, it's almost midnight, there's a coach outside that's threatening to turn into a pumpkin. Prince Charming comes to you, remember? You don't go to him.'

'Nick has to dance!' she yelped, pointing somewhere in the vicinty of Nick. 'He needs to do dancing!'

'I'll make sure he dances,' Kekipi promised, carrying

her away from the lights. 'Third rule of dance club – if it's your first time at dance club, you have to dance.'

'What are the other two rules?' I asked Makani.

'First rule of dance club is never talk about dance club,' he replied.

'And the second rule is never talk about dance club?'

'No, the second rule is drink until you can't remember dance club.' He spun me round suddenly and I was so glad not to be wearing my heels. 'That way you can't talk about it, even if you wanted to.'

'You've thought of everything,' I yelled over the music before I felt a pair of hands on my waist pulling me away from my dance circle. 'What do you think you're doing?'

'Nothing nearly as inappropriate as what you did earlier,' Nick said, pressing his lips into my hair. 'Take these clips out. I want your hair down.'

'I want never gets,' I said, pushing him away, but he just grabbed my wrists and pulled me back. 'Let me go.'

'You don't want to talk to me?' he asked. 'No more questions?'

'I'm all out,' I said, trying to ignore the growing burning sensation that was not caused by the fact that my jeans were too tight and I needed a wee. Even though they were and I did. 'I think I know everything I need to know.'

'I agree.' He let go of one wrist but spun me round with the other and trapped me against him. 'We should just go back to yours.'

'Why would I do that?' I looked down at my chest. So that was what a heaving bosom looked like. 'After you walked out on me last night.'

'Why wouldn't you do that?' he asked. 'After you kissed me this afternoon?'

'I don't know you, Nick.' I noticed the rest of the partygoers had formed a subtle circle around us and were keeping a close eye on proceedings. Fantastic – now I was the official entertainment at a gay, Gaga-soundtracked luau. Truly this was a week of firsts. 'I don't know why I did what I did earlier. Maybe I'd had too much sun.'

'Vanessa.' He stopped dancing and gripped me tightly around the waist. 'I don't do games.'

'Good job I didn't challenge you to a round of Boggle, then.'

Bothered and bewildered, I slapped his hands off me. I seemed to be breathing awfully heavily.

'Come on, it's my first night at dance club,' he said, smiling and holding out his hand. I hated that smile. Definitely more of a smirk. 'I have to dance.'

'I'm sure there are plenty of takers.' I knocked his hands away and walked off, leaving him to the mercy of Kekipi's friends.

The tricksy combination of racing hormones and too much rum left me burning with a furious temper that wasn't even slightly cooled by the giant glass of water I downed the second I stepped through the door. Bathed in the half-light of the fridge, I stood and chugged, really wanting to swap the crystal-clear goodness for another cocktail, but more than anything I didn't want to wake up with a hangover. I wanted to wake up with a beautiful man and some intimate chafing, but that wasn't going to happen.

A quiet knock on the door disturbed my filthy thoughts, and, half hoping it would be Nick, I set down the water, pinched my cheeks and opened up. It was Kekipi. What a waste of a pinch.

'I just wanted to make sure you were home safely,' he said, calm and professional. Even at a party, business Kekipi was never far away. Although business Kekipi smelled a little bit of sick and I had to assume that had something to do with his new, more sombre attitude. 'I saw your light from Miss Sullivan's cottage. Can I get you anything at all?'

My vagina was so sad that it was him and not Nick at my door but there was really nothing he could do about that. 'No, I'm just going to go to bed. Aren't you going to go back to the party? It felt like it was just getting started.'

'It was and I am,' Kekipi confirmed, the glint back in his eye. 'Those boys are animals. You won't join me?'

'No, no,' I said, shaking my head. 'It's bedtime for me.'

'Of course,' he replied. 'With or without Mr Miller?'

I wanted to look shocked, but I couldn't do it. Instead I just laughed as if the very idea were ridiculous. 'I'm not that kind of girl,' I assured him. 'I don't think so.'

'I don't see why not,' Kekipi shrugged. 'He's very attractive, he clearly thinks you're very attractive, there's some chemistry there. Why wouldn't you?'

'Because I'm not a gay man?' I suggested.

'And that's what's wrong with the world,' he said, starting back down the path but leaving my door wide open. 'Man, woman, straight, gay. There's nothing wrong with wanting someone. We're all adults.'

My immediate reaction was that while Kekipi and I might be adults, Nick was a petulant man-child who needed a good slap, but every other part of my body was screaming something else. Every other part of my body was reminding me that Nick was a very attractive, solid slab of man who invoked the kind of animal lust in a girl that made me want to climb him like a tree. I clutched the door handle, fully intending to shut it, lock it and go to bed. Instead, I just stood there, closed my eyes and took a deep breath. Why shouldn't I go back? Kekipi was right. Why was it such a big deal for me to admit I wanted to eff the hell out of this man?

'Because good girls don't do that,' I whispered, arguing with myself. 'Because you don't.'

OK, so I barely knew him, and admittedly what I did know I didn't necessarily love, but it wasn't like sleeping with someone I'd been smitten with for ten years had worked out entirely according to plan, so, really, what was the point in a plan? It wasn't as if overintellectual-izing my decisions had got me anywhere. Kekipi was right. I had only five more days in Hawaii, and after that I never had to see Nick again. God knows I wanted him, and against all laws of God and man, he seemed to want me too. I should do it. But still – I took one more breath in and fluffed out my hair – if I was going to do this, there had to be some ground rules for myself. No emotions, no sobbing the morning after. I would go in, get laid and then go back home to bed. All business. All I had to do was screw my courage to the sticking place. Or stick my courage in the screwing place. Or something.

As if by dirty, dirty magic, when I opened my eyes I saw Nick sitting two feet away in one of the white wooden chairs by my cottage and jumped out of my skin. If my heart hadn't been racing before, it was now.

'I really need to know what you were thinking about,' he said, resting his elbows on his denim-clad legs and looking up at me from underneath his messy, beachy hair. 'That's quite the expression on your face.'

I held still for a moment, concentrating on breathing and not falling over. Falling over wasn't sexy. Nick, however, was sexy. Even in the delicately lit darkness of the bay, there was no way around the fact that he was a very handsome man. And he was looking at me that way again. No one looked at me that way.

'I was thinking about coming to see you,' I said, standing as still as possible. I wasn't sure what would happen if I moved. There was every chance I would run and lock myself in the bathroom. Again. 'About this afternoon.'

'To apologize?' he asked, rising from the chair, his forearms flexing against the rolled-up sleeves of his shirt. I really was a mug for those forearms.

'No.' I managed to get the word out before he was in front of me. It was just as well. Once he was only inches away, I seemed to lose the power of speech. Nick was not my type. He was barely taller than me. His eyes were too blue and he had too much of a tan. He was blond. He was arrogant. I didn't know him, I didn't love him, I didn't like him. He wasn't Charlie. And I had never wanted to have sex with anyone so badly in my entire life. 'I'm not going to apologize.'

'Good,' he replied, pushing me back against the door, knocking my head against the wood and kissing me deep and hard without asking permission, without pausing to see if I was OK. I was more than OK. My body lit up under his touch, excited to be doing something, or someone, so new, and started to explore the man pressing against me. Nick didn't waste time with his kisses, moving from my lips to my throat and all the way down to the neckline of my T-shirt before I could even blink, and somehow, with eyes closed, I concentrated on the sensation of his fingertips tracing patterns all over my body and tried to remember to breathe. His hands coiled themselves up in my hair and pulled my head back sharply, making me gasp. I heard him laugh. He did not stop. Instead, his hands slid down my back, feeling out the fastest route into the waistband of my jeans and slipping inside. This was not his first time. Gasping for air, I wrapped my arms around his neck and hung on for dear life as he pulled me away from the door, pushed me into the cottage and kicked it closed before tearing at my button fly.

'These are in the way,' he whispered.

He was right, but they weren't in the way for long. With no chance of turning back, I wriggled around, my back against the closed door, and helped him remove my extraneous clothing while reaching for his belt buckle. Two could play at this game. I just hoped he wouldn't notice my amateur status when he was quite clearly a pro.

It was an unnecessary concern. Making love to my soulmate might have scared me senseless, but when it came to a filthy throwdown with a near stranger, it seemed I was a natural. I kicked and stamped my way out of my skintight denim, all the while pushing and pulling and bucking against my lover, lips already raw, cheeks chafed from his stubble and the taste of him in my mouth. My brain had long since switched itself off, leaving a previously unknown dirty girl autopilot in charge. There were no thoughts, no arguments, no concerns. All I knew was that I wanted this man inside me as soon as humanly possible, and there was nothing else. I heard the rustle of denim, the clank of his belt hitting the floor and felt the burn of Nick's fingers on my thigh, lingering at the edge of my underwear. He paused, pulled away and looked at me, our noses almost touching, both of us breathing so hard I could hardly bear it. His eyes were deep and dark, and, panting back at him the way I was, I knew I must look feral. But messy hair and worn-away make-up didn't matter any more. He kissed me again, crushing his lips against mine. His hand slipped around my waist and grabbed my hips, lifting me up, locking me in. I curled myself around his waist and buried my face in his neck. He smelled warm and dark and delicious. I could already smell his sweat on my skin.

We only made it as far as the sofa before he threw me down, tore off his shirt and knelt down between my legs. Everything was hot and hard and wet and humid, and the last thing I remembered before losing myself completely was the soft sound of his laugh, the flicker of his fingers and the whirr of the ceiling fan. For the first time in my life, being in control seemed overrated.

CHAPTER ELEVEN

It was still dark when I woke up, and it took a moment for my eyes to adjust. I was in my room, I was in my bed, but I was very, very naked. Oh no. I rolled over to the edge of the mattress and patted the floor until I could find something underwear-shaped. But when I held them up to face height, they were not my pants. They were man pants. Instinctively I threw them across the room – no one wanted a pair of boxers that close to their face unless they were being worn by Michael Fassbender – and turned over very slowly, very carefully, to see Nick lying beside me. Sliding my legs over the side of the bed, I followed the trail of clothes back out to the living room, wincing at the assorted sex injuries that made themselves known as I moved. If shagging Charlie had been like riding a bike, then Nick was a mechanical bull. Fast asleep, face down in a mound of pillows, he looked so different. All I wanted was to get back into bed and stroke his hair gently until he woke up and shagged me senseless again. I was romantic like that.

Replaying the action in my mind, I pulled on my

knickers as well as a T-shirt I picked up en route and surveyed the damage. The apartment was quite a scene. We'd knocked vases off tables, tipped over chairs, and there were cushions everywhere. I placed a hand on the small of my back, gingerly pressing to test bruises and friction burns. How had I managed friction burns in a cottage with hardwood floors? I glanced back towards the bathroom. Ahh, bath mat. Wow, we really had given the entire place the once-over.

'Hey.'

Nick was awake. In the darkened bedroom, his voice sounded softer than before. Husky. From sleep or sex – I wasn't sure which. Either way it made me want his hands on me.

'Hi,' I replied, still standing in the living room, staring back into the bedroom. I was so pleased about the darkness: he couldn't see me blushing.

'So I feel like I should mention it now, before it's a thing . . .' He sat up and stretched. Hot, hot, hot. 'But you know, this is just what it is. I'm a much better shag than I am a boyfriend.'

I stared. I felt a bit sick. I nodded.

'I know we're on the same page, anyway,' Nick said, patting the empty bed beside him. 'It's just usually best to make everything really clear. Just in case.'

'Just in case?' I asked.

'Well, I wouldn't want you to go falling in love with me,' he said with a laugh. 'Come back to bed.'

'Actually, I'm really tired.' I picked up his jeans and threw them at him. 'And I sleep a lot better alone.'

'Seriously?' Nick grabbed the jeans and clung to them, showing no sign of actually putting them on. 'You're kicking me out?'

'I wouldn't want you to get the wrong idea,' I replied, burning with anything but desire and making a beeline for the bathroom. 'You can see yourself out.'

I sat myself down on the toilet and angrily scrubbed at my face with a cleansing wipe until I heard the front door slam. How dare he warn me not to fall in love with him? How dare he think I would get ideas? How dare he assume we were 'on the same page'? Even though we were. Definitely. What an arsehole. I stopped rubbing when my face started burning from something other than shame and leaned back against the cold porcelain of the toilet cistern. Tossing the face wipe into the bin, I went back into the bedroom and straightened up my messy bed. I shook out the sheets and turned over all the pillows. The last thing I wanted to do was turn over in the night and get a whiff of wanker. I'd wanted a one-night stand and now I'd had a one-night stand. Tick box. And now it was time to sleep. But of course I couldn't sleep. There was only one thing for it. I picked up my phone and asked Siri to call the only person I had left to talk to.

'Tess?'

'Amy,' I said. 'I'm a knob.'

'Me too – I shouldn't worry,' Amy replied, her voice all tinny and far away. 'Any particular reason? Above and beyond the obvious?'

'I shagged a bad man.' I rolled over and stared at the empty space beside me, pressing my hand into the pillows where Nick's head had been.

'I know.'

'Oh no, another one,' I clarified. 'Here in Hawaii.'

'That's fast work.' Amy sounded horribly impressed. 'Who? Where? How? I want all the gory details. I haven't had sex in months, and you've been shagged twice in a week? I'm horribly jealous.'

'He's a journalist for the magazine,' I replied, eyes locked on the handprint in the pillows, imagining Nick still lying there, still asleep. 'I have a horrible feeling I may have just shat were I intend to eat.'

'You are talking figuratively, aren't you?' she asked. 'Just making sure this isn't the start of a different story.'

'Figuratively,' I confirmed. 'And it was stupid. He's a complete twat.'

'Hot twat?'

'The hottest.'

'Oh my God, your life is turning into a Taylor Swift song. This is amazing.' She didn't sound too concerned. 'Really, Tess, what's the problem? You shagged a hot man. It's good – it's sorbet sex. Palate cleanser. Get the taste of tit-face Charlie out of your vag.'

'That's so poetic.' She was disgusting sometimes. 'Have you heard from him?'

'No,' she answered. 'And don't change the subject. Tell me about this foxy wanker who charmed your iron knickers off.'

'I have no idea what happened, really. I think pretending to be Vanessa is getting to me,' I said with half a yawn. Hearing Amy's voice was like having a warm bath and a hot chocolate. 'I saw him, I hated him, and then I wanted to have sex with him. And then I did. I didn't even really have to try. It was mental.'

'Women don't really have to try – how many times have I told you?' she said. 'You just need to be, like, oi, big boy, let's have it. And if they don't respond, they're not worth having. Or gay. Or both.'

'I'm not sure I agree with that, but OK,' I muttered,

trying to remember whether or not I'd called Nick 'big boy' at any point in the past two days. It wouldn't have been inaccurate, but it would have been indelicate at best. 'I'm just mad at myself because he's such a knob. I don't even like him.'

'So hate-fuck him until you go blind, come home and never think about him again,' Amy suggested as though it were completely rational. 'And you're always mad at yourself. Or feeling guilty. Or feeling guilty about being mad. You are allowed to just enjoy yourself, you know.'

'I am?' That was a scandalous new concept.

'Really, Tess, you've got to stop calling me from fucking Hawaii and complaining. Ooh, I'm in paradise. Ooh, I've shagged a gorgeous man. Ooh, I just found a magical pony that shits diamonds. Just get on with it.'

'I haven't found a . . .' It took me a second to understand what she was getting at. 'Fine. Sorry. I just feel a bit gross, that's all.'

'Because you had sex with a hot man?'

'Because I had sex with a hot man who I don't know and don't like.'

'Honestly, Tess Sigourney Brookes.' Amy was starting to get annoyed. 'It's like feminism never happened with you sometimes.'

'How is this feminism?' I was starting to wish I'd never called. 'How am I progressing women's rights by letting a bad man put his penis in me?'

'Have you never seen *Sex and the City*? And I'm fine. Thanks for asking.'

Oh, bloody hell – of course. Amy had lost her job. I'd completely forgotten.

'I'm sorry, I'm just so tired. It's like five in the morning or something, isn't it? I wasn't thinking. Are you OK? Have you found a new job yet?'

'I don't really want to talk about it right now,' she snapped, and then sighed, softening at once. We weren't very good at being mad with each other. 'Don't worry about it. Don't worry about any of it. Come Sunday, you're never going to see any of these people again, are you? So just have fun before you have to come home and live in the real world again.'

She'd made a good – and worrying – point.

'Thank you for being amazing,' I said, fighting full-on yawns by now. And rightly so. I was jet-lagged, mentally exhausted from All Of The Lying, and physically exhausted from All Of The Sex. 'I don't know what I'd do without you.'

'You're welcome,' she replied. 'And you'd die. You'd actually just die.'

'I'm going to sleep.' I was smiling again. 'Talk to you later.'

'Not if it's to tell me you found Aladdin's lamp,' Amy said. 'Love you.'

'Love you too,' I said, waiting for the double beep to tell me she'd hung up before I set my phone back on the nightstand and fell fast asleep.

The thing I'd learned first about Paige was that she was not shy about personal boundaries. Having already demonstrated how very comfortable she was with letting herself into my cottage, she had clearly decided it was perfectly reasonable for her to come into my bedroom while I was still fast asleep.

'Morning, sleepyhead,' she said, tapping me briskly on the top of the head until I opened my eyes, a steaming mug of coffee in her hand. Not for me. 'How are you still asleep? It's almost ten.'

'Oh shit' I rubbed my eyes and tried not to upset any of my injuries. I was sore everywhere and I didn't really want to have to explain why to Paige. 'What time are we meeting Bennett?'

'We're not,' Paige said with a frown. 'He's cancelled. Again. We're meeting his son in half an hour, though. It would seem Daddy dearest is being a bit of a diva and his son is going to explain what's going on.'

'He has a son?' I was a bit surprised. But then, as Amy often liked to remind me, even Elton John was married.

'Yeah, he's taking over the business. Has taken over the business. I don't know, actually, I'm only the art director. They tell me naahthing.'

'So Nick's going to interview the son?' I was confused. And still so very tired. It was all I could do not to swipe that coffee cup out of her perfectly manicured hand.

'I don't know.' Paige shook her head. 'If it's all we get, it's all we get. But will anyone care? I mean, who wants to know about the business brain? How often do you read about Robert Duffy compared with Marc Jacobs?'

'Who?' I asked.

'You are funny,' she said. 'I keep forgetting you're not actually Vanessa. Or in fashion. Or a photographer.'

Exactly what I needed to be reminded of first thing in the morning.

'Not that I've got time to worry about that.' She slapped my duvet-covered arse and stood up. 'Come on, out of bed. Up and at 'em.'

'You're looking very fresh considering the state of you last night,' I commented on my way into the bathroom. Paige followed. Surely she didn't think we were going

183

to chat while I had a shower? She sat down on the toilet, lid down, and looked up at me, wide eyes bright and sparkling. Oh. She did.

'Berocca, eye drops and four of these,' she said, holding up the coffee. 'And I work in fashion, darling. If you can't get your shit together the morning after, you may as well fuck off to the teen mags where no one cares what state you're in.'

'Nice.' I turned on the shower, waited for it to steam up the glass screen and pulled my clothes off as quickly as possible, disappearing under the stream of red-hot water and rinsing off all the residual sleep and sex.

'Anyway, what state did you come home in?' Paige shouted over the shower. 'Why are your clothes all over the living room? Did you get lucky or are you just a scruffy cow?'

'Scruffy cow,' I yelled as fast as I could. 'I was just so tired I couldn't wait to get into bed. And drunk. I was drunk.'

I hadn't forgotten Paige throwing herself at Nick the night before. Conveniently, I had completely forgotten it while I was having all of the sex with him, but now it was a very clear memory, shining brightly in the front of my mind. And it did not fill me with joy.

'Is Nick coming to the meeting?' I asked as casually as humanly possible.

'In theory.' Paige's reply was full of equally feigned nonchalance. 'I sent him a text. He wasn't answering when I knocked on his door. I hope he isn't dead.'

'Ha, me too,' I agreed, not entirely sure I meant it. 'So, tell me how you know him?'

'Oh, we've worked together a few times over the years – different mags and stuff, you know? He's always been a bit of a flirt, I've always been a bit of a flirt. Nothing serious, though – he's just not that kind of bloke.'

'What kind of bloke?' I scrubbed myself red-raw with coconut-scented shower gel to get every last trace of him off me in case I didn't like her answer.

'The decent kind,' she laughed. 'The kind that takes you out for dinner and says nice things and texts in between shags.'

'So you've slept with him?' I poked my head out of the shower and grabbed a towel, suddenly feeling very sick. This must have been exactly how Vanessa didn't feel when she realized we'd both had sex with Charlie.

'Oh no.' She flapped her empty hand around her face. 'Not for the want of trying. I don't know – I really like him, but he doesn't do girlfriends. Everyone knows that and I'm not one of those girls who shags the guy she likes, even though he's a tosspot, and hopes he'll eventually realize how great she is. That's just asking for trouble.'

'What if it's a guy you don't like?'

'Entirely different matter.' Paige stood up and ventured back into the bedroom. 'Get dressed, we're going to be late. We can discuss my plan to make an honest man out of Nick Miller later.'

'Can't wait,' I said weakly.

Bleurgh.

I could hardly believe how fresh-faced Kekipi looked when we got to the main house. Even though I hadn't been that drunk and had managed to grab at least six hours of decent sleep, I was fully aware that I looked like shit, whereas he and Paige looked like they were fresh out of the spa. And I never looked like shit because

I always got a full eight hours' and I never spent Tuesday nights drinking cocktails with fifteen gay strangers and banging a bad man. Either someone was going to have to teach me how to use concealer or I was going to have to go back to my old life sooner than anticipated.

'Can I get you anything else to eat?' Kekipi asked, the very model of professionalism, while gesturing towards the spread already laid out on the table. 'Mr Bennett will be with you momentarily.'

'I'd take your arm off for a fried-egg butty,' Paige muttered, turning her head away from all the sushi on the table. However fresh she looked, she clearly didn't feel it. 'Fish? For breakfast?'

'Mr Bennett's request,' Kekipi explained. 'One fried-egg butty. And Miss Vanessa?'

'Oh, that's me,' I said, just slightly too loudly. Paige quirked an eyebrow and shook her head. 'I'm fine, actually. Thank you.'

As soon as he was gone, I grabbed a plate and piled it high with tiny sugary-looking pastries. I needed carbs and I needed them now.

'Before we start, are you actually going to be able to pull this off?' Paige asked, looking me dead in the eye. 'This whole Vanessa thing?'

'Yes?' I didn't even sound like I believed myself. 'It's fine.'

'Good,' she replied. 'Because if you fuck up now I know, we'll both be in for it.'

'Really, though . . .' I choked down a mini Danish and shrugged. 'What would happen if someone found out? How bad could it be?'

'Bennett would probably pull the interview altogether. I'd get fired. The magazine would probably sue Vanessa's agent. They'd definitely sue you.' she started to tick off the options on her fingers. 'Bennett could sue us. The possibilities are endless. They mostly involve people getting sued.'

I lowered the pastry back down to the plate.

'I really hadn't thought past Vanessa kicking the shit out of me,' I whispered. 'Bloody hell.'

'And that's assuming the photos are good enough to use in the first place,' Paige smiled sweetly. 'If they aren't, assume all of that and more.'

'Good photos.' I stared at my feet. 'Gotcha.'

'Amazing photos,' Paige corrected. 'The best photos anyone has ever seen.'

'But Vanessa isn't actually a very good photographer,' I pointed out. 'Surely adequate photos would be enough.'

'The best photos anyone has ever seen,' Paige repeated, slowly this time. 'Or you won't need to worry about Vanessa kicking your arse because I'll have already handed it to you on a plate, yeah?'

'On a plate.' I nodded to show I understood. 'Best photos ever.'

'Glad we're clear,' she replied. 'Ah, Mr Miller, at last.'

I hadn't expected to have a physical reaction to seeing Nick, but as he strode up the path, all grumpy face and Wayfarers, I wanted to get up from the table and dive into the sea. His pale blue shirt was creased to hell and his khaki shorts looked like they weren't buttoned up properly at the fly. He did not look like a man who had enjoyed a good night's sleep in a luxury villa in Hawaii. He looked like a man who had spent the night shagging someone rotten and then spent a couple of hours tossing and turning until the sun came up.

Interesting.

He leaned across the table, right in front of me, just to make me jump. Without a word he grabbed the coffee pot, poured a full mug then threw in several sugar lumps in complete silence. Paige glanced at me, trying not to smile, as he took the seat at the far end of the table as far away from the two of us as possible.

'Where's Bennett?' he asked after two long sips of coffee. 'He's late.'

'So are you, sunshine,' Paige replied. 'Bad night?'

Even though he didn't take off his sunglasses, I knew he was staring straight at me.

'I've had better,' he said with an entirely straight face, while I coloured up from head to toe. 'I've had worse.'

'Looks like you went through the wringer.' I was determined not to let him win. 'Sometimes it's best just to let sleep come naturally. When you try too hard, you just end up frustrated.'

'Oh, don't worry, I'm not frustrated,' he replied swiftly. 'But you don't look so clever yourself. Maybe you could do with trying a bit harder.'

'Now, now, children,' Paige intervened, entirely oblivious to the extreme level of bitchy subtext flying across the table. 'Let's not have fisticuffs. We need to sort out this Bennett sitch, and I don't really want to have to do that on my own. Can we kiss and make up?'

Nick turned up one corner of his mouth and nodded. 'I'm game if you are, Vanessa.'

'I think she means figuratively,' I said, adding cream to my coffee. 'I'm a professional.'

'Really?' He rested his elbows on the table and pushed his glasses up over his eyebrows. 'I probably owe you some money then.'

Before Paige had time to question Nick's jibe or my

look of outrage, the glass door to the house slid open to reveal a tall, slender man wearing a Hawaiian shirt and cargo shorts. Despite his ensemble, I knew it was Mr Bennett Junior right away. He was the spit of his father. The clothes were casual but tailored to his body perfectly, his grey hair was stylishly cut, and even though he had to be somewhere in his mid-forties, he was a striking man. And not just because he had the most amazing handlebar moustache I had ever seen. On cue, he twirled one of the ends and waited until he had our full attention.

'*Aloha.*' Mr Bennett the younger held his arms out as he approached the table and made his way round to shake everyone's hand. 'Apologies for my lateness. I hope you haven't been waiting too long.'

His accent seemed to be American, but he was attempting to affect something of a little British lilt and it wasn't quite working. Nonetheless, he was an imposing figure. Just ever so slightly funny at the same time. It could have been the moustache.

'Not at all.' Paige answered for all of us. 'We were just saying what a wonderful way this is to start the day.'

No we weren't, I said silently. We were just trading badly concealed barbs across the table and one of us was basically calling the other a whore. But it didn't seem like saying that out loud would really propel the conversation forward, so I just smiled.

'I'm Artie Bennett.' Our host sat down at the head of the table and let Kekipi pour his coffee before piling a ton of sushi onto a plate. For breakfast. Gross. 'Shall we do introductions?'

'Paige Sullivan.' Paige flashed her loveliest smile. 'I'm the art director with *Gloss*. I'll be overseeing the shoot. And this is Vanessa, our photographer.'

'Hi.' I raised a hand in an awkward half-wave. Clearly she didn't trust me to introduce myself. Fair enough, really.

'Nick Miller. I'll be writing the piece on your father,' Nick interrupted, not giving me any more time to add to my hello. 'When do you think I might be able to meet with him, Artie? These constant cancellations are getting really quite frustrating.'

Wow. Bolshy. I held my breath, waiting for Artie's response. Looking over at Paige, I saw she was doing the same.

'Well, Mr Miller.' Artie failed to return Nick's informality but matched his attitude entirely. 'We do have a bit of a problem there. I was hoping we could eat breakfast and get to know one another a little before getting down to the work chatter, but if you'd rather get it out of the way—'

'I would,' Nick confirmed. 'Is he going to do the interview or not?'

Artie put his plateful of sushi down on the table and shifted in his chair to face Nick square on. Taking a deep breath, he placed his elbows on the table and tented his fingers under his chin, taking his time and considering his response. The tension was killing me.

Clearing his throat and sitting straight back in his chair in such a way that clashed horribly with his casual clothes, Artie gave Nick a brittle smile. 'As of this moment, Mr Miller, he says he is not.'

Paige let out a horrified gasp, as if the moment wasn't already dramatic enough, while Nick simply looked to the skies and then rubbed a hand over his face. I stayed silent. There was no way for me to make this situation any better.

'So what do you propose?' Nick asked as Artie picked up his chopsticks and started on an admittedly delicious-looking piece of salmon sashimi. 'Are we all just supposed to sit around here until he stops sulking? We all flew halfway round the world just to talk to your dad and now he doesn't want to play?'

I had always been a big believer in the idea that you catch more flies with honey than with vinegar, but it seemed Nick did not agree. I was half expecting him to vault over the table, slap Artie Bennett with a glove and challenge him to a duel. He looked pissed off. Paige looked terrified. I looked ambivalent. I couldn't deny it – the first thing that had crossed my mind when he said Bertie didn't want to do the interview was that if there was no interview, there would be no pictures. It was starting to look like I could potentially get away with this whole charade scot-free.

'I'm going to talk to my father later today,' Artie said once he had chewed and swallowed his food. 'I have impressed upon him how important this interview is for the company, how important it is to me, and I have explained to him that you have travelled a very long way to meet with him.'

'Well, that's very big of you.' Nick stood up, his chair scraping along the terracotta tiles of the veranda. 'If you could maybe call me when he thinks he might be ready, that would be great.' He turned to Paige and tossed down his napkin. 'This is what happens when you make arrangements with the monkey instead of the organ grinder.'

Without waiting for a response, Nick stormed off back towards the cottages. He was definitely not in the best mood ever. You'd have thought he'd be a bit more chipper, given the night he'd had.

'Mr Bennett, I am so sorry,' Paige said, standing up but going nowhere. 'I can't apologize enough. I don't know what could have come over him. He's a very passionate man and I think he's not feeling well and—'

But before she could finish, Artie cut her off with a full, throaty laugh.

'Oh, Ms Sullivan, please sit down.' He waved his hand at her, still chuckling to himself. 'There's nothing like a little drama at breakfast. Mr Miller is obviously frustrated. I don't blame him. I had a very similar reaction when my father declared his intentions to me last night. I do, however, somewhat object to being called a monkey.'

'I'm so sorry, seriously.' Paige couldn't have looked more embarrassed. 'I really apologize, I do. Nick is just, he's just . . .'

'He's just a bit of a knob,' I interrupted. 'Really. Can't be helped.'

'He is a bit of a knob.' Artie began laughing again, this time squeezing a couple of tears out of the corners of his eyes. 'Oh, that was funny, Ms – oh, I'm sorry, I didn't catch your name?'

'Vanessa,' I offered with a relieved glance at Paige. 'Vanessa Kittler.'

'Vanessa, yes,' he repeated as though to commit my name to memory. 'He is a bit of a knob. Very eloquently put. I had very much hoped I wouldn't have to come with this news today, but at the moment my father is being quite difficult.'

'If you don't mind me asking,' I started with caution, 'how come your dad arranged all this if he didn't want to do the interview? Seems a bit silly.'

'In short, he didn't arrange it,' Artie replied, getting right back into the sushi. 'I did. My father was against it from the beginning, but after a while he seemed to be persuaded. It was only after Mr Miller arrived on Monday morning and I went to check in that he decided he wasn't interested any more. And it's very difficult to talk my father into something that he doesn't want to do.'

'I suppose that's why he's been so successful?' I suggested. Nothing like a bit of flattery to grease the wheels. 'Because he knows his own mind?'

'This is true,' he agreed. 'But this is a very opportune time for an interview. Not to get into family politics, but this is something we have been discussing for a while – his retiring, my taking over the store, the brand. This piece is really quite important to me. If Mr Miller had stayed to discuss things a little longer, I would have made assurances that the interview will be salvaged somehow.'

'That's wonderful news,' Paige replied. 'Thank you so much, Mr Bennett.'

'Artie, please,' he offered eventually. 'Failing all else, I can pull clothes for the fashion shoot and we'll work around the interview somehow.'

Paige's face lit up while my smile sank. I was so not getting out of taking those bloody photos.

'Well, the idea of the original shoot was that we would have your dad as sort of the king of fashion,' she explained with enthusiasm. 'We were going to shoot at the palace, have him in the middle of the set on a throne with all the gorgeous nature and historical culture clashing against the more modern fashions. Perhaps we do the shoot with you as the heir apparent? The prince regent?'

'That could definitely be arranged.' Artie stood up gracefully while Paige and I scrambled out of our chairs.

I half expected her to start bowing. 'If you would excuse me, do enjoy your day. I believe we should have everything back on track tomorrow. I apologize in advance if things end up being a little rushed, but I'm sure we'll make things work.'

'We will,' Paige said. 'If nothing else, the models arrive this evening. Perhaps we could take a look at the clothes this afternoon or this evening and pull for the shoot?'

'I'll see what I can do,' Artie replied with a gracious nod and disappeared back into the house, his plate still full of almost untouched sushi.

'Models?' I looked at Paige.

'For the clothes?' She looked right back. 'How did you think you were shooting clothes without models?'

'Coat hangers?' I squeaked.

'You're a moron,' she sighed, sinking back into her seat and banging her head gently on the table in front of her. 'I'm fucked, aren't I?'

All I could think was that she wasn't fucked. We all were.

For the want of a more positive answer, I ate another pastry and kept my mouth shut.

CHAPTER TWELVE

So, another free day in Hawaii. We could do anything. We could go anywhere. And all Paige wanted to do was get back into bed.

'I'm knackered,' she whined on the way back to the cottages. 'The caffeine is wearing off and I need to call the magazine and tell them about the changes.'

'But shouldn't we do something?' I looked around at the beachy paradise. 'Shouldn't we go sightseeing or something?'

'You need to go and take some photos,' she pointed out. 'Maybe practise taking pictures of actual people?'

'Fair point,' I grumbled, my mind having been on something altogether more touristy. I'd read some very exciting reviews about a wolphin at the Sea Life center. He was half whale and half dolphin! When was I going to get a chance to see that again? But she was right. I did need to practise taking pictures of people. 'But I don't have a model?'

I batted my eyelashes at her and made an effort to look as pathetic as possible. Not too hard.

'Tess, I'm tired,' she replied with a dramatic yawn. 'I think not.'

'Please?' I pressed my hands together in prayer. 'I really do need the practice. You said so yourself.'

'I did, but I'm tired and I'm pissy and I need more caffeine before I can do anything,' she said, pulling her hair up into a high ponytail before letting it fall back down around her shoulders. 'Actually, that makes me the closest thing you'll find to an actual model for miles.'

'Just an hour,' I promised, rushing inside to get my stuff. 'We'll just do an hour and then you can go and have a nap and I can go and see the wolphin and we'll both feel better about the shoot tomorrow.'

'Fine – I'll be by the pool,' she called after me. 'Just get me more coffee.'

Behind our cottages there was a great big kidney-shaped pool surrounded by sunloungers and brightly coloured parasols. I had barely registered it before, given that there was an entire ocean only a few feet away, but it was perfect for our faux shoot.

'So where do you want me?' Paige emerged from her cottage in a dazzling white bikini and huge sunglasses, her blonde hair loose and shiny. It was beyond me how normal people looked like that in swimwear, but then I remembered Paige wasn't normal people – she worked for a fashion magazine. That was why she was wearing huge neon-pink wedges and red lipstick to hang out by a swimming pool.

'Um, over by that wall?' I pointed towards a short white wall covered with climbing vines and beautiful, colourful flowers. Looking up at the sun, I waited until she was in position, checked my light meter and pulled out an assortment of reflectors, lenses and back-up batteries that I'd nicked from Vanessa. It never hurt to be overprepared. 'Right, so just stay there, keep your face towards the light, but don't, like, do any posey stuff for the camera. I just want to do a few test shots.'

'I really hate having my picture taken,' she complained, picking a bright pink bloom and carefully placing it in her hair. 'I look awful.'

'Yeah, you look really disgusting,' I agreed, seeing something quite different through my viewfinder. Paige was pretty in real life, but through the lens she was beautiful. Honest to God gorgeous. When I zoomed in, I could see the green flecks in her blue eyes and a tiny smattering of freckles that she had tried to cover up with make-up. I snapped away as she stroked the petals of the flowers and wrinkled her nose self-consciously.

'Can we start soon? I just want to get this over with,' she shouted, shielding her eyes from the sun after ten minutes of mindless snapping. I was so in the zone I'd forgotten to tell her I'd already started.

'You're brilliant,' I shouted back. 'Just carry on doing what you're doing. I've already got loads of shots.'

But as soon as I spoke, she froze. It was as though someone had swapped her for a waxwork. Everything that had come alive for my camera died.

'Paige, you've gone weird. Can you just do what you were doing before?' I called, trying to work out what was wrong.

'What was I doing?' She sounded as awkward as she looked, shoulders stiff and hard, her face a mask of panic. 'I don't remember.'

'You just looked normal.' I didn't know what else to say. 'Just relax.'

'I am relaxing,' she replied in a voice that did not support her statement. Turned to face me, arms straight sticks be her side, Paige pulled her shoulders up to her ears. 'Is this OK?'

It was not OK.

'Why don't you sit down on the sunbed?' I suggested. 'Give me something else to try.'

Nodding, and clearly relieved, she took herself off to the nearest sunlounger and collapsed on her improbably flat stomach. I consoled myself a little with the fact that she wasn't fitter than me, just hungrier. After rearranging my equipment, I crouched down on the floor in front of her and started snapping. She still looked about as life-like as one of the Kardashians. I had to get her to stop thinking about the pictures.

'Tell me about when you met Nick.' I shuffled onto my bum and snapped as quietly as possible. I hoped that if I kept her talking, she would be distracted enough to stop worrying. And also I wanted to pump her for information about my one-night stand without fessing up.

'Oh, it was a couple of years ago.' She squinted at me and pursed her lips. 'Well, the first time would have been a lot of years ago, but I was with my ex then. And he was with his.'

So Nick did have a serious ex. Interesting.

'But then I ran into him at a Christmas party just after me and Stefan broke up and, you know how he is, he just looks like trouble.'

'Yes, he does.' I couldn't have agreed more. I'd had that stupid Taylor Swift song running through my head ever since Amy had mentioned it on the phone. 'So . . . you two, what, got together?'

'Oh no.' She smiled and her shoulders dropped half an inch. 'Didn't quite manage to get that far. Anyway, we were chatting at the bar and he's all hand on my leg and, to be honest, full disclosure, I probably would have gone home with him, but just when everyone was clearing out, he leans in and he says to me, "Before we go, I should probably tell you I'm a complete arsehole, so you shouldn't go falling love with me."'

Paige dropped her head onto the sunlounger and laughed out loud. My fingers, not connected to my brain, carried on taking pictures. My brain, not connected to anything, packed its bags, waved goodbye and tried to make a hasty exit out of the fire escape.

'Classy line, isn't it?'

Thankfully, Paige couldn't see my face for my massive black camera. It was a classy line. It was also one I'd heard less than twenty-four hours earlier.

'Thank God I came to my senses, laughed in his face and went home alone. But for some reason I've always sort of regretted it. Maybe that's why he says it – gets girls' backs up. Makes him a challenge. And of course every time I've seen him since, he hasn't been the slightest bit interested in me.'

'Yeah, but you wouldn't be interested in him either, surely?' I crawled over to the sunlounger next to Paige and sat down for a moment, camera in my lap. 'You must have loads of blokes wanting to go out with you.'

'We always want what we can't have, don't we?' She sat up and hugged her knees. 'Or at least what we know is bad for us. I've been more or less single since Stefan. Still can't believe he did it.'

'I'm sorry.' I turned my attention to the screen on the back of my camera. Those last few pictures were so pretty. The ones when she was talking about Nick. 'Really.'

'I know you're pretending to be Vanessa, but you're not her, remember?' She rested a hand on my wrist and squeezed. 'You didn't shag my fiancé a month before my wedding, did you?'

'No?' I probably should have sounded more certain about that.

'I had my dress and everything.' She let go of my wrist and wrapped her arms around herself. 'We'd have been married three years this September. I thought I'd have kids by now.'

I thought back to three years ago and wondered whether or not Vanessa had ever brought Stefan to our apartment. Had I met him? Had I made awkward conversation with him in my kitchen on a Saturday morning? It was more than possible.

'But who wants babies when they're trapped in Hawaii with a really hot man and endless cocktails?' she said, snapping out of her trance and clapping her hands on her thighs. Which did not even quiver. 'Totally going to bang Nick, totally going to break my curse.'

'I don't think that would be a very good idea,' I choked, wishing we had some of those cocktails to hand. 'He's clearly got some problems.'

'Yeah, and I want to be one of them,' she replied with a sly smile. 'Don't worry, I won't go falling in love with him. But he might accidentally fall head over heels for me.'

'Shall we take some more pictures?' I suggested with forced brightness, scrolling through the terrible posed pictures and deleting them as quickly as I could – anything to distract myself. 'Just a couple?'

'Can I have a look at what you've done so far?' she asked. I nodded, nervous. Not only was I dealing with a woman who disliked having her picture taken, I was also dealing with my boss.

'Oh God, I look awful.' She screwed up her face and kept clicking through. I knew what she really meant was 'your pictures are awful'. 'I look like my mum.'

'Not a good thing?' I asked.

Paige shook her head, skipping through the shots too fast to really take in just how terrible they were. Until she reached the ones on the sunlounger. Finally she slowed down.

'This one is quite pretty.' She paused on a shot of her laughing, halfway through her Nick story. 'And I don't hate this.'

Slowly, she cycled through all the shots we'd taken until we got to the first few, the ones she didn't know I'd been shooting at all.

'Oh, Tess, these are beautiful.' Paige looked up at me with something new in her eyes. It looked strangely like respect. Mixed with surprise. 'Like, really, really beautiful. The light, the expression you've captured. These are great.'

Carefully she handed me my camera and smiled.

'You're going to be great at this,' she said, nodding. 'I'm not worried at all.'

'Are you just saying that so you can go and have a nap?' I asked, blushing.

'A little bit,' she replied. 'But those pictures are genuinely beautiful. They are so hot, I would totally let you tag me in them on Facebook.'

Wow. Now there was a compliment.

*   *   *

'*Aloha*, Vanessa,'

A couple of hours later, still bathing in the glow of not quite hating myself as much as I had when I woke up, I opened my cottage door to find Kekipi standing on my doorstep with a giant wicker picnic basket in one hand and a white envelope in the other.

'*Aloha*.' I eyed the picnic basket like a rabid Yogi Bear. I'd been so busy editing Paige's pictures, I had completely forgotten to eat lunch. 'How are you?'

'Since Mr Bennett cancelled once again, there was a suggestion that you might enjoy a tour of the property. The boat is ready and I have a picnic.' He waved the basket at me and my eyes followed it, tongue almost hanging out of my mouth. 'Sound like fun?'

'Sounds amazing!' I clapped my hands together like a little girl and jumped from foot to foot. 'Can I just run in and change my battery pack? I want to take my camera.'

'*Wiki wiki*,' he said, handing me the envelope. 'That means be quick. I'll wait right here.'

I nodded and wiki wiki'd myself into the house. The note was from the main house and confirmed that Artie would have everything ready for the fashion shoot tomorrow. So things were actually happening. Confidence buoyed by my test shoot with Paige, I left the card on the kitchen top and didn't think any more about it. The only thing on my mind was how many awesome selfies I could take to post on Facebook with the caption, 'Hey, Charlie, you wanker, I'm in Hawaii having the best time of my entire life and not even thinking about you at all.' Or something.

I was already suffering from sunburn so I pulled on a long black T-shirt over my bikini, but abandoned my shorts. There was nothing more disgusting than sitting in damp denim – I'd learned that lesson the hard way after one too many turns on the log flume as a kid. It was Amy's favourite ride. The T-shirt wasn't fooling anyone into believing it was a dress, but I figured Kekipi wouldn't be that offended by the sight of my arse. Or at least he'd be too professional and polite to say otherwise. Piling my hair on top of my head and grabbing my camera bag, I was ready to go. Just as I was about to leave, my phone started beeping. I yanked it out of my bag and stared at the screen, frozen to the spot.

Charlie Wilder.

I looked at the screen for a moment, looked at the letters in his name, looked at the tiny photo that had popped up, the whole situation so unwelcome. Unable to take another second of it, I pressed answer and felt three days of progress disappear.

'Hello?'

'Tess?'

'Who else would it be?' Well, perhaps I had managed to hang on to a touch of attitude.

'I . . . I just wanted to call you. It's been ages.'

'Right.'

Standing in the middle of a kitchen that wasn't mine, on an island in an ocean that was far, far away from the island and the ocean I had grown up on, I didn't know quite what to say. If I'd been in my kitchen, on my island, in my ocean, I had a feeling I'd be crying by now. But something was stopping me.

'You wanted to call me to say what?' I asked, reaching out to steady myself on the kitchen counter.

Even though I knew the smart thing to do would be to hang up, there was a sickly softness in my stomach that was begging him to tell me he loved me. No matter where I was or what I was doing, ten years weren't that easily undone. If he would just say that he needed me.

'Just to say, you know, hello and everything,' he said, laughing with nerves. 'I think this is the longest we've gone without speaking since we met.'

'It *is* the longest we've gone without speaking since we met,' I replied, picturing him rubbing his eyebrow, biting his lip. 'I'm sorry, I've got to go.'

'But I wanted to tell you . . .' he said hurriedly. 'I meant to say . . .'

'Meant to say what?' I asked, holding my breath and hoping.

'About work. I've heard the company is in loads of trouble. Apparently it's not the economy or anything; it's just that Michael has pissed loads of money away and we're going under. Or something. And they didn't have the budget for the job he'd promised you any more. Anyway, that's what I heard.'

'That's what you wanted to say?' I couldn't quite believe it. My grip on the kitchen top tightened and I watched my knuckles turn white. 'That's all you wanted to tell me?'

'Yeah?' He didn't sound quite sure. 'I know you're really upset about your job and stuff and I don't want you to be. Upset.'

'Charlie?' I squeezed my eyes tightly together and ignored the prickling tears. 'Please don't call me again.'

'But I miss you,' he said in a broken whisper. 'I miss my best mate.'

And that was enough to make me hang up. I unclenched my fists and placed my palms on the cool kitchen counter. Leaning forward, I fought the sick feeling in the back of my throat. I fought the desire to get into bed and never get back out. I was better than this. The things he was talking about were Old Tess problems. New Tess didn't care. New Tess had better things to do. Like eat loads of cheesy snacks on a boat.

Confused and close to tears, I stumbled out of the door, slipping my sunglasses over my reddening eyes and hoping Kekipi wouldn't mind if I went in for a hug. But instead of finding my presumed boat buddy, I found Nick. Holding the picnic basket. And a huge bag of Cheetos.

'Can't have a picnic without crisps, can you?' he asked.

'Where's Kekipi?' I asked, glad I'd grabbed my sunglasses 'You're not coming?'

'Kekipi has gone back to do whatever it is Kekipi does, and, yes – yes, I am,' he said, looking impossibly pleased with himself and dangling a set of keys from his thumb and forefinger. 'You're with me, kid.'

'Because you know how to drive a boat?'

He nodded.

'And you know your way around Hawaii?'

He nodded.

'There's no way I'm getting in a boat with you.' I crossed my arms and gritted my teeth. 'I saw *Shirley Valentine*.'

'Then you'll know exactly why you should get in a boat with me,' he said, slipping the keys into his pocket and holding out his hand. 'For fuck's sake, Vanessa, I'm not going to feed you to the sharks.'

'There are sharks in there?' I eyed the ocean suspiciously, pushing all thoughts of Charlie, of Donovan & Dunning, of the Old Tess right out my mind. 'Now I'm really not sure about this.'

'I am and you're coming.' He grabbed my hand and started to pull me along the beach. 'Because I need some company and you need a shag.'

'I do not need a shag,' I replied, trying to shake off his hand and ignore the way my skin burned as soon as he touched me. 'And if you need company, why not take Paige?'

'Why would I take Paige?' he asked, seeming genuinely nonplussed, as he dragged me along to the little pier beside our cottages. At the end, the world's smallest motorboat bobbed up and down on the ocean. 'Can't think why I'd take her.' I couldn't take my eyes off his arse as he leaned over to drop the picnic basket into the boat. He looked so big and manly as he unravelled the rope that tied the boat to the pier I was worried my ovaries were going to burst. Traitors. 'I've got a feeling she might be mad with me anyway.'

My brain and my vagina hadn't quite reconciled on where I stood with the whole Paige thing. Nothing had happened between them and it really didn't seem like anything ever would. But I still felt as though I should have told her about this. Whatever this was. Obviously, because I was a massive wimp and didn't want her to hate me, I hadn't, so the natural conclusion would have been just not to hang out with Nick again. That was easier said than done. 'Maybe because you were a complete cock at breakfast?'

'I don't like being messed around.' A brief darkness crossed his face before it was replaced with his annoying grin. 'Hope you don't get seasick.'

'How come you're suddenly in such a good mood?' I let him take my hand and help me into the boat, trying to ignore the sudden flashbacks to the night before. 'Forget to take your meds this morning?'

'I never forget to take my meds,' he replied, and I had no idea whether or not he was joking. 'I lost my temper earlier, I know. It was unprofessional, but it's been a pretty stressful few weeks. I didn't need Baby Bennett's shit.'

'He was actually quite nice about you after you flounced off like a little girl,' I said, remembering, after my bottom hit the wooden bench, that I wasn't wearing any shorts. Oh cock. 'So you might not get fired after all.'

'And if they fire me, who's going to do their interview?' He jumped behind the wheel of the boat and slipped the keys into the ignition. I hated the fact that both his arrogance and ability to operate a small seafaring craft were epic turn-ons. Maybe he didn't just look a little bit like Daniel Craig; maybe he actually was James Bond. 'Not that I give a shit. When I'm done here, I'm going home to do a real job.'

'What's that supposed to mean?' I grabbed hold of the side of the boat as the engine sputtered into life.

'Don't talk to me while I'm driving,' he said, Wayfarers down, eyes on the horizon. 'Unless you want to end up in an episode of *Lost*, I need to concentrate.'

Staring at him from behind my sunglasses, I narrowed my eyes and fought the urge to kick him in the back of the knee. Why had I got into the boat? Kekipi was going to pay for selling me out. We pulled away from the pier and away from the beach and headed out onto the clear blue seas, but instead of looking out at the beautiful, breathtaking scenery, I couldn't take my eyes off the captain. I quietly wondered if Amy would fancy him. He was definitely more her type than mine. Stocky, solid. Not so much buff as just really well put together, like he played a lot of sport rather than worked out. And he wasn't terribly tall – maybe five ten, five eleven if he was lucky – but he did definitely have that rugged, hot blond thing going on. There weren't many men who could get away with being so impossibly arrogant. Maybe Michael Fassbender, possibly Bradley Cooper, but that was it. But still, really not my type. So why was I imagining repopulating the world with him after a zombie apocalypse and simultaneously resisting a strong urge to kick him in the balls so badly that he turned into a lady? With a resigned sigh, I reached over to the picnic basket and grabbed the Cheetos. If in doubt, cheese was always the answer.

We were only on the water for fifteen minutes or so, but it was quite long enough. I peered over the edge of the boat pretending to be absorbed in the sealife under the waves. In reality I was just trying to avoid an embarrassing vomming situation. It turned out I did get seasick. I really was learning something new about myself every day. Thankfully, Nick barely acknowledged me while he captained our teeny vessel, though to be fair to him, sitting together in silence was a lot more companionable than any conversations we'd had so far.

Eventually we slowed down and began to head inshore. I leaned over the edge, hoping Nick wouldn't push me in and sail away. The water was crystal clear, just like on TV, and I could see tiny fish darting around the sides of the boat. Brighton never looked like this. My bath water never looked like this. Further out, the ocean was dotted with smaller, rocky-looking islands jutting upwards and occupied by an assortment of interesting-looking birds. Back towards the mainland, the huge green mountain behind Bennett's estate dominated the skyline, towering above the coconut palms and banyan trees. I couldn't believe how breathtaking Hawaii looked from the water, and every time I blinked or wiped away some spray, I was slapped in the face by the soft, sweet smells of the island. The edge of saltwater just made the delicate floral breeze that much more wonderful, like sea-salt caramel ice cream. It smelled so clean. I wanted to bottle the scent and wear it for ever. Or bottle it, sell it and make so much money I could come and live here for ever.

'Do you actually know where we're going?' I asked Nick as he jumped out of the boat, barefoot, into ankle-deep water and dragged us both onto the beach. Manly. Hot. 'Because I saw that film where Madonna got cast away on a beach for ages.'

'No one saw that film,' Nick replied. 'And yes, of course I know. I'm not about to get stranded on a deserted beach with you, love.'

It took me a moment to decide which insult to deal with first.

'Lots of people saw that film,' I grumbled and held out my hand for him to help me out of the boat, but instead he just grabbed me round the waist and hauled me onto land without getting my feet so much as damp. My heart pounded and my knees felt weak. Colour me a lost cause. 'Why did you bother bringing me in the first place?'

'That,' he said, wading back to the boat and recovering the picnic basket. And the half-empty bag of Cheetos. Two-thirds empty, 'is a very good question.'

'Just fancied having someone around to take the piss

out of?' I suggested. 'Or maybe there's something heavy you need me to carry?'

Nick stood three feet in front of me and frowned. 'I wanted to come here. I thought you would like it. Zero ulterior motive. Why did you get in the boat?'

'Vitamin B deficiency?' I suggested from the safe place behind my sunglasses. 'Jet lag? Morbid self-hatred?'

He took a step closer. I took a step back.

'Are you always like this?'

'Like what?'

'An unrelentingly cynical bitch?'

It was fair to say I was a little stunned. Nick just stood there waiting for an answer. His blond hair was all mussed up from the water and I badly wanted to smooth it down. Sailing hair looked a lot like sex hair and it was incredibly distracting, but he had just called me a cynical bitch so I wasn't feeling quite so weak at the knees any more. Just inches apart, I stared at him. No one had ever called me a bitch before in my entire life. Not even Amy. Doormat, yes. Walkover, on occasion. Regularly a martyr. Admittedly I was hardly Pollyanna, but a cynical bitch? Me?

'Sorry, that was out of order,' he grunted, breaking off the awkward stand-off, and started down the beach and into the trees beyond. 'It's this way.'

Smiling, I followed.

For as long as I could, I trailed Nick in silence. It was easy to be distracted – the valley was breathtaking and I kept stopping to touch everything. Flowers, leaves, trees, birds that were too slow to get away from me. After getting my wrists slapped twice, I stopped running my fingers through the bougainvillea and plumeria and stayed close to my stoic tour guide. We wandered through some beautiful trees, down a beautiful path, up some less beautiful rocks and finally down a desperately unbeautiful mud bank that tested my ability to hike in flip-flops.

'Nick?' I called as I faltered halfway down the path, flapping around like a drunken mountain goat. I clawed at the slippery stones either side of me and felt my feet slipping further and further apart. 'A little help?'

'Oh, shit.' He darted back, took hold of my wrist and hoisted me down the path. Once my feet were on solid ground, he didn't let go. 'I'm sorry.' He looked as though he meant it. 'I get carried away.'

'I'm not really an experienced hiker,' I said, annoyed with myself at having to ask for help when I was so enjoying giving him the silent treatment. 'If I'd known we were climbing mountains, I'd have worn proper shoes.'

'That was hardly a mountain.' Nick's fingers slid down my wrist until we were holding hands. 'And did you even bring proper shoes?'

I looked down at our hands and blushed.

He smiled and reached behind me to pluck a soft pink flower from a tree and tucked it behind my right ear.

'Wearing a flower behind your right ear in Hawaii means you're looking for a mate,' he said, fingertips trailing from the flower down my cheek. 'On the left side it means you're already spoken for.'

Without saying anything, he pulled it out from behind my right ear, combed out my hair with his fingers, and placed it behind my left ear.

'You cheesy bastard,' I said, gingerly touching the soft petals and threatening myself not to blush. Nick gave my fingers a squeeze and then turned away quickly, dropping my hand.

'Come on.' He started walking faster. 'It's right around here.'

'What's right here?' I was trying to watch where I was going, not lose my flower and work out when was the last time I'd held a boy's hand, all at the same time. It was not easy. 'How do you know where we're going?'

'This is right here,' he said, standing back and gently pushing me in front of him. 'And I know because I've been here before. And when you've been here once, it's very hard to forget.'

I turned a corner at Nick's nod and pushed my way through a thick, rubbery bush, following the sound of running water.

'Oh. Oh, wow,' I whispered, grabbing his hand again, squeezing it tightly. 'Oh, Nick.'

In front of us was a small pool about the same size as the mill pond back at home. But that was where the similarities ended. The blue-green water was surrounded by tall cliffs that stretched up so high, covered in green vines and trees, and sheltered us with a canopy of trees. Sunlight found its way through the branches and dappled the water, making it sparkle and glitter, and directly opposite us a narrow white waterfall danced down the black rocks from somewhere unseen up in the sky. It was too much.

'How did you know this was here?' I asked, my voice low and reverential. I was waiting for mermaids to come out and tell me to be quiet or at the very least start singing a Disney medley.

'I spent a summer in Hawaii a few years ago,' he said, leading me down the gently sloping pebbled shore to the water's edge. 'Me and my girlfriend were travelling, and one day I went out exploring the island and found this place.'

I tried not to flinch at the use of the word 'girlfriend' and the distinct lack of a qualifying ex in front of it. He said he was single, didn't he?

'Can you believe we're still on Bennett's property?' Nick set the picnic basket down on a large, smooth stone and kicked off his shoes to paddle into the water, never letting go of my hand. I followed, abandoning my flip-flops, and followed suit. The water was so cool and refreshing, the horrors of the hike were immediately forgotten. Dozens of tiny tadpoles darted around my feet in the shallows, disappearing as we got deeper. 'Technically, you could say I was trespassing the last time.'

'Technically?'

'I was trespassing.' He was up to his knees in the water and I watched as the edges of his shorts darkened. Tess would have pointed that out, but Vanessa kept her mouth shut and concentrated on his story. 'It's one of the reasons I took this job, actually – I've wanted to come back for so long but never had the chance. It seemed fortuitous.'

We stayed where we were, knee-deep in the water, holding hands and staring up at the waterfall.

'You didn't want to come back with your girlfriend?' I asked with as light a voice as I could conjure up. 'Wouldn't this be a "you and her" place?'

'We broke up just after we came here,' he replied just as casually. 'And she didn't come with me to the waterfall. I tried to get her to come back after I'd found it, but she was more of a lie-by-the-pool girl than a walk-through-fifteen-minutes-of-beautiful-forest-to-see-something-extraordinary kind of a girl.'

Somewhere in my cold, black little heart, a spark flared for just a second, warmed by the fact that Nick had chosen to share this special place with me and only me. Not that he'd told me there was going to be a fifteen-minute walk. If he had, there would have been no guarantees I would have done it.

'I thought, since Bennett cancelled on us again, he owed us this,' he said, turning towards me and peeling off his T-shirt. Fuck a duck, he was so handsome. And romantic. Maybe he was something special after all. 'And I thought, after last night, you owed me round two.'

And then I remembered that he was an arrogant twat and this was just a one-week sexathon, nothing more, nothing less.

Not that I was about to stop him. There was something about Nick's hands on my body that made me lose all sense of myself. They were big and strong and hot and they made me feel small and weak in the best way. I had had a lifetime of liaisons that had been awkward at best. There hadn't been a single sexual encounter where I hadn't spent at least half the foreplay desperately trying to manoeuvre myself into a flattering angle or, better yet, under the covers. Even with Charlie I hadn't been able to banish the thought of the gargantuan size of my arse from the back of my mind, but with Nick I was too busy revelling in the sensation, the firmness of his touch, the intention behind every move, to worry whether or not he thought I could stand to lose half a stone from my rear end. Everything about the moment – his tight, tense breathing, his half-closed eyes, his warm lips pressing against my neck as he coiled my hair into a knot around his fist – said he didn't give a shit. He wanted me. He made me feel desired, and nothing had ever turned me on so much in my entire life.

'Are you sure there's no one around?' I whispered as I watched my pink flower float away towards the water-fall. I barely recognized my own voice when I was with him. I barely recognized myself when I was with him.

'Do you really care?' he asked, one hand disappearing into my bikini bottoms.

'No.' I breathed in and clung to him, my lips on his lips, my thighs on his thighs, and my knees very close to giving way. 'Just don't stop.'

And he didn't.

'So, are you excited to get to work tomorrow?' Nick asked afterwards. I basked in the afternoon sunlight and the warm afterglow of ridiculous sex, stretched out on a beach towel like a happy copper-haired walrus. I'd managed to keep my bikini about my person, but my T-shirt, soaked through, was drying on a large, flat rock across the way, along with all of Nick's clothes. 'Are you dying to take some pictures? Are you desperate to put some six-foot mutant in a five-thousand-quid dress and tell her how to pout for half an hour?'

'Can't wait,' I moaned, burying my head in the sand. Literally. 'Are you excited to meet the elusive Bertie Bennett?'

'After everything we've put up with so far?' Nick lazily traced figures of eight around my bare lower back. 'I can't wait. If it actually happens, it's either going to be one of the most interesting interviews I've ever done, or he's going to be one of those absolute bastards who won't say a word.'

'Isn't that hard?' I kept my eyes closed and tried to

concentrate on asking sensible questions. I had a very hard time keeping my wits about me immediately after sexytimes. 'When people don't want to talk to you?'

'Is it hard when people don't want you to take their picture?' he bounced the question back.

'That's never happened to me,' I replied. Brilliant, another thing I hadn't thought to worry about until now. Just add it to the list.

'Lucky you,' Nick said, sitting up and rummaging through the picnic basket. 'You must be a better photographer than I am a writer.'

I hoped he was right. I worried he was not.

'When you came to Hawaii the first time,' I asked, rubbing my finger and thumb over a big green leaf that hung right above my head, 'with your girlfriend . . .'

'Yeah?' He pulled out a Tupperware box of pineapple, frowned and put it back, rifling around for something else.

'Was it for work?' I wasn't sure what I was trying to find out, but I figured I'd know when I heard it.

'No, we were on holiday,' he answered, placing a bottle of water in the sand beside me and twisting off the cap. 'She lived in LA, I'd been working in Australia for a few months, we met here. It's in the middle.'

It all sounded so jet-set and romantic to me. Three years ago I had decided I was going to get over Charlie and fall in love with an accountant from Wimbledon, but after three dates, the thought of forty minutes on the District line was enough to dampen his ardour. Not quite *Romeo & Juliet*.

'What happened?' I asked. I couldn't imagine Nick sending sweet text messages or whispering sweet nothings down the phone to his long-distance American lover, but I wanted to know more. I needed all the details so that I could accurately obsess about it later. And possibly Google-stalk the shit out of his ex. 'With the two of you?'

'Nothing exciting.' He nudged the water towards me. I took the bottle and sipped. 'I loved her more than she loved me. It happens.'

'Yes, it does,' I agreed, the familiar stab of pain and betrayal threatening to ruin a perfectly shagtastic afternoon. 'So she's still in LA?'

'I don't know where she is,' he shrugged. I stole a look at him, at the droplets of water in his hair, the crinkles around his blue eyes as he squinted at me. Eurgh. It was like seeing him again for the first time. 'Don't see a lot of point in keeping tabs on someone who didn't give a shit about me.'

I nodded, making a mental note to stop checking Charlie's Facebook page every night before bed. And when I woke up. And whenever I looked at my phone. The phone call. He missed me. No, he missed his best friend.

'Was she your last girlfriend?' I wondered how many questions I could get away with before he clammed up. I shifted slightly on my towel, tugging at my bikini bottoms. I wasn't sure, but I thought my bum might be burning, and that couldn't be a good look.

'Why?' He pulled sunscreen out of the picnic basket and squirted it directly onto my backside. Impressive mind-reading techniques. 'Does it matter?'

'I'm just asking,' I replied, defensive, realizing that it totally mattered. 'Was she?'

'She was.' As he leaned over me I felt his shadow block the sun overhead and shivered, very, very slightly.

'After her, I realized I'm not cut out to do the girlfriend thing. Any more searching questions?'

'I'm not the professional question asker,' I said. 'As we've already established. I'm just curious.'

'About me?' He took the bottle of water back and sipped thoughtfully. 'What do you want to know?'

'I just think it's weird that we're, you know, doing this –' I felt myself blushing as I spoke – 'and we hardly know each other.'

'What is there to know that you don't already know?' Nick shrugged. 'What do you need? Middle name? Parents' occupations? Blood type? You don't need to see someone's birth certificate to enjoy having sex with them, Vanessa.'

'You're not curious to know more about me?' I asked, trying not to let his answer sting. It was just sex. He'd made that very clear. We'd both made that very clear. 'I mean, in general. I don't have my birth certificate on me.'

'I find the more you get to know about a person, the more disappointed you end up,' he replied. 'Right now, I like you, you like me, we're having a good time. A very good time. I say we leave it at that before someone finds out something they don't want to know.'

I nodded, but really he was just making me want to ask more questions. This was just bravado – it had to be. No one was so incredibly nonchalant about these things. And he was so full of contradictions. One minute he was putting flowers behind my ear, telling me he wanted to share his special place with me, and the next he wasn't 'cut out to do the girlfriend thing'? Mixed messages, anyone?

'I just feel like I should know more about you,' I said,

trying to sound as flippant as possible. 'Since this keeps happening.'

'Should is a terrible word,' he muttered, running a finger across my collarbone. 'Never do something just because you think you should.'

'What about doing something because you know you shouldn't?' I asked, the last four days flashing in front of me, my skin burning in the wake of his hands.

He was quiet for a moment, his expression reflective before it transformed with a wolfish grin. 'I only do the things that I shouldn't. Like you.'

Now it was my turn to be quiet. I knew I wasn't playing fair, but it was one thing for me to choose to have a fling and quite another to have your chosen lover rub the fact that he had no emotional interest in you in the slightest right in your face.

'What was the last thing you did that you shouldn't have?' Nick asked, lying back down beside me, allowing the sun to cover my body again in a warm glow. He looked like he belonged there in paradise. And that only served to remind me that I didn't. 'Aside from me.'

'What makes you think I count you?' I pulled the leaf from the tree and watched it snap back. I refused to look at him. I didn't want him to know I was upset. 'What makes you think this is a big fat tick in the mistake column? Maybe I think it's a brilliant idea.'

'Oh, I'm definitely a mistake.' His voice took on a shade of self-importance and arrogance that I didn't especially enjoy. I'd heard it before and it didn't suit him. 'I'm just a really fun one.'

'You're adorable,' I replied. 'Do you genuinely feel better about yourself when the women you're sleeping with think you're a complete tosspot?'

'Yes, I do.' Nick looked at me closely. 'You haven't answered my question. What's the last thing you did that you shouldn't have?'

I took a deep breath and turned onto my side so that I could see him properly. His handsome face and solid, tanned body were so close, the warmth radiating from his skin was hotter than the sun overhead, but I couldn't quite make out his features – the bright mid-afternoon light silhouetted him against the waterfall.

'The last thing I did that I shouldn't have done was sleep with my best friend,' I said, quickly and loudly. 'I should not have done that.'

'Best friend?' He perked up immediately. 'Female?'

'Male.' I gave him my best wry smile. 'Sorry.'

'Why shouldn't you have slept with him?' he asked, not a trace of jealousy or concern on his face. 'Was he in love with you?'

'No.' I shook my head and stared at my fingernails.

'Were you in love with him?'

Staring at my nails, I realized I should have given myself a manicure. Vanessa would never go out with nails like this. I imagined Paige was tweeting about the state of my cuticles at that very second.

'Oh, you were.' He leaned forward and pushed my hair out of my face. 'Are you still?'

I looked up but I couldn't look him in the eyes. Instead I focused on the tiny patch of grey that was starting on his temple.

'Are you still in love with him?' he asked again, more softly this time, looking directly into my eyes.

'It doesn't matter either way,' I said, shaking my hair out of his hands. 'He doesn't love me.'

'Oh, now I get it – you've never been in love before.

You're an emotional virgin.' Nick made a clucking noise and rolled his eyes at me. 'Or worse, you're an emotional eunuch and you've cut off your own balls. Which is it?'

'Neither, knobhead.' Sometimes he said the most ridiculous things. The most ridiculous, accurate and hurtful things. 'I have feelings. I've been in love.'

I had. I knew I had. So why did the words sound hollow even to me?

'Why did you sleep with him then?' He looked away for a moment before leaning back on his elbows and looking back at me with professional interest on his face, the muscles in his arms bulging just enough to make me want to give them a gentle squeeze. 'Did you think it would make him feel differently about you?'

'I thought he did feel differently,' I replied, suddenly uncomfortable. 'This is weird, talking about this with you. Do you work out?'

'I run a lot, and no it isn't,' he replied without missing a beat. 'So you slept with him thinking it would make him fall in love with you when presumably you've known him for years and he hasn't shown any interest before?'

I gave him a sharp, stern glare. 'Your point being?'

'You're not the first.' He cocked his head to one side and gave me a standard-issue condescending smile. 'You won't be the last. Have you talked to him? Asked him why it happened? I'm assuming you didn't march up to him in a bikini on the beach in Hawaii and stick your tongue down his throat.'

'He said he didn't know.' I ignored the burning in my cheeks and his adorable reference to our first kiss. 'And now he says he wants to be friends again. I just can't work out why he did it at all.'

'Why did Hillary climb Everest?' he shrugged. 'You

were there. Men are explorers. Once you've got to the top of a mountain and put the flag in, why would you bother climbing the same one again? There are a lot of very exciting mountains out there – there's always a bigger one round the corner.'

'I don't want to be a mountain,' I said, trying not to whine and failing. 'And that's bollocks. If that was true, no one would ever get married.'

'Well, climbing mountains gets tiring after a while,' he reasoned, his expression perfectly even. 'I think one day you find one that's got a really good view, you end up hanging around for a bit and before you know it, you've set up base camp and you're going nowhere. Doesn't mean you don't look at the other mountains, though. Mountains are pretty.'

'None of this is reassuring,' I replied. 'And you're not exactly making me feel good about myself.'

'If it helps, you're one of the most fascinating mountains I've ever met.' He rested a hand on my knee and stroked my skin gently. 'Sometimes blokes are just blokes, even if they are your best mates. He's clearly an idiot.'

'For sleeping with me?' I asked in my quiet voice.

'For not setting up camp,' Nick replied.

We sat in silence for a moment, Nick's hand on my leg threatening to burn a hole right through my flesh. I was so confused. How could I be sitting here, heart hurting like hell for Charlie, and desperately wanting Nick to throw me down and shag me senseless? I shook my head and looked down at the sand again, feeling silly. Feeling like the old Tess.

'Maybe he wasn't man enough to get all the way to the top of your mountain,' Nick said, breaking the quiet and taking away his hand. I missed it immediately. 'Maybe he realized you were too much of a challenge.'

'What, and you are man enough?' I asked with a laugh that was slightly more bitter than I liked the sound of. 'I thought this was just sex, Nick?'

'It is,' he said. 'But you are giving me more pause for thought than I'd anticipated.'

I hopped up off my towel and brushed away the sand along with his words. He wasn't helping. 'Swim?' I asked, turning towards the water before I got a reply.

It was posed as a question but it was definitely more a statement. I wanted to wash away the conversation and pretend it had never happened. This split personality of Nick's was getting to be too much. One minute he was the devil-may-care playboy, the next an insightful sweet-heart. He was funny, then he was crass. He was sweet, and then he was arrogant. And talking about Charlie, stirring up genuine emotions, only made it harder for me to sort through what was real and what was fake. I was having a hard enough time remembering what my name was supposed to be.

I walked into the water, ignoring the shock of the cold as it crept up my legs. Baking in the sun had warmed me through, and now the lagoon that had been so refreshing before felt icy. Without looking back, I swam towards the waterfall and looked up. I wondered where the water came from, where it went, how it stayed so clean and fresh. Nick gave me a whole two minutes' peace before I heard him swimming over to me with a strong, straight stroke.

'What happened with your ex?' I asked as he reached me. 'Really?'

'Shall we just agree exes are off the agenda?' he

suggested. The fact that he wouldn't tell me only convinced me that there was something to tell.

'I'm just curious.' I bobbed up and down in the water, starting to enjoy the freshness again. 'Sorry.'

'Maybe we just shouldn't talk at all,' Nick said. 'Stick to what we're good at.'

'Maybe we should just stop everything altogether,' I suggested, kicking my legs underneath me. 'You do your interview, I'll take my pictures, and then we all go home.'

'And what happens after we go home?' he asked, wiping his face and treading water.

'After we go home?' I was confused.

'Yeah.' Nick swam closer and our feet touched under the water. 'When this is over. What's on the agenda for you when you get back to reality next week?'

'Oh.' I smiled sadly and ducked my head. 'Reality.'

Home. London. Amy, Charlie, Vanessa. Tess again. Of course. I glanced around at the lagoon, the vine-covered cliffs, the palm trees, the golden sand, the blue-green water and cascading waterfall that almost drowned out his words. It was all too good to be true. This wasn't reality for someone like me.

'Wake up, realize this was all a dream,' I said. 'Find my dead husband alive and well in the shower. You?'

'New York,' he replied. 'Maybe Hong Kong the week after. Still waiting to confirm.'

'Don't you ever stop?' It all sounded like such hard work. 'Don't you get tired of moving all the time?'

'I don't like to stay in one place too long,' he said, kicking backwards towards the waterfall, away from me. 'Don't like to let the grass grow under my feet.'

I waded towards him, just a half-step, and stopped.

'How do you have any sort of life if you're always on the move? How do you cope?'

'When you've only got yourself to worry about, it's not so difficult – I'm fine,' he called back as he swam away. 'You worry too much.'

I watched him vanish under the crashing water, my heart in my mouth until the moment he reappeared. He was fine, of course he was fine, and of course he was right – I did worry too much. But for the first time, while I was sure he was fine, I was starting to think he wasn't entirely happy.

CHAPTER THIRTEEN

The rest of the afternoon passed too quickly. We lazed on the beach, Nick read, I devoured everything Kekipi had put in the picnic basket and we silently agreed not to ask each other any more difficult questions. We also spent so long kissing that by the time we made it back to the cottages my lips were so chapped I thought they were falling off. When we parted ways on the beach, without so much as a goodbye, and trotted back to our respective homes, I paused by the door, looking back at him to see if he was looking back at me. He wasn't. Without a second glance, Nick let himself into the cottage and closed the door behind him. My heart sank a little but my brain gave me a gentle slap and pushed me inside. I still couldn't quite work out how things could be so insanely fabulous with someone I hardly knew, someone I barely liked and someone I would most likely never see again in four days' time. Maybe Nick was right – maybe I did worry too much. But to be fair, I had quite a lot to worry about.

And the first thing on the list was the note I found

from Paige scribbled on a piece of kitchen roll and stuck to my fridge. At first I smiled – writing on kitchen roll was such an Amy thing to do – but once I'd registered what the makeshift message actually said, I felt a little less warm and fuzzy and considerably more queasy.

'I wish she would bloody stop letting herself in here,' I muttered, casting my eyes over her scrawl.

The models had arrived.

There were models. On the same island as me. Not that there weren't always models on the same island as me. I lived and worked in East London, for God's sake – there were usually models on the same bus as me – but these were models I was going to take pictures of. And I was so scared that they would take one look at me, smell the fear and know. Models were like horses. I'd be holding the camera wrong or I'd ask them to smile instead of smize and the jig would be well and truly up. Whenever we did shoots at the ad agency, I always sent one of my team to deal with the models – they were altogether too intimidating and, hilariously, they always reminded me of Vanessa. We just didn't see eye to eye. Literally, in some cases. The rest of the kitchen-towel message was no more reassuring. I read it a couple of times over, just to make sure I wasn't missing anything.

– Models arrive at 6.00, staying in cottages next 2 u.
Pls go and say hi.
– I have 'plans'. Meet outside 2moro @ 7.00 a.m.
– We are shooting w/Artie NOT Bertie
Paige xx
P.S. bring camera

Next to the last bullet point was a huge winky face.

Oh good, it was supposed to be a joke.

So I was the model welcome wagon. What could Paige possibly be doing on the island of Oahu that was so important she would trust me to go and deal with the models on my own? On the upside, when I looked over at the sofa, I noticed the badly written message wasn't the only thing Paige had left in my cottage. Thrown all over the settee was what looked like three suitcases' worth of clothes and another note that read, 'Your wardrobe made me sad.' I was insulted. And a little bit giddy. Paige's clothes were much nicer than Vanessa's clothes. I held up a couple of the dresses and shirts that she'd tossed so carelessly and did the mental 'will I get my boobs in them?' test. For at least fifty percent of her offerings, the answer was no. But for the other fifty percent, with the right bra and a positive attitude, I could probably make them work. I recognized some of the designer names from the magazines I'd pored over obsessively on the plane and from the stiff paper carriers that Vanessa left lying around our flat.

Barely breathing, I pulled out a beautiful silk shift from 10 Crosby, all powder-blue background with a ridiculously pretty coral and white flower design. Very Hawaii. I gently laid it down on the armchair and worked my way through the rest of the pile. After twenty minutes of feeling like a kid in a very swanky sweet shop, I had a colourful collection of silk and satin and the softest cotton dresses I'd ever seen. My pile of borrowed ensembles made Vanessa's wardrobe at home look like the floor of Primark at the end of a particularly brutal Saturday. Clothes had never really been high up on my agenda; I was always too busy worrying about everything else in the world. Mostly I just wanted to be taken seriously and not show stains. I spilled a lot. But while I was in character, I might as well be in costume. Selecting a pretty, soft-looking cornflower-blue Phillip Lim dress from the pile, I strode purposefully into the bathroom to wash away my perfect afternoon and prepare for my model evening.

After treating myself to a long, steamy shower and a good talking-to, I stood in front of my neighbour's cottage and steeled myself. I was in a nice dress, I was wearing a lot of eyeliner. My camera didn't exactly go with my outfit, but I figured it made a good prop and, if necessary, a decent weapon. What was the worst that could happen? So yeah, OK, they were models; but they were also girls on a jolly in Hawaii. Surely they would be as blown away as I was when I'd first arrived? Surely they would be happy and excited?

'And they're only people,' I reminded myself under my breath. 'They stand in front of cameras and pout for a living. I managed to convince half of the UK to start using a different kind of teabag by making up a singing teaspoon voiced by Barbara Windsor. This is nothing.'

With one last worry about my non-existent manicure, I rapped on the door and waited. And waited. And waited. One more deep breath and I knocked again. Harder and louder and longer. This time I heard a shuffling noise inside, an awkward rattling at the lock, and eventually the door swung open to reveal what was either some sort of demon or a very, very angry model.

'What?' she snapped, straw-blonde hair tied up in a topknot and a pair of absurdly big blue eyes red raw and narrowing right in on me. 'Did I not tell you I was going to sleep?'

'Um, *aloha*.' I waved a hand in a futile gesture of friendliness. 'I'm Vanessa?'

'Yeah, definitely told you I was going to sleep,' the model nodded, clinging to the door like she might fall down if I took it away. 'Can you just fuck off?'

'We haven't actually met,' I said hurriedly before she could shut the door on me. I pointed at my camera and tried a toothy smile, 'I'm the photographer. For the shoot. Tomorrow.'

'Whatever.' She yawned without covering her mouth. 'I've just got off a plane that I've been on for nearly twenty-four hours, so unless you want to take pictures of the crypt keeper tomorrow, I suggest you go away and let me sleep.'

And with that, she slammed the door.

'Nice to meet you,' I said, still holding my hand up in a wave. '*Mahalo*.'

So . . . that was one of the models. I turned to face the last cottage. No lights on. No sound coming through the windows. Maybe I'd just let that poor little lamb rest.

All dressed up with nowhere to go, I weighed up my options. I could go for a walk, discover a little bit more of the island. I could go back to my cottage and edit some of the photos I'd taken that afternoon. I could probably find Kekipi and ask him to reenact my favourite scenes from *Joe Versus the Volcano*. Or I could go to Nick's cottage and look at how pretty he was. Life was full of tough choices.

'Where are you taking me?'

I was just about to slink over to Nick's when I heard Paige giggling. For no good reason I hid round the corner of the models' cottage, pressing up against the wall and peeking out to see who she was talking to.

'I thought we were just going to get dinner?' She was still laughing. It gave her voice an infectious, attractive lilt, the kind of girly voice that made men melt. Something I'd never quite mastered. 'Why do we have to go in the boat?'

'I want to show you something,' her dinner date replied. 'So just be quiet and get in the boat.'

It was Nick. Paige was getting into the boat with Nick. Just like I had got into the boat with Nick. All at once my heart sank, my face burned and I felt sick to my stomach.

'I'm not dressed for a boat,' Paige mock whined as I watched her climb aboard in a tiny black strappy dress, her high, high heels in Nick's hand as he helped her aboard with that half-smile I recognized so well on his face.

Oh my God, I was stupid. And in no position to be upset, I reminded myself, as I fought back angry tears. In fact, I was stupid to even be surprised. Of course he had moved on to Paige. Hadn't he explained all of this to me this afternoon? Paige was a proper mountain. Paige was Snowdonia or something. I wasn't even a hill. Maybe a hillock. Because it rhymed with pillock, and that was what I was. Nick had planted his flag and moved on to the next expedition.

I stayed exactly where I was until I heard the chug of the boat motor fade away. I didn't want them to see me. I didn't want Nick to know that, against all my better judgement, I gave a shit. Wiping black tears away from underneath my eyes, I briefly considered knocking on the cottage door again. Death by model might be better than having to look at the two of them across the breakfast table tomorrow. Paige all loved up, Nick all smugged up. What a clever man – he'd managed to bang both of the girls on the job before he'd even met the models. Get the amateurs out of the way before you move on to the professionals, presumably.

Without a plan, I stormed up the beach away from the cottages, away from the lights, away from the mess I'd got myself in. Perhaps I could just keep walking until I found a house and claim amnesia. It almost always worked on telly and when did telly ever lie? I frisked myself for my phone but I'd left it charging by the bed. I was distractionless. No phone, no music, no book, no nothing. Just my stupid brain thinking its stupid thoughts. Nick, Charlie. Charlie, Nick. I wished I had an ad campaign for loo roll to distract myself with. But all I had was my camera.

'Calm down,' I whispered to myself, closing my eyes and breathing deeply. 'All that really matters is that you take a good photo tomorrow.'

I opened my eyes and felt a stillness that had been missing. Hands clamped onto my Canon, I looked around for a suitable subject. A little way down the bay, sitting next to an unlikely-looking surfboard, was Al. He was too far away to shout to but close enough to snap. He looked deep in thought, his tanned face creased into a dignified mask of lines and wrinkles. Underneath his big white beard, his profile was strong and regal – he looked like a lion of a man. I was sure he must have been ridiculously handsome when he was younger, but at that exact moment, caught on camera, he just looked so sad. I wondered if he was thinking about his wife. Or his job. Or if he was thinking about all of it at once, like me.

'*Aloha*, Vanessa,' he shouted, still staring out to sea. 'Get any good pictures?'

'Um, I did actually,' I shouted back, walking as quickly as I could on sand to where Al was still settled. 'Sorry. That was really rude of me.'

'An artist finds her inspiration in many strange places,' he said with a welcoming smile, patting the sand beside him. 'And who am I to stand in the way of art?'

'Thank you.' I folded my legs underneath me, careful not to show my new old friend my knickers, and nodded towards his board. 'Been surfing?'

'I have,' he nodded. 'I think it keeps me young. My son thinks it will get him his inheritance sooner. So how is it all going? The photo shoot?'

Wincing, I stroked my camera and shrugged. 'I haven't actually taken any proper pictures yet. Lots of random stuff, but there's been a bit of a cock-up with the job and so we're waiting for everyone to sort it out. I'm supposed to do the shoot with some models tomorrow and I'm bricking it.'

'You don't like models?' he asked. 'That's got to be hard for a fashion photographer?'

'I have a confession.' I rested my camera on my bare knees and wrapped my hands under my legs. 'I haven't actually ever worked with models before.'

'Oh.' Al had the decency to look concerned, but his eyes were still sparkling and I had a very strong feeling that he was about to laugh. 'So you really haven't been back in the photography game for long?'

'Not that long, no.' I looked at the screen on the back of the camera and flicked through the shots of Al. It was easier than looking him in the eye. 'I was in advertising. And I lost my job. And now I'm here.'

He really didn't need any more details than those.

'You didn't want to get another job in advertising?'

'Um, this came up quite suddenly,' I said, not strictly lying. 'So I thought I'd give it a shot, no pun intended.'

'Let me see those pictures of me.' He held his hand out for the camera and, once again, I handed it over. He scrolled through quickly, umming and ahhing, occasionally shaking his head and then nodding. 'Did you love your old job?' he asked, passing the camera back to me. 'Were you good at it?'

'I loved it,' I said. 'And I was *so* good at it. But I got made redundant. No reasoning behind it. It didn't make any sense.'

'Well, that is hard,' he replied with a thoughtful look. 'I do understand how you must be feeling.'

'It's just shaken me a bit,' I admitted. 'I've always known what I've wanted. Or I thought I did. There was a plan. Now I don't know.'

'Perhaps it's time for a new plan,' Al suggested. 'Maybe it was just time for a change and you didn't realize. I know I said this yesterday, but your pictures really are very good. You've a talent, Vanessa – you're a very bright girl.'

'I don't feel that bright at the moment.' I took the camera back and nursed it in my lap.

Folding his arms and stretching out his legs, Al clucked and tutted. 'I feel like that all the time – everyone does. You'd think things would get easier as you get older, but they don't.'

'Have you made a complete cock of yourself over a rubbish man as well?' I asked, only wondering afterwards as to whether or not I should use the word 'cock' in front of my Hawaiian granddad.

'Sort of. Probably not in the same way, though.'

'It's so embarrassing.' I rested my head on my knees, unable to look directly at him. 'I can't believe I fell for it.'

'This is a man here on the island? Not someone back at home?' he asked. I nodded. 'Holiday romance, then?'

'Something like that,' I replied, still face first into my own knees. 'I thought I could do the whole fling thing, but turns out I can't. For some reason I keep on thinking I can do things and then it turns out I can't.'

'I'm probably not very good at giving young ladies advice on the modern man,' Al said, patting my shoulder in an awkward dad way that was oddly reassuring. 'I was married for a very long time and I wasn't much of a cad before my Jane, but I can't see what good it's doing you walking up and down the beach at sunset crying over someone after three days.'

'I know you're right,' I said, looking up and running a finger under each eye. Why was today the day I'd decided to experiment with eyeliner? 'I'm just being stupid. Maybe I'm still jet-lagged or I have pineapple poisoning or something. It's probably just that I'm stupid, though.'

'Never call yourself stupid,' he said, looking stern. Or as stern as it was possible for a man with a big white beard to look. 'What would your dad tell you to do?'

'I honestly don't know,' I shrugged. 'We don't really talk. Haven't seen him in years.'

'I didn't talk to my son for a long time,' Al said with a sympathetic smile. 'He was always much closer to his mother.'

'Are you close now?' I asked, twisting my curls into a long ponytail and fluffing the ends. 'With your son?'

235

'I wouldn't say close,' he said. 'After his mother died, we didn't seem to have an awful lot to say to each other.'

'It can't be easy, being a parent.' I was trying to be diplomatic, but really I couldn't imagine someone not loving having Al for a dad. Mine had always been more interested in his football and *Star Trek* than me and my sisters, but then mine was a bit shit.

I watched as Al scooped up a handful of sand and let it run through his fingers. 'It isn't easy. But it's not easy being the child sometimes either, is it?'

The powdery white sand filtered back onto the beach and I was sad for a moment that he would never be able to pick out exactly the same handful ever again. Rubbing my dry, sandy fingertips against my temples, I was starting to think I might be missing the bigger picture. My life had been so tiny and so utterly consumed by Charlie and my work that I'd let everything else slip past me without even noticing. I even used worrying about Amy as an excuse not to worry about myself. Now, sitting here on the beach with my stand-in granddad a million miles away from home, it was much easier to see that what had really changed in all of this was me.

'Ahh, look at that,' Al sighed as the sun finally tipped over the horizon, blending the pretty teal sea into the deep, dark blue sky. 'Beautiful. How can we be sad when we're looking at that? Now, let's see if we can't put a smile back on your face.'

'I'm just being stupid.' I looked up at the sky, already streaked with red and pink and dotted with stars starting to sparkle. My head was beginning to hurt from too much thinking and not enough mai tais. 'Like you said, it's only been a couple of days. How upset can I really be over someone I've known a couple of days?'

'I asked Jane to marry me a week after we met,' Al said, stroking his beard. I couldn't say why but it really did seem to give his statement more gravitas. 'I knew right away that she was the one for me.'

'You proposed after a week?' I blew a stray strand of hair away from my face and smiled. 'That's incredible. You just knew? Both of you?'

'Well, she didn't say yes right away.' He laughed like Brian Blessed and it made me so happy. 'It took me another three months to wear her down.'

'What made her change her mind?' I asked, trying to imagine a young Al courting his sweetheart. Nope, couldn't do it. All I could see was Santa down on one knee in front of Mrs Claus.

'She said she'd never met anyone who made her so angry and so happy at the same time,' he said with a wistful smile. 'And really, I didn't give her a lot of choice. Once I set my mind to something, I don't let it get away. Life's too short for dilly-dallying.'

'Isn't it a bad thing when someone makes you angry?' A memory of my mum and dad screaming at the kitchen table while I tried to eat my spaghetti hoops in peace popped into my mind. 'I mean, aren't you supposed to marry your best friend?'

'She was my best friend,' he replied with a firm nod. 'Doesn't mean we always agreed on everything. But we understood each other. She brought out the best in me, challenged me to keep going. You've got to have that spark, that little kick, otherwise it gets boring.'

I wrinkled my nose and wondered whether or not he was right. Amy always said the reason she and Dave didn't work out was because they were too alike, that she was bored; but that was what made me love Charlie so much. I loved that he could finish my sentences; I loved that he knew how I wanted my tea without having to ask. We never fought. He never made me sad. Well, not intentionally. Charlie always told me how clever I was, how he was so impressed by whatever I was doing. He knew everything about me and I knew everything about him. We were the perfect fit. But now, with Nick . . . I couldn't think of anyone who made me so mad so easily. He clearly thought he was much more intelligent than I was, that he knew better than I did, that he was some sort of sexual superman. But I wanted him so badly. The idea of him and Paige together at the waterfall made my skin crawl. I could live with knowing he wasn't mine, but the idea of him being with someone else, right now, was another thing altogether. I looked down at my hands, curled into tight little fists. All the better to punch him with.

'Tell me about the photos you've been taking.' Al interrupted my reverie with a cough and a question. 'You must have got some beauties around the island?'

'I have,' I nodded. 'This place is gorgeous. But I am not looking forward to tomorrow.'

'Ah, the models.' He pulled a thoughtful face. 'Well, won't that be interesting?'

'It will be interesting,' I confirmed. That was an under-statement. 'The art director has this ridiculous concept planned . . . I don't know. It feels weird to me. But what do I know?'

'You are the photographer,' Al reminded me. 'So I should imagine you know quite a bit?'

'This is true,' I said, taking a breath. 'I am Vanessa the photographer. Good point.'

'I do like you, Vanessa,' he said, giving me another

blast of his booming laugh. 'You're a little bit odd, like all the best people.'

'Thank you.' I laughed back and felt myself relax just a fraction. 'Let's hope the models feel the same. I'm starting to panic a bit. Pre-shoot nerves, I suppose.'

'You'll be fine. You know you will. You're definitely someone who doesn't walk away from something until it's right, I can tell,' he said. 'Takes a perfectionist to know one.'

'I guess.' He would definitely have been right about me once upon a time. I bit my lip and looked him right in the sparkly old eye. 'I just . . . I don't know. I've had so much stuff go wrong lately. I really, really need this to go well. It's like, if I can get this right, maybe everything else will be all right as well. If I can just make one thing perfect, I can get the rest of my life back on track.'

'That's a lot of pressure to put on one photograph,' Al said. 'I don't want to worry you, but I'm not entirely sure that's the way life goes.'

'Well, in that case,' I said, breathing in through gritted teeth, 'let's just hope the models don't tear me to tiny little pieces.'

'Models.' He made a noise that sounded a bit like a cat throwing up. 'I'll never understand it. Such a funny thing. Women are odd creatures.'

'Models?' I asked. 'I don't think they actually count as women. They're a different species. I honestly think it must say so on their passports.'

'It just never made sense to me,' he said with a chuckle. 'Male models aren't as rich as female models because men don't want to look at a better version of themselves in a jumper they're about to buy. And yet women insist on putting these perfect-looking creatures in clothes that have been pulled and pinched and altered beyond all recognition and then spend six months out of the year starving and crying because they don't look like the model in the dress when they buy it. Of course they don't look like the model! No one looks like a model. You're all mad.'

'No, I'm with you.' I couldn't really argue with the man – he was perfectly correct. 'Fashion magazines are not my friends.'

'Really?' He looked at me and smiled. 'I'd keep that to myself tomorrow if I were you.'

I blushed and nodded. I wished there was a Wisdom of Al app for my iPhone. If nothing else, maybe I could just record his laugh and play it whenever I got a bit down.

'Now, I've got to go and see a man about a dog,' he said, jumping up and yanking his surfboard out of the sand. I made a mental note to enroll in yoga classes when I got home and hoped he hadn't heard my knees crack as I staggered to my feet. 'And I imagine you have to go and do some fabulous fashiony photography things.'

'Not really, but I could pretend I have if that would help?'

With a surfboard under one arm, he gave me a scouting salute with the other. 'Have a lovely evening, Vanessa. I do believe this chat has given us both quite a lot to think about.'

He was not wrong.

CHAPTER FOURTEEN

Starving, emotionally exhausted and without a drop of booze in the entire cottage, I called the main house in search of something to eat and lots of things to drink, but instead of sending down dinner, they sent down my fairy gayfather. Fifteen minutes later, Kekipi had selected me an outfit from the clothes Paige had left, brushed my hair out into loose waves and waited patiently while I cack-handedly applied as much make-up as I knew how. If I was going to hag it up in Hawaii, I was going to do it properly. I knew I'd achieved the look we were going for when I emerged from the bedroom to a double thumbs-up from Kekipi.

'You look like a princess,' he confirmed, hurrying me out of the door before I could look in a full-length mirror. I did not look like a princess. I looked like someone wearing a too-tight-in-the-boobs black lace dress that was so short I was fairly certain you could see where babies came from, and enough make-up to make the average *Real Housewife* gasp in horror.

'Where are we going?' I asked, pressing my nose against

the glass of the black town car he bundled me into as we cruised out of Bennett's giant gates and onto the open road.

'Waikiki,' Kekipi replied. 'My job is to keep you entertained, and I can't think of anything more entertaining than filling you up with cocktails and seeing what happens. Especially since your fellow fashion compadres are all either AWOL or knocked out on Night Nurse.'

I made myself laugh. I didn't care what Paige and Nick got up to. I just wished Paige had better taste in men. And I wished Nick's penis would shrivel up and fall off.

'So if we're going to Waikiki, where are we now?' I was not very clear on my Hawaiian geography and was becoming increasingly upset about leaving the beach behind for what looked suspiciously like Doncaster town centre. In the fifteen minutes we'd been in the car, we'd already passed three McDonald's drive-thrus.

'Hawaii 101.' Kekipi brushed some imaginary dust from the shoulder of his impeccable navy blue polo shirt and then fanned out his hands. 'The state is made up of hundreds of islands, but there are eight main islands. Of those, the most densely populated is Oahu, which is where you are now.'

'You hate giving this lecture, don't you?' I asked, brushing some very real dust off my shoulder and fanning my hands out to check for grubby fingernails. I shouldn't have bothered.

'Yes,' he replied. 'The Bennett estate is in Kailua, a small town on the windward side of the island, and around twelve miles to the south of Kailua is the city of Honolulu. Waikiki is a neighbourhood in Honolulu. With me?'

I nodded.

'Waikiki is famous for its beach. It's where the majority of Hawaii's tourists visit and where most of the nightlife is on the island.'

'So it's a good place?' I asked, shaking out my long, loose waves. 'It's cool?'

'That I did not say.' Kekipi slapped my hands away from my hair and pulled it all over one shoulder. 'But it's better than going to play half-price games at Dave & Busters in the mall. Just barely. There. Now don't touch your hair again or I will have to slap you.'

'Yes, boss.' I placed my hands in my lap and pressed my lips together, gnawing nervously on the bottom one. And then remembered I was wearing lipstick for the first time in eleven years and stopped. Then immediately did it again. Being a girl was hard.

'Now, tell me everything that's happening with Mr Miller.' Kekipi leaned across the small, glass-topped table and opened his wide brown eyes. 'Should I be picking my maid-of-honour dress yet?'

'Before I start lying, can I ask whether or not there are security cameras in the cottages?' I groaned. His big, beautiful eyes lit up and his fluffy eyelashes fluttered.

'Two mai tais, please?' Kekipi ordered before our waiter could even open his mouth. Instead he gave us an unconcerned shrug and headed right back to the bar. 'They're both for you. Now, tell me everything.'

'I don't really know where to start.' I drummed my fingers against the table and looked to the heavens for an answer. They presented me with a clear, blue-black sky bedazzled with the brightest stars I'd ever seen, but they did not provide an answer. Bastards. 'It's all such a great big pile of bollocks.'

We were sitting at some swanky hotel pool bar by a beautiful marina in the center of Waikiki, as if Bertie Bennett, his Barbie dream house, Nick, Paige, the water-falls, the models, all of it, didn't exist. When you couldn't see the mountains, the flowers and the fruit and the endless miles of beach, you could be anywhere in the world. Well, anywhere with a marina full of beautiful sailing boats and dozens of so-hip-it-hurt American tourists. I'd spent so much time with Nick and Paige that it was easy to forget I was technically in America and not on the set of a very special episode of *Made in Chelsea*.

Kekipi took my silence with good humour for all of seventeen seconds, letting me soak in the ambience of the bar and the marina, before he could be quiet no longer.

'Vanessa, have you had sex with him or not?' The words literally exploded out of him, attracting the attention of at least four neighbouring tables. 'Because, yes, we do have security videos, but do not make me look at them. I don't want to see anything I don't have myself.'

'Good news, everyone,' I announced to my new friends at the other tables. 'I have had sex with him.'

'Is he hot?' an Australian girl with short blonde hair sitting two tables away asked loudly.

'He's *so* hot,' Kekipi replied before I could, 'that I've thought about drugging his coffee, just so I can sneak in and take a peek. If you know what I mean.'

'Everyone knows what you mean,' I hissed before turning to offer the Australian girl an awkward, all-teeth smile. 'He is quite hot.'

'Good on you, girly.' She held up her drink in a toast. 'Give him one for me.'

Where were my mai tais? I really wanted a drink.

'OK, so you've hit that.' Kekipi slapped the table to regain my attention. 'And while I will be needing each and every dirty detail, it seems as though you're conflicted, young grasshopper. For what reason I cannot even possibly begin to imagine. What's going on?'

Even though Kekipi was a thirty-something gay Hawaiian man sitting here waiting for cocktails and sharing boy banter, it almost felt as though I was back on the sofa at home with Amy. He had an amazing ability to make me feel comfortable, despite the fact that half the bar was still discussing my recent shag action, and so, for no good reason, I told him everything. Everything about Nick, anyway.

'It's so weird,' I said, gratefully accepting my drink, immediately inhaling the wedge of pineapple off the side and gulping down half the glass. I could not get drunk. I had to take photos of models in twelve hours. But one or two would be good – calm my nerves, help me sleep. 'I genuinely wasn't interested. That first night at dinner, I was like, yeah, he's handsome, but he's such a twat, and twat has never really been something that's done it for me.'

'I wish it didn't do it for me,' he replied, sipping his drink at half the speed I was making my way through mine. 'Something of a flaw of mine. It's not my fault, though – I'm gay.'

'Does being gay mean you only fancy arseholes?' I asked, pushing my drink ever so slightly away. Kekipi pushed it right back.

'Drink. And yes, of course it does. Now carry on.'

'Well, yeah, I didn't fancy him.' I sucked on the straw and peeked out at my date from under heavily made-up

245

lids and lashes. 'Right, OK, I fancied him. Objectively, I knew he was fanciable, but I didn't have designs on him.'

I felt myself making air quotes around the word 'designs' and stopped myself right away. It was an Old Tess thing to do.

'Clearly at some point you developed designs,' he said, copying my air quotes. 'What changed?'

'I've had a load of really shitty stuff happening at home,' I said. I felt that covered losing my job, shagging my best friend, telling him I loved him, him telling me he didn't love me, finding out he'd shagged my awful flatmate and then assuming her identity and stealing her job. No need to go into specifics. 'And, I don't know – he got under my skin. And when I snapped, he was there. So I kissed him.'

'You kissed him?' Kekipi squealed. He was a man secure enough in his homosexuality that he had no interest in not reinforcing gay stereotypes. 'Just like that? Just kissed him?'

'Yes?' It clearly sounded just as unlikely to me as it did to him. Probably more so. Here was a man who had met a woman three days ago, and the only solid facts he had to go on while weighing her up was that she had shagged a complete stranger she was supposed to be working with and she really liked eating Cheetos. I was actually doing a much better job of being Vanessa than I could have anticipated.

'And then what? Why is it a problem? Or rather, why is it a great big pile of bollocks?'

'Because it's just sex.' I could barely say the words. It really was a miracle that I'd actually been able to do it in the first place. 'It is a press trip fling. It is purely physical.'

'But you like him,' Kekipi said.

'I don't know,' I replied, being as honest as I could possibly be. 'Because I love someone else.'

'Ah.' He winced. 'I see.'

'And I'm fairly sure –' I sighed heavily and downed the rest of my drink. It was practically just juice. I could barely taste any alcohol at all – 'he's shagging Paige as well.'

'What makes you think that?' He made the same concerned face as Amy. Half, *Tess, I'm listening*, and half, *Tess, are you being a paranoid psycho again?* 'Just because they're not home doesn't mean they're shagging.'

'No, but she basically told me she was planning to shag him, and then I saw them getting into the boat together, and I'm fairly certain he'd shag you if you were the only willing partner around. No offence.'

'None taken,' he said with conviction. 'So Paige likes Mr Miller? That doesn't mean Mr Miller likes Paige. I'm sure they were just . . . doing something.'

'Doing something?' I quirked an eyebrow so high I heard it ping off the moon.

'Something else,' he qualified. 'Work related. But more importantly, you saw them together and you were jealous?'

I half shook my head, half shrugged, and picked a great big glob of mascara out of the corner of my eye. 'I didn't say that.'

'Oh, you were.' He purred the last word as though he was the cat that had caught the canary. Or got the cream. Or eaten the canary and then had some cream for afters. 'So even though it's just sex and you are in love with someone else, you don't like the idea of him being with someone else. Interesting.'

'No it isn't,' I said, even though it clearly was.

'We'll put a pin in that.' He pinched his shoulders and moved on. 'What exactly did Paige tell you about Mr Miller?'

'That she likes him, that he's a professional shagger, that I'm a horrible person for sleeping with him when she likes him,' I replied. 'I added that last part.'

The waiter sauntered back towards our table, yawned loudly and picked up my empty glass.

'Could I have another, please? When you've got a minute?' I asked as politely as possible.

He looked at me, looked at Kekipi, and walked away without answering.

'Everyone here is an asshole,' Kekipi said, just loudly enough for the waiter to hear. Not that he reacted. I assumed he was either really high, really rude or semi-lobotomized. 'But they really do have the best cocktails. When we're smashed, we'll go across the street to the horrible dive bar and sing karaoke.'

'I can't get smashed,' I said with a tiny hiccup that hardly supported my argument. 'I've got the shoot tomorrow.'

'You'll be fine,' he promised. 'I won't let you get too wasted. But back to the story – tell me more about this man at home.'

'You don't think I'm horrible for sleeping with Nick when I knew Paige liked him?'

'I don't think we're in tenth grade, so I don't think it matters. They're not together, he didn't cheat, you didn't cheat.' He rapped his knuckles against my forehead. 'And I think if a man that hot was coming on to me – and make no mistake about it, Vanessa, he was coming on to you at dinner on Monday night; I was there, I saw

– then I think someone would have to hit me with a truck to stop me sleeping with him.'

But I still couldn't shake the thought that I had cheated on Paige. I knew she'd be pissed, especially after the real Vanessa had boffed her ex. I was becoming altogether too good at playing my part.

'Tell me more about this man you're in love with. I'm assuming it's not a happily-ever-after-type affair?' Kekipi drank the last dregs of his cocktails as the waiter wandered back over with our fresh drinks and held out the empty glass without a word. The waiter took it and stood beside us, silent, staring.

'Is everything OK?' I asked. He looked like someone had just run over his cat.

'I need, like, a credit card or something?' He blinked at me once and held out a hand. 'And, uh, do you want food?'

'We do not want food, and here is a credit card.' Kekipi handed him a black American Express card and waved him along. 'Honestly, I hate being rude to wait staff – I have been wait staff – but I'm really worried he's off his medication.'

I laughed, wondering how many waiters on Oahu had black Amexes, but nodded along all the same.

'So, man at home, wiki wiki.' He clapped his hands again. 'On a scale of one to Nick, how hot? And what's the relationship status?'

'Definitely Nick hot. Just, different. Just, not Nick.' I found it really hard to compare the two in my mind. Nick was all fire and physical and total frustration. Charlie was . . . Charlie was everything. 'He's my best friend, I've been in love with him since uni – since college – and we finally did the deed a week ago and then I told him I loved him and then he said he didn't love me. Oh, and I found out he's been shagging one of my mates.'

Once again skipping over the details on anything Vanessa-related.

'Hmm, tough one.' He leaned back in his chair and pursed his full lips. 'But I'm going to say your friend is a douchebag and you should probably fake a pregnancy to make Nick marry you.'

'Considered, practical advice,' I said, nodding slowly, a smile on my face. 'My friend is a douchebag.' It felt so good to say it. 'But I think Nick probably is a douchebag too.'

'Nick is definitely a douchebag. If he met the douchebag tribe out in the jungle, they would worship him and make him their king. But, and I say this with love –' he gestured at me to drink my drink. I didn't need telling twice – 'it sounds to me like your baby box is lonely. It's sad and it's lonely. It needs a friend and I think you should let him be that friend.'

'You remind me so much of my Amy,' I laughed. Second hiccup. What was in these drinks? 'She would agree with you.'

Speak of the devil and she showed her horns. I peered inside my bag to see my phone lit up with two missed calls and a voicemail from my best friend. I wanted to call her back right away, but I didn't want to be rude to Kekipi. One day my mind was going to explode from trying to make everyone happy. Placing my bag back on the table, I decided to concentrate on the gay at hand and call Amy first thing in the morning. She would totally understand.

'Amy's not the best friend, right? I'm not missing

something very important here, am I?' he asked, a look
of concern on his handsome face.

'Nope, she's the other best friend. The only best friend
now, I suppose.' I was starting to feel very strongly about
everything I said. These cocktails were the best. 'She's
amazing. I love her.'

'You love everyone.' Kekipi flapped a hand at me.
'You'll be proposing to me next.'

'One more of these and I will,' I agreed. 'So, tell
me more about this karaoke bar.'

'What are you going to sing?' I shouted as loudly as I
possibly could over a group of three Japanese tourists
merrily murdering an Adele song. The karaoke bar was
everything Kekipi had promised. Dark, dingy and, most
importantly, attached to a twenty-four-hour diner. While
I was fine with my frozen pineapple daiquiri for the time
being, it was good to know that I was never more than
seven minutes away from some bacon.

'I don't know,' Kekipi wailed back. 'I don't want to be
a cliché.'

'What do you want to be?' I asked.

'Fabulous?' he suggested, complete with jazz hands.
'Obviously.'

'You're such a cliché,' I said with a half-hug. 'Just bust
out some Cher and be done with it.'

I left him poring over the song book and took myself
for a wander around the bar. Not that there was that
much bar to wander around. Sipping on a neon-pink
straw and bobbing my head to the music, such as it was,
I tiptoed through the groups of sunburned American
tourists chugging beers and the not-at-all-sunburned
Australians chatting away to some happy-looking locals

while a group of Japanese men in suits and loosened ties studied another copy of the massive song book. Other than the professional karaoke-goers, I saw so many men in Hawaiian shirts. And there was me thinking that was just on the telly. Pulling at my hem and pawing at my hair, I found an empty bar stool and decided it was time for a sit-down. Nana was tired. And a bit tipsy.

'But only a bit,' I said out loud to a passing cocktail waitress with a pretty blue flower behind her ear. What had Nick said about flowers? I couldn't remember. Not that it mattered. 'What does Nick know?'

'Sorry?' An exceptionally tall, exceptionally blond and, if you liked the square-jawed six-pack surfer type, exceptionally good-looking man sat down on the bar stool next to me. 'Nick?'

'He thinks –' I poked the icy bits left in the bottom of my glass with my straw – 'that he is so clever. He thinks he knows everything.'

'Right.' The guy laughed. I eyed him carefully and tried to decide whether I had heard an Australian accent or whether he just looked so much like Vinnie from *Home and Away* that I was adding one into the hot mix. 'That Nick, eh?'

Nope, he was definitely Australian. I had always had a soft spot for an Aussie. Most of the Australian men I met in London were tall. I liked tall. Most of them were gorgeous. I liked gorgeous. Most of them weren't interested. I didn't like that as much.

'He's a complete cock,' I confided in my new friend. 'But you know, whatever.'

'I believe you.' He held out his big, strong hand and I shook it, trying very hard not to giggle. 'I'm Owen.'

'I'm . . .' I paused and looked off to the left. 'Vanessa?'

'Is that a made-up name?' Owen asked, signalling to the bartender. 'You don't sound so sure about it.'

'It's not made up.' I shook my head vehemently and almost immediately fell off my stool. I covered up with a cough and casually slipped back up onto the pleather upholstery. 'It's definitely my name.'

'All right then.' He shifted his whole body to face me and leaned one very brown elbow on the bar. 'What's that you're drinking?'

'It's delicious,' I replied, slurping the last little bit through my straw. 'But I do not remember what it is called.'

Owen took the glass from me and knocked back the icy remains, never once breaking eye contact. All of a sudden, I was all of a fluster. I wasn't good at talking to boys and I was even worse at talking to men. Where was Amy when I needed her? In stupid England, that was where. She was so selfish.

'Pineapple daiquiri, delicious. Can I buy you another?' Owen asked, interrupting my chain of thought. He had very pretty blue eyes. Like Nick. Only not, because he wasn't a knob. Probably. He could be. Most of them were . . .

'Vanessa?' He leaned in a little closer.

'That,' I poked him gently in the shoulder, 'is my name.'

'OK then.' Despite the slightly troubled look on his face, he turned to the bartender and ordered two more daiquiris and then turned back to me. 'What brings you to Hawaii, Vanessa?'

For a reason I couldn't quite put my finger on, hearing this great big strapping surfer address me with Vanessa's name really made me chuckle. It took me a moment to choke down a laugh and compose myself well enough to answer.

'I am a photographer,' I replied with a winning smile. Or at least I hoped it was a winning smile – there was a chance I had lipstick all over my teeth. 'And I'm taking pictures for a magazine.'

'That's interesting,' he said, paying the bartender for our grown-up Slush Puppies and brushing his hair behind his ears. He had sexy ears. 'You're not a surfer, then?'

'I am not,' I confirmed.

'Right, right.' He took a deep breath in through his nose and exhaled slowly. 'I'm a surfer, myself. Chasing the waves. Waikiki has the best waves in the world.'

'Isn't the best surf up on the north shore?' I asked, not exactly sure how I knew that. 'And isn't it better in winter?'

'Uh, nah, definitely down here.' Owen pushed my drink towards me and held his up in a toast. 'To Hawaii.'

'Hawaii,' I repeated, searching my memory banks for the source of my stellar surfing knowledge. Was it from *Point Break*? Charlie loved *Point Break*. Actually, I loved *Point Break*. But no . . .

'And to new friends,' he added before taking a massive swig of yellow slush. 'Christ, that's cold.'

'Oh, that's my friend.' I buzzed into life and pointed at the stage with teenage-girl excitment as Kekipi took the mic. 'I came with him.'

'Came with him, came with him?' Owen raised a concerned eyebrow. Also blond. Pierced. Again, very sexy.

'Well, no.' I looked at him like he was very stupid. Which I was starting to realize in all likelihood he was. 'Obvs.'

'Obvs?' He didn't seem to understand until Kekipi screamed out, 'Whitney Houston, gone but never forgotten,' before giving what was actually a surprisingly good performance of 'I'm Every Woman'.

'Oh, obvs.' Owen seemed to get it quite quickly once Kekipi started dancing. Very well. 'He's gay?'

'He's gay as a goose,' I nodded.

He seemed confused. Again. 'Are geese gay?' he asked.

'I don't know.' I looked into my lurid yellow drink and was suddenly overcome with the intense desire to not be drinking it any more. 'It seemed right when I said it.'

'Yeah, I guess like you thought you knew about surfing,' he said with an extraordinarily patronizing laugh. Before I could decide how I felt about it, I watched him place his large, tanned hand on my thigh. My eyes travelled slowly from said hand, up his muscular arm, across his broad, tight-T-shirt-covered chest and up to his handsome face. 'Am I right, Vanessa?'

I stopped and breathed for a moment. It shouldn't have been so hard to think clearly – I'd barely had anything to drink. Or at least I couldn't remember having had that much to drink. Maybe I'd lost track once me and Kekipi had started the boy talk. And we did have those shots while he was telling me all about his ex, the male burlesque dancer.

'Vanessa.' Owen squeezed my thigh a little bit higher up than I was entirely comfortable with. 'How about we finish these drinks and get out of here? I reckon your mate can do without you, don't you think?'

I was torn. Tess would make an awkward excuse, go to the bathroom and try to sneak off home without him seeing her. Vanessa would have gone to the bathroom as well but only to take off her knickers and save him a job in the taxi.

'I don't feel very well,' I replied, slipping off the stool with all the grace of a drugged monkey and pushing people out of the way until I got to the ladies' loos. I dug through my handbag, spilling lip balms and old receipts and sticks of chewing gum all over the floor, trying to find my phone. After poking everything in the bottom of the bag and breaking an already manky nail into the bargain, I bashed something that lit up and pulled it out. I had four missed calls from Amy. Backing into a stall and flapping at the lock at the same time, I sat down on the toilet seat and pressed redial. I needed to hear her voice.

'Thank fuck for that,' she yelled. 'I thought you were dead!'

Maybe I didn't need to hear her voice.

'What are you doing? You were supposed to call me every day?' She didn't even pause for breath. 'What's going on? Are you in prison?'

'I'm in a karaoke bar,' I whispered as loudly as I dared. I was suddenly gripped with the fear that Owen would come into the toilets looking for me. 'Why would I be in prison? Are you OK?'

'Why can't I hear karaoke then?' Amy wanted her own questions answered before she got to mine. 'Hmm?'

'Because I'm in the lav?' I offered.

'Tess Brookes, if you are having a slash while you're on the phone to me, we're going to fall out.' Once again, she was using a volume and a pitch that a pre-puberty Justin Bieber would have found difficult to emulate. 'Call me back, you filthy mare.'

'I'm not having a . . .' I couldn't bring myself to say

it. 'I'm just in the toilet. I'm hiding from a man. My friend is singing Whitney.'

'Friend?' She was immediately suspicious. 'Is this the hot guy?'

'He's gay,' I replied.

'The hot guy is gay?' she asked.

'No, not my hot guy guy.' I answered. 'But the gay guy is hot.'

'And where is your hot guy?'

'He's not my hot guy. I'm with the gay.'

'So you're out with a hot gay guy and not the hot guy who isn't gay?'

Now I was confused.

'Why would I be in prison?' I pressed my entire face against the cold metal of the toilet stall and sighed. It felt lovely. And then I remembered I was in a toilet stall and that was disgusting. I rubbed at my cheek with toilet paper and made a very unattractive face. I was almost definitely going to throw up.

'Um, the whole identity theft thing?' she reminded me.

'I don't think you can go to prison for that,' I said, a hot feeling flushing across my face, followed by a very unpleasant cold sweat. Bleurgh. 'I haven't, like, taken out credit cards in her name or anything.'

'No, you've just stolen loads of her stuff and are using her name to get a job,' Amy reasoned. 'Totally legal. Anyway, tell me everything. I need an update.'

'Aims, I've got to go,' I said, now desperate to puke and convinced that Interpol would be outside with a warrant for my arrest. Oh, to go back in time by five minutes when the only thing I had to worry about was a vaguely rapey Australian who knew nothing about surfing. 'I'll call you later.'

'You won't, though,' she wailed. 'Talk to me now. I miss you.'

'Amy, seriously.' I retched as delicately as possible and crashed forward, kneeling on the floor and trying to wheel around in the tiny cubicle. It was like trying to get a Chieftain tank to do a three-point turn in a phone box. 'I've got to go. I'll call you later. I love you.'

I just managed to get my phone back in my bag and pull my hair up behind my head before I let out a spectacular technicoloured yawn into the toilet bowl. Sitting back against the metal partition, I panted, dabbing delicately at my mouth with toilet paper. I was such a lady. Even my puke was neon yellow.

'Nick told me about the surf,' I told the little white toilet paper dispenser, my voice full of awe. 'He told me this afternoon at the waterfall.'

'Of course he did,' the toilet dispenser said back to me in a squeaky, judgemental voice, 'because Nick knows everything.'

'Nick does know everything,' I agreed, hoping the toilet dispenser was taking the piss, like I was. I would be so mad if the inanimate object I was talking to was Team Knobhead. But it didn't have another answer. And so I leaned over the toilet, threw up once more, rinsed out my mouth at the tap and gave a very confused-looking Hawaiian woman a very serious nod on my way out.

'*Mahalo*,' I whispered.

Back in the bar, Kekipi was still on stage. The crowd didn't seem terribly enthused with his performance, which as far as I could tell was quite good. Then I realized I'd been in the toilets for fifteen minutes and he was singing a different song. Kekipi had taken the stage and he was not giving it back.

'Hey, Vanessa.'

Someone reached out and grabbed my arm. That someone was Owen.

'I wondered where you'd gone.' He loosened his grip slightly but did not let go. I did not like it. 'Where were you?'

'Throwing up,' I answered. Owen let go of my arm. 'I think I should go home.'

It was fascinating to watch whatever internal drama was going on inside his head play out on his handsome, simple face. Still sitting on the bar stool, I saw him weigh up his options. It was late, there weren't really any other girls in the bar, he had already bought me a drink and, to be fair, I'd been quite flirty. But I had also vomited. What would he do?

'Fuck it, let's go back to mine.' He tightened his grip again and hopped off his stool. 'Come on.'

'I don't want to go to yours,' I said, shaking my arm loose. 'Get off.'

'The lady said get off,' a voice boomed across the room, backed by a Casio keyboard version of 'I Don't Know How to Love Him'. 'Don't make me come over there.'

'Yeah, right,' Owen said with a wildly unattractive snigger. 'Gay as a goose.'

'What did you just call me?' Kekipi tossed the mic down on the stage and was across the bar in a heartbeat. Before six-foot-something Owen could react in any way, the five-foot-five estate manager had him bent backwards over the bar with a fistful of T-shirt in one hand and a fistful of punches in the other.

'Actually, that's my bad.' I flapped around, trying to insert myself in between the two men before any fisticuffs were actually thrown. 'I said it first. I may have got it from my nana. I am sorry.'

'Oh, don't worry, doll, it's adorable.' Kekipi released his grip on Owen and let him crumple to the floor. He slipped his arm through mine and, with the entire bar watching in complete silence, minus the Andrew Lloyd Webber soundtrack, we moseyed on out of the bar. 'How does the word McDonald's make you feel right now? I'm fricking starving.'

'I did a sick.' I tried to whisper but didn't seem to have a lot of control over my volume. 'But that sounds very nice.'

'Fucking fag and his hag,' I heard Owen mutter from the floor as we walked away. Pressing my hands down on Kekipi's shoulders to calm him, I held up one finger, turned back into the bar, and delivered one very firm, very direct kick straight to Owen's balls. The entire bar winced in unison.

'That's from the hag. Think yourself lucky the fag isn't going to knock you out,' I said before scrabbling to pull my hair over one shoulder and returning to an admiring look from Kekipi. 'So, you were saying something about McDonald's?'

CHAPTER FIFTEEN

I was halfway through my second McChicken Sandwich, curled up in the back of a big black limo and cruising along the starlit coastline, when Kekipi stopped slurping down his strawberry milkshake, carefully folded the empty cardboard box that had held his deep-fried banana pie, and threw it directly into my face.

'Vanessa Kittler?' he shouted.

'Yes?'

'You have to be one of my favourite guests ever to visit the estate,' Kekipi announced with some ceremony. 'You've been here for no time, you've already banged a hot guy, thrown up out of a moving vehicle and kicked another hot guy in the balls. You are a superstar. I'm totally going to add you on Facebook.'

'Oh, I'm not on Facebook,' I said, lying so smoothly, even I believed me. 'I hate that stuff.'

'Total superstar,' he said with absolute certainty. 'I wish I had your appetite for life.'

'I wish you had my appetite for fried food,' I grumbled, still gorging on the sandwich. 'I'm going to be seventeen stone heavier when I get home. I just threw up – why am I eating this?'

But if eating a McDonald's when you were drunk was wrong, I didn't want to be right.

'It's not like I've had a bad life,' Kekipi mused, ignoring me and staring out of the darkened glass. 'I love my job, I love my home, I love singing karaoke until people shout at me. But, you know, I kind of wish I'd done more. I wish I had as much confidence in myself as you have.'

'Me?' I stopped eating and looked around the back seat of the car. There had to be someone else he was talking to, surely.

'Absolutely.' He looked as though whatever he was getting at was obvious. 'You jet around the world taking photographs in glamorous locations, a handsome lover here, a handsome lover there, heartbreak at home and love on the horizon. You're fun, you're smart, and when you actually make an effort, you're very cute. Add in a feisty kick to the nuts and you've got one hell of a woman. You could be the Grace to my Will. Hell, if we got you some new shoes, you could be the Carrie to my Stanford.'

'That is the nicest thing anyone has ever said to me,' I replied with a sniff. And it more or less was. Shame it was all a load of bollocks. 'But really, three hundred and sixty days out of the year, I'm just your normal, boring girl, standing in the kitchen eating Dairylea Triangles in front of the fridge because she can't be arsed to decide what to make for dinner.'

'I don't know what a Dairylea Triangle is,' he said, one hand held out in front of him as he spoke. 'And I don't care to. I do have one question, though.'

Imagine a world without Dairylea . . .

'Which is?'

'Aside from him being a rapey, homophobic asshole, how come you didn't make out with the hot guy in the bar?'

'That's not reason enough?' I asked.

'If someone that cute was hitting on me, we wouldn't have had an involved enough conversation for any of that to get in the way,' he shrugged. 'I saw you talking to him for a while. How come you didn't just pounce like the sex panther I know you are.'

'Firstly, I'm more of a sex sloth,' I explained. 'And secondly, I actually don't know. There was just something bothering me. Bar hook-ups have never really been the thing that floats my boat.'

'Because you're a smitten kitten for the boy back home?' he asked.

'I don't know,' I replied. I thought of Charlie and felt a little bit sick.

'Or because you're a smitten kitten for Mr Miller?' he asked.

'I don't know,' I replied. I thought of Nick and felt very sick.

'Interesting.' Kekipi took a sip from the biggest Diet Coke I had ever seen and wriggled his eyebrows. 'Very interesting.'

'Stupid,' I groaned and munched on the last bit of my sandwich. 'Very stupid.'

Somewhere between my second fried chicken sandwich and an existential crisis, I passed out in the back of the limo and didn't stir until the door I was leaning against opened abruptly and I tumbled out onto the soft, fresh grass.

'I'm awake,' I yelped as Kekipi hauled me to my feet. 'But I think I might die. What time is it?'

'You won't die,' he promised, even though he didn't sound entirely sure. 'And it's not even two a.m. You really are a lightweight.'

'I love you too,' I smiled and pawed his face. My hands were sticky. He did not smile back. 'I like it when you sing and everyone else hates you.'

'That's almost fifty percent compliment,' he replied. 'Oh. Well, look at this.'

I wasn't sure what I was supposed to be looking at, given that I was far too busy trying to put one foot in front of the other until I was in my bed. Really, I was more tired than drunk, but neither was a great look on me.

'And what have you two been up to?'

With a very loud sigh, I rolled my head off Kekipi's shoulder, opened my eyes and groaned. Nick. He was sitting on the white wooden chair in front of my door, battered paperback book in hand, still in the same clothes I'd seen him wearing earlier that evening. When he was getting into a boat with Paige.

'Oh, God,' I muttered under my breath. 'Piss off.'

'Mr Miller.' Kekipi resumed his calm, reassuring, professional tone and nodded genially at Nick while sticking an elbow in my ribs. 'Could you possibly help me with the door? Ms Kittler is a little fatigued this evening.'

'So I see,' he replied. I couldn't bring myself to look at his face, but that annoying, bemused tone was back in his voice. 'Rough day, Vanessa?'

'I've already kicked one bloke in the bollocks tonight. Give me a reason to make it two. Please.'

'You know what, Kekipi, I can take it from here.' Against my will, I felt Nick manhandle me out of Kekipi's arms and scoop me up like a rag doll. Which would have been hot if I weren't super pissed off, covered in Kekipi's milkshake and about seven minutes away from throwing up again. The second my feet lost contact with the floor, my stomach lost contact with every single thing that was inside it. 'I'll make sure Ms Kittler gets to bed.'

'Of course,' he replied courteously. 'Good night, Ms Kittler. I'll bring coffee with your wake-up call.'

'Bring drugs.' I felt my entire body roll with nausea as Nick tossed me over his shoulder. 'Hard drugs.'

'I've been waiting out here for hours,' he said, pushing through my door and stalking straight into the bedroom. 'Why didn't you answer your phone?'

'You didn't call my phone?' I said carefully as I observed his bottom from this interesting new angle. And tried not to throw up on it. 'I had it with me all night.'

'I called you three times and left a message.' He set me down on the bed and pushed my hair back off my face. 'What is all this shit in your hair?'

'McFlurry.' I flapped my hands at him to push him away. Ahhh, bed. Sweet, wonderful bed. 'You did not call me.'

'Vanessa, I did call you.' Nick looked stern. 'Your voicemail sounds weird.'

Oh dear. Oh dear me.

'How did you get my number?' I asked, already knowing the answer. Oh dear-dear-dear-dear-dear.

'From the call sheet,' he said, pulling off my shoes and rubbing my feet gently. It was annoyingly lovely.

Nick was right – he had called Vanessa. But he hadn't called me. And now her dead BlackBerry, sitting on her

265

nightstand back in London, was full of voicemails from a man in Hawaii trying to have sex with her. Or me. I couldn't help but think even she would be a bit confused by that. It's not like she was a stranger to the booty call, but a man in Hawaii she'd never met before? That was really pushing the envelope, even for Vanessa.

'Oh.' It was very hard to think fast enough to cover my tracks. Or think at all. 'That phone is not here.'

'It's an old number?' Nick asked, coming up with an obvious solution that I couldn't quite manage. 'An old phone?'

'Yes.' I patted his leg and smiled. Clever boy. 'Old number. Night-night.'

And with that I rolled face first into my pillows and closed my eyes.

'Don't you think you should probably, I don't know, wash that mess out of your hair before you go to sleep? Or have a shower?' he suggested, pinching my toes. 'You'll never get it out in the morning.'

'There's nothing in my hair,' I said from within my pillowy sanctuary. 'Go away.'

'Looks like booze, but it could be puke, I'm not sure,' he replied. 'And I used to have a Mohawk that I set with sugar water, so I know. You will literally never get it out if you don't wash it now. Come on.'

Once again against my will, Nick picked me up and carried me into the bathroom. I could hear myself making reluctant mewing noises, but I didn't fight him. Because I couldn't. Regardless of the E-numbers in my drinks and the obscene calorific value of my Maccy Ds, I had zero energy. He set me down on a the chair in the bathroom and started running the hot tap.

'Maybe take your make-up off as well,' Nick said,

holding a white wash cloth under the running water. 'You look as though a very angry toddler has been at your face with a pack of felt tips.'

I looked in the mirror. He was right. I kind of liked it.

'Yeah, well, I'm not Paige, so blah blah blah.' I wrinkled my nose and pulled my head backwards every time he tried to rub the warm flannel on my skin. It was too hot but I didn't have enough control of my vocabulary to tell him that. Or anything else, really.

'So blah?' He persevered with the flannel, tenderly wiping away whatever make-up was left underneath my eyes. 'What are you on about?'

'You and Paige.' I wiped my eyes dry with the backs of my sticky hands so I could look at him properly. 'You went to the waterfall with her.'

'No, I didn't,' he said, rubbing the dirty marks off the back of my paws altogether less tenderly. 'Seriously, what have you been drinking?'

'You got in the boat with her – I saw you,' I said, grabbing the flannel from him and scrubbing at my face until it was both ice cream-free and red raw. 'So why are you here?'

'I did get in the boat with her,' he agreed. 'But we didn't go to the waterfall. She wanted to go to some ridiculous romantic place for dinner, but because I didn't want to lead her on, I suggested a boat ride.'

'Oh, because a boat ride around Hawaii isn't romantic, is it?' I said, pressing my palms to my cheeks. There was a chance I'd been a bit too enthusiastic with the flannel. It was possible that when I took my hands away, I wouldn't actually have any skin left.

'Not when I know she gets seasick,' he replied, sheepish. 'We were on a job together once in Croatia and everyone went on this boat thing at the end, but she spent the entire trip with her head over the side. I know it was a dick move, but I didn't want to piss her off.'

'You couldn't just say "Sorry, Paige, not interested" and move on?' I looked in the mirror over his shoulder. I appeared to be doing a pretty good impression of Macaulay Culkin in *Home Alone*. Sort of ruined my credibility in the conversation. 'You had to propose a lovely sunset boat trip.'

'Well, there's every chance I'm not thinking straight at the moment,' he snapped. Ooh, testy. 'What with sitting around like a wanker waiting for this old mental to decide whether he's going to give me an interview, not knowing whether I'm coming or going when it comes to you, not to mention not even knowing where I'm going to be living next week. I'm sorry if my shit solution to my awkward problem doesn't work for you.'

'What do you mean you don't know whether you're coming or going when it comes to me?' I released my left cheek. Nope, not ready. Ow-ow-motherfucking-ow. I must have caught the sun at the waterfall this afternoon. I hoped that was all I'd caught.

'Let's not have this conversation right now.' Nick's tone shifted immediately. He laid his hands over mine and leaned towards me until our noses were almost touching. 'Let's not have any conversation right now.'

I closed my eyes and parted my lips, just ever so slightly. He smelled good. He felt warm. Through the warm, fuzzy rum haze my body reacted and suddenly woke up. Luckily, so did my brain.

'No,' I said sharply, pushing him away. Dear God, my face was sore. I tried to stand up but was too confident in my abilities and immediately fell back down onto the chair. 'No, I am not having sex with you.'

'Why not?' Nick was still doing his best to sound playful but I could see he wasn't sure whether or not I was teasing. 'Come to bed, Vanessa. I've been thinking about you all evening. I think I might actually be going mad.'

'No,' I repeated, looking at the floor. I wasn't sure I was going to be able to stick to my guns if I actually looked at him. The shock of the pretty was still too powerful. 'You don't just have sex with people. You think you do, but you're sad and I'm sad and you don't.'

'All right, you're just not making sense now,' he said. Even his feet were good feet. I looked at my feet. They were not good feet. 'Let's just get you into bed and I'll leave you in peace, OK?'

'I can get myself into bed,' I replied, slapping his hands off me as he tried to pull me upright. 'You're not in charge of me. You don't know best. You're not my boyfriend. You're not anything.'

'You are a fun drunk,' he groaned, pressing my wind-milling arms to my side and directing me towards the bedroom. 'Fingers crossed you're a forgetful one. You're not going to feel good about this in the morning.'

'You're not going to feel good about this in the morning,' I repeated. As insults went, it wasn't my best of the evening. Eventually I gave up and let him walk me back towards the bed. I was shattered. 'You think you can just do it and it'll be fine because you're hand-some and clever and blah blah blah, but it's stupid because you don't love me and it's stupid. You shouldn't have sex with people you don't love because they love you and then everyone is sad and you're sad. And stupid.'

'Is this even about me?' Nick yanked the covers off the bed and plonked me onto the mattress, sans ceremony. 'Or is this about your mate back home? Because I genuinely have no idea what you're on about now. Do you want some water?'

'Not Charlie,' I said, pulling a most attractive face. I wrestled with my dress, trying to pull it over my head gracefully, but the tiny fraction of my brain that was sober and awake knew that ship had already sailed. 'We don't talk about Charlie.'

'His name is Charlie, then.' I heard a zip unfastening and then felt my dress whizzing over my head. Oh. It had a zip. Nick dropped the dress onto the floor and draped the covers over me. 'I'm going to get you some water and you're going to drink it all. Then you're going to sleep, right?'

'I might be sick,' I said in a tiny voice. All the fight had gone out of me, and when I closed my eyes, the room spun round and round and round.

'You won't be sick,' Nick sighed, kissing my forehead before disappearing off into the kitchen. 'I promise.'

He hadn't even started running the tap before I realized that was not a promise that he could possibly be expected to keep. Because I was absolutely, positively about to be sick. With new-found energy I pushed away the covers, scrambled into the bathroom and managed to lose my entire late-night snack into the toilet before he realized what was happening. I flushed quickly, not wanting Nick to see, and sat sweating on the cold tiles, waiting to see if there would be a second wave.

'Well.' Nick stood in the bathroom doorway, glass of water in one hand, bottle of Advil in the other. Damp, pale and red-eyed, I looked up at him and sniffed. Tall, tanned and hopelessly handsome, he looked down at me and smiled. I could have been mistaken, but it even seemed to be a real smile that made it all the way up to his eyes. 'Feel better?'

I shrugged, trying not to let any mewing sounds escape from my mouth, and held my hand out for the water.

'Sip it,' he ordered, passing me two Advil. 'Bed?'

'Bed,' I confirmed, handing the glass back and letting him help me to my feet without struggling. 'I want to go to sleep.'

We walked back to the bed in silence, Nick turning out the lights as we went and holding my hand until I was safely off my feet and in the bed. I lay in the semi-darkness, watching him unbuckle his belt and step out of his shorts. He pulled his shirt over his head without unbuttoning it and laid both things carefully on the back of my leather office chair.

'I'm staying to make sure you're OK,' he said, pulling the covers back on the opposite side of the bed. I rolled over to look at him with big, watery eyes. Oh, the crazy emotional rollercoaster that was a night on the lash. 'I'm not going to try to have sex with you because I'm sad.'

'I'm sorry,' I whispered, pulling the sheets up underneath my chin. 'I don't know what I'm doing.'

'Neither do I,' Nick said with a sigh, curling his arm underneath my shoulders and resting my head against his warm chest. 'Neither do I.'

CHAPTER SIXTEEN

In all of my days, I'd never been a good drinker. The
first time I'd ever got properly wasted was at university
during Fresher's Week. A sophisticated combination of
Archers and lemonade cocktails mixed with shots of
Aftershock led to my first ever puking-in-the-park
extravaganza. The only reason I knew that I'd passed
out in the student union toilets with my knickers round
my ankles after dancing on the bar and singing 'Oops!
. . . I Did it Again' by Britney over and over and over
was because Amy took lots and lots of photos. I lost
the will to live and she lost a shoe. After that, I tried
to lay off the sauce as much as was humanly possible
for a student, but I was terrible in the face of peer pressure and Charlie and Amy were not good peers for a
bad drinker.

So it shouldn't have been a surprise that I woke up
on Thursday morning with a headache that felt like it
could only be cured by a guillotine. Prising one eye open,
I turned off an alarm I didn't remember setting and rolled
carefully over to squint at my empty bed. Wasn't there

someone else in it when I fell asleep? I was almost certain
I hadn't imagined Nick's nursemaiding, but then again,
I was entirely certain I could pull off a red PVC catsuit
ten years ago. And I could not. Regardless, he definitely
wasn't there now. I peered under the covers to see that
my underwear was still safely upon my person, and even
though I felt like I might actually just die at any second,
I did have both my eyes open and, seemingly, full control
of all my faculties. Slowly, the events of the night started
to come back. Cocktails, Kekipi, karaoke. McDonald's,
shouting, puking and then sleeping. Yep, Nick had definitely been in my bed before. And now he'd vamoosed.
What a shock. I just wished I could remember the perti-
nent details of our conversation aside from my yelling,
his sighing and my throwing up. I had a nagging feeling
we'd discussed something important – I just didn't know
what it was.

When I regained the ability to focus properly, I looked
at the phone in my hand and saw several missed calls
from Amy. As well as three voicemails, there were more
than half a dozen texts, emails and Facebook messages
that were borderline death threats. I felt like calling my
mum and telling her I was being cyberbullied. Then I
remembered me and my mum weren't talking and I just
stuck the phone back on its charger and had a little cry.
It lasted for about seven seconds before I realized I needed
a wee far more than I needed to cry and I only had
enough energy to do one thing at a time.

'*Aloha*, Vanessa?'

From the bathroom I heard a knock at the front door,
followed by a familiar voice that split my head in two.
I grabbed onto the bathroom sink while washing my
hands and retched, but nothing happened. At least I

273

seemed to be fully puked out. Silver lining to every desperately pathetic cloud.

'I have coffee and breakfast and many headache remedies.'

The look on Kekipi's face as I appeared in the doorway was priceless.

'Are you dying?' he asked. 'Did you and Mr Miller do crack after I left?'

'I think I just shouted at him a lot and then threw up on myself a bit,' I said, staggering over to the coffee. It smelled so good. I had no idea whether or not I'd be able to keep it down. 'Thanks for this.'

'No problem.' He took a short step backwards. 'The cars are leaving for the shoot in forty-five minutes. Are you going to be OK? I feel dreadful.'

He felt dreadful? Wait, what? Cars? It took a moment before it dawned on me what he could possibly be talking about. The cars were leaving. For the shoot. The shoot was actually happening. Oh dear God.

'I will not be OK,' I said, pouring the coffee and trying to suppress the rising panic that was threatening to give me a heart attack. 'But I'll be dressed and holding a camera and hoping that somehow this thing gets cancelled again today.'

'Sadly, I don't think you're going to be so lucky,' he said, heaping three giant spoons of sugar into my cup and stirring for me. 'It would seem Ms Sullivan and Mr Bennett Junior have decided to press ahead without Mr Bennett senior.'

'Brilliant,' I muttered and took one tiny sip of the sugary sludge in my cup. It was magical. 'Well, it's not like I haven't got this far on horrible decisions, is it? Who knows, I might be a better photographer when I'm hammered.'

'I'll make a hangover picnic, and you make this human again,' he replied, waving his hand in my general direction. 'It's going to be a great day. And at least you don't smell of vomit.'

Once I was certain I could keep the coffee down, I drank it as quickly as I could and chased it with a sip of water and two headache tablets. After scrubbing myself down and cleaning my teeth for about seventeen minutes, I plaited my hair, pulled on my jeans, a little black T-shirt and my Converse, then carefully applied as much mascara as my eyelashes would hold. Putting on make-up seemed to be the only way to prove that I actually had eyes. With five minutes to go, I checked my camera bag. I had a million battery packs fully charged, I had all my lenses, all my memory cards, my tripod, my reflectors, light monitor, flash and a few other things that I wasn't entirely sure of but assumed were something a professional photographer was supposed to have. It was time.

'Right then,' I said to the mirror. My reflection, laden with bags, looked resolute and, oddly, not nearly as bad as I felt. But to be fair, that probably wasn't actually possible. 'Everything's been fine so far, hasn't it?'

My reflection didn't reply, but it did throw me a look that just seemed to say, 'Really, Tess?'

'Look at you,' Kekipi declared when I reappeared in the kitchen fully dressed and not on the verge of falling down. 'You look just like someone who went out and got wasted last night but is almost certainly capable of doing an adequate day's work.'

'That's the best I could hope for,' I replied, grabbing another cup of coffee and a second pastry. Pastries were good. Cocktails were bad. 'Are the cars here?'

'They are,' he said, craning his neck to look out of the

window. 'You're in with Ms Sullivan. The models are in together and I'll be travelling with Mr Bennett.

'You're coming?' I asked. He nodded and clapped. 'I'm so glad. If I go missing at all, can you just tell everyone I'm dead?'

'Sure thing,' he replied. 'But don't worry, really. You'll be fine – you're just a little hungover. Everyone's a professional here. What's the worst that could happen?'

'Oh my God, this is a complete fucking disaster.' Paige buried her face in her hands and stifled a scream. 'Tell me this isn't happening.'

'It's not happening?' I offered, resting my hand on her back and making small soothing circles. 'It's definitely not happening.'

But it was happening. As it turned out, I really shouldn't have been worried about my hangover. What I should have been worried about was an unforecast tropical storm, a model so doped up on whatever sleep aids she'd taken she couldn't stand up straight, a wardrobe selection so horrifying they made Lady Gaga's stage costumes look too conservative, and a location that had seemingly forgotten we were coming. There was something about a soggy, obese man from Arkansas in a neon-orange bumbag that really took the shine off an haute couture photo shoot. By eleven a.m. I was still in the back of the SUV drinking my fifth cup of coffee, and I hadn't even taken my camera out of its bag. Apart from to take a picture of the obese man from Arkansas. You didn't see a sight like him round Old Street.

'I don't know what to do,' Paige whispered at me, her face fearful and tear-stained. 'I'm amazing at this. I've directed shoots on the top of volcanoes, I've had the

Eiffel Tower closed down so Naomi fucking Campbell can have her picture taken in peace, I did an entire editorial on a yacht on Lake Como with an entirely Italian crew. I don't speak a word of Italian and I had violent seasickness all the way through it and still came home with the best pictures the magazine had ever seen. What am I going to do?'

As a photographer, there was really nothing I could say that would help. As a creative director, I was in agony for her. I'd had shoots and projects go wrong, but this was just chaos. She had managed to pull a feature out of her arse when Bertie went AWOL, and now she was stuck in the back of a car with no location, an amateur photographer, a stoned model and a disgruntled middle-aged man who had brought half of Lily Savage's wardrobe with him. I looked out of the window at the Iolani Palace. All the way here, Paige had been telling me about her concept, how amazingly beautiful it was, how we would have the models and Artie reclining on the white stone steps, leaning against palm trees, posing in the throne room. That it combined all the elegance and glamour of high fashion with the cultural significance of Hawaiian royalty. Right now, it looked like a wet weekend in Brighton. Even the fountain on the driveway looked sad. It must be tough to be a water feature when you're competing with a storm so scary. I was a little bit afraid our car might wash away.

'Ms Sullivan.' The car door opened and Kekipi stuck a soggy head inside. 'I've spoken with the manager on duty and he says he has no record of the booking and can't get in touch with the events coordinator. I think we're going to have to find a second venue.'

'I had one.' Paige rubbed her temples and closed her

eyes. 'But we're so behind schedule, I didn't reconfirm. Shit, I had a third and fourth venue, but they're all outdoors. And I can't rely on this stopping, can I?'

'I think it will, but we shouldn't bank on it,' he replied, looking up at the dark grey sky. 'I have an idea. Wait just a moment.'

'Not bloody going anywhere, am I?' she muttered, pulling out an iPad and scrolling madly up and down an email inbox. I had a feeling it wasn't really helping but I didn't want to say. I didn't dare say.

'You look nice.'

If in doubt, go with compliments.

'Thanks,' she replied without taking her eyes off the screen. 'It's Rag & Bone.'

'What did you get up to last night?' I asked, adding a little yawn to show how casual I was about the question. I didn't quite know whether or not to believe Nick's version of events when he'd shown up on my doorstep, but given that he was on my doorstep in the first place, I had to assume things hadn't gone quite to Paige's plans. 'Anything fun?'

'I don't really want to talk about it right now,' she said, looking up at me at last. Her black liquid liner and scarlet lipstick hadn't even thought about smudging, even through her tantrum. Cow. 'Can we get dinner tonight? If I don't kill myself and everyone on the shoot?'

'Absolutely,' I promised. 'Can you make mine a quick death?'

'Absolutely,' she promised.

'I think I have a solution.' Kekipi opened the door with a big smile and jazz hands. 'My friend is the events manager at the Royal Hawaiian. It's very old Hawaii, very stately. They have a space we can use and some props. It might take a little creativity, but we have a location.'

'Kekipi, if it wouldn't turn your stomach, I would kiss you,' Paige said, her face a picture of relief.

'Ms Sullivan,' he replied, 'if we could take a picture and send it to my grandmother, I might let you.'

'Shall we have a look at the venue first?' she suggested, slipping the iPad back in her bag. 'And we'll pose for engagement photos later.'

'Yes, boss,' he said, closing the car door and banging on the roof.

'If you could just turn to the left a little?' I called to the blonde model. 'So I can see more of the feathers?'

Kekipi had come through on the location. The hotel was almost as palatial as the actual palace. Unfortunately, it was also pink. Bright, Pepto-Bismol pink. We were stuck in a courtyard right off the beach, which would have given me great light to shoot with if we'd been there three hours earlier, but instead, all I had were doomsdayesque shadows from the overhead midday sun. The storm had passed but that was the only thing that felt like it was going our way.

Our blonde model, Ana, had woken up from her sleeping pill haze, and, if it were in any way possible, was behaving even worse than she had during our brief meeting the night before. She swore at the local make-up artist, she gave me the finger when I went to say hi, and she actually hissed at Paige. Hissed like an angry cat. The other model, Martha, a stupidly beautiful black girl with eyes so enormous I kept worrying that she was hypnotizing me, just looked like she might cry. Whether something was wrong or Ana was pinching her while we weren't looking I wasn't sure, but I suspected the latter. Paige had tried to talk to her approximately eighteen thousand times, but she just sniffed, shrugged and sat there quietly having her mascara reapplied. Again. And again. And again.

As if the location, the lighting and the personnel issues weren't bad enough, I also had the pleasure of trying to make the wardrobe look like it hadn't just been dragged out of Joan Collins' 'Save it for best circa 1982' closet. The clothes that Artie had picked out of the Bennett vault couldn't possibly be indicative of the fashion nous that had made his dad so successful. Unless his dad was exclusively clothing drag queens and the cast of *The Muppets*. Currently we had Ana in a baby-blue feathered affair that grazed her knees and dipped so low at the back that the make-up artist was having a wonderful time trying to cover up her tramp stamp. Martha had fared no better, stuck in a dropped-waist canary yellow silk number that had shoulder pads so big she could have just leaned her head over and had a little nap. Maybe that's why she was so sad.

There were one or two outfits that had made Paige squeal with delight – some late eighties Gaultier, and a dress that she held up with such reverence I had to wonder if it was the Turin Shroud; but no, it was just vintage Valentino. I thought she was going to slap the taste out of my mouth when I responded with an 'oh'. Sadly for the beautiful dresses, they were every one of them either red, pink or emerald green, all of which looked ridiculous in front of the pink palace, and so, instead, the models stood there, looking like someone had puked a rainbow against the wall. And it was my job to capture that rainbow.

'Ana, to me,' I called again. 'More feathers.'

I did not really want to see more of the feathers. All I wanted to see was the inside of my eyelids and possibly the bottom of a toilet bowl. This was officially joining the day I got fired, the day things went to shit with Charlie and the day I dropped my favourite My Little Pony out of a speeding Ford Escort somewhere on the M1 and my mum wouldn't stop to get it as one of the worst days of my life.

'I'm just not sure it's working,' I said quietly to Paige, flicking through the images on my camera screen while the poor local make-up artist tended to beauty and the beast. 'It just looks so forced.'

'Then make it look better,' she replied just as quietly. 'Don't fuck me over, Tess. Do not fuck this up. Artie is getting pissed off, I can tell – we don't have much longer.'

I looked up at her, a little startled. Me? What had I done? Oh, right, I wasn't a real photographer and therefore the shitty pictures had to be my fault. Nothing to do with the fact that all I had to take photos of was a grumpy middle-aged man in a nasty suit lounging on a papier mâché throne, flanked by two models who would apparently rather be poking sticks in their eyes than getting paid to hang out in Hawaii wearing designer clothes *for money*.

'OK, um, Martha, could you maybe sit down on the steps and pull the train out behind you?' Oh yes, the yellow dress had a train. Martha did as she was told like a sad puppy and looked up expectantly.

'Ana, I need you to give me something really solid, something really strong,' I shouted.

Anything to offset the tragedy of the man on the throne, I thought to myself. I've taken better pictures in a photo booth. To Ana's credit, after muttering something obscene under her breath, she struck a pose and it seemed to work. I fiddled with the camera for a moment, adjusted the height of the flash that would hopefully light up Artie's face a touch better than his non-existent smile, and started shooting again.

'Ladies, I'm really not terribly comfortable in this crown,' Artie bellowed from his seat, disrupting the first half-decent shot I'd got out of the lot of them in over an hour. 'I think it would be better not to use it.'

'But the crown is the lynchpin of the whole concept, Artie.' Paige used her most soothing tone of voice to try to convince Bennett Junior to keep his hat on. Personally, I thought he looked like he'd just crashed a fashion shoot on his way home from a boozy trip to Burger King, but my input was not required. As Paige had already told me several times. Every suggestion I'd made had been shot down. Any confidence I'd managed to build in my ability as a photographer, the confidence that she had worked so hard on helping me with, was completely shattered. But I had to remember Paige was in charge. Paige was the art director. I was the photographer. I was just there to do as I was told. And it was grating on my last nerve.

'Looks . . . interesting?'

And just when I thought things couldn't get any worse, Nick arrived.

'I'm busy, we're busy,' I replied, not taking my eyes away from the camera and ignoring the prickling sensation running down my back. 'Closed set.'

'No, it isn't. Anyway, I'm here to talk to Artie.' He came nearer until he was close enough to whisper in my ear. 'Feeling better, lover?'

'If you don't back up immediately, I'm going to throw up on you,' I replied. And it wasn't a lie. He had that effect on me. 'Please let me get on with this.'

'They look ridiculous, you know,' he said, stepping aside and folding his arms. I took a precious second away from my camera to glance over at him. Messy hair, scruffy stubble, grey-blue eyes against a golden tan. And the outfit hardly hurt – bright white V-neck T-shirt and perfectly fitting khaki cargo shorts. Bugger me, he looked good in shorts. Men hardly ever looked good in shorts. 'What is Paige thinking?'

'Why don't you ask her? I'm just the camera monkey.' I tightened my plait and looked back at the scene in front of me. It did look ridiculous. Mario Testino couldn't have made this look good. Maybe Agent Veronica should have sent a chimp with a camera phone after all – there was every chance he might have seen something in it that I couldn't.

'Memory card's full. Give me two minutes everyone,' I called over to my models. And Artie. 'One more set-up, I promise.'

Me and my shadow went over to the table where I'd set up my laptop and plugged in my camera. More and more upsettingly average pictures of a depressingly tragic set. I couldn't see a single one I was proud of.

'It's not your fault, you know,' Nick said quietly, one hand on my back. 'They aren't bad pictures. This . . . all this . . .' He waved his hand around at the hotel, at the models, at a foaming-at-the-mouth Paige. 'It's not exactly working for you.'

I looked up from the screen and out at the ocean. Waikiki beach was full of holiday-makers sunbathing, running in and out of the waves, building sandcastles

283

and basically having a very lovely time. I wondered what would happen if I just cobbed the camera at Paige's head and started running. I could reinvent myself as one of the slightly scary ladies wandering up and down the sand selling bits of mango. It was a good life.

'I think we need to make more of the Hawaiian feeling,' Paige announced, snapping me out of my daydream and slapping Nick's hand off my back. 'We need to add more fun, more playfulness. Kekipi, let's do it.'

I was fairly certain that the playfulness was already very well communicated in the slightly off-kilter crown Paige had put on Artie's head and in the fact that our models were wearing outfits it looked like they'd made themselves, but no. To Paige, 'Hawaiian feeling' and 'playfulness' could only be communicated by adding two girls in grass skirts holding ukuleles and a pile of pineapples.

'Oh dear God, shoot me now,' I whispered, wide-eyed and afraid.

'If I could, I would,' Nick replied.

'Paige,' I started with caution. 'Are you sure about this?'

'Yes,' she shouted, her voice brittle.

'It's just . . . I mean, it's not clichéd?'

Big mistake. Huge.

'I'm really fucking stressed right now, *Vanessa*,' she said with an awful lot of emphasis on my name. 'So if you could try and take a half-decent picture out of what we've got, we can all get out of here before Christmas, yeah?'

'Hey, Paige, I know you're stressing, but don't take it out on Vanessa.' Nick leapt to my honour before I could say anything. And it did not help matters in the slightest.

Paige paused in her direction of the hula girls and turned to face us fully. I took a tiny side-step away from Nick and looked at the floor while whispering 'please don't let her be the violent type, please don't let her be the violent type' to myself.

'Nick, could you be a love and fuck off until you're needed?' she said sweetly. 'We're trying to get something done and you're not helping. Vanessa can't be distracted while she's creating her masterpiece. Isn't that right, Van?'

'Vanessa can probably speak for herself,' he responded, not moving. I shook my head, still focusing on the grass beneath my feet, and prayed for the ground to open up and swallow me. Why weren't there active volcanoes in Hawaii? Where was a flowing river of molten lava when you needed it?

'Vanessa probably could,' she agreed. 'But seriously, not the time or place. Nick, do one. We're busy.'

My refusal to make eye contact with anyone other than the little brown bird that was pecking the ground beside my feet was probably a touch out of character as far as Nick was concerned. I felt his eyes on me, waiting for a snappy comeback or at least a 'fuck you' for Paige, but instead I shrugged, clicked a couple of buttons on my camera and kept my mouth shut.

'Fine,' he said, defeated. 'I'll be in the bar. Send Bennett in when you're done.'

I met his eyes briefly, trying to explain without an explanation, but he just looked a little pissed off and a lot confused.

'If the look you're going for is that bit in *The Jungle Book* where Baloo dresses up as a monkey, then you're right on the money. If it's not, you're buggered. Have fun, ladies.'

I looked at Paige. Paige looked at me. We both looked at the hula girls.

'Lose the girls,' Paige bellowed. 'Keep the pineapples. Now let's take some pissing pictures so we can all go home.'

The two dancers sashayed sadly away, their grass skirts swishing as they went. Even though I was this close to bursting into tears, I felt a chuckle bubbling up inside me. It was like someone had said something hilarious in science class and I had lost all control over myself.

'Don't you dare laugh,' Paige warned me, taking a red lipstick out of her handbag and reapplying it perfectly without a mirror. 'Just don't.'

'Thought hadn't even crossed my mind,' I said in the squeakiest voice possible. 'Shall we just get this done?'

'Yes.' She pushed a long, Veronica Lake wave out of her face and breathed out purposefully. 'I need a cocktail. Sorry. I just want this done.'

'And I need a miracle,' I said, turning back to the set. Still shit. 'But I will settle for a cocktail.'

CHAPTER SEVENTEEN

'Crap, crap, crap, crap, crap, even crappier, mega crap, crap . . .'

What felt like days later, I scrolled through the fruits of my photographic labour back in the cottage. I had downloaded – hundreds of shots to my computer – hundreds, and every single one looked shit. 'Crap, crap. Mega crap. Super crap. The crappiest piece of crap I've ever seen. Oh, awesome, this one's just regular old crap.'

I curled my legs up underneath myself and continued to scroll through the pictures, trying not to sob. I had a throbbing headache from last night's cocktails and the epic quantity of coffee I'd mainlined to keep me conscious during the shoot. All I wanted to do was fill a bucket full of crystal-clear water and dunk my head in it, but there wasn't time. Paige was due to come over and look through them with me any minute, and I couldn't bear the thought of her seeing such shit. Objectively, they looked fine, I told myself. Objectively, there were shots where the models looked amazing, where Artie looked regal and elegant, where the hotel looked kitsch but classy at the same time. Photos where you could barely see the pineapples. Sadly, none of these elements occurred in the same photo. Not even once. I hoped someone back at *Gloss* was very, very good at Photoshop, because I wasn't. I had no idea how Paige was going to react. I paused on a particularly awful picture of Ana posing on one leg, Martha sobbing and Artie checking his phone. At least my hangover hadn't mattered. I could have turned up to the set, shot up in front of everyone and still struggled to get a usable image. It was almost funny. I'd been so worried about being the weak link in the chain, it hadn't occurred to me that the chain would be about as strong as a roll of soggy Andrex in the first place.

'All right, let's see them.'

For a shocking change, Paige had let herself into my cottage without knocking. In her hand was a huge silver travel coffee mug which she held out to me. I shook my head.

'It's got whisky in it,' she explained, holding it out again.

I took it, swigged it, retched ever so slightly and shuffled up the sofa so she could see the laptop.

'Oh dear,' she said, taking the cup back. 'Oh dear.'

It wasn't nearly as bad a reaction as I'd anticipated.

'I know they're awful,' I said, starting slowly and holding my hand back out for the spiked coffee. It was amazing how quickly it took away my headache. 'But I'm sure there must be something we can do.'

'They're not awful,' Paige replied with as much diplomacy as she could muster. 'They're not my favourite pictures in the world, but they're not awful. They're not actually as bad as I thought they were going to be.'

I could tell she was trying to be nice after her outbursts on set. It was touching but unnerving. I sat looking at her, biting my bottom lip and waiting for her to shout, 'Fooled you!' then punch me in the face.

'What do we do?' I asked, letting her move the mouse back and forth until she settled on one shot for more than a second. It was one of the better images. For just one moment, almost everything had come together. The lighting looked soft and beautiful, Ana's steely gaze set off the sad, faraway look on Martha's face. Artie, on the other hand, just looked like a tosspot. 'Is there anything we can do?'

'This is what we've got,' she replied carefully. 'I'm just going to have to suck it up and go with it.'

It wasn't really the gushing compliment I'd been hoping for, but it was better than the slap I'd been expecting.

'That crown was a mistake, wasn't it?' Paige pulled a face and placed her thumb over the offending accessory. 'I wonder if we can Photoshop that out.'

No one likes to hear 'I told you so', so I didn't say it. At least, I didn't say it out loud. In my head I was bouncing up and down, shouting it in her face and doing a very unappealing dance, very Tom Cruise on the Oprah sofa.

'I'm sorry I was such a dickhead – I just panicked. And I never panic.' She highlighted a couple of the pictures, the same ones I'd mentally cleared as 'not the most awful', and nodded slowly. 'If you can do a bit of a clean-up on these, just basic stuff, I'll send them over to Stephanie and she can get back to us. Nick should be able to file his interview tonight, and then we're done. Thank fuck.'

'We're not doing the portrait?' I asked, boldly adding

one of my least hated pictures to the approved collection.
'With Artie?'

'After this afternoon, he suddenly doesn't want to do
it,' she explained. 'So right now, no. Honestly, I have no
idea what's going to happen when I speak to Steph
tomorrow. The whole point of this feature was a
retrospective on Bertie, not a big old wankfest over Artie.
Everyone in fashion loves Bertie – he's, like, one of the
last of the old guard. But Artie . . . he's got kind of a
horrible reputation. I heard that once Anna Wintour
called him a brat.'

'Wow. Given what he's like now, I can only imagine
what he was like as a little boy.'

'Oh no, this was in Milan last season.' Paige raised an
eyebrow.

'I'm sorry, I wasn't really helping earlier,' I said. I
could tell she was on the verge of giving up and I just
couldn't let her. If Paige went down, we all went down.
I couldn't let it happen. 'I was just so worried about not
cocking up the photos, I hadn't really thought about the
big picture.'

'And I was focusing on you not cocking up the photos
because I couldn't deal with thinking about everything
else,' she said, rolling her eyes up to the ceiling and
giving a wan smile. 'I'm sorry I made it so hard for you.
I know this didn't exactly come about in a conventional
way, but I'm glad it's you here and not Vanessa. And not
just because she's an evil demon bitch from hell. You're
a really good photographer, Tess. I mean it. Shit, look at
what you managed to drag out of this trio of defects.'

She waved towards the laptop and I felt a tiny glow
light up inside me. Her words were almost all compliment,
and it had been a while since anyone had had anything

nice to say to me. Well, except for Al. And Nick. And when I thought about it, how long had it been since three different people had compliments for me? Hmm. It was a pleasant change not to hate myself for just a moment.

'I'm sure Steph will understand,' I said, not sure in the slightest, but it felt like the right thing to say. 'I don't see what else you could have done under the circumstances. You're going back to London with a story and a photo spread. You can't be held responsible for the invisible man, can you?'

'No, I know.' Paige leaned back against the sofa and knocked back the rest of the coffee with a whisky-fuelled wince. 'But she's fired people for less. And I like my job.'

'I liked mine and they fired me for nothing.' I pursed my lips and put the laptop to sleep. 'It won't come to it, you know it won't – but seriously, if they fire you over you working your arse off to try and save a disaster situation, then bugger them. You'll find someone else who actually appreciates what you do.'

'Is that what you said when you got laid off?' she asked, sitting the coffee mug on the white wooden side table.

'I didn't get out of bed for a week, got hammered at a family christening, shagged my best mate in my childhood bedroom – on a bunkbed, Paige, a bunkbed – and then ran away to Hawaii,' I shrugged. 'So I've set the bar pretty high for unpredictable behaviour in the face of a firing. I can't see you doing quite so badly.'

'I blame men,' Paige announced. 'Is there anything else to drink in here?'

'There's wine in the fridge,' I said, watching her slink off in search of more booze. She really was perfect looking. If I hadn't known what a neurotic crazy she was, I would have hated her guts. 'I have to work on these pictures, though. I'm OK.'

A loud popping sound suggested she wasn't really listening to me, unless she was planning to drink an entire bottle of champagne by herself. Not entirely impossible, I reasoned.

'We should get some food,' I suggested as she moseyed back over with an open bottle of Veuve Clicquot and two glasses. My headache coughed quietly in the back of my head, reminding me of our precarious truce, and my stomach rumbled so loudly, I was almost sure it would start a tidal wave and wash the island away.

'I'm trying not to eat too much at the moment,' Paige, the world's skinniest girl who still had boobs, replied. 'I've got to lose five pounds before fashion week. I know it's clichéd, but seriously, if I want to go to the New York shows, I more or less need to look like I'm in recovery for something or I'll get eaten alive.'

'Which is ironic because there would be nothing on you to eat,' I said, reluctantly accepting the champagne and wishing I wasn't so painfully polite. Thank God no one had ever thought to offer me crack; I wouldn't know where to put myself.

'What's more delicious, Tess – food or compliments?' Paige asked.

'F– ompliments?' I offered. The look on Paige's face suggested I had not got the answer correct. 'No, it's definitely food.'

'I know it sounds horribly pro-ana, but I work in fashion,' she went on, sipping the champagne and making such intense happy noises, I felt a little bit uncomfortable. She needed to get laid even more than I did. 'I think it was Kate Moss who said, "Nothing tastes as good as being thin feels."'

'Kate Moss is incorrect,' I said, mentally telegraphing Kekipi to come over with some pork or sushi or chicken or a mouldy slice of bread he'd found on the side of the road a week ago. I was so ridiculously hungry. 'Kate Moss has never eaten an entire Domino's pizza.'

'Coke does do wonders for curbing the appetite,' Paige admitted before eyeing me awkwardly. 'Allegedly.'

'Allegedly,' I echoed and clinked my glass against hers in a toast. 'So. Why are we blaming the men for today's debacle? Aside from the Bennett boys being a couple of tosspot drama queens?'

Emptying her first glass of champagne while she contemplated her answer, Paige rested her head against the arm of the sofa and stretched her long, denim-clad legs out over my lap. I looked down at them, not knowing quite what to do. Good to know we were back on friendly terms. She really was just another Amy in a slightly shinier package. And just as crazy, as she had proven at the shoot that afternoon.

'Oh, Tess.' She sighed my name and threw her hand against her forehead like a Jane Austen character. A rubbish, secondary Jane Austen character whose spunky sister would end up having to defend her honour and marry her off to some soft twat who had an income of more than a thousand a year. 'I feel like such an idiot.'

'Hands up who here doesn't?' I looked around the empty room. No hands up.

'No, I've been a total moron.' She dropped her head even further back so that her hair cascaded all the way down to the floor. 'I told Nick I've got a crush on him.'

Oh noes.

Even though I sort of knew she was going to say something along these lines, even though I was kind of pushing her to admit it, hearing it first-hand did not feel good.

'You, Paige Sullivan of undetermined age, told Nick Miller, thirty-six, that you have a crush on him?' I asked. Just to make sure.

'I'm thirty, so fuck off, but yes, we were supposed to go out for dinner last night, but he made me go on this stupid boat ride and I threw up over the side and he was so lovely about it that it just sort of came out.' She loved a run-on sentence, did Paige. 'And he was totally lovely about it, but he so isn't interested, and now it's dead awkward and I feel like I'm fourteen or something.'

'He's not interested?' I asked, picking out what I considered to be the keynote of the rushed speech. 'How do you know?'

'Well, aside from the fact that I more or less threw myself at him, and even though we're in Hawaii, and even though there's no one else here for him to fancy . . .' She paused for breath and to take in my slightly angry thin line of a mouth. 'What?'

'No, there's no one else here. Carry on,' I said tightly.

'Well, no – it's just he's not into models, I know that,' she explained, only succeeding in making matters worse. 'And you're all in love with that bloke back home, aren't you?'

Her rationale was sound, and I understood why she would think that I wouldn't be into Nick when I was supposedly so head over heels in love with Charlie – I was head over heels in love with Charlie after all, I reminded myself – but I couldn't help but think she'd disregarded me as competition very easily. Not that I could blame her – she was beautiful, she was successful, she was funny and clever when she wanted to be, her hair was incredible, and when they were together, she and Nick looked like an ad for a very expensive denim brand. Like those really annoying print ads you always saw on the underground for Uniqlo that had 'real' people in who were a thousand times more attractive than anyone you ever saw on the Tube. I totally would have cast them in an ad to sell high-end kitchenware. Me and Charlie would probably have been booked for a job advertising Nando's or something.

'Go on,' I said, taking one more tiny sip of champagne, just to see how it felt.

'Well, yeah, so I threw up and he was being all lovely and funny and brought me water and stuff, and I said that he was going to make someone a lovely wife one day, and he said he should be so lucky, and I just sort of laughed and said, "Oh, I'd marry you," and then we both laughed, and then I put my hand on his, erm, leg, and then he went a bit quiet, and then he said that he was "sort of seeing someone", and then I laughed too loudly and said I was only joking and he said of course he knew that and then I left because I was absolutely mortified.'

It was a lot of 'and thens' for one sentence.

My first reaction was 'poor Nick'. He'd come all the way to Hawaii to interview someone who didn't want to be interviewed, and then spent his entire trip looking after girls who kept throwing up. It was not a dream come true. Unless you had a very particular fetish.

My second reaction was, 'he was sort of seeing someone'. Wha?

'Have you spoken to him since?' I asked.

'Only when he showed up this afternoon,' she said, sitting back up to drink her champagne. 'It's fine. I just have to stop falling for knobheads.'

'Oh, just that little tiny thing.' I patted her leg. 'Piece of piss.'

'You can talk,' she snarked, kicking me back. 'Excellent choices you've been making lately.'

Oh dear God, I thought, forcing myself to laugh loudly. If only you knew.

'You're not, like, really, really into him, though, are you?' I asked, my conscience really hoping for an answer that would help me sleep through the night. 'Nick, I mean.'

'I don't know.' She twirled a lock of hair around her finger and shrugged one shoulder. 'I just haven't really even fancied anyone since my ex, and Nick is just so, you know. He's such a bloody man. And I know he likes to talk a load of shit, but my mate Jackie's boyfriend is mates with his friend Steven, and Steven reckons he hasn't had a girlfriend since this girl he went out with in America years ago.'

'Right,' I said, adding this information to the profile I was building slowly. The LA ex. The one who was too lazy to walk to the waterfall. 'You don't think that might be because he's a filthy shagger who can't keep his trousers on?'

'I definitely think he's a filthy shagger who can't keep his trousers on.' Paige's eyes lit up and she looked positively thrilled at the prospect. 'But men like that, they're just waiting for the right girl. I know that sounds naïve, but you get to a certain age and you realize it's true.'

She seemed so convinced, I didn't have the energy

or the heart to argue with her. But who was right, Paige or Nick? Were men just sitting around in their cave, scratching themselves and waiting for the love of a good woman, or were they out climbing mountain after mountain after mountain until they just couldn't be arsed any more? Either way, it seemed like Cupid was out of a job. The recession really had hit a lot of people.

'So you do really like him?'

'You know, my heart says yes, but my head says probably not,' she replied with a scrunched-up face. 'Although my vag says something altogether different. Maybe I actually love him. Maybe I just want to cover him in Nutella and lick it all off. I don't think anyone can actually make sane decisions about their emotional state when they're wearing sunscreen. Just the smell of it makes you crazy.'

'I've heard worse theories about holiday romances, actually.' I had to admit, she might have been on to something.

'I reckon when you get home, Charlie is going to be all turned around on this situation,' Paige said, sitting up, pouring herself another glass of champagne, and topping me off, despite my refusals. 'He's going to be all freaked out that you went off and did something amazing without him, and he'll be so jealous and so worried about missing out. Absence makes the heart grow fonder, Tess.'

'Does it?' I wasn't so sure.

'Yeah, definitely,' Paige said, agreeing with herself so aggressively that she was spilling champagne all over the settee. I surreptitiously grabbed a bit of kitchen towel and dabbed at the wet mark while she wasn't paying attention. 'Or at least, absence makes the dick get harder.

Not to be coarse or anything. He'll be all over you like a rash. A hot rash. He's hot, isn't he?'

'He is.' I folded up the damp paper and tossed it onto the coffee table, trying very hard not to think about Charlie's penis.

'Let me see a picture.' She scrambled onto her knees and passed me my laptop. 'Come on, just one. I want to see what's so special about him.'

With all the enthusiasm of a beached whale, I logged onto Facebook and immediately found a thousand different pictures of me and Charlie. I'd been doing so well. It had to have been at least twenty-four hours since I'd looked at them, and now it did not feel good.

'Oh, he is cute,' Paige said with approval. 'Tall, too. Really, like, boy-next-doorsy. I bet he'd be dead good at changing light bulbs and playing sport. You make a really cute couple.'

'Hmm,' was just about all I could manage.

'Oh, shitting hell – I'm sorry,' she said, slamming the laptop shut. 'I'm doing it again. I'm not thinking. But really, I do think he probably just needs a bit of space to adjust to things. Coming here was the best thing you could have done.'

I nodded. Getting on a plane and flying to Hawaii may well have been the best thing I could have done. I'd found a great new friend in Paige, I'd remembered how much I loved photography, and, more importantly, it turned out that I was actually pretty good at it. That made me really happy. But I'd also effed my new friend's crush, lied about my name and stolen my flatmate's job. That made me a little bit concerned. So: swings and roundabouts.

My plan not to get wankered so I could work on my

pictures was offset nicely by Paige's plan to get absolutely obliterated so she could get right on my tits. Within an hour, she was three years deep into my Facebook photos and two bottles of champagne into her own personal pit of misery.

'You all look really happy,' she said with a telltale snort. 'You and your mates. My mates are all arseholes. All my mates were my ex's mates and now all I've got left are fashion mates. No one is mates in fashion, not really.'

'But magazines?' I tried to give her a glass of water, but she pushed it away and poured more champagne. Badly. I had to remind myself this was not my sofa and I was not responsible for the stains. 'Aren't there fun journo girls?'

'I came in from the fashion side, though.' She shook her head, clicking on a pic from Amy's twenty-fourth birthday party. I took her to the Natural History Museum to see the dinosaurs. She did not have as much fun as I did. 'All the writers have known each other for ever. I don't know, I don't make friends that easily. Girls don't like me.'

I took a momentary step back and watched the beautiful yet shit-faced woman knocking back booze on the sofa, still looking like she'd stepped off her own fashion shoot. She didn't have so much as a wrinkle on her tissue-thin sweater, and it was white, for God's sake. I was only allowed to wear white shirts on the days I only drank clear liquids. 'I can't think why,' I replied.

'Oh, it's because I'm, you know . . .' She waved a drunken hand at her general appearance. 'Whatever. It's fine.'

If nothing else, you had to admire her honesty.

'I like you,' I offered, taking the dead bottles of booze into the kitchen and putting on the kettle. Paige might be halfway to hangover heaven, but I was knackered and I still had stuff to do. 'And I'm a girl.'

'Yeah, but you don't care, do you?' She rested her head against the back of the sofa and gave me a sloppy smile. 'You're not competing.'

'Right.' I slapped my hand on her thigh, hard. 'I think it's time you nicked off back to your cottage and I got some work done. I'll have the photos over to you in the morning.'

'Fine,' she said from inside the wine glass. A bottle and a half ago, she had realized she could get much more champagne in a red wine glass than a champagne flute. 'I'm tired anyway. What is it, two a.m.?'

I glanced at the clock on the kitchen wall. It was half past eight in the evening.

'It's very late,' I replied gravely. 'You should probably go to bed.'

'Yeah,' she nodded, hoisting herself off the squishy sofa. 'I'll see you tomorrow. Thanks, Tess.'

'Get back safe,' I called as she tottered out in her heels. The cow still looked amazing.

'I'm going thirty feet away,' she laughed, reaching for the door frame and missing. 'You worry too much.'

Even as she was saying it, I was trying to work out the likelihood of her falling in the pool and drowning on her way home.

As the door swung shut, I closed my eyes, breathed out and thought, for all of fifteen seconds, that I might be allowed five minutes' peace. Until my phone started to rattle across the tabletop. It had been on silent since the shoot and I'd forgotten all about it while I was managing my favourite new alcoholic, but now she was gone and there was no one loudly complaining about how hard it was to be so beautiful, I heard the quiet buzz of vibrating iPhone against paperback book and spotted a flashing screen over on the bookcase, where it was charging. All I wanted to do was let the kettle finish boiling, make my tea and pretend I hadn't seen it. But it was Amy. And I had already hung up on her once in twenty-four hours. Twice absolutely would not fly. Better to just get it over with.

'Hey.' I pulled the charger out of the phone and flopped down on the settee, stretching out from top to bottom. 'Dear God, today was horrible.'

'Hi, Amy! How are you, Amy? Have you got a new job yet, Amy? I'm so worried about you, Amy.' She started her rant before I had even finished my sentence. 'I'm doubly sorry I've been ignoring your phone calls and haven't been in touch for days, and I'm even more sorry that today you found out that your ex-fiancé got engaged again because his new girlfriend of half a fucking second is pregnant.'

'Ohhh.'

'But no, please do go on. Tell me all about your horrible day.'

The silence that followed was not comfortable.

'Amy, I'm sorry.' I didn't really know where to start. I'd only been away for five minutes and it felt like a lifetime. 'Are you all right?'

'Of course I'm not all right,' she said with a choking sob. 'He's engaged. He's having a baby. I haven't got a job, my mother hates me, and I haven't got a clue what I'm doing with my life. Come home, I need you.'

'I'll be home on Sunday,' I promised. 'Don't get this upset over someone so rubbish. You don't want to marry him, you don't want to have babies with him. He's crap, remember?'

'I don't know,' she sniffed, her voice still woolly and unreliable. 'It wasn't that bad. I wasn't unhappy.'

'You weren't happy,' I reminded her, telling her everything that she had told me when she'd dumped him in the first place. 'You were settling. You ended things because you're brave and you know what you want and you're better than a miserable relationship in a sad semi in Ruislip with a man you don't love.'

'It was a nice semi,' Amy replied. 'And how are things better now? Honestly, Tess?'

'You're not wasting your life?' I wanted to shake her so badly. Amy wasn't one to get maudlin and self-indulgent, but when the mean reds really took hold of her, it was impossible to drag her back out without a metaphorical kick up the arse and, on occasion, a literal slap. 'You're not plodding on day in and day out with someone else's plan?'

'I'd rather be with Dave than be on my own,' she whispered.

It was a good job I was thousands and thousands of miles away. I really would have booted her up the backside for that one.

'No, Amy. Just no.'

She let out one more reflexive howl, and I waited until her crying calmed to a ragged squeak.

'I'll be home on Sunday,' I said again, closing my eyes and trying very hard not to think about what that would mean. 'Don't work yourself up over Dave. It's been years. You know you're happier without him.'

'But how come he's getting married and having a baby and I'm not getting married and having a baby?'

Ahh. Now we were getting somewhere. Her tears gave way to a temper tantrum and the volume of her voice went right up to eleven.

'What did I do wrong? Why don't I have someone?'

'You know there isn't an instruction manual for life, lovely.' I was trying to calm her down, to sound as comforting as possible. My best friend needed a hug and I wasn't there to give her one; it felt horrible. 'Everyone gets there in their own time. I'm hardly waltzing down the aisle either, am I?'

'Yeah, but that's because you're fucking stupid,' she said bluntly.

'Sorry?' So much for trying to calm her down.

'Oh, you know what I mean.' I could hear her trying to flap away her insult down the line. 'You don't have a boyfriend because you've been waiting for Charlie to wake up and realize he's in love with you for the last decade, and now what – the second you decide you're over him, you've got some random bloke drooling all over you? I don't exactly feel sorry for you.'

'What, so I don't deserve to be in a happy relationship because I've got legitimate feelings for someone?' Didn't seem exactly fair. 'Sorry I haven't been shagging my way around London for the past ten years, hoping to accidentally fall on The One's penis.'

'Are you calling me a slag?' Amy went from loud to quietly pissed off. 'Don't beat around the bush, Tess, just say it.'

'I didn't call you a slag,' I replied. I was far too tired and too stressed to have this conversation. 'But it's not like you haven't done your fair share of research in the boyfriend department, is it?'

'Oh, fuck off,' she snapped back. 'I know you're happy being a sad nun, but some of us actually have a life. I'm sorry if that's upsetting to you.'

'I don't want to fight with you,' I said, and realized as I chose my words that they were more of a warning than an apology. 'Today has been shit. I'll be back Sunday. Either we can talk about this calmly now, or we can fight about it then.'

'Oh, yeah, I forgot – please do tell me more about your dreadful day in paradise.' Apparently she wanted to fight about it now. 'Has everyone worked out you're not actually a photographer? Probably didn't take long. Were you as shit at that as you were at your amazing job that you were so amazing at that you got the sack for nothing? Or did your new boyfriend bin you off like Charlie?'

I didn't even reply. Instead, I hung up and threw my phone across the room. And immediately regretted it when I heard the clunk, chunk, shatter of a broken iPhone.

'That wasn't about you,' I said out loud, my blood pressure building and building until I thought I might actually start shooting Popeye-style steam out of my ears. 'She was being mean on purpose. She was trying to hurt you.'

And she had succeeded. How dare she say that to me? She knew I was stressing out about all of this; she knew I was scared. In a heartbeat, I went from being so tired I could have slept on the kitchen floor to being so full of rage that every limb felt like it was going to shoot off in a different direction. My shoulders shook and my hands were clenched tightly into tiny little fists. If only there were something or someone in the vicinity to punch. I paced the kitchen and the living room, opening kitchen cupboard doors and slamming them shut again. Not even snacks could calm me down. It was serious. I wanted to do something drastic like cut all of my hair off or send her Gwyneth Paltrow's head in a box. Or maybe something in between that didn't involve a sharp blade. In my temper, the light, airy cottage seemed too small and utterly claustrophobic. Not bothering with shoes, keys or any of the other dozens of items I usually couldn't leave my house without, I stormed out of the door and out into the night air. The freshness of the ocean hit me like a wet slap with a cold kipper and stopped me dead in my tracks. *Breathe*, a quiet voice said in the back of my mind. *Calm down and breathe.*

'All right there?'

Nick was sitting outside his cottage, book in one hand, drink in the other, his laptop on the table beside him and a bemused look on his face.

'Something wrong?'

'Everything,' I replied, feet still frozen on the wooden slats of my veranda.

'How are the photos?' he asked.

'How is the interview?' I deflected.

'Shit.' He shrugged and picked up a pipe from the ashtray on his table. An actual, honest-to-God pipe. 'Artie is an uninteresting, self-important tosspot.'

'Photos are shit too,' I admitted, the ragey wind starting to leave my sails. 'They don't look right. It's just not what it's supposed to be.'

'The whole thing was bollocksed from the start.' Nick struck a match and I watched as the orange flare lit up his features for a moment before fizzling down to a soft, golden glow. 'Don't feel bad about it. There'll be other jobs.'

I laughed softly and felt my fingers unfurl. Easy for him to say.

'I just wanted one thing to go right,' I said, facing away, looking at the ocean. 'All I wanted was to come here, do this and know I'd done it well. I wanted to know that despite everything else that's been so utterly shit lately, I could do this.'

'I'm sure it isn't your fault,' he said. 'You get really stressed really easily, don't you?'

'I don't know.' I was trying very hard not to cry. It was a long time since I'd looked in a mirror and even longer since I'd applied so much as lip balm. Bright red eyes weren't going to make me any more attractive. 'I needed this one thing to go right for me.'

'One shit shoot doesn't make you a shit photographer, Vanessa,' Nick replied, missing the point entirely. 'It just means the next one will feel like a holiday compared to this.' He waved his pipe around our luxury accommodation and smiled. 'Which is, when you think about it, ironic.'

The sky was clear again, with dozens of constellations I didn't recognize stretched across the sky as far as I could see. When we were little, Amy and I used to sneak off into the fields around the village on summer evenings and lie on our backs making up stories for all the stars. It was weird to think these were the same stars. I walked a little way onto the beach and lay down in the sand. It was still warm from the sunny afternoon that had been and gone. I couldn't remember a time when I hadn't wished on the first star I saw every evening, and I could barely remember a time when that wish wasn't 'please make Charlie fall in love with me'. As angry as I was with Amy, as upset as I was with everything in my life,

I could at least see one thing clearly. It was time for a new wish.

'Do you have a nickname?' Nick lay down beside me and looked up at the sky.

'A nickname?' I asked, quiet alarm bells starting to sound in my mind. Had he heard Paige calling me Tess?

'Yeah, you can't be Vanessa all the time to everyone, can you? It's so dramatic.' He laughed a little and flashed his hands above his head. 'Vanessa.'

'No nicknames,' I replied. I wanted to tell him the truth so badly. I wanted to roll onto my side, prop myself up on an elbow and say, 'Listen, it's a funny story, but my name is actually Tess . . .' But I didn't. Because I was terrified. I just didn't know why.

'I'll have to come up with one then.' He crossed his legs and kicked off his shoes, burying his bare feet into the beach.

'Were you really smoking a pipe?' I asked. 'Like, a proper old-man pipe?'

'I was smoking a proper old-man pipe,' he confirmed with that grin that made my entire body fill with helium and hyperactive kittens. 'I find it relaxing.'

'I bet you like jazz too,' I said with a smile. He was so close, I could smell him. He was like a cross between catnip and prozac – just being near him made everything else seem totally insignificant. I was completely calm and buzzing all at once.

'I love jazz,' he said, his voice full of smiles. 'Am I enough of a cliché for you?'

His fingers found mine in the sand and we lay there, quietly holding hands, not saying anything. I let my head fall to the side and rest on his shoulder, half expecting him to pull away and hoping that he wouldn't. He didn't.

'So, a couple of nights ago,' I whispered, not wanting to talk over the sound of the waves. Seemed rude. 'You were telling me what an absolute bastard you were. Is that part of the jazz-loving, pipe-smoking bollocks?'

'Ha ha.' He knocked his head against mine gently and I buried myself into his shoulder. 'I am a complete bastard. All of this is just a ruse to work my way into your good graces before I steal all your granny's silver.'

'My granny hasn't got any silver,' I said. 'She's got a lot of Argos catalogues and figurines of geese, but that's about it.'

'Why the geese?' he asked.

'Who knows?' I replied. 'Paige said you were seeing someone.'

Nick rolled onto his front, showering me in a light dusting of powdery white sand, and looked at me with narrowed blue eyes. I pulled my hand away from him and pushed it underneath my body to keep it warm.

'Did she?'

'Yeah.' I didn't know why I'd said it. I didn't even know where it had come from. 'I thought you might have mentioned it. You know, to me.'

'If there was something to mention, I would have.'

'Right.'

It wasn't really an answer and I wasn't sure I felt any better. Either he was lying to me or he was lying to Paige. Awesome. All I had managed to establish was that Nick Miller was a liar. I'd never had to deal with issues like these when I was sitting behind a desk for eighty hours a week, pining after my best mate and coming up with wacky slogans to sell cling film.

The evening was warm and quiet, and everything that had happened before I stepped out onto the beach felt like a million years ago. Fighting with Amy, hanging out with Paige, taking hundreds of terrible photos . . . for ever ago. The only thing that registered was lying on the beach with Nick and not wanting to move. It was not very Tess-like. Old Tess would have been back on the phone to Amy apologizing, whether she was right or wrong. She would have been sitting playing Bejeweled on her phone in Paige's bed while Paige slept, just to make sure she didn't choke on her own vomit in the middle of the night. Old Tess wouldn't be crossing her legs and tensing her shoulders to force her body to stop thinking about how soon she could be having sex with this man she'd met four days ago. I looked upwards at Nick's stubbly jawline and full bottom lip and wondered what he was thinking about.

'So, any word from that bloke back home?' he asked. Ohhh.

'Nope.' I replied. 'Not a peep.'

'Are you going to call him?' Nick rolled over onto his back again, moving slightly closer to me. I followed like a magnet, and for the first time in my life I did not want to talk about Charlie Wilder.

'Was the interview really that bad?' I asked, changing the topic as quickly as I could without even answering. 'Artie was really that terrible?'

'Really that bad, really that terrible.' Nick apparently didn't need an answer. 'Nothing I can do now. Just like your pictures.'

'Don't remind me,' I groaned, an image of Artie with his plastic crown and grumpy face flashing in front of my eyes. 'I hate not being able to fix this. I hate being so out of control.'

'Maybe you shouldn't have let Paige take charge at the

shoot,' Nick suggested lightly. 'Too late to try and play the control freak now.'

'You're not helping,' I instructed, pursing my lips and wondering whether or not he was right. What would I have done differently? 'Paige was the art director, it was her concept – what was I supposed to do?'

'Oh yeah, you only had the camera in your hand,' he said, pulling sharply on my hand. 'What could you have done?'

'Shut up.' I could feel myself getting annoyed, and I didn't want to be annoyed. I wanted to be orgasmic. Then hungry, then eating Cheetos, and then asleep. And then maybe orgasmic again. 'You don't know.'

'Actually, I think it's going to be good for you not to get your own way for once.' He pushed his messy blond fringe back out of his eyes. 'You clearly have some control issues that we need to work on.'

'I don't know what you're talking about,' I replied. I believe my tone could have been referred to as 'haughty'.

'It's beyond me how you haven't gone mad yet, if you let every last little thing get to you as much as this job has,' he went on. 'I know a lot of photographers who are perfectionists, but you're taking this so personally. I don't get why you're so angry about stuff you couldn't change when you didn't change the things that you could have.'

'Like what?' I demanded. 'What could I have changed?'

'You could have told her the props looked like a joke instead of waiting for me to do it,' he said. 'You could have told her the clothes looked like shit. You could have got rid of that fucking crown.'

'She really wanted the crown,' I muttered, angry only because I knew he was right. I should have said something, I'd just been too afraid. 'She thought it was a good idea.'

'Well, Paige thinks a lot of things are a good idea,' Nick said. 'She's not always right.'

'Fine, I should have said something,' I accepted, folding my arms over my chest. 'It's all my fault that the shoot was terrible and the pictures are awful and Paige is probably going to get fired. OK, is that better?'

'Yeah, I think you've probably gone a bit too far,' he relented. 'It's hardly your fault Bennett dropped off the face of the earth, is it?'

'Not as far as I know,' I shrugged. 'Might be.'

'And you couldn't have been prepared for Paige fucking up the location. Or a freak rainstorm? Let alone those God-awful clothes Artie the Arsehole turned up with.'

'It just stings that there's nothing I can do now. If you're dedicated and you work hard, you'll always get to where you need to be,' I said, repeating words I'd told myself over and over and over. Usually on the Saturday nights when I sat in the office ignoring Amy's texts to come out and meet her. 'I should be able to fix this.'

'So everyone who works hard succeeds, do they?' he asked, pulling my arm from across my chest and taking my hand in his again. 'No one ever gets shafted, no matter how talented they are or how many hours they put in?'

Oh. Hmm. Bugger.

'Because I worked really hard on this interview, and it's still a piece of shit.' Nick seemed to be losing his temper a little bit. This did not bode well for my getting laid. 'And regardless of what I do or how late I stay up to work on it or what research I manage to pull out of

311

my arse, it's still going to be shit. It's still going to be published and people will still read it and think I did a shit job.'

'Maybe they won't?' It was the best I had.

'Maybe they won't think your photos are shit and maybe you won't be embarrassed to see your name next to them.'

This definitely wasn't the time to go into the whole 'by the way, I'm not actually Vanessa' thing.

Nick sat up, resting his arms against his thighs and staring out at the sea. 'The last time I was here,' he said, 'I thought I had it all figured out. How is it that the older we get, the less we know?'

'Since I'm so much younger than you, I should have an answer to that,' I said, thinking that Al had said almost exactly same thing a day earlier. 'But I don't.'

He looked over his shoulder at me and gave me a half-smile that didn't quite make it up to his eyes as I sat up to join him. It was too dark to really read his expression, but I could see he wasn't happy and I knew there was so much more going on than he was going to tell me. Rather than say another word, he sighed, leaned forward and kissed me. I closed my eyes, letting the soft sweetness wash over me, and leaned into him, but his soft kiss turned into a determination that took me by surprise, and his second kiss knocked me back into the sand. He pushed down on top of me, his heavy, solid body holding me in place, and pinned my arms above my head while his stubble scratched against my face and his legs wound their way around my own. It was a blessing and a curse that we were both wearing jeans.

'We should go inside,' I said with a little cough to

clear my throat. With dark eyes, Nick nodded, making a gruff agreeing noise.

'I'll be a minute.' He rolled off me and stood up, looking away. 'Wait for me in the bedroom.'

Wait for me in the bedroom?

What did he have to do that was so important – smoke another pipe? Before I could come back with a witty retort, he turned to me and raised that bloody eyebrow.

'Don't start without me.'

Muttering under my breath, I stood up, brushed off my jeans, and, on shaky legs, made for the bedroom in his cottage. I was in so much trouble.

CHAPTER EIGHTEEN

It was almost dawn when I gave up trying to sleep and rolled out of Nick's bed. I wanted to stay. I wanted to wake up all flowing hair and glowing skin and fantastic morning sex, but I was wise enough to know that the reality was all knotty tangles, sunburn and morning breath. Besides, sleepovers weren't our thing. Sleepovers were something couples did, and we weren't a couple.

Clutching my sandals in my hand, I rested my fuzzy, tired head against the door frame and looked back at the bed. Nick was still fast asleep, curled up in a corner on the edge of the mattress, the white sheets wrapped around his waist, tangled up in his legs. We might not be a couple, but I was starting to think I was going to be sad when whatever this was was over. Since his unanticipated one-eighty turn into a normal human being, I was more than a little confused about him and about myself. It didn't help that I hadn't got a wink of sleep and desperately needed my own bed. There was too much to process, and I wasn't going to be able to work anything out within a thirty-foot radius of his penis. It was basically a homing beacon of temporary insanity.

I opened my door and slipped inside with a sigh. It was strange how soon somewhere could start to feel like home. Nick had been clear about things in the beginning – this was just a very fancy version of a sales conference shag. And even if I went completely mad and decided I wanted something more from him, it just wasn't possible. As far as Nick Miller was concerned, he was sleeping with Vanessa.

On my way into the bedroom, I caught a glimpse of something small, black and shattered resting on the floor by the door. My phone. It had not fared well from being lobbed against the wall in a fit of temper. Even though the screen was still working, it was completely destroyed, the background picture of me and Amy sliced into a thousand tiny pieces. I just couldn't have nice things, even when they were given to me by a neo-Nazi mugger. He'd think twice before giving me another phone if this was the way it was going to end up. I looked over at my laptop, still plugged in but fast asleep, just like I should be. Masochist that I was, I paused on my way to the shower to swipe my finger across the trackpad and bring the screen back to life. There were the photos, large as life and twice as shitty. They hadn't magically got any better while I'd been otherwise indisposed. And there I'd been, hoping the Photoshop elves might have come and magically replaced them with, well, I didn't know. Anything good would have done. Camel in a top hat. Dogs playing poker. Even the wolphin. Anything would have been better.

The shower was, as ever, hot and steamy when I

stripped off all my clothes and carefully unplaited my hair. I hated washing it at the best of times, but when it was full of sand, like today, it was an actual nightmare. I would rather have taken photos of Evil Ana for another day than prop myself up against that shower wall and tease out every tangle with half a bottle of conditioner. Being a woman was so hard. Well, being a woman or Brian May. The bruises I'd acquired on Tuesday had left little dark blue dots on my arms and shoulders and were only just starting to fade away to a yellowish blur. It was all very *Fifty Shades of Grey*.

'Which he has totally read,' I announced to the shower-head. 'Wanker.'

It took far too long, but eventually I was clean and dry, my hair was as fresh as a daisy and I was wearing clean underwear.

'And all before the sun came up,' I announced to my bed before falling face down onto it. 'Well done, Tess.'

Even though I thought a lie-in was thoroughly well deserved, the universe did not agree. It felt as though my head had only just hit he pillow when my shattered iPhone started shrilly demanding attention from the other room. So not only had I broken the screen, I'd also destroyed the silence function. Brilliant.

'Vanessa fucking Kittler, why haven't you answered my fucking email?'

Oh, how charming. It was Agent Veronica.

'Morning, Veronica,' I replied as bravely as I could. 'Because it's about seven in the morning and I haven't seen it yet?'

'Don't be fucking smart with me,' Veronica carried on yelling. She did not care for Vanessa's sleep patterns.

'What's going on? Why haven't I seen any fucking photos? Send them to me right the fuck now.'

'They're not quite ready to go out.' I was not kidding. 'I'm just doing some edits with the art director, and then I'll get them over to you in an hour.'

'You better not have cocked this up, Kittler,' she warned, her voice oddly cheerful given the fact that she was putting the fear of God in me. 'Because if you have, I will personally come around to your fucking flat and string you up by your tits. Got it?'

'I have got it,' I confirmed, crossing one arm over my chest. 'Talk to you soon.'

Veronica hung up before I could, leaving me in my underwear, sitting on the edge of the settee, staring at a big black screen on a silver laptop.

'Right then,' I said to no one.

Five minutes earlier, I would have happily slept through a hurricane, but now, with a very real threat of physical violence levelled against me and my boobs, I felt strangely wired. Like, five cups of coffee and a Mars bar wired. Gathering my thoughts and, more importantly, a banana, I slipped on my sunglasses and went outside. The ocean was calming. Maybe I could find a little spot where I could sit down and meditate. And by meditate, I meant freak out quietly.

It was still early, but the sun was already heating up, warming my skin through my hastily pulled on T-shirt and stroking the back of my neck. I pulled my hair over one shoulder and twisted it into something like a ponytail, while I wandered and collected my thoughts. Playing with the ends, I noticed the sun had brought out some pretty blonde strands that I'd never seen before, and even though my hair had suffered the sun and sea, altogether it just looked healthier, shinier. Flying out to a tropical island probably wasn't a cost-effective way of getting nice highlights, though. I hoped there was a more affordable middle ground for a failed photographer and unemployed ad gal back in London. Maybe they still made Sun-In.

At home I sulked if I had to walk more than five minutes to a Tube station, but here I found I could wander along for an age without getting bored or annoyed or shoved in the back of the ankles by a push-chair. By the time I thought to turn round and see how far I'd come, the cottages were so far behind me I could barely see them.

'Probably best to get used to that,' I reminded myself, turning towards the water and wading ankle-deep into the gentle waves. In forty-eight hours I'd be looking back at the job centre, neck-deep in trouble. Altogether less enticing. From out of nowhere, I felt a tear trickle down my left cheek. Followed by another. And then, not to be outdone, my right eye decided to join in, and before I knew what was happening, I was openly sobbing in the middle of the beach.

'Stop it,' I sniffed. 'You're not a cryer. You don't cry.'

But as I had to keep reminding myself, it was a week of firsts. Getting on that plane had seemingly opened the floodgates to every emotion that I'd supressed for the past twenty years. I didn't even know why I was crying. I was a very practical woman – I didn't weep in the sea wearing nothing but a T-shirt and my knickers. Bending over, I dipped my hands in the cool water and pressed them against my face. Ah, the simple pleasures of not wearing make-up.

'Good morning, Vanessa.'

Ah, the simple pleasures of not wearing make-up and looking like shit when you bump into someone you aren't expecting to see. Emerging from the trees, my spirit guide, Al, gave me a wave and a smile. At least I assumed he was smiling – it was hard to tell behind his awesome, in every sense of the word, mega-beard.

'Hello, Al.' I waved back and turned away from the sea. I was going to miss it. I was going to miss everything. 'How are you today?'

'Oh, been better, been worse,' he said, waving a hand in the air.

Today he was sporting a knackered old Rolling Stones T-shirt and some neon-yellow shorts. Very Shoreditch twat, I thought. If only he were a twenty-seven-year-old marketing exec instead of a seventy-year-old widower, he'd be so on trend.

'Do you want to see something wonderful?' He cocked his head to one side and nodded down the beach.

'Yes,' I nodded, wiping my face with the back of my hand and marching over to him with purpose. 'Yes, I do.'

'Then come with me.' He held out his arm like a true gentleman and escorted me along the sand. I was going to miss Al. And bloody hell, here came the tears again. 'You all right?' he asked.

'Yep,' I replied curtly, biting the inside of my lip until my face stopped leaking. Vanessa wouldn't have cried because an old man was nice to her. Vanessa would have been very busy trying to work out how to get into his will and then make him have a heart attack. I figured I'd settle for the middle ground of just being polite. 'What are we looking at?'

'Well, we can't get too close, but over there – look.'

Al let go of my arm and pointed towards a big grey rock in the middle of the beach.

'Um, OK?' I shielded my eyes with my hand and stared at the rock. 'What am I looking for?'

'You're looking right at it,' Al laughed. 'You can't see it?'

'I can see a rock?' I squinted and looked around the rock. And then the rock moved. And then I nearly shit myself.

'It's a giant sea turtle,' Al explained. 'They come out onto the beach for a bit of sun sometimes. We're not actually meant to go within six feet of them – they're federally protected – but I don't think there are any policemen around here, do you?'

'Unless you're a policeman.' I followed him on tiptoes towards the turtle. 'And this is a very elaborate sting operation?'

'Ha, yes,' he replied in a low voice. 'I'm actually Magnum, PI.'

'Magnum P what?'

'The youth of today,' he moaned. 'Ask your mum.'

Mum. Another sneaky tear crept down my cheek.

'Hello, turtle.' I knelt down a couple of feet away from the great big greyish creature and held my breath. 'How do I know if it's a boy or a girl?'

'The easiest way is to turn it over,' he explained. 'But I don't fancy it much, do you?'

I looked at the giant, slightly slimy looking turtle and it looked right back.

'No, you're all right,' I muttered.

For roughly three months, when I was seven, I told everyone who would listen that I was going to be a mermaid when I grew up. We were two months into my obsession when my mother began restricting my viewing of *The Little Mermaid* to twice a day, and I was banned from wearing my sleeping bag-slash-mermaid tail to the dinner table after only a week. My sea shell bra, painstakingly crafted from two tubs of I Can't Believe It's Not Butter, mysteriously vanished while I was in bed one night, and all requests for a crab for Christmas fell on deaf ears. But I still knew all the words to 'Part of Your World' and I still loved sea creatures. Or the cute ones, at least; you could keep your sharks. I was very, very excited about meeting a turtle. He or she seemed less excited about meeting me.

'So, Miss Vanessa,' Al said quietly after five minutes of patiently watching me stare at a turtle while it stared right back at me. 'What were those tears for back there?'

'I feel like it can see into my soul,' I whispered, reaching one finger out to touch the turtle's shell. Ew. Slimy.

'It can't,' he replied bluntly. Way to sugarcoat, Al. 'Is everything all right?'

'Not really,' I shrugged, eyes still trailing up and down the turtle's beautifully patterned shell. I wanted to touch a flipper but I didn't dare. 'It'll be fine, though.'

'What if it isn't?' Al asked. 'Sometimes it isn't. Did the photo shoot not go well?'

'The photos are shit . . . sorry, they're rubbish,' I blushed as I checked my language, but Al just smiled and waved for me to carry on. 'My friend says the interview he did is terrible and he's really freaking out about it because it'll be so bad for his career, and then there's all the stuff I have to deal with when I get home and I just don't really know where to start.'

The turtle lifted its head very slightly and gave me a sympathetic wink. That or it was trying to tell me I was rambling.

'And what's happening with the chap?' he asked. 'The one who's so wrong for you?'

'Yeah, that's sort of a mess too.' My ponytail sprang out of its coil and scattered curls all around my face. I pushed them out of the way and sighed. 'He's the one doing the interview.'

Al and the turtle shared a concerned, furrowed brow.

'So I've messed up the pictures, messed up with Charlie, messed up with Nick, Paige is going to be furious, Amy isn't talking to me, my mum isn't talking to me, I won't have a job when I get back, and that's without even getting into the flatmate shenanigans.' I took a deep breath in and tried to let it out evenly without tears creeping into my voice, but I heard it thicken and break. 'I don't know what I thought was going to happen if I came here, but I didn't think it would make things worse.'

I coughed, rubbed my eyes with the sleeve of my shirt and looked away at the sea. I didn't want Turtle to see me like this.

'I don't really know who any of those people are, but maybe things aren't as bad as you think,' Al said in his most conciliatory tone of voice. 'It's possible, isn't it?'

'Anything is possible.' I never wanted to leave this beach. 'But the only people who are still talking to me won't be for long. One thinks she's in love with the man I've been seeing, and said man thinks I'm someone I'm not. It's a very long story.'

'Most people think we're someone we're not,' Al reasoned. 'How do you know he's not right and you're wrong? Maybe he knows you better than you know yourself.'

'That is pretty deep,' I said slowly. 'Still, doesn't help me have decent photos or get Nick a good interview.'

'What was so awful about them?' He pulled at a loose thread on his T-shirt and shook his head slightly. 'And why was your friend's interview so bad?'

'The photos are just bad.' I didn't know if I had the energy to get into it again. 'You know I said Bertie Bennett cancelled on us? Well, his son did the piece instead but he pulled these really awful clothes, and I haven't read the interview, but Nick said he was just really awful and full of himself, and he was really struggling to make it sound like he wasn't, well, a massive twat.'

'Bloody hell.' Al rubbed a hand over his face and all the way down his beard. 'Sounds about right.'

'Yeah. He's a bit of a knob. Nice, but sort of a knob. I just wish his dad hadn't cancelled. Or at least hadn't said he'd do it and then changed his mind when we got here. Nick is really, really upset. I wish I could fix it.'

'Quite the dilemma.'

I made a squeaky groaning noise and wished Turtle would give me an answer.

'There are fights you can win and fights you can't.' He clearly hadn't quite given up. I wished he would. Only fifty percent of what he said actually made me feel better. 'You can't fix everything for everyone all of the time.'

'I do realize that it has not worked out especially well for people in the past,' I acknowledged.

'Good,' he carried on. 'And your job isn't who you are. I think I was right before – you say this Nick chap thinks you're someone you're not, but honestly, do you actually know who you are?'

'The Nick situation is a bit more literal than that,' I replied, stroking Turtle as I spoke. 'But no, really, I am my job. I always have been. Before that, I was the girl who did well in school, the girl who always stayed in to finish her homework. If I'm not my job, I'm not anything. I don't know how to be anything else.'

'I think that's the bigger problem here,' he said with a half-smile. 'And I think it's something I understand. So how about we do a deal?'

'A deal?' I eyed him suspiciously. What could Al possibly have that would help me?

'I'll help you resolve this photo nonsense, but you have to work on finding out who Vanessa is.'

'Finding out who Vanessa is really is a very big part of the problem for everyone,' I said, briefly wondering whether or not I could ride Turtle back into the ocean and live in his underwater kingdom if I wasn't technically a mermaid. It worked in *Splash*.

'Come on.' Al wasn't having any of it. 'Let's go and find your friends and sort this mess out.'

'I think I want to stay here,' I said, visions of being dragged into my sister's room to apologize for eating her last Easter egg hovering before my eyes. 'Thanks, though.'

'You don't think your friend will want to redo the interview?' Al asked. 'You don't want another go at the photos?'

'Well, yeah, but I – what?' I reached up and took the hand that Al held out to me and leapt up to my feet. Turtle opened his mouth to say something but just tutted and sighed before starting to shuffle back into the ocean. 'How are we going to do that?'

'I know you're very busy with your own identity

crisis,' Al said, linking his arm through mine again and giving me a casual salute with the other hand, 'but I've been having a little one of my own. I feel I should introduce myself properly. My name is Albert Bennett. Lovely to meet you.'

CHAPTER NINETEEN

'Oh. Hello.'

It was safe to say that Nick was not nearly as pleased to see me when I knocked on his door fifteen minutes later as he was when I'd passed through it fifteen hours earlier.

'Hello,' I replied, more than a little awkward. Al loitered a few feet away, carefully examining a knot in the wood of one of the chairs on the veranda and demonstrating very impressive not-listening skills. 'I've got good news.'

'Is that why you had to sneak off in the middle of the night?' he asked, striding across the room and pulling a T-shirt over his bare torso. Which was a shame. 'Clearly it wasn't because you were self-conscious about your hair looking a mess.'

Ouch. He really was annoyed. I raised a sad hand halfway up to my sad hair before shaking my head and reminding myself why I was there. Not to bicker and argue but to make something right. For a change.

'Clearly not,' I agreed. I took a cautious step into his

cottage and waited to see what he would do. Nothing. 'I went for a walk.'

'Well, that makes much more sense,' he replied. 'Totally understandable.'

'Hang on a minute, you weren't around when I woke up yesterday. I thought you didn't do sleepovers?' I planted my hands on my hips. I'd come to make things better, not get into a fight, but it didn't look like he was going to give me any choice.

He opened the fridge door, pulled out a carton of orange juice and gulped it loudly for an uncomfortably long time. I noticed his juice had pulp; mine did not. Kekipi must be some sort of idiot savant when it came to juice preferences.

'Nick, you can kick my arse in a bit, but right now I need you to get your bloody Dictaphone and your pen and your little pad and come outside. I've got someone who wants to talk to you.'

'I don't have a little pad,' he snapped back. But journal-istic curiosity was too much for him and he turned around slowly. 'Who am I supposed to be talking to?'

'It's good.' I bit my bottom lip to keep in a smile. According to the thunderous expression on his face, it was still too soon for smiling. 'It's really good.'

He placed the empty juice carton on the side, brushed his hair away from his face and gave me a disbelieving look.

'Oh, just come with me.' I grabbed his arm and dragged him back towards the open door. 'My friend Bertie Bennett would like to have a little chat with you and then we're going to take some pictures. Does that sound OK?'

'But how . . .' Nick's eyes lit up and a huge smile

broke out across his face. In an instant he'd become someone else, switching from mean and moody to eager and excitable. And as much as mean and moody Nick made my knickers twitch, eager and excitable Nick did something incredibly worrying to my heart.

'Actually, fuck it, don't tell me. Where is he?'

'Outside.' I moved a step to the left so he could see Off-Duty Santa, who was now whispering to himself while he picked at something I couldn't see on the top of one of the tables with his thumbnail. I hoped Kekipi wasn't in trouble. 'Ta-da.'

'That's Bertie Bennett?' Nick mouthed in surprise. 'Seriously?'

'Well, that or he's some delusional old mental I met on the beach who is pretending to be Bertie Bennett.' I started to laugh and then stopped. Nick met my terrified expression with one of his own. 'Oh shit.'

'No, no.' He reached a hand out to my shoulder and squeezed gently. 'I'm sure he's not some random crazy. And even if he is, I'm pretty certain he'd give me a better interview than Artie.'

'This is true.' I breathed out and placed my hand on top of his. Nick smiled. I smiled. It was a little bit nauseating. I liked it. 'God help me with the pictures, though.'

'I might stick around while you do those.' He nodded, laughed and leaned in to kiss me softly on the lips. 'Thank you, Vanessa.'

And just like that, the spell was broken. I shrugged off his hand, sighed softly and ignored the confused look on his face. What else could I do?

'You're welcome,' I said on my way out of the door. 'Now come and meet my friend, Al.'

*   *   *

But it seemed as though our interviewee was legit. When our little party arrived at the main house, the woman dusting the pinball machine almost had a heart attack. Within seconds, every pair of eyes inside the four walls had snuck a look at us. Only Kekipi had yet to make an appearance and I had a feeling he wouldn't be far away. Al popped a disembodied head out from inside a rainbow of dresses and smiled.

'So how did you get into fashion in the first place?' Nick asked while Al rummaged through a walk-in wardrobe so big I could have lived in it. And in twenty-four hours, I might have to, I thought quietly in my corner.

'Women,' he said, tipping Nick the wink. 'My dad ran a gentlemen's outfitters in Leicester, and I used to work there every Saturday. I'd see the wives come in with their husbands and then I'd have to take the chaps into the changing room and measure them up while the ladies sat outside waiting. I was about fourteen when I realized my father had it all wrong. When I took over the buying, I convinced him that we should start carrying women's fashions. I found the more I knew about the clothes, the more I had to talk to the female customers about, and the more you talk to women, the better your odds are. Am I right, Nicholas?'

'You are right, Mr Bennett,' he replied with a smile.

We had locked ourselves in Jane Bennett's dressing room and it was epic. The walls were lined with mirrors, and against one, there was a white leather fainting couch that held the dresses Al had already pulled out, and in the corner, Nick made himself at home in a chair sitting in front a vanity unit so incredibly pink, Barbie herself would have turned her nose up at it on grounds of stereotyping. He was such a picture of uncomfortable masculinity, I had to snap a photo. His khaki cargo shorts and loose white T-shirt clashed against the prettiness of it all. He looked huge and awkward and out of place. I was worried he would break something just by existing.

'It's Al, really. Mr Bennett is my son.' He stretched an arm into the far reaches of the wardrobe and, with a strained expression, pulled out a huge clothing bag with a flourish. 'Vanessa, could you take this?'

I took it, I unzipped it and I gasped at the most beautiful ballgown I had ever seen.

'Archive Valentino,' Al explained as I held the hanger over my head and made the dress dance. It couldn't have been more different from the last Valentino dress I'd seen. Acres of lipstick-red silk and ruffles flurried around me and whispered just how much better my life would be if I owned something so very beautiful. 'One of Jane's favourites.'

'Jane Bennett, like in Austen.' Nick smiled at me. Of course Nick read Jane Austen. Obviously I didn't read Jane Austen, but unfortunately for him, Jane Bennett was a character in the mini-series that had Colin Firth coming out of the pond all piss-wet-through and gorgeous, so he could piss off if he thought he was going to make me look stupid.

'It was her favourite,' Al nodded. 'Always said I was her Mr Darcy. Tall, dark and bloody annoying.'

'How did you two meet?' Nick asked while I mooned over the love story and the Valentino.

'Like I said, it's a numbers game.' He gave us both a sad smile and disappeared back into the racks while I carried on staring. 'Sometimes your lucky number comes up. Jane came into the shop one Saturday morning in

May with her fiancé. They were looking for a suit for their wedding.'

'Al,' I admonished, tearing my eyes away from the World's Most Beautiful Dress. 'You didn't?'

Nick gave me sharp look and pressed his finger to his lips. Oh, right. I was supposed to be a silent observer of the interview. Some hope of that.

'Vanessa, I did.' He waggled his white eyebrows up and down. 'She was the one. I knew it as soon as I saw her, all tall and beautiful with that bright red hair and such a furious look on her face. All I wanted to do was make her smile. And I'll have you know, I was so good at my job, her ex didn't even return the suit when she called off the wedding.'

'And when did you make the move to New York?' Nick was tapping away at his laptop while Al continued to toss bag after bag of beauty at me. I glanced over at my phone to see if Paige had returned any of my calls, but there was nothing. I'd knocked for her on the way up to the main house, but a large sheet of white paper torn out of a notebook and taped to the front door declared she was 'SHOPPING' in large, back scrawl. Shopping and not checking her phone, clearly. I hoped her phone call with the magazine hadn't gone badly.

'Jane wanted to get away after the scandal.' Even now, Al clearly couldn't contain his delight at winning his wife. The tiny, ebbing glow of romance left in me thought it was sweet, but the cynical, weary London woman wanted to roll my eyes and declare him a typical man. 'And she had some family over in America. Her mother was Irish and they'd come over in the twenties. We came, we set up a little shop, and, well, that was it, really.'

'I'm not sure anyone is going to let me let you get

away with calling Bennett's a "little shop",' Nick said, scratching his head with a grin. 'I've been to Bennett's. Bennett's is a behemoth.'

'It is now,' Al agreed. 'But when we moved to New York, it was a little shop. Just one floor, just three racks. Still on Madison, but Madison and 83rd. About twenty blocks away from where it is now.'

'And what was the secret to your success? Couldn't just be luck.' Nick gave a non-commital shrug when Al held up a deep teal evening gown that rustled when he flicked his wrist. Al silently shook his head and put it back in the racks. I pouted.

'No secret,' he said, brandishing a black garment bag and throwing it directly at me. 'It was Jane. She loved fashion and I loved her. That really was all there was to it.'

'She must have had quite the eye.' Nick watched as I pulled down the zip on the most glorious little black dress with a full silk skirt and acres and acres of netting underneath. 'These are all hers?'

'Dior,' he said with a happy sigh. 'And yes. She did. And they are. But she didn't like the limelight or the drama of the fashion world, so I did all the outside business while she picked all the clothes. After a while, her taste started to rub off on me, thankfully. After she had Artie, she wasn't nearly as interested in the store any more. She still loved clothes, though. She always looked stunning, did my Janey.'

I swallowed a lump while Nick cleared his throat in a very manly fashion and sat up in his chair. His pink padded gilt chair that was sitting at a pink padded gilt dressing table. It really was an adorable scene.

'That's what so many people get wrong about fashion now.' Al clucked and passed me one more bag. I pressed it against my chest and waited for him to finish speaking. 'It shouldn't be about the trends or the size zeros or who's using fur and who isn't; it should be about love. It should be about a woman walking into a shop, seeing a dress and her face lighting up, just like yours, Vanessa. And as the buyer or the designer or even the shop assistant, you've got to know that. If you don't love what you do, love seeing that look on a woman's face when you've found her the perfect frock or her dream pair of shoes, then you're in the wrong business. It shouldn't be a popularity contest. It's about love.'

At Al's encouraging, I unzipped the final bag and gasped. Somewhere deep inside me, the dying romantic stuck herself with a shot of adrenaline, knocked back a Red Bull and punched the cynical London bitch in the face.

'Oh, Albert Bennett,' I gasped. 'We can't use this in the shoot.'

'Yes, we can,' Al said, overruling me and reaching across Nick's crossed legs to pick up a silver frame from the crowded dressing table. Amongst the matching trinket boxes and hairbrushes that sparkled in the sunlight as though they had been polished that very morning (and I was almost certain they had) was a wedding photo. Smiling as if he had just found out that his football team were guaranteed to win the FA cup every year for the next century, a beardless and considerably younger Al stood beaming beside a tall, beautiful redhead who was wearing a distinct look of happy resignation on her face, as well as the most gorgeous dress I had ever laid eyes on. It was the dress I had in my hands. 'It's my article and I get to pick the dresses. Every single gown I chose after the wedding was influenced by this one. We have to include it.'

The dress was a masterpiece in simplicity. Holding it up by the hanger, it didn't look like much. Off-white, heavy but simple. A straight neckline ended in cap sleeves and the full skirt emphasized a waist so tiny, my still empty stomach started to eat itself. All wrapped up in itself, it was only half possible to see how wonderful the dress might look on the right woman, but in the photograph Al held so carefully, it was clear that the right woman made the dress look spectacular. The black Dior sobbed quietly in the corner.

'It's Givenchy couture,' Al intoned with appropriate reverence. Even Nick was holding his breath. 'Elizabeth Taylor wanted it, but I said no. Audrey Hepburn wore a knock-off in *Funny Face*.'

'Audrey Hepburn wore a knock-off?' I squeaked, suddenly shaking as I realized that this dress was probably worth more than my life.

'Not a knock off per se.' He waved one hand in the air and brushed his thumb along the glass of the silver frame unconsciously. 'Hers was Givenchy too. But tea length instead of a full ballgown. And she didn't have quite so much of an underskirt. My Janey was taller; pulled it off better, if I do say so myself.'

For a moment, there was nothing more to say. I pulled the zip back up on the garment bag and gave it a hug. Mostly because I wanted one.

'I'm going to go and get Martha.' I hung the dress on the to-shoot rack we'd set up by the door and gave myself a shake. 'I'll be back in about half an hour with my camera.'

'We'll be here,' Al said with a cheerful smile.

'Can't wait to see what you're going to pull out your arse,' Nick said with a sarcastic smirk.

'If you get your head out of yours, you'll be able to see,' I said, skipping off down the hallway of the Bennett mansion before he could reply.

That man.

'Martha,' I called quietly, knocking as loudly as I dared on her front door. While I wanted my favourite model to come and help out with the reshoot, I did not want to deal with Ana. It was after ten in the morning but her curtains were still shut, and I was hoping she was a heavy sleeper. It was beyond me how anyone could sleep through a day in Hawaii, but I supposed she was used to visiting exotic locales on other people's money. And also, it was worth remembering she was a complete bastard. 'Martha, it's Vanessa. Are you awake?'

'I am,' a voice snuffled from behind the door while the lock rattled. These doors locked? In London, I had to put the deadbolt on before I could even run to the toilet for a drunken wee, but it hadn't even occurred to me to lock the doors here. 'Is everything all right?'

Even red-faced and puffy-eyed from lack of sleep and sobbing so relentless that she couldn't stop it to say good morning, Martha was obscenely beautiful. Even a paper bag over the head wouldn't help – it would probably just bring out her swan-like neck. But this wasn't the time for pointless jealousy; this was the time for cold teabags and hopefully some very expensive eye cream to work their magic.

'Everything is fine.' I clutched at my camera bag and tried not to drop my tripod. I'd had the best idea for the shoot and was so excited I couldn't stand still, but I needed Martha's help. If she wasn't up for it, I was left with Ana. And that wasn't happening. 'Are you all right?'

What a stupid question.

Rather than do something obvious like answer with words, Martha burst into deafening, heart-wrenching sobs and buried her face in my shoulder. I slid my tripod onto the floor, ignoring the unpleasant clattering sound as it struck the ground, and patted her back.

'Don't cry, he's not worth it,' I told her in between comforting taps. I'd been managing a team of almost entirely women for five years. I knew an on-the-job boy breakdown when I saw one.

'I've been trying to hold it together, but I just caaan't,' she wailed. 'He's seeing someone else. He's coming home to me every night after he's been out shagging someone else. I don't know what to dooo.'

Wow. Men even cheated on models? There really was no hope for us mere mortals.

'That's awful,' I said as sympathetically as I could manage, prising her arms off me. 'And we should have a drink and talk about it, but, I was wondering, is there any way I could borrow you for a couple of reshoots?'

'Oh shit, yeah, of course.' In a heartbeat, Martha snapped into professional mode. Professional model with a runny nose. I couldn't have loved her any more. 'When?'

'Now?' I held up my camera bag. 'And, um, there's no make-up artist and I sort of thought we'd do it without Ana.'

'Thank God,' she sniffed and tossed her long black hair out behind her. 'I can't stand that cow. Let's do it. Anything is better than sitting around here. I just can't seem to stop thinking about him. What's the plan?'

'I'll tell you on the way.' I sighed with relief, understanding exactly how she felt. 'Prepare yourself for some pretty epic dresses.'

'Better than preparing myself to dump that wanker when I get home, isn't it?' she said sadly. 'Lead the way.'

'She looks amazing,' Nick whispered as I moved Kekipi's arms into just the right position with my light reflector. He tutted, sighed and tossed his head like an angry pony, but he did as he was told. As photographer's assistants went, he was – well, he was terrible, but he was willing, so that was something.

Martha was sitting at Jane's dressing table, gazing into the mirror as she touched up her impeccable make-up – someone had been paying attention over the years – wearing the red Valentino dress. Al stood in the wardrobe, still in his board shorts and T-shirt, beaming with his memories of Janey wearing the dress. I wished we could have opened up his head and scooped them all out, but the way his smile shone through the lens of my camera, it was almost as though I had. 'This is perfect.'

'The way Al was talking about it all,' I said, not taking my eye off the scene, 'it all just made sense. The pictures needed to be intimate, they needed to be about him and Jane, and this room is her.'

'Yeah. I felt a bit weird being in here at first,' Nick said, peering over my shoulder at the image showing in the back of my camera. 'It's like when people make the bed for their dead husband or set a place at the table every night ten years after they've carked it, but this just feels right. Really happy.'

'I know.' I paused to signal to Kekipi to lift up the reflector. Lazy bastard. 'Did you notice how all her silver brushes and frames and things look brand new? But it's not weird.'

337

'Which is, oddly enough, a bit weird,' Nick said, placing a gentle hand on my waist. 'These photos are going to be perfect. Thank you.'

I blushed and made an awkward shrugging motion, waving him away, not knowing what to say. 'Um, Martha, I think we've got this dress. Shall we try the next one?'

'The wedding dress?' She sounded as though she was asking if she could finally have a ride on a pony. 'The Givenchy?'

The second we'd walked into the dressing room, Martha's heartbreak was forgotten. She still had a slightly preoccupied, wistful look in her eyes in the images, but the look on her face when she'd seen Jane's wedding dress was unbelievable. I'd considered getting her to call her boyfriend and break it off then and there, she was so consumed by it, but instead I just let her make breathless squeaks at Al and jump up and down, arm stretched out but never quite touching the fabric of the dress. It was a fashiongasm. Al seemed quite pleased.

'Are you sure about this, Al?' I asked. I had my reservations. Everything else looked so incredible. The magazine wouldn't know they weren't getting this and it just seemed so personal. 'Really?'

'Really,' he nodded, handing the dress to a practically vibrating Martha. 'The look on her face, that's what I was talking about earlier. And Janey would be furious if we didn't include her favourite dress.'

'She wouldn't be mad that you're letting someone else wear it?'

'No, it's right,' he said, sounding very certain. 'Janey wasn't one to hide things away and hole them up. She wouldn't want her things to be locked away and turning into rags; she'd want everyone to enjoy them. She'd want them to have a life.'

'She'd want her things to have a life?' I pursed my lips and raised my eyebrows. 'She wouldn't want to hide them away? Maybe not just her things?'

'Oh, very clever, young lady,' he chuckled. 'And yes, you're right. Women usually are. The sooner you learn that, the better, Nicholas.'

Nick gave him a nod and squeezed the hand that was still sitting lightly on my waist.

'I needed a bit of time to think about things, and I've had that. I am still sad that Jane isn't here any more – heartbroken really – but more than anything, I'm glad that I had her while I did. I'm glad we didn't waste a minute.' He stopped speaking as Martha popped out of the bathroom wearing the dress.

The ivory fabric glowed against her dark skin and she'd pulled her hair up into a simple knot, letting strands fall down against her cheeks. She looked incredible. Al stepped back, took a proper look at her, then readjusted the slightly skewed neckline and offered his arm. Martha took it, smiling so broadly there was a good chance she'd been shooting up in the bathroom. I'd never seen anyone look so happy because of a dress. And I had been to a lot of weddings.

'This will not be the first time anyone's said this to you,' Al said, giving a desperately weeping Kekipi a stern look, 'but there isn't enough time to waste in this life. So don't.'

'I'd better finish taking these pictures then,' I said, purposefully obtuse.

CHAPTER TWENTY

The shoot didn't take long. Martha and Al got on like a house on fire, and all remaining thoughts of her rubbish boyfriend were temporarily forgotten just as soon as Martha got a glimpse inside Jane Bennett's fabled wardrobe. I left the two of them playing dress-up with Kekipi and went back to the cottage to work on the photos. As soon as I pulled them up on my laptop, I knew we'd done it. They looked amazing. Al looked happy and proud; Martha looked stunning in every shot. Each dress told a story, and happily, Nick now had those stories. And alongside the beautiful fashion pics, I'd pulled the photos I'd taken of Al on the beach. They were perfect. Honest, sweet and real. And not a ukulele in sight. Somehow, we'd pulled off the impossible. Before I could think better of it, I picked my favourites and emailed them to Agent Veronica. One job down.

'While I'm dealing in miracles,' I muttered, reaching for my phone. Reluctantly, the fucked-up phone dialled out, rang several times and eventually went through to voicemail. I cleared my throat and closed my eyes. I felt horrible. We'd never fought and gone so long without making up before. I couldn't believe she hadn't called me. I couldn't believe I hadn't called her. I had no idea what I was going to say.

'Aims, it's me,' I started, not knowing where to go next. 'I am a massive cock. I deserve to be punched in the boob and I love you very much. I'm sorry I've been so useless, I'm sorry I went complete batshit mental, and I'm sorry I'm not there when you need me. Hopefully you're just down at G.A.Y. dancing on a table to Rhianna and not in the bottom of the Thames. I'll be home Sunday evening, about five-ish. I'll call you then? If you're not dead?' I paused, minimized the Photoshop window on my laptop screen and stared at the picture of me, Amy and Charlie that I used as my wallpaper. Weird. 'So yeah, topline summary, I love you. I'm coming home. Vanessa's probably going to kill me in my sleep, so if you don't hear from me again—'

Before I could finish my round-up, the call waiting tone chimed loudly in my ear.

'Someone's trying to call me and I'm hoping it's you. So I'll talk to you in a minute. Bye!'

But I couldn't talk to her because my phone was officially a piece of shit. I stabbed at the shattered screen again and again but it stubbornly refused to switch calls, and because I'd made such a beautiful modern artesque job of destroying the thing, I couldn't even see for sure who it was that was calling.

'I hate you, iPhone,' I yelled, furious at being refused a chance to make things up with Amy properly. Voicemail messages always sounded hollow and worklike. No one left voicemails any more. Apart from me and whoever had just tried to call me, it seemed, as a green box flashed up underneath a criss-cross pattern of shattered glass announcing a voice message. Out of sheer perversity, I jabbed at the box and, lo and behold, it connected immediately.

'Of course you did,' I hissed, picking up my technological nemesis and holding it to me ear. 'You little shit.'

'Hello, um, Tess?' Bugger me backwards, Bob, it was Charlie.

'Yeah, just checking in. Again. Wanted to see if you're all right or not, or talking to me again. Or not. I tried to call Amy, which was probably a mistake. She's not very happy with me, but when is she? Anyway, um, I've got some news. My football team won on Wednesday night. That's not the news, but, well, I suppose it is news . . .'

He sounded so uncomfortable and so strange that I felt sick. I was doing this to him. Me not talking to him was making him sad. I'd spent ten years trying to make Charlie Wilder happy and now I was hurting him so much that he was making feeble jokey comments about his football team on my voicemail. 'But call me back, yeah? Really need to talk to you. I know I'm a massive twat who doesn't deserve a phone call even, but I, um, yeah, I really, really need to hear your voice.'

It wasn't a long message and it definitely wasn't a coherent one, but it was enough to make me turn off my phone (after six attempts) and rest my head on my forearms. Silly me thinking everything would magically be sorted out by a half-decent photograph. Or several amazing photographs, if I was really going to toot my own horn. Eurgh.

'Vanessa?'

A quiet knock on the door announced my visitor before they spoke, so I knew it wasn't Paige. Sniffing quickly and rubbing my face on my arm, I looked up, blinking into the daylight. Staring at a screen for so long had made me dizzy.

'Kekipi.' I tried to look pleased to see him, and not just because he had a picnic hamper in his hands. 'How is the happy couple?'

'I haven't seen Mr Bennett happier for a very long time.' He smiled right back at me. 'They were still up to their eyeballs in haute couture when I left.'

'Think they both needed a bit of a boost,' I said, eyeing the picnic basket like the honey badger I was. I hadn't eaten anything all day, and now the nervous energy that had carried me through the morning was about to blow up into one giant fist of fury.

'From the looks of things, so do you.' He set the basket down on my couch and came closer, unwittingly risking life and limb. 'Trouble in paradise?'

'Trouble, definitely.' I looked at my phone again, looked at the computer screen and yawned. It was all too much. 'I'm really bloody hungry. What's in the basket?'

The words were out of my mouth before I could stop them. My nan would have been appalled.

'Nothing to eat.' Kekipi frowned and made straight for the kitchen. 'I'll make you a deal. You go and shower, shave, do whatever it is that girls do, and I'll prepare something light and delicious."

'Why do I have to shower to eat something light and delicious?' I looked down and poked my soft belly gently. Maybe I had gained a couple of pounds while I'd been away, but still, insulting much?

'Because I'm taking you somewhere special for dinner, and that picnic basket is full of things to make a woman

343

beautiful,' he said, turning to fix me with an unmistakeably judgemental eye. 'Things that you do not currently own.'

I would have been offended, but he was quite right. I was still using the Nivea for Men I'd nicked from work because I hadn't had time to go out and buy proper moisturizer. Anyone going through my toiletry bag would think it belonged to a travelling salesman. 'I'll just be a minute.'

'You will be a minimum of ten,' he corrected. 'Don't wash your hair, I like it like that.'

'Yes, boss.' I pushed myself up out of my chair and sloped into the bathroom, weak from lack of munchies and the tyranny of an impending gay makeover. Hopefully he wasn't taking me to a live taping of *RuPaul's Drag Race*. Or, actually, I hoped that he was.

When Kekipi finally unveiled his handiwork, I gasped. His flair for the dramatic meant that he had covered every mirror in the cottage aside from the giant one in the bathroom, and I was forbidden to see myself until he was happy. And, scarily enough, when it came to make-up, this time what made him happy made me happy. My skin looked soft and airbrushed with a rosy pink glow rather than bronzed tiger stripes, my lips held just a whisper more than their natural colour, and, thanks to the very liberal usage of smokey eyeliner and individual false eyelashes that I was really, really looking forward to picking off when I got home from wherever we were going, my eyes looked enormous, but not creepy. I almost looked as pretty as him. 'Thank you, lovely.'

'You're very welcome,' he said, tapping me on the nose with a powder puff. And his work was complete.

'I used to do Jane's make-up. When she wasn't well enough to do it herself.'

'Sounds like she was amazing.' I returned his sad smile with one of my own and gave his knee a squeeze. 'I wish I could have met her.'

'She was incredible,' he confirmed. 'But she was also a massive ballbuster and had very little tolerance for anyone not doing as they were told. Unless you were Artie, of course. He could do no wrong.'

'Is that why he and Al don't get on?' I had so many questions about the Bennetts; it was like stepping onto the set of a Hawaiian *Dynasty*. 'Because she let him get away with murder?'

'If he murdered someone, she would have buried the body and torn the tongues out of any witnesses,' he replied. 'There was nothing that boy could do that was less than perfect in her eyes. Sometimes that doesn't sit well with both parents.'

'Sad,' I pouted, swinging my legs on the high stool. 'I wish they could make up. Al's so cool.'

'He had his moments as well,' Kekipi said with a satisfied sigh, hands on his hips. 'But maybe they'll make up now. Now Mr Bennett seems to have snapped out of his mood.'

I nodded slowly, thinking about my mum. I hoped she was OK. I really had to call her when I got home. These things were never easy.

'Shall we get you dressed?' he asked, vanishing out of the front door and reappearing with a black garment bag. 'I have something special for you.'

'Ohhhh.' I clapped my hands together and jumped off the stool, clipping my black fluffy towel to me by the power of my armpits. 'What is it?'

345

'I knew you wouldn't sit still while I did your make-up if I brought it in, so I left it out there,' he said. 'Mr Bennett picked it. I had the final say. And yes, before you ask, it will fit.'

I pressed my hands over my mouth and tried not to cry as he pulled down the zip to reveal the red Valentino ballgown I'd been cooing over during the shoot. It really was remarkable. We'd had to pin it to Martha during the shoot, so there was a tiny sliver of a chance that Kekipi was right, that the dress would go on me. Jane Bennett had easily been as tall as I was, but we definitely did not share the same proportions. Her waist was offensively tiny and no amount of light and delicious food was going to change that.

'What if I sit down and Hulk out?' I whined as he pulled down the concealed zip in the back of the dress and beckoned for me to step into the skirt. 'I'm deceptively fat. I get away with it because I'm tall.'

'You are not fat,' Kekipi snapped back. 'Frickin' women, always thinking they're obese because they have an arse.'

'Wasn't thinking about my arse, actually,' I said sulkily. 'But thanks for the feedback.'

'Shut up and put out your arms,' he commanded. The dress felt surprisingly light and the skirt fell about my legs, fluttering lightly and demanding a twirl. I had to mentally staple my feet to the floor to stop myself from spinning. So this was how it felt to be a princess. Screw you, Kate, it was my time to shine. I felt absolutely beautiful. 'And anyway, Jane wore this while she was pregnant with Artie. It's empire line, so there's plenty of room in the waist.'

And suddenly I felt like a fatty again.

But it didn't matter. As soon as Kekipi parked me in front of the mirror, all was forgotten. If this was maternity wear, then someone needed to knock me up, pronto. The lipstick-red shade of the fabric made my lack of a tan an asset rather than an embarrassment, and the loose, soft waves that Kekipi had teased out of my hair made the whole thing look soft and romantic rather than uncomfortable and formal. I wasn't afraid to move; I wasn't scared I would rip it. We were a team – the dress breathed when I did. Floor-length layers of red silk floated in front of me and a deep, sleeveless V-neck bodice flattered my boobs and cinched in my waist. And Kekipi was right. The high empire line waist wasn't too tight, and more importantly, I could already tell it was going to allow for eating. Hurrah.

'Oh God, you've got to take a picture of me in this,' I said, not able to look away from the mirror. 'My friend Amy will never believe it.' Not that she'd called me back yet.

'Done and done,' he replied, hands on my shoulders. 'I think you're ready, Cinders. I need to get you to the ball.'

'We're going to a ball?' I was utterly non-plussed.

Kekipi shook his handsome head. 'Not exactly, but you do have somewhere to be, and if I don't get you there before midnight, Prince Charming will likely be pissed.'

'My date isn't with you?'

'Honey, even dolled up like this, you're just not my type.' Kekipi took my hand and walked me to the front door. 'You don't need your shoes. Follow me, lover.'

So transfixed was I by my own reflection that we were locked in the back of one of Al's SUVs before I realized

I had still not eaten anything, either light or delicious. I pressed a sad hand against my empty belly and sniffed. So this was how models stayed so skinny.

No matter how pretty, graceful and grown-up I looked, when my stomach was rumbling, I was complaining. Kekipi fished around in the back of the SUV and managed to come up with two packets of biscuits wrapped in cellophane which I inhaled without bothering to ask where they had come from or how long they had been in the car. I did not care. I was so hungry. By the time the car rumbled to a halt, I was covered in very un-Valentino crumbs that Kekipi was obsessively picking off me in a very disgruntled manner.

'I knew we shouldn't have put you in something so elegant,' he muttered under his breath. 'There were some perfectly good mumus in that closet.'

'Oh, shut up,' I sang, hopped up on a tiny amount of sugar and arrival giddiness. I still had no idea where we were and Kekipi wasn't parting with any details, but I'd deduced, from his Prince Charming comment, that Nick was most likely involved, and I couldn't wait for him to see me in my dress. 'Where are we?

'You shut up,' he snapped back, grumpy but smiling. 'Get out of the car and you'll see. Honestly, the things I do for love.'

The driver opened my door before I had a chance to and I gave him as pretty a smile as I could manage, given that all I really wanted to do was jump up and down and do the Snoopy dance of joy. The entire afternoon had vanished in a vortex of photo editing, make-up application and mystery road trips and, wherever I was, the sun was setting, casting a pinkish orange glow through the low, lush trees that hung overhead. Somewhere nearby, I heard water running. It was all very familiar but not.

'That way.' Kekipi nodded towards a narrow sandy path leading into the trees. 'I'll see you later, princess.'

'Am I being sacrificed to a giant monkey?' I asked, my nervous energy turning into flat-out nerves. 'Because no dress is worth that.'

'Go away.' He flicked a hand at me and hopped back into the car. 'Call me when you're engaged.'

And just like magic, my nerves turned into complete and utter, all-consuming terror.

'He's joking,' I whispered to my dress as I made my way down the path. 'It's just not a funny joke.'

Somehow I managed to keep my feet moving one in front of the other. The sound of water changed from running to rushing, the smell of the frangipani flowers swam all around me, and as I peered between the trees, I started to see little tealights appear. At first it was just one or two grouped together on the left or right side of the path, but as the path turned into a stairway, the candles became more common. Each step was lit with three tiny white candles in little glass jars. One or two had already blown out, but it was still beautiful. Ever so slightly cheesy, but very, very beautiful. It took me too long to work out why the sound of the water was so familiar, and I was almost at the bottom of the steps before I saw the waterfall. Right where we had laid in the sand was Nick. The self-satisfied smile on his face melted away when he saw me.

'Wow,' he whistled.

'Yeah,' I exclaimed, hands above my head. 'I know.'

By the water, Nick, and presumably Kekipi, had set up a small round table that was covered in food and looked almost as good as my date. I stopped at the bottom of the steps and gave myself a moment to take it all in. The heavy scent of the flowers, the rush of water, all the little glowing candles and, in the middle of it all, the man who had done this, just for me. His hair was still a mess – by now I'd realized it always was – but his shirt and jeans were smart, and his eyes sparkled all the way across the beach. When he wasn't looking smug, his smile was infectious, and I felt a happy grin spread across my own face. I couldn't help but feel a little overdressed, compared with Nick's ensemble, but at the same time, it was a very pretty dress. Probably not the best for swimming in, though. Probably ought to stay out of the water.

'You found your way, then?' Nick called, giving me a wave. 'Are you coming down or not?'

'Did you know there was a footpath to this bloody place?' I bellowed, looking back at the steps I'd just descended with so very much grace and breaking his spell. 'I nearly broke my neck on Wednesday and there's a bloody staircase back there, Nick Miller.'

Nick smiled, said nothing and picked a bottle of champagne out of a silver ice bucket.

'In the interests of this evening going well, I'm just going to ignore you,' he said, popping the cork and pouring out a glass – just the one – and taking a sip. I remained on the other side of the beach. 'Have you got any idea how long it takes to carry and light two hundred candles?'

'Half of them have gone out.' I flipped my hair and strode as agitated as was possible in a floor-length ball-gown, on sand, and sat down at the table. The lure of food was irresistible. I was powerless in its presence.

And Nick didn't look half bad either. 'Maybe you should run back up and relight them while I have my tea.'

'Maybe you should be quiet,' he replied, filling up a second glass of champagne and handing it to me, his fingertips just missing mine as I took it, but even the potential for skin-on-skin contact made me shiver. I breathed in deeply, breathed out slowly, and sipped my drink. 'Nice frock,' he said.

'It's all right, isn't it?' I fanned the skirt out around me and tried to steady my pulse. Between being completely famished and totally overwhelmed by what was happening, I couldn't rely on my voice to stay calm. And there was nothing sexy about a squeaky comeback. 'Just something I keep for hanging out at the beach.'

'It works,' Nick nodded, sitting down in the chair next to mine, his knee touching my knee. 'You should wear it more often.'

'Thinking it'll look good down the job centre on Monday.' I took a sip of my champagne and immediately realized my mistake. That was Tess's problem not Vanessa's. 'Because I'm never going to work as a photographer again,' I added quickly.

'Those photos you took this morning were beautiful,' he said. 'You know they were. I told you everything would be OK if you just trusted yourself. You didn't need Paige directing you; you needed Paige gone.'

'It wasn't Paige's fault,' I replied, feeling the faint twang of betrayal as Nick loaded my plate with bread and fish and, blee, salad. 'It was everything. Today was better because we had Al. If he'd been around since the beginning, none of this would have happened.'

'If he'd been around from the beginning, I probably wouldn't be here now,' Nick replied. 'I'd been planning to change my flight to leave as soon as I'd got the interview.'

'Something exciting to rush home for?' I asked, popping a piece of marinated pork in my mouth and trying not to make inappropriate noises. Fuck me, it was delicious. 'Hot date?'

Nick didn't say anything. Instead he made a disgruntled sighing noise and gave his head a shake before his expression hardened. Satisfied he'd plied me with enough food and booze, he started to serve himself. In silence.

'Did you refile the interview?' I asked.

'I did,' he said. 'Did you send the photos?'

'I wanted to show Paige first. She's been missing all day. I haven't been able to get hold of her.'

Nick laughed, his blue eyes softening a little. 'She's been off shopping all day. You should have sent them to Steph yourself. She should know it was your idea.'

'I don't want to stab Paige in the back,' I said, silently adding, 'any more than I am right now.'

'I'm guessing this is why our paths have never crossed before, Vanessa Kittler.' Nick raised his glass in a toast. 'You're too nice.'

'Vanessa Kittler, you're too nice,' I echoed, touching my glass to his and taking the tiniest sip. 'Words that have never been uttered before and will likely never be uttered again.'

'You really have got it in for yourself, haven't you?' he said, rolling up the sleeves of his dress shirt. Apparently we'd been smart for as long as we needed to be. 'OK, since this went so well last time, let's play a game. I want you to choose five words to describe yourself.'

'Hungry, tired, overdressed and . . .' I glanced round

at my surroundings for inspiration. 'Annoyed that we didn't use the stairs on Wednesday. Your turn.'

'That's more than five words,' he admonished, flexing his forearm as he reached out for more bread. I resisted the urge to bite it. Just barely. 'I'll go after you.'

'Such a gentleman,' I said, huffing and cramming an entire chicken skewer into my mouth. I hoped Kekipi was prepared to send care packages once I'd left – every mouthful of food was delicious. 'Fine. Hard-working, loyal, dedicated and still tired and hungry.'

'You don't believe all that any more than I do,' Nick responded, leaning back in his chair and giving me a full headshake this time. 'Are they honestly the best attributes you can come up with, or are you just being stupidly self-effacing? Because I can't decide which is more irritating.'

'Well, I'd add in stone-cold fox, but I'm worried I'd seem a bit full of myself,' I replied through a mouthful of pig. 'Your turn.'

'Clever, perceptive, funny, loyal and quick.' He counted his words off on his fingers. 'And obviously a stone-cold fox.'

'This is not the first time you've played this game, is it?' I asked. 'I feel cheated.'

'At least you feel something other than the heavy burden of other people's expectations,' he said, deftly dodging my hand as I swung out to punch him in the arm. 'See? I'm quick.'

'And too bloody clever for your own good,' I said, soothing my bruised ego with another well-earned sip of champagne. No matter how hungry I was, if I was going to get through another battle of wits with knobhead, I was going to need a cocktail or two.

'You really don't see yourself, do you?' Nick asked. 'You really do think you're just this sad workhorse, slogging away.'

I coughed, choking on too much dry bread. Note to self – never be in too much of a rush to eat to forget butter. 'Thank you for such a beautiful image.'

'I'm serious,' Nick said seriously, wearing his serious face. 'I'm really good at reading people. It's kind of why I ended up in the job I'm in, but I cannot get a proper read on you. You're definitely not the girl I thought I was meeting, and you're really not the martyr you think you are. So who are you?'

'I don't know what you're talking about,' I replied, wishing there was a toilet I could excuse myself to. Not because I needed to go, but because the conversation was becoming increasingly uncomfortable. And at some point I was going to need to go.

'I'm talking about you hiding who you are under this "poor me"' act,' he went on. 'You put all your focus on what other people think, on work, on that stupid man in London who doesn't know how fucking lucky he is, but when you let all of that go, you're amazing.'

'I'm amazing?' I met his eyes, expecting to see a light of laughter, but there was nothing. Just painfully bare honesty. I felt myself blush and shifted in my seat. 'Nick, you don't know me.'

'Yeah, I do,' he argued. 'The look on your face today when you were taking the pictures, when Al was talking about his wife. When you forget to try, you're so beautiful. It's the same when you're with me. I love the look on your face when you know you can't win a fight.'

'I never know I can't win a fight,' I rallied, knocking back almost an entire flute of champagne. Hic. 'And really, you don't need to say all this just to get in my pants. I think we're a bit past that.'

'That's the other thing,' he laughed. 'As soon as things get even the tiniest bit real or honest, you make a joke or you say something bitchy. It's all a defence, Vanessa. I've been interviewing people for long enough to know when they're trying to keep me out.'

I looked up at the sky and watched as pale pink and peach streaks washed over the light blue twilight. 'And why would I be trying to keep you out?' I wondered aloud.

'I'm trying really hard to do something nice.' I felt Nick's hand cover mine on the table. Out of politeness, I let go of the piece of bread I was holding and curled my fingers around his. 'I know I was a total dick. I've been a massive dick to everyone for a really long time, and I basically forgot how to be anything else.'

'So why stop now?' I asked, still not quite meeting his eyes.

'Damned if I know,' he replied, a hint of a laugh in his voice that didn't really ring true. 'Been trying to work that out myself. Thought of a thousand reasons: being back on Oahu, just had my birthday, haven't had a shag in ages.'

He sat quietly for a moment, waiting for me to say something, but I had nothing. With one hand I cradled my glass in my lap, and with the other I squeezed his warm fingers. It was meant to be reassuring. I hoped that it was.

'I've got a horrible feeling it's actually because I really like you,' he whispered.

'Because I'm loyal, dedicated and hard-working?' I asked.

'Because you're passionate and fierce and caring and creative and so funny and so beautiful and totally naïve, and you've got so much hair, and you're completely fucking oblivious to all of the above,' Nick replied, leaning closer towards me. 'Apart from the hair. And because you took me on and won.'

I'd won?

'And because you're not afraid to tell me the truth.'

He had to go and spoil everything.

I wanted to melt, I wanted to kiss him hard and ask him to say things like that to me every single day, but I couldn't. Because the day after tomorrow, the girl he was talking about wouldn't exist any more. And the girl that would take her place didn't know how to tell him the truth. Instead I let go of his hand and let my head fall backwards, as far as it would go, covering my eyes with my hands. I needed a moment, just a moment, to work this out.

I should just tell him. I should just laugh and take his hand and say 'funny story . . .' It wasn't that big a deal, was it? It was only a name. I remembered something from my GCSE English: A rose by any other name would smell as sweet. Except things hadn't worked out so well in that instance. Oh bugger.

'Vanessa?'

I'd tell him in the morning.

'I haven't really opened up for a while,' Nick said, gripping my wrist tightly to get my attention. I uncovered my eyes and looked at him. His jaw was set and the sparkle in his eyes was burning. It was all too much to bear. 'So you can understand why this is a bit uncomfortable for me right now. Should I not have said that?'

'I just don't know what to say,' I whispered, eyes wide and prickly. 'I don't know what to say to you.'

'Then I'll just stick with my earlier comment,' he replied, leaning in to press his lips to mine. 'In the interests of this evening going well, I'm just going to ignore you.'

I woke up in Nick's bed, in Nick's arms. The rest of the evening had passed perfectly, just as Nick had planned. I quietly relived the kissing, inappropriate touching, some champagne-fuelled skinny-dipping and fifteen minutes of drunkenly blowing out tealights on our way back to our car and driver, me wearing Nick's white shirt, him carrying my precious dress. If he was hurt by my less than positive reaction to his confession of like, he did a fantastic job of hiding it. I looked down to see I was still wearing his shirt, with almost every button done up wrong. The rest of my clothes were scattered across the room, the Valentino was draped across the chair opposite the bed, giving me a sly wink. I felt as though I'd done her proud.

'Go back to sleep,' Nick murmured as I stirred again. His body was hot and solid, curled against mine, and I willingly pushed back against it, feeling the tension in his muscles. It made me smile. His knees moved up, pulling me in towards him, and he coiled his legs around mine, our hands and arms already entwined.

'I should go back to mine and pack,' I sighed in response. 'We fly out this afternoon. I haven't sent the pictures to Steph yet, and Paige still hasn't seen them. There's too much to do to stay in bed.'

'But you're really only agreeable in bed,' Nick replied. 'As soon as you get out, you start opening your mouth, and that's when you get annoying.'

'I know,' I agreed. 'But there's really not very much I can do about that.'

'You could come back to New York with me,' he suggested in a voice barely louder than a whisper, speaking right in my ear. 'We could stay in bed for days.'

I let him kiss my ear, my neck, my shoulder, before I replied. Was that throwaway pillow talk or a genuine offer? Not that I could just up and run off to New York, could I. Could I? I'd already upped and run off to Hawaii. What was one more week? And maybe when we got there, I could explain everything and he would understand. Probably. I bet New York was full of pathological liars. I bet everything sounded more charming in the shadow of the Empire State building. I'd be like a modern-day Meg Ryan. Without the plastic surgery. Oh, how we'd laugh . . .

'You want me to come to New York?' I said with a squeak as one of his hands let go of mine and started to work its way down my thigh. 'With you? Today?'

'Why not?' he replied, his voice thick with sleep and desire. 'You keep saying you have nothing to go home for.'

'This is true.' I closed my eyes and let a very speedy procession of images flash through my mind before giving in to Nick's dexterous fingers. 'But I shouldn't.'

'Because?'

I smiled and let out a tiny yelp.

'I don't really know,' I said, rolling over to face him. 'Why don't you give me a couple more reasons why I should.'

Half an hour and two very good reasons later, I lay in bed listening to Nick shower, making no moves to head back to my own bathroom. I really should, I told myself – there was too much to do. But rolling around on the silky soft sheets with my eyes closed was too tempting.

As soon as I opened up my suitcase, I had to admit that this week was over, and as soon as I admitted this week was over, I had to stop having fun and start making some very difficult decisions. Probably. Unless I went away with Nick.

Giving myself one more minute to wrap myself up in Nick's sheets, I breathed in, storing away each and every memory as safely as I could. The smell of the ocean, of Nick, that lay on top of crisply laundered bedlinen. I had replayed the moment he had kissed me by the water-fall so many times that it was burned into my brain. It was already starting to feel like something I'd seen in a movie rather than something that had happened to me. The sound of the shower running in the bathroom echoed the rush of the waterfall, and, making myself a nest of pillows, I hid my face from the morning sun. Just one more minute. Just one more minute here, and then . . .

And then my phone started to ring.

And that's when things really started to go wrong.

CHAPTER TWENTY-ONE

'Paige, wait,' I wailed, following her out of Nick's cottage, trying to pull his white shirt over my underwear before we hit civilization. None of the gardeners or housekeepers wanted to see me in my pants. Literally, none of them. Kekipi had hired half the gay population of Oahu. 'Can I try to explain, please?'

'Um, no,' she shouted without looking back. 'You can fuck off and die.'

'Maybe you can explain to me?' Nick grabbed my arm and pulled me back. I glanced down reluctantly and breathed an unlikely sigh of relief that he had found his boxers before leaving the bedroom. 'What is going on, Vanesssa?'

'Her name's Tess,' Paige reminded him. 'Although she might as well be Vanessa, given what a filthy, lying skank she is.'

Oh, that was a low blow. Not that I didn't have it coming.

'I can't believe you would do this. Which just goes to show how stupid I am.' Paige looked furious. 'You did a really good job of pretending to be my friend. Well done.'

Oh God, I was a horrible person.

'I am your friend,' I protested. 'Honestly, this is . . .'

'Exactly what it looks like?' she countered. 'Friend?'

'Paige, wait.' I shook off Nick's hand and gave him a desperate look as she ran off. 'I can explain to you in a minute – just let me go and explain to her and then I'll come back.'

'You don't think I deserve an explanation first?' He looked furious. Confused and furious. 'Because Paige seems to know your actual name, which is one step ahead of me.'

'Oh God.' I pressed my hands against my face and made a frustrated mewing noise. What should I do? What was I supposed to do? 'OK, my name isn't Vanessa; it's Tess. Vanessa is my flatmate. She's a massive cow and I sort of borrowed her camera and her job and, well, her name to come out here because I got the sack, I got fucked over by Charlie and I may or may not have had a very small mental breakdown. That's the short version. Can I come back and give you the long version in five minutes?'

'Go and talk to Paige,' he said in a strained voice. 'Tess.'

Well. If I'd known it was going to be that easy to shut him up, I could have told him the truth a week earlier. His fury changed to shock and his shock, if I was being brutally honest, looked an awful lot like a confused goldfish. Not his most attractive expression. Still hot, though.

'I was going to tell you,' I replied weakly. 'I wanted to tell you.'

'Go and talk to Paige,' he repeated. 'Go.'

Thinking of the right thing to say was impossible, so I simply nodded and ran up the steps, following Paige towards the main house.

'Paige, wait,' I bellowed, struggling to run and shout at the same time. I really was too out of shape for this much drama. 'Just one minute.'

But it was pointless. She was on a mission and I had a horrible feeling that nothing good was going to come out of it. For me, anyway. When I finally heaved myself over the top step, I saw Paige animatedly lecturing Al and Artie, who were sitting together at the huge table on the veranda while Kekipi looked on, a delighted look on his face. It was quite the sight, to see the two Bennett men together. Resuming his rightful role as Bertie had done nothing to alter Al's appearance. Even back at the head of the table, he was still ninety-five percent beard and still wearing a faded old T-shirt and a pair of knee-length shorts, and Artie, sitting to his left, was resplendent in a full three-piece suit at nine o'clock on a Saturday morning. In front of the glamorous mansion, in the broad sunshine, it was difficult to say who looked more out of place.

'And so, yes, I'm so sorry, Mr Bennett . . .' I was finally close enough to hear Paige as she got to the end of her story, hands pressed against her chest, painfully earnest look on her face. 'And Mr Bennett. It's all just been such a terrible mix-up. Obviously we'll be dealing with Miss Brookes when we return to England, but, really, I just wanted to reassure you both that *Gloss* had absolutely no idea about any of this and we will do whatever it takes to make things right.'

'Well, well, well.' Al stood up and gave me the biggest,

sunniest grin I had ever seen. 'You weren't kidding when you said you weren't who we thought you were.'

I stood still at the top of the stairs, very, very aware that I was only wearing my knickers and a badly buttoned-up man's shirt with last night's make-up smeared all over my face. Kekipi gave me an elaborate wink, a silent clap, and then motioned for me to wipe the mascara smears away from under my eyes.

'I don't know what to say.' I took a step forward and then froze, crossing my arms in front of me, feet rooted to the spot. Paige turned an icy glare my way and sat down at the table opposte Artie. He mostly looked confused. 'I'm really sorry.'

'You can say you're sorry to our lawyers,' Paige intoned without turning to look at me. 'Or the police. I'm not sure exactly how this is going to work.'

'Oh, Miss Sullivan.' For some reason, Al seemed to think this was all terribly funny. He was actually laughing. 'I don't think there's any need for that. Besides, I'm not entirely convinced our friend – Tess, is it?' I nodded and wished very hard for the earth to open and swallow me whole. 'I'm not sure Tess has actually broken any laws. Besides, if I hadn't made her acquaintance, I wouldn't have been able to sit down with Mr Miller yesterday and do your interview in the first place.'

'You . . . you did an interview?' Paige's head spun so quickly, her perfect blonde hair was just a blur. 'With Nick?'

'I left you so many voicemails for you to call me back.' I couldn't remember a time when I'd felt more frustrated with myself. 'I emailed you.'

'And we took new photos,' he confirmed. 'I think they probably turned out quite well, didn't they, Tess?'

'They did,' I said quietly. 'I can show you? They're on my laptop. I already sent them to my agent. I thought you'd want to send them to Steph yourself.'

She shook her head slowly, face like thunder.

'I tried to call you loads of times, but you didn't answer,' I explained. 'And then I couldn't find you.'

'And I couldn't find you last night,' she replied tartly. 'But that's because you were busy.'

'I'm sorry.' Artie finally found his voice to interrupt. 'I think I'm missing something here. So?'

'No.' I took another tiny step forward. 'I'm Tess. And again, really, really sorry.'

'In all honesty, it doesn't much matter to me,' he replied. 'I'd just like to know what is actually going in the magazine. My interview is running, yes? Father?'

'Artie, I really want to make things right with us,' Al said with a sigh, pouring a cup of coffee and beckoning me over to the table to sit beside him. I tiptoed over, careful not to flash my knickers, and sat down, keeping my knees firmly together. Paige looked livid. If her hair had been shorter, I was pretty sure we would have been able to see steam coming out of her ears. 'I miss your mum and I miss you. But I had Mr Miller email me his interview with you, and, I won't lie, son, it's bloody awful. So, no, I don't think they're going to be using it.'

The tension round the table could have been cut with a knife. Paige looked like she wanted to throttle me, Artie looked like he wanted to punch out his dad, and Kekipi looked as though he wanted to leap onto the nearest chair and burst into song. Keeping quiet in the corner was killing him.

'You agreed that we would do this interview to announce your retirement from the company,' Artie reminded his father, pulling on the end of his tie as his face grew redder and redder. 'Are you telling me that's no longer the case?'

'I am still retiring,' Al replied calmly. 'The business is all yours. I made you a promise and I will never, ever go back on a promise to you. But I agreed to the interview because Dee-Dee asked me to do it. It was your idea to use it to announce my retirement. Not mine. However, it's done. Don't worry.'

'Who's Dee-Dee?' I asked when Artie didn't say anything in return.

'Delia, my god-daughter,' Al explained, not taking his eyes off his son. I was certain we were all a bit worried he might have a stroke. 'She owns the magazine, um, *Gloss.*'

'Oh.' I stole a quick glance at Paige, who appeared to have gone catatonic. 'Couldn't put a good word in for me, could you?'

'I certainly could.' He laughed again and it was a re-assuring, booming noise. 'Much easier now I know your real name.'

'If you'll all excuse me.' Artie pushed his chair away from the table and gave a curt nod. 'I need to make a few calls. Father, I'll speak to you later.'

'We're having dinner together, whether you like it or not,' Al called after his retreating son. He turned back to us. 'His mother would be furious if she could see us bickering like this.'

'You'll fix it, though?' I picked up my coffee cup, eyes still trained on Paige, just in case she decided to jam a screwdriver in my neck.

'I hope so,' he said, picking up a piece of bread and cheese and putting the entire thing in his mouth, artfully avoiding dropping crumbs on the beard. 'But I think we both know these things can be very complicated.'

'I'm going to pack.' Paige excused herself. 'Thank you for being so understanding, Mr Bennett.'

'Paige.' I jumped up and grabbed hold of her hand. She snatched it back before I could get a good grip. 'Just please let me explain.'

'What's to explain?' she asked, and for the first time, she didn't look angry, just really, really sad. 'I trusted you. You lied to me. You've made me look stupid and it's all worked out beautifully for you, hasn't it?'

I had nothing to say.

'You must have learned more than you realized from living with your flatmate,' she said, tears spilling over her cheeks. 'You're a natural, Tess.'

Sniffing delicately, she jogged down the staircase and onto the beach. I stood there watching her go until she disappeared into her cottage. The slam of the door echoed all the way up to the veranda.

'Oh. My.' Kekipi declared as the silence became too much. 'Tell me everything.'

'Kekipi,' Al said with a warning tone. 'I don't think this is the time.'

'It's absolutely the time – she's leaving in an hour,' he argued. 'Vanessa, Tess. Whatever your name is. Details.'

'I'm only doing the short version,' I said, sinking back into my seat, face first into my cup of coffee. 'And after this, I'm just not doing it ever again. So, I have this flatmate called Vanessa . . .'

The short version of my story took almost twenty minutes with all of Kekipi's questions and interruptions. To his credit, Al stayed quiet throughout, only adding the odd tut or sigh to show support. He really was the best stand-in dad a girl could ask for. If Artie decided he didn't want him, I would totally sign him up.

'But really, I never do things like this – the Nick thing, the spur-of-the-moment thing, lying in general.' I chewed on my bottom lip and tried to look as honest as possible. 'When I was fourteen, me and my friend went to see *The Exorcist*, even though my mum said I couldn't, and when we got back, I had to go and wake my mum up because I felt so guilty. I can't lie. I can't even tell people they look good in a pair of jeans if they make them look fat.'

'But didn't you say you work in advertising?' Kekipi asked, pouring himself a very generous mimosa. 'Isn't that professional lying?'

'Exactly, professional lying,' I pointed out. 'Completely different kettle of fish.

'I know you want us to tell you what a terrible person you are and lock you in the stocks at midday,' Al said, stroking his chin through his beard and sniffing with contemplation. 'But I'm not entirely convinced of that.'

'Not following,' I replied. 'Paige is never going to forgive me for the Nick thing. Nick is never going to forgive me for any of it. And that's before I even try to unravel the mess back home.'

'If they're real friends, they'll forgive you,' he argued. 'And if they don't, you have to accept that. As you get older, you'll realize there isn't enough time to waste regretting the things you've done. Apologize, explain, wait for them to come to you. You can't rush forgiveness, but you can't waste your life waiting for it either.'

'I can't believe you're being so understanding,' I said. 'I wish I didn't have to leave.'

'I'd tell you to stay, but I think you need to go back

and work a few things out,' Al replied. 'And come back when you've worked out who you're going to be next.'

'I think I'd just like to go back to being Tess.' I raked my hands through my hair, pulling it all over one shoulder and slowly working away at the tangles. 'I wish I could just go back to how it was before.'

'No, you don't,' Al smiled. 'You weren't any happier then than you are now.'

'True,' I admitted. 'But things were a lot easier.'

'Take a breath,' Al advised. 'Work out what you really want before you do anything. And not what you think you should want or what other people tell you to want. Really think about it, Tess. Now's the time.'

It seemed strange that someone should be telling me to think about myself after everything I'd done.

'Sometimes we have to try on a few different personalities before we find ourselves,' he said. 'Admittedly, not everyone does it in such an extreme way as you, and they usually get it out of the way a couple of years after university, but still. I think you've probably learned something.'

'Odds are good,' I agreed. 'Still trying to work out exactly what, though.'

'You'll get there,' he said, cutting himself some more cheese. 'You'll get there.'

Even after Al's words of wisdom, I felt heavy and exhausted when I got back to the cottages. Kekipi had promised to ride with me to the airport, presumably just to squeeze out more information on the Nick front, but I wasn't complaining – I was looking forward to the company. It would be nice to stock up on smiling faces while there was still one around. But before I could throw all my-slash-Vanessa's things into my woefully empty suitcase, I had to talk to Nick. I said I'd be five minutes and I'd been ages. Who knew what kind of conclusions he'd come to in my absence.

I pushed my hair into something approaching a reasonable shape, bit my lips and rubbed my cheeks, well aware that this entrance was about as far removed from my entrance at the waterfall last night as it was possible to be. Gone was the Valentino; gone were the eyelashes and the carefully combed-out curls. Gone was Vanessa. All that was left was Tess. I hoped she was enough.

I knocked on the door and waited. Nothing. I knocked again, pre-flight and pre-fight anxiety building inside me. When he didn't answer my third knock, I opened the door and let myself in. It's what all the cool kids were doing, anyway.

'Nick?' I called quietly. The cottage was so still, even my softest voice sounded intrusive and rude. 'Are you there?'

It was a stupid question. He was gone. All of his things were gone. There wasn't a single trace of him anywhere in the apartment. His pens, his notebooks, the stack of dog-eared paperbacks I'd knocked over by the couch last night. All gone. I wandered through the rooms, trying to find a memory that would convince me he had been there in the first place. I took a deep breath before opening the bedroom door, hoping I would walk in to find him sleeping, just too tired to hear me knocking. The bedroom was empty, the sheets stripped from the bed, screwed up in a ball and tossed in a corner of the bathroom. Wherever he was now, Nick Miller had left this place as a less-than-happy camper.

Sinking onto the bare mattress, I ran my hand over

369

the plush fabric and sniffed a little, feeling sorry for myself. It was my own fault, I knew that. I could have told him the truth before things got away from me. I could have told him the first night we were together. I could have told him over dinner at the waterfall. But by then it was too late. And before it was too late, it was too soon. He went from being an arsehole to being everything so quickly, I didn't have time to catch myself. And now, here I was, sat on his bed, wearing his shirt, wondering where he had gone. Well, I couldn't say he'd lied about being unreliable, I thought, lying back and imagining him there beside me.

I just wished I could say I hadn't lied at all.

CHAPTER TWENTY-TWO

The living room was exactly how I'd left it. The remote control sat on the arm of the chair, the curtains were half drawn, and an empty coffee mug was gathering dust to the left of my foot as I sat, coat still on, hunched up in the middle of the settee. My suitcase, once again hastily packed with Vanessa's things, was parked by the door, and the entire place was silent and still. Through my overtired, jet-lagged fug, I heard doors slamming and horns blowing outside, people shouting in harsh London accents, buses roaring down the main road and splashing in the rain. Because, of course, it was raining. Staring straight ahead out of the window and onto the chimney pots of my neighbours, I curled my hands back into the sleeves of my coat. It felt like I'd never been away.

All the way home, I'd tried to think about what Al had said – how I needed to work out what my next move was, who I wanted to be – but I couldn't move on with myself until I'd fixed everything with everyone else. First, though, right now, I needed to sleep. I tried to summon the energy to take off my coat and drag myself into my bedroom, but it was too hard. I'd checked the devil's daughter's room – nothing had moved in there either, so it looked as though she was still away on her own adventure. There was always the slim chance she'd seen the error of her ways and gone off to become a nun or a Tibetan monk or something. A girl could dream.

'I could just sleep here,' I whispered, sliding sideways onto the settee until I was completely horizontal, feet still on the floor. 'Vanessa isn't here. She won't know.'

As my eyes slid shut and I used up my last drop of energy to haul my legs up onto the settee, I heard a rattle at the door. A key in the lock.

Fuck.

It was too late to make a run for my bedroom – there was no way I could get past her in time. I could roll myself into the bathroom and lock the door, but then she'd know I was home for sure. Maybe if I just lay very still on the settee she'd think I was dead already and leave me out for the Alsatians.

'Tess? Are you in there? I can't get the fucking key to work.'

Sweet Jesus, Mary and Joseph, it wasn't Vanessa. It was Amy. It was wonderful, foul-mouthed, fantabulous Amy. I'd taken my phone out to call her a thousand times after leaving the cottage – on the way to the airport, during the interminable three-hour wait in the departure lounge and every two minutes on the cab ride back to the flat. But I hadn't a clue what to say.

'Just push it harder,' I said as loudly as I could manage, face first in the cushion. 'It gets stuck when it rains.' Well, that was something.

'It gets stuck when it's sunny, it gets stuck when it snows – it's a piece of shit,' she shouted. I heard something hard strike something heavy and then a very small person clatter through a doorway and onto the floor. 'But it doesn't like being kicked, do you, you bastard?'

I loved that she talked to my door. I loved that she was sprawled across my living-room floor with a Tesco bag in her hand, effing and blinding at an inanimate object.

'So you're back then?' she said, dusting off her skinny jeans and leaping on top of me. 'I have missed you, you daft mare.'

'I thought you hated me?' I tried to find the energy to roll over and hug her, but it wasn't so easy when she had me pinned. 'I'm so sorry.'

'You don't get rid of me that easily, Brookes.' Amy wrapped her arms round the back of my neck, contorted herself into a horizontal piggyback and started dry-humping my legs. If we had been naked and covered in jelly, there would probably have been some money to be made. 'I lost my temper. I'm the one who's sorry. Anyway, you're back! It doesn't matter!'

'I'm back,' I repeated, once again freaking out at the overwhelming feeling that I'd never been away. 'And you're OK?'

'It was weird that everything happened while you were away,' she said, shuffling over until we were comfortably spooning. 'It was like, if you'd been here, we would have gone out and I would have got drunk and you would have been dead sensible, given me a lecture and sorted me out.'

'You're making me sound like a right barrel of laughs,' I interrupted. 'I'm not your mum.'

'No, I didn't mean it in a bad way,' she said, slapping me round the back of the head. I shut up. 'I meant you would have made it better in a Tess way, so I wouldn't really have had to work anything out on my own. But because you weren't here, I did. And, yeah, I think it's OK.'

I pouted into my pillow. 'What did you do? Or should I be too afraid to ask?'

'I went for a drink with Dave,' she said. 'And it was nice.'

'Oh, Aims.' I could see it all now – one too many glasses of wine, reminiscing about old times but conveniently forgetting that time she threw a melon at him in the middle of the big Asda on the A3. 'You didn't?'

'Have a little faith, knobber,' she replied. 'Actually, I had one drink, I went to the loo, and I thought, what would Tess do?'

'So you got on a plane and vanished to Hawaii under an assumed name?'

'No, I thought, Tess would give him a hug, tell him congratulations, and then go home. So that's what I did. Via the supermarket for a massive bottle of wine and all the Dairy Milk I could carry.'

'Wow, that's pretty sensible.' I patted her on the head, impressed.

'I know. I did wonder if we'd accidentally made a wish and, like, swapped bodies or something, but I think, actually, I just had to grow up a little bit because you weren't here to be the grown-up.'

'That's terrifying,' I said, pulling a stray strand of hair out of my mouth. 'I haven't really had that much influence over your decisions for the past twenty-seven years, Amy.'

'Yeah, you have.' She shrugged and gave me a squeeze. 'But I didn't really give you much of a choice, did I? You were the sensible one and I was the crazy one. Looks like we'd both had enough of our assigned roles at exactly the same time.'

'You mean, now you're the sensible one and I'm the crazy one?' I asked, fighting sleep with every breath.

'Maybe we could go fifty-fifty,' she suggested. 'Let's be honest, I shouldn't be left to my own devices for too long.'

'And as it turns out, neither should I.' I yawned loudly. 'What time is it? Can I go to bed yet?'

'You're not getting a wink until you tell me everything,' she said, rubbing my shoulders. 'Everything. Every word of it. Hot man, Hawaii, photographs, all of it.'

'Amy, I am literally going to pass out. Literally.' My voice was thick and even making words was a chore. 'I swear I'll tell you everything if I can have an hour?'

'Fine. One hour, and only if I can watch your *Buffy* boxset while you pass out,' she bargained.

'Fine, but you have to make me a cup of tea first.' I pushed her off my back and dragged my sorry arse into the bedroom, pulling my suitcase of stolen goods behind me. 'Sugary. Very sugary tea.'

'One diabetic builders' coming right up,' she confirmed. 'I'm glad you're home, Tess.'

'Well, that makes one of us,' I muttered, trying to smile as I collapsed on my beautiful bed. 'Which is better than nothing.'

Jet lag was a cruel mistress. I was fast asleep before Amy could even bring me my cup of tea on Sunday evening, but I was wide awake at the crack of dawn on Monday while she snored beside me, resplendent in my ancient Snoopy T-shirt and a pair of neon-pink knee-high socks that I had to assume she'd brought with her. They certainly weren't mine. I'd managed to regain consciousness for a short time exactly one hour after I'd fallen asleep, when Amy turned off the telly, started poking me in the arm and didn't stop until I opened one eye and told her absolutely every last detail of the past seven days. When she was finally satisfied she'd had the whole story, she patted me on the head and turned the TV back on. Just before I went back under, I was pretty certain I heard her say she was proud of me.

Fishing the remote control out of the covers, I flicked off the TV she'd left playing, which explained why I'd had nightmares about vampires chasing me through the ocean, and rolled out of bed without disturbing my sleepover pal, a skill I'd really honed over the past week. Waking up in my own bed, wandering into the kitchen in my knickers and going through the motions of my morning tea ritual didn't make anything feel better. It was almost as though I'd woken up from a dream but couldn't quite shake it, only I couldn't work out which was the dream, London or Hawaii. Or the seafaring vampires. The past seven days felt more real to me than the past twenty-eight years in England. Despite the drama and the anxiety, they had been fun, and I already missed everything about them. I'd been challenged and excited and things had felt new. And for the first time in a long time, in Hawaii, I'd been happy.

'Post-holiday blues,' I told the toaster. 'It was a holiday. It was a break from reality, all of it. It's done. Back to real life now.'

But the toaster didn't look convinced.

'Fuck off, toaster,' I muttered, taking my tea back into

the living room and settling down on the settee to watch the sunrise.

I thought watching *BBC Breakfast* might help me feel more present, but after two hours of suffering relentlessly smug non-news, I started to feel like it might be a good idea to get out of the house. And so, after my third cup of tea and fifth slice of toast, I showered, dressed as quietly as possible, picked up my bag, still full of my laptop, my passport and five bags of chocolate-covered macadamia nuts, and ventured outside, into London. As I locked the door, I pulled out my phone and patiently tapped and prodded at the shattered screen until it pulled up the number I was looking for.

'Hello?' Charlie answered right away.

'Hi, it's me,' I said, concrete feeling very odd underneath my hard-soled shoes. It had been a while. 'Can you meet me? Starbucks by the office?'

Better to get this over with, I rationalized as I flagged down the bus. And all the better to do it with coffee and cookies, before Amy got involved and while I was still half out of it with jet lag. It was a perfect plan. Get in, get out and go back to bed. Piece of piss. What could possibly go wrong?

'Wow.'

Charlie walked into Starbucks in his black skinny jeans and the navy blue Jack Wills jumper I'd bought him for Christmas, his hair brushed back away from his big brown puppy-dog eyes and a leather man bag I didn't recognize thrown across his wiry chest. Without thinking, I stood up to hug him and realized right away that it was a mistake. He looked like Charlie, he smelled like Charlie, he felt just like Charlie, but something was off. I let go, sitting down and grabbing my giant coffee with both hands. That was my second wow in a week. Actually, my second wow ever.

'You look great.' Charlie looked genuinely pleased to see me while I struggled to assemble an expression that wasn't one of complete shock and horror. I did not feel great – I felt sick to my stomach.

'I look exactly the same,' I replied, pushing my plait over my shoulder. 'You just haven't seen me for a week.'

'Longest week of my life,' he said, reaching his hand across the table towards mine. I pulled away and shook my head, eyes trained carefully on my coffee cup. 'Right. I'm going to get a drink. Do you want anything?'

I shook my head again.

'What could go wrong? she said. How bad could it be to see him? she said,' I muttered under my breath. 'What an idiot.'

I could just imagine Nick sitting at the next table, hiding behind the *Guardian*, shaking his head at me and Charlie, dying to tell me what a moron I was, what a loser he was. Just imagining his presence, hearing his voice in my head, was enough to make me squirm in my seat. It was almost forty-eight hours since I'd seen him and I still had no idea what to do about the situation.

'One regrettable shag at a time, Tess,' I told myself as Charlie wandered back over with a huge steaming cup and two chocolate muffins.

'I know you said you didn't want anything, but when have you ever turned down a muffin?' He pushed one towards me, and, taking a cautious sip of his latte, he immediately started rubbing his eyebrow. I immediately felt queasy. 'And it's my bargaining chip. To keep you quiet while I make a proposal.'

'A proposal?' I choked on the giant chunk of muffin I had already shoved in my mouth. 'What?'

'A business proposal! A business proposal,' he corrected himself quickly. 'I don't know if you got my voicemail, but I said I had news and I really do. Donovan & Dunning has gone under.'

'It's what?' I didn't think I'd heard him right. Gone under?

'Closed down. Apparently Donovan has been skimming money off the top for the past couple of years, ever since things went a bit quiet, and, you know, firstly that's illegal, and secondly, he skimmed too much. HR came in with the bank on Friday morning and sent us all home. You should have seen Raquel's face – she was so bloody confused. So happy she got to fire a load of people, but then at the end of it, she sort of had to fire herself. It almost made the whole thing worth it.'

'Wait – so the entire agency has just closed down? It's gone?' If I hadn't felt sick before, I certainly did now.

'Yeah, gone.' Charlie nodded. 'Aparently he tried to get the bank to extend the loans – that's why they laid you off. He wasn't allowed to hire anyone, and technically you were a new hire, but when they got hold of the books, they just came in and shut everything down.'

I couldn't process it. That place had been my entire life for so long. Of course I was still angry about being fired, but to see all my friends out on the streets, to see all my work gone to nothing . . . It was so sad.

'But what about all the clients?' Visions of dancing teaspoons, talking toilet brushes and unrealistically happy furniture shoppers flashed in front of my eyes.

All for nothing. 'Who's looking after the clients?'

'I am glad you asked,' he said with a very self-satisfied smile. Almost Nick-like, really. 'We are.'

Huh?

'Huh?'

'Me and you.' He waved his hand between us. He was doing his very best to sound confident and together. It had never occurred to me in ten years that he wasn't really either of those things. 'And probably a couple of other people, but listen, Tess, we should do this. Wilder & Brookes. Or Brookes & Wilder. Or something entirely different. I'll handle the accounts, you head up the creative. I've already called a couple of the clients – they're interested. If it's me and you, they're keen. Why wouldn't we do this?'

Why wouldn't we do this?

I stared at Charlie, my hands tight around my red-hot cup, burning slightly but only enough to remind me that the world outside my mind actually existed. Here was the boy I'd loved for ever offering me the chance to be the creative head of my own agency. To work with him on our own accounts, with our own clients. Professionally, it was all I'd ever wanted. Personally, it was probably the best I could have hoped for – a way to keep Charlie in my life, in my every day, for the foreseeable.

'Charlie, that sounds amazing, but . . .' I tailed off slowly, half stopping myself before I could say something stupid and half stopping myself because I had no idea what I was actually going to say. 'But I don't know.'

'I know things might be weird for a little bit,' he said, stumbling over his words. He seemed so awkward and young, and I missed Nick. 'Because I know I messed up.'

'You slept with Vanessa,' I clarified. 'That's not messing up; that's shagging Satan.'

'I'm not talking about that,' he said. 'Well, I suppose I am, but when I say I messed up, I don't mean with her. I mean with you.'

I said it before he could. 'Because it shouldn't have happened. I know.'

'Because it shouldn't have happened like that,' he corrected me softly. 'This past week without you has been horrible. All I've done is think about how I fucked up, how I hurt you, how I ruined everything with my best friend, and all I wanted was for you to give me a hug and tell me everything was OK. Because that's what you do.'

I nodded for him to carry on, concentrated on breathing and let him talk.

'But you weren't here to make everything right this time, and I realized that I've been letting you make everything right for a really long time. No matter what I do or how I cock up, you always just make it better.'

'Seems like you and Amy would have been a lot happier if I'd vanished years ago,' I said, laughing nervously and picking the edge off my muffin. 'Epiphanies all round.'

'I can't speak for Amy, and after the conversation I had with her on the phone, I don't think she's speaking to me anyway,' he said, hunching his shoulders at the memory. 'Not that I didn't deserve it. She was right. I am a cockwomble.'

'She told me she hadn't spoken to you?' The minx. 'And also, wow. That's her most offensive term. Congrats.'

'Thanks.' He laughed. 'I thought it was colourful. Maybe there's a future for her at our agency.'

'Perhaps.' I rubbed my eyes until I saw little sparks dancing in front of them. This was too much for someone as tired as I was. And I still didn't really know what he was saying. 'I'm so tired right now, Charlie. Can we talk about this tomorrow?'

'We can,' he said. 'But I need to move fast on the clients, and most of them just want you. They don't give a monkey's whether or not I'm there – you're the creative genius, you're my Lady Draper. They just want you.'

'Always nice to be wanted,' I sighed, slugging my coffee. Of all the things I'd thought he might say, this was the most unexpected.

'But in principle yes?'

'In principle I don't know.'

He nodded, wisely declining to force the issue.

'And what about the other thing?' he asked, speaking slowly. 'Does that need to wait until tomorrow as well?'

'Other thing?'

'Other thing,' he replied, reaching out for my hand again. This time I didn't pull away. 'Me and you?'

'Hang on, have I missed something?' My heart was pounding. Had I blacked out during a very important part of this conversation? Me and him?

'Oh God, I've had ten years to get this right and I'm still cocking it up.' Charlie moved his chair closer to mine and pressed my hand harder. 'I am a cockwomble. Tess, if you still want to, I think we should give it a shot. You know, going out. Being together.'

'What?'

I realized I was shouting when the next three tables all jumped out of their seats at the same time.

'You want to what?' I hissed. 'Are you serious?'

'I'm totally serious,' he said looking around, a little

embarrassed. 'Weren't you listening? I've had a week to think about it. I missed you so much, and not just as my friend. I know we didn't exactly start things off right or in any sort of way Amy will ever approve of, but I don't care. I'm sitting here talking to you and all I want to do is kiss you.'

'Really?' I wouldn't have wanted to kiss me. I looked like shit.

'Maybe that's not all I want to do, but we are in public and I think that sort of thing is frowned upon in Starbucks,' he replied.

Well. I was wrong. Out of all the things he could have said, *this* was the most unexpected. Not the shagging in Starbucks, but suggesting we give it a go. Me and Charlie. Boyfriend and girlfriend.

'You're going to make me wait, aren't you?' Charlie pushed up the sleeves of his jumper and pulled his whiny face. It was the same one he gave me when I wouldn't let him eat ice cream before his dinner, even though I always ended up giving in. But not this time.

'I've waited ten years, Charlie,' I sighed. All. Too. Much. 'You can wait until I'm awake.'

I pushed the rest of the muffin away and stood up. He hopped to his feet, towering over me in a way that had always made me feel safe and small before, but as he leaned down to kiss me chastely on the lips, all I could think of was the way Nick's eyes burned directly into mine in the second before we kissed. And there was nothing chaste about any of his kisses.

'I'll call you later,' I promised. 'I have some stuff to sort out.'

'OK, I'll text you,' he said. 'Or I'll just wait for you to call. But I'll probably text you.'

I nodded, my brain exploding with too much information as I walked back out into the cool summer sunshine.
I was so tired, but so completely wired from the ridiculous
quantities of caffeine I'd consumed in the past three
hours that I knew I wouldn't be able to sit still. Checking
my phone as I walked down Theobalds Road, away from
an office that was no longer there, I saw a text from Amy
wanting to know if I'd run off to the Caribbean and could
she come with me, and a missed call from Agent Veronica.
Of course she'd heard the news. Drawing up every last
ounce of courage, I pressed redial and hoped she didn't
have a sniper using my phone as a tracking device. Of
course, if she did have me killed, or as she'd so eloquently
threatened, strung up by my tits, at least I wouldn't have
to deal with the Charlie dilemma. So that was a plus.

'Tess motherfucking Brookes.' Agent Veronica looked
exactly how I had imagined. Short hair, fag hanging
out of her mouth, dressed in black and wearing very
expensive shoes. What I hadn't expected was for her to
stand up as I slunk into her office, walk round her desk
and give me a bone-crushing bear hug.

'Are you going to kill me?' I asked, my arms pinned
to my sides while I nervously folded and unfolded the
Wispa wrapper in the pocket of my jeans. It was a shit
last meal, but it was all I'd been able to wolf down on
my way over to Veronica's office. 'Is this like a mafia kiss
or something?'

'Are you fucking kidding me?' Agent Veronica was
apparently insane. 'I got your photos on Saturday. And
then I got a phone call from *Gloss* this morning. It took
me a minute to put two and two together and come up
with something other than forty-fucking-two, but I got

there. You were the one in Hawaii taking the pictures.'

'Yes,' I admitted as Veronica finally let go of me and sat back down. She pointed at the empty chair opposite her. I checked it very quickly for hidden explosives and took a seat.

'And it was you I spoke to on the phone?'

'Yes.'

'Should have known it wasn't that cockmuncher Kittler. Never answers her phone – always emails. Nasty bitch, that one.'

I wasn't going to argue with that, but I still felt a bit bad.

'Veronica, am I in trouble?' I asked. 'Paige was furious.'

'Well, that's because you shagged her fella, didn't you? You dirty mare.' She let out a foul, hacking laugh and slapped the desk. 'She isn't happy with you. But I'm fucking ecstatic.'

'Yay?' I whispered.

'Those pictures of Bertie Bennett were amazing,' she said, suddenly switching gears. 'As soon as I saw them, I knew Vanessa hadn't shot them. She hasn't done anything as good as that since I've had her on my books. Even the pictures that made me sign her weren't as good as those.'

'I keep hearing about these amazing pictures.' Fear of violence fading, I relaxed a fraction into the uncomfortable visitor's chair. 'Do you have them?'

'Yeah, they're in her book – give me a sec.' Veronica lit another cigarette, clamped it between her bright red lips and spun around to a bookcase full of portfolios. 'Now, obviously you're going to be signing an agency agreement with me before you leave this office, since I've smoothed everything over with *Gloss* and I've got your first job lined up already.' She handed me a thin, light brown pleather book with Vanessa's name printed on the side in silver type. Mmm, tacky. 'You're welcome.'

'I'm sorry, I'm not following?' I said, flipping through the pictures. I very nearly felt bad saying it, but they really weren't great. Vanessa was not a natural photographer. 'A job?'

'Bertie Bennett, aka your best friend in the entire world, other than me,' she announced with a flourish, 'wants you to go to Milan and work on his retrospective. He's putting together some sort of exhibition with someone. He's doing a book – the whole shebang. Shenanigans ahoy. He wants you to do all the pictures, document the entire exercise. It'll be three months at least. Starting as soon as.'

If Bertie's proposal hadn't left me speechless, what I saw in Vanessa's portfolio would have done the job.

'These are her pictures?' I breathed out without breathing in again.

'Oh yeah, they're the ones. There are, like, four of them? She really caught something there.' Veronica took a drag on her cigarette and then flicked the ash over her shoulder. 'Other than an STD, for a change. That's why I took her on. I thought she knew how to tell a story, but all I've had off her since is bollocks.'

I couldn't speak. The photos were beautiful. The first one showed an old couple sitting beside a pond at sunset, smiling at each other and feeding the ducks. The next one showed the same couple walking off down a country road, holding hands, silhouetted by the low light. The next two were more of the same – a mother and baby smiling at each other, two teenage girls giving each other filthy looks.

'Intimate,' she said. 'Honest. Bit like your Bennett pics.'

'That's because I took these,' I said, my words stilted and uncertain. 'Veronica, these are my pictures. I took them years ago. They must have been on the memory card when she took my camera.'

'Fuck. Right. Off.' She looked absolutely delighted. 'You're serious? You're fucking serious. That sneaky cow.'

'I don't know what to say,' I breathed. It was becoming something of a catchphrase of mine. Perhaps I should get it printed on to a T-shirt to save my breath. 'But these are totally mine. It's the mill pond in the village where I grew up. I can't believe she would do this.'

'You can't?' Veronica didn't seem quite so surprised. 'I can.'

'I just . . . she knew how much I loved photography and she still took the camera, but to steal my pictures, pass them off as hers and make a career out of it? That's something else.'

'Yeah, that's even more mental than pretending to be your flatmate, nicking off to Hawaii and shagging the journo on the job,' she replied, leaning across the desk and snapping her fingers in my face. 'Tess, this is the past. We are looking at the future. Your future, my massive commission. Say yes to the job. We'll book your flight right now. You get to go and play dressing-up with your mate Bertie and even use your own name. How exciting is that?'

'It's so exciting,' I said, still staring at the photographs in my lap. 'Um, can I have a day to think about it?'

'What?' She didn't sound nearly as understanding as Charlie had. 'What is there to think about?'

'I'm just really tired and jet-lagged, and I think I need

a minute.' I slapped the portfolio shut and threw it onto the desk, suddenly disgusted by it. 'I think I need some sleep before I make any big decisions.'

'Your journo friend is back in New York,' Veronica said with a casual wink. 'Heard he didn't take your big reveal that well.'

'How do you know he's in New York?' I sat up straight, my plait swishing behind my head. 'Do you know him?'

'Passing acquaintances.' She screwed up her face and clucked. 'And he was in on the emails from the magazine. Bennett wants him to work on the retrospective as well.'

'Has he said he will?' I could barely sit still at the mere mention of his name. My heart was beating hard, and not just from the jet lag and the caffeine. If we were both working with Al, he'd have to talk to me.

'He hasn't confirmed yet,' she said. 'Seemed very keen to know whether or not you'd be there, actually. Email him. Tell him your side of the story and see what he says. If nothing else is true, I do know that man loves a story.'

I pulled out my crappy knackered phone and opened a new email. But what was I supposed to say?

'I didn't mean do it now, you wanker.' Veronica clapped for my attention. 'Go home and cry over your love letter there. You made quite an impression on everyone, you did. Not sure if that's good or bad, but I do know you're a fucking good photographer and I want you on my books, Brookes.'

She slapped her desk hard and cackled. 'Ha! It rhymes. Now fuck off home, get some sleep and call me in the morning to apologize for making me wait an entire fucking day before I book this job.'

I stood up again, nodding like the Churchill dog, and

stumbled towards the door in a complete daze.

'Come on, Brookes,' Veronica yelled over her shoulder. 'I've just offered you a job and a shag in a oner. How often does something like that come around?'

'You'd be surprised,' I said, pushing the door open, and wished I had another Wispa to eat on the way home. Or some crack. I imagined some crack might be nice about now. 'You'd be really surprised.'

CHAPTER TWENTY-THREE

'I have no words.' Amy sat cross-legged on the settee, clutching her neon-pink ankles, her face a picture of shock. 'No. Words.'

Stretched out on the hardwood floor of the living room, I gently knocked the back of my head against the floorboards and pressed my feet into the sharp edges of the TV cabinet. Nope. Still couldn't actually feel anything.

'I know.'

'No, really, all of it.' Amy grabbed the remote and turned off the random episode of *The Vampire Diaries* that she had on mute. This was serious. 'The agency, the cockwomble finally bloody growing a pair, Milan, that's all awesome. But fuck me, Tess, I cannot believe she is such a complete and utter psycho.'

'I know.'

For the last two hours, all I'd done was think about what might have been. What if Vanessa had shown my photos to her agent but admitted they were mine? I could have been a professional photographer for years. I might have left the agency and had a life. I might not have spent so long hung up on Charlie that I didn't know how to have a functional relationship with another human being. Jesus, forget the relationship – I didn't even know how to have a conversation about a relationship. Everything might have been different. She'd stolen my life.

Which was funny when you thought about it.

But, then again, everything might not. I might have said thanks for the offer, but I'll stick with my torturous, low-paying, zero-regard office tomb, thanks, because that's what my mother wants me to do. There was no way of knowing, and as Al had said, life was too short for regrets. It was, however, not too short for swift and violent retribution. If only I knew where she was.

'So what are you going to do?' I could tell Amy was feeding on the drama. I hardly ever gave her anything to get her teeth into, so this was like all her Christmases come at once. 'What does your gut say?'

'My gut says I need to not eat any more pineapple for about a year,' I replied. 'I don't know. I'm too freaked out right now. I'm having more feelings than I knew one person could have at one time.'

'Have some more wine,' she said, grabbing the open bottle of white and pouring it into my Snoopy mug. 'That'll help.'

'It won't help because it's half past twelve in the afternoon,' I said, taking a swig. 'But I will have some anyway because I don't really know what else to do.'

'You do seem very emotional,' Amy said with as much sympathy as she could muster. 'Like, more conflicted than when *Jersey Shore* finished, and I know how hard that was for you.'

'I was just really worried about what would happen

to them when the cameras stopped rolling.' I sloshed my mug back onto the floor, trying not to spill any of the half-bottle of wine Amy had poured into it. 'What life will they have now?'

'So do you think you'll go to Milan?' She poured her own wine, switching the subject right back to where we started. 'And are you going to call Nick? And tell him you love him?'

'I don't know.' I needed so much more wine than there was in the universe. 'And I don't love him.'

'Yeah, you do,' she said, kicking me in the hip. 'But I think you probably still love Charlie too.'

'I don't know,' I said again. And again. And again.

'Yeah, you do,' she said again, this time kicking me in the head. 'But that's definitely more of a Stockholm Syndrome love. I'm team Nick. Deffos Team Milan.'

'And what will you do if I go off to Italy?' I asked, unfastening my plait and fanning my hair out around my head. 'You going to stay here and get more and more sensible?'

'No way,' Amy yelped. 'I'm coming with you. I want to meet this uber-amazing crazy sex wizard that's finally shagged some sense into you.'

'That is the most interesting interpretation of what's gone down over the past week that anyone could come up with,' I said, staring up at our manky ceiling. It needed painting so badly. 'A different kind of sense, yeah?'

'Of course the sensible thing to do would be to start the agency with Charlie,' she explained, as though it was a thought that hadn't crossed my mind a million times in the past hour. 'But the amazing thing would be to go to Milan with Nick.'

'What you're forgetting,' I pointed out from the floor,

'is that Nick isn't talking to me. So there's not necessarily any Nick in the equation. And there shouldn't be any Charlie in the equation, at least not in a sexy way. Not until I've decided what I want to do workwise.'

'Want you want to do or what you think you *should* do?' Amy asked. 'Close your eyes and tell me what staying here and opening the agency looks like.'

'It looks good,' I said, flexing my toes. 'It looks familiar. I know the work, I know the clients. It would be fun, owning the business, and maybe I wouldn't get quite as drawn in as before. Maybe I'd be able to keep a better work–life balance.'

'Yeah, right,' she scoffed, her disbelief echoing around her own mug o'wine. 'And what does going to Milan look like?'

'I don't know,' I said, a small smile in my voice. 'I'd be taking photos, living somewhere new, working with Al. It could be incredible or it could be awful.'

'Pretty sure even awful things are amazing in Italy,' Amy said dreamily. 'The telly says so.'

'And the telly never lies,' I confirmed solemnly.

'So it's head or heart, Tess,' she replied. 'What's it going to be? And leave your baby box out of this, because we both know she's Team Nick too.'

'I need more wine.'

We lay in our respective positions, quietly drinking, Amy presumably planning our Italiano adventures and me flipping back and forth between the easy thing and the new thing. Charlie or Nick? Photography or advertising? What if I'd got lucky with the pictures in Hawaii? I might be terrible at the next shoot and then I'd be out of a job again. And it wasn't like starting my own advertising agency with ready-made accounts and super-keen clients was a runner-up prize. I worked too hard and I forgot I was supposed to have a life outside the office, but I loved my job and I was good at it. There was no doubt or nerves there. And, yes, Charlie had made an epic, epic mistake by shagging Vanessa, but if he said he wanted to be with me, then he meant it, didn't he? Whereas Nick didn't even want to talk to me. I needed to email him, but I still didn't know what to say. I needed all the information before I made a decision.

'We need more wine,' Amy announced from her perch on the settee. 'That bottle's dead.'

'We've only just opened it.' I looked over at the empty green glass beside my head in disbelief. 'We are such drunks.'

'We are modern women on the horns of a dilemma,' Amy corrected. 'We are culturally conditioned to drink. It's Bridget Jones's fault, not ours.'

'There should be a bottle of sauv in the fridge then,' I called as she hopped over me and vanished into the kitchen. 'And bring the biscuits. I'm culturally conditioned to be greedy as well.'

I flapped my arms out by my side, making an imaginary snow angel, and carried on staring at the ceiling. It didn't have any answers for me. Just like the stupid toaster. It really was time the flat started pulling its weight in the decision-making around here. But while the ceiling wasn't great at telling me how to live my life, the front door was spectacular at providing an early warning system. Amy was in the kitchen. I was on the floor. There was only one other person it could be.

'What are you doing down there?' Vanessa stood over me, hands on her skinny hips, her hair falling in a perfect blonde curtain around her face as she stared down at the floor. 'Have you had a stroke?'

'No, but I feel like I'm about to,' I said, not moving. 'Where have you been?'

'Ohh, I was at a spa,' she sighed, shrugging off a shrunken leather biker jacket I didn't recognize and throwing it on the sofa. 'After all that shit I had to deal with last week, I needed a break. No phones, no Internet, no TV. It was amazing. Spiritual.'

She sat down and pulled her non-shattered, brand-new iPhone out of her pocket, sighing dramatically as she scanned her emails. I wondered if she even remembered that she had a BlackBerry in her room.

'Gingernuts or Hobnobs?' Amy shouted from the kitchen.

'Oh God, she can piss off home,' Vanessa spat, flicking at the iPhone screen. 'I haven't just spent three grand learning how to relax to have to deal with that mentalist when I get home.'

Even though I knew she could only be seconds away from something on her phone that would give away a hint at my adventures, I just couldn't seem to get off the floor. Instead, I rolled over onto my side, curled into the foetal position and waited for Amy to come back into the living room.

'I went with Hobnobs,' she said, holding the packet in one hand, and the open bottle of wine in the other. 'Gingernuts and wine seemed a bit tacky. Oh, look, you're home. Amazing.'

Whatever witchcraft was stopping me from getting up and running for the hills froze Amy to the spot in the middle of our living room. Vanessa looked up from her phone, perplexed.

'Have you two been doing mushrooms or something?' she asked. 'I'm going to bed. Fingers crossed you won't be here when I wake up.'

'*You stole Tess's photos,*' shouted Amy as loud as her little lungs would let her, pointing a finger at the accused.

'What?' To her credit, Vanessa looked completely and utterly flummoxed. 'I did what?'

'When Tess sold you her camera, you said her photos were your photos and that's why you're a photographer and you're not really – you're shit.' She punctuated the 'shit' by slamming the full bottle of wine down on the tabletop beside her.

And yet still I could not seem to move.

'Huh.' Vanessa crossed her long, leather-covered legs and cocked her head to one side. 'And how have you worked all this out, Sherlock?'

'Might have, sort of, borrowed my camera back?' I whispered from the floor.

'Did you now?' She was starting to sound a bit peeved. And I didn't like it when she sounded peeved. It usually ended in something being broken. But still, best to get everything out in the open.

'And there's a chance I sort of pretended to be you and went on a shoot to Hawaii for Veronica, and then she called me in and I looked at your portfolio and that's how I know.'

'OK, I'm totally not following you now.' She blinked twice and put down her phone. 'You did what?'

'She went to Hawaii and she took amazing photos and fell in love with an amazing man and you are a complete demon,' Amy wailed.

'There's no way.' Vanessa paled, very, very slightly, underneath her make-up. 'There's no way you did that. You probably haven't moved off the floor since I left.'

'It doesn't really matter who did what or where I was or whether or not I used your name and stole a job.' I felt eerily calm as I explained all of this from my ball on the floor. 'What matters is you stole my pictures. You kind of stole my life. I think I'm going to be moving out.'

'I'm calling Veronica,' she snapped, grabbing her phone. 'You better start packing. You need to find somewhere else to live, like now.'

'Ooh, put it on speakerphone,' I suggested. 'I think we'd all like to hear what she's got to say to you.'

Vanessa did not put the call on speakerphone, but it didn't matter. Agent Veronica – my agent, Veronica – did a fine job of amplifying her own voice. I couldn't quite make out the entire conversation, but it definitely included the words 'you're fucking fired' and 'you filthy, talentless little shitbag'. It was a bit like *The Apprentice* only not. Most importantly, Vanessa's face was a picture.

'I get it.' She kicked off her heels and pulled her hair back into a ponytail. Uh-oh, she was styling for a fight. 'This is because I shagged your boyfriend. You're all in on it. It's some weird revenge fantasy that you've cooked up between you.'

'As if anyone would go to that much effort for you.' I waved a hand in her general direction. From the floor. 'Nope. Totes went to Hawaii. Totes took some pictures. They were totes better than yours.'

'Bertie Bennett wants Tess to go to Milan and take pictures for his book and his exhibition because she's amazing,' Amy was shouting again. 'And Charlie doesn't love you anyway; he loves Tess. Nobody gives a shit about you because you're literally the worst person in the entire world. And you've got fat thighs.'

'Oh, that's it.' Vanessa jumped up, leapt over my prone form and gave Amy a good, hard shove. The Hobnobs went flying. I was very relieved she'd already put down the wine. 'Get out of my flat right now, you little psychopath.'

'You're the psycho,' Amy argued as Vanessa grabbed hold of a handful of her hair and started dragging her towards the door. 'You stole Tess's photos and passed them off as your own. That's psycho!'

'Not to defend her,' I said, finally rousing myself to duck as they passed me on their way outside, 'but what I did was a bit mental.'

'Not helping, Tess,' Amy squealed.

It was, as the gathering neighbours would attest, quite the scene. A barefoot Vanessa, in black leather leggings and a cropped baby-blue silk shirt, staggered down our front steps, still with a good handful of Amy's bob. But that wasn't to say Amy was losing the fight. Vanessa had a lot more hair to get hold of and Amy wasn't missing any opportunity. As they hit the street, she leapt onto Vanessa's back, still wearing nothing but a Snoopy T-shirt, her knickers and her neon-pink knee-highs. Finding my feet, I rushed to the top of the steps and slapped a hand over my mouth.

'I'm going to kill you,' Vanessa screeched, her arms wheeling around wildly.

'Good luck,' Amy yelled back, clamping what looked like a sleeper hold around Vanessa's neck. Who could have known that all those Saturday afternoons spent watching wrestling with her granddad would come in handy in the end.

The pair of them scrambled up and down the street while people whipped out their camera phones and started filming. I didn't know what to do. I knew I should stop it somehow, but where to start? Vanessa's arms and legs shot out, trying to knock Amy off her back, but my best friend was too tiny and too quick. She looked like a rabid spider monkey trying to take on a bitchy giraffe. And this wasn't her first fight with someone bigger than her.

'What is going on?'

I was so engrossed in the action, not to mention the group of schoolkids on their lunch who had now surrounded the girls and started a very popular 'fight, fight, fight' chant, that I didn't even see Paige coming up the steps.

'Is that Vanessa?' she asked, pointing at the tumble of shrieking limbs that was about to run right into a bus shelter.

'It is,' I said, the hand that had been clamped over my mouth moving down to my heart. 'Paige, I'm so sorry. Please—'

'Let me speak.' She held out a thick brown envelope and shook her head. 'There is a chance that I overreacted in Hawaii.'

'No,' I said quickly. 'I should have told you about Nick. Or I shouldn't have done what I did. Girl rules – you were right: I'm just as bad as Vanessa.'

'You didn't sleep with my fiancé,' she said, looking a little bit embarrassed. 'You fell for the irresistible charms of legendary man whore, Nick Miller. He emailed me, told me everything – that he made all the moves, that it was before we'd even met. So, yeah, I might have overreacted a little bit.'

'I still should have told you,' I replied as the fight rolled back past us again. The language on those two. 'I'm really sorry.'

'Then we're both sorry. We can agree we both have terrible taste in men and we can forget all about it. And can you please take this bloody envelope,' she said, waving it at me again before turning to watch the show. 'Friend of yours?'

'That's Amy,' I said, opening the packet and pulling out several large glossy prints. 'They've had a disagreement.'

'She just went straight to the top of my Christmas card list,' Paige said, leaning against the low wall outside our front door and settling in for the show. 'Can she take her?'

'Amy could take down an ox. Vanessa's been on borrowed time for years. All this,' I flapped the photographs in their general direction, 'is just the excuse she needed.'

'I like her already.' She looked back at me. 'When she's done, we should go and get a drink. I took the afternoon off to bring you those.'

As much as I wanted to watch Amy bash Vanessa over the head with a randomly acquired bottle of 7UP that I suspected had been supplied by the schoolchildren, I couldn't take my eyes off the photos. They really were beautiful. Al looked happy, Martha looked stunning, the colours, the lighting, the story behind each outfit – it was all there, ringing through the pictures.

'They're really good, Tess.' Paige interrupted my quiet moment of wonder. 'And not a pineapple or a ukulele in sight.'

Before I could reply, a blur of blonde hair and black leather came tearing up the stairs.

'Hi, Vanessa,' Paige said, offering her a casual wave. With a black eye and a bloody lip, my flatmate paused on the steps, looking confused, angry and, more than anything else, terrified. 'How's it going?'

'You're all fucking mental,' she spat, slamming the door to the flat and snapping all of the locks. 'Do not even try to get in here. I'll call the police.'

'OK,' I called back. 'Let me know when you're out and I'll come and get my stuff.'

'We've left a bottle of wine in there,' Amy pouted, skipping up the steps entirely unscathed. 'Hi, I'm Amy.'

'Paige.' The considerably less offensive blonde beauty offered her hand to my best friend and shook it heartily as the crowd in the street dispersed, disappointed. 'Cocktail?'

'Cocktail,' Amy agreed, looking down at her outfit. 'Probably going to have to be somewhere in Shoreditch, though.'

'I know just the place,' Paige said, pulling out her phone. 'I've got a car waiting.'

I kept flipping through the photos – the black Dior, the Givenchy wedding dress, the red Valentino . . .

'They're beautiful,' Amy said, taking them from my hands one by one. 'I'm so proud of you.'

'Thanks,' I said, eyes trained on the Valentino. I pulled out my own broken phone and scanned my emails. And there it was. Nick Miller. I pressed as hard as I could on the screen to open the message before I lost my nerve. All that was there was a US phone number and two words.

Call me.

I blinked, checked again and smiled. Still there. I hadn't hallucinated it. He had emailed me.

'This is our car, ladies,' Paige said, pointing at a big black people carrier pulling round the corner. 'Shall we?'

'Are you sure you don't want to go back inside and, I don't know, sort things out?' Amy asked. 'What if she goes mental and bins all your stuff?'

'All my stuff is shit,' I said with a shrug. 'We'll get new stuff.'

'I didn't want to say anything,' she said, hopping from neon foot to neon foot, 'but yeah, it is. And you'll need new stuff for Milan.'

'Or for the agency.' I gave her a tiny but genuine smile and followed Paige down the steps, really not caring what we must look like. 'Or whatever I end up doing. I don't need to know everything right now, do I?'

'Ha,' Amy breathed, linking her arm through mine. 'Who are you and what have you done with my best friend?'

'I'm Tess Brookes,' I replied, giving her a squeeze. 'Pleasure to meet you. Now, how about that drink?'

London or Milan?
Charlie or Nick?

If you're dying to find out who Tess chooses
and where she ends up, look out for Lindsey Kelk's
next book in this series:

What A Girl Wants

Coming Summer 2014!

Acknowledgements

I'm worried the list of people I must thank is getting dangerously close to becoming longer than the book itself, but here goes. As always, I couldn't have done this without my brilliant agent and even better friend, Rowan Lawton (especially on that day you told me to shut up, close my laptop and have a bath) and Liane-Louise at Furniss Lawton. Thalia, I don't know how you managed to stay so calm throughout this entire process, although I imagine it had something to do with not being at all calm when I wasn't looking. Thank you for being dead good. There are so many people to thank at HC – Martha, Lucy, Elinor, Kate and, of course, Lynne. Thanks for not punching me in the face. Yet. More uber-thanks to everyone who was lovely to me (or even mean about me behind my back; I don't mind) at HarperCollins Australia, especially the wonderful Kimberley Allsop – dinosaur lovers of the world unite. And thank you to Leo and all my HarperCollins Canada family. It really means a lot to me that you publish my books *and* I can pop into your office to steal sweets from Paul Covello when I'm in Toronto.

There aren't enough words to express how much I love everyone on Twitter and Facebook and the Internet in general, although I ought to be able to do it in 140 characters. Cheers to Amy Portess for lending me her name as well as Claire (wherefore art thou, Margs?), Rachel Campbell, Amanda Harper, Edelle McGinn and Kay Parker for suggesting words when I had run out. I couldn't not give a book hug to Carly Thompsett and the rest of Team Kelk (you know who you are, you crazies) and Kevin Loh – twinsies fo' lyfe.

Writing really does induce a special state of madness and it's thanks to these ladies that I didn't feel quite so alone in it this time – Ilana Fox, Katy Regan, Pippa Wright, Sarra Manning, Mhairi McFarlane, Kiera Cass, Katie Fforde, Meg Sanders and Lucy Robinson, as well as obligatory token boy writer WillHillAuthor. And when I'm not online, these poor bastards have to deal with me in real life – thank you SO MUCH Della Bolat, Terri White, Beth Ziemacki, Ana Mercedes Cardenas, Georgia Adey, Jackie Dunning, Sarah Donovan, Julie Allen, Rebecca Alimena, Erin Stein, Sam Hutchinson, Sarah Benton and Ryan Child. Mahalo (bitches), Emma Ingram. Hawaii wasn't ready. I have to thank my family for only asking me when I'm going to stop living my silly life and pop out a baby after I'd finished writing, and big thanks to Beyoncé, Detectives Eliot Stabler and Olivia Benson, Sour Patch Kids, Hendricks Gin, CM Punk and the WWE Universe (but not Vince – you're a bad man), Camera Obscura, Sam Cooke, Etta James and The National. I know Sam and Etta aren't around any more but it would be rude not to thank them. They were involved.

And thank you to JM for cracking the metaphorical whip. Now stop gloating.

Q&A with Lindsey Kelk

We said you could ask Lindsey anything – read on for her answers to your burning questions...

Edel Salisbury: What was your favourite book when growing up that you would still read now?

I've always been an epic reader so there are many! When I moved to NYC I brought four with me, *The Secret Garden*, *Remember Me To Harold Square* by Paula Danziger, *Frog and Toad Together* by Arnold Lobell and *Setting Up Home at Willowtree Cottage* by Elizabeth MacDonald which is a beautiful story about the trauma of living with terrible roommates that really never made sense until I had them.

Michelle Pickles: In *I Heart New York*, Angela peed in her fiancé's expensive wash bag. What I want to know is, where did that great idea come from?

At the time, the scene just came from my overactive imagination but it may or may not have inspired me to pee on my ex's toothbrush. For which I apologise.

Izzy Rowland: Favourite author besides yourself?

There are so, so many but I've always been a big fan of Donna Tartt, Bret Easton Ellis and Michael Cunningham. When I was a teenager, I was obsessed with Paula Danziger and Virginia Andrews. And vampires. Big fan of vampires. Thank god *Twilight* didn't publish until I'd learned to control myself.

Helen Antill: Are the books based on your life experiences, or purely from imagination?

Bit of both. The storylines are totally imagined but sometimes some of the scenes are inspired by real life events. Like colouring Rachel's hair red in *The Single Girl's To-Do List* and the pole dancing scene in *I Heart Vegas*. For shame… Sorry, Mum.

Kimberly Golden Malmgren: If you could steal away to anywhere in the world with anyone in the world to get inspiration for your next book, where would you go and who would you pick as your companion?

Right now, I'd nick off to Hawaii with every single one of my girlfriends and never come back. It's paradise. If I had to visit somewhere new, it would be Russia or Japan with a certain gentleman friend. Really want to visit both countries.

Amy Keen: What one piece of music do you need in your life when you are busy writing?

I have a writing playlist that goes on for about four hours pre-loaded onto my iPod and iPhone! It's full of stuff by The National, Camera Obscura, Tegan & Sara, Sleater-Kinney, The Pains of Being Pure at Heart, Tanlines and tons and tons of soul and Motown. I'm a sucker for a bit of Smokey Robinson and Etta James. And Fleetwood Mac. Who doesn't love Fleetwood Mac?

Kate Bain: Would you rather have a dog that can rap or a cat that sings you to sleep every night?

Oh my god, I'm SO TORN. The dog would be best at parties but I'm selfish and I think the cat might be soothing. Although that might be awkward on occasion: I don't think it would go down well with the chaps? But still, the cat. We could watch Buffy together and then have a singsong. Amazing.

Kevin Loh: If NYC was under siege what would you stock up on? Only THREE things!

Pizza, Diet Pepsi and Ben & Jerry's. I could go for months on that. Or at least until I had a heart attack.

Megan In The Sunshine: Do you have any lucky underwear? Or a lucky anything?

I have a Marc Jacobs watch necklace that I wear every single day even though the battery died months ago but I can't bear to be away from it to have it fixed. And while I don't have lucky undies, I do have a first date dress… It has an excellent success rate.

Bridget Siegel: What's your favourite type of character to write?

I love writing all of them. The main characters, Angela, Rachel and Tess, are always the most like me so they can be quite hard – being honest with them is like being honest with myself – whereas writing all the others is like trying on a new personality. It stretches my imagination to be a boy or a bitch. OK, maybe it doesn't stretch it that much to be a bitch for a few hours…

Ellie Rooke: Would you rather be a giraffe-sized ant or an ant-sized giraffe?

Ant-sized giraffe! I'd be adorable!

Jade Marie Johnston: Do you ever get your own back on people by calling them out in your books in a Taylor Swift-like fashion?

Ha! No… I've definitely been inspired by a few people but I never write someone directly into a book. It would be too weird – who wants to spend that much time constantly thinking about someone after a break up? I'd much rather move on.

Kelly Cooke: If you could have a super power, what would it be?

I fly all the time and while I love being on the plane, there's far too much time wasted in airports when I could be doing something fun! So I would definitely pick being able to fly. That way I could nip back home for a cup of tea with my mum whenever I wanted. Bliss.

There are lots of ways to keep up-to-date with Lindsey's news and views:

Check out Lindsey's new website at lindseykelk.com

Like her on facebook.com/LindseyKelk

Follow her @LindseyKelk